Materials for a History of the Wither Family - Primary Source Edition

Reginald Fitz Hugh Bigg-Wither

MATERIALS FOR

A HISTORY OF THE WITHER FAMILY.

MATERIALS

FOR

A HISTORY OF

THE WITHER FAMILY,

BY THE

REV. REGINALD F. BIGG-WITHER, M.A.,

Rector of Wonston, Hants.

Winchester:

WARREN & SON, 85, HIGH STREET.

1907.

WINCHESTER:
PRINTED BY WARREN AND SON, THE WYKEHAM PRESS.

Dedicated

to the Memory of the Author's Father,

and of his Son Arthur Sergius.

PREFACE.

IN the early sixties a young Oxford undergraduate, preparing for the history schools, as he leant Sunday after Sunday during the long vacation over the edge of the high family pew in the unrestored parish Church of Wootton St. Lawrence, near Basingstoke—gazed with increasing interest at the following monumental inscription on the opposite wall:—

"WILLIAM WITHER ESQUIRE
died Oct: 31 1789 aged 86.

. . . .

On his death, all the male issue
Of an ancient and well respected family,
Who had resided at Manydown
During the space of four centuries
Became extinct."

"Four centuries" in 1789, that takes one back (he said to himself) to the reign of Richard II. I wonder what the succession of the Withers of Manydown was, and what sort of life a country squire lived in those days. Visions of the manorial system; of the estate divided into two portions, that in demesne and that held by the villagers in villenage; of the manorial courts and of the lord dispensing justice—rose before him. "Some day I will write a history of the family and of the manor."

Time passed. After Oxford came residence abroad. Then Holy Orders with exacting ministerial work. At length, through an enforced winter's rest, came the opportunity of putting into shape materials that had for years been collected for a history of the Withers of Manydown and of their offshoots at Oakley Hall, Theddon Grange, and other parts of Hampshire, and of prefixing to it a sketch of the origin of the family in Lancashire and, in the nature of an appendix, to add some particulars of its ramifications in other parts of England and of America.

The result is the present volume.

The title *Materials for a History of the Wither Family* is an admission of incompleteness. It is hardly possible in the lifetime of a busy man to collect and adjust *all* available facts concerning an ancient family, that dates back to the twelfth century, and then to weave them into a history proper. As it is, the search for ancient records in the Public offices, the examination of old family deeds, of wills at Somerset House and elsewhere, of Church registers all over the country, has taken up already too much time in a life set apart for more important occupations. The writer, however, is confident that the information here presented will interest many who bear the family name, and many members of allied families: moreover he is assured that it will usefully serve the wider purpose of illustrating the history of his own county of Hampshire.

The Wither family may not have produced any, or many, world-famous men and women; but it is not without just pride that its representatives to-day look back to forbears of distinction in all branches of Church and State, of literature, law and commerce; and especially to a long succession of country "squires" living on their estates, "good old English gentlemen," serving their country as magistrates, their parish as benefactors, honoured by their neighbours, and beloved by the poor.

As the sheets were going through the press the author of this family history experienced an irreparable loss in the death, at the early age of eighteen, at Winchester College, of his only surviving son. This fact may be a sufficient excuse for some errors in correcting proofs.

It remains for the author to thank those relatives and friends who have helped him in his congenial task. To his cousin, Mrs. Norsworthy, whose skilled pen has drawn the coats of arms from which the heraldic illustrations are printed, his thanks are especially due; also to Mr. Frank Sidgwick, of the publishing firm of Bullen & Co., for great help in connection with the life of George Wither, the poet, and for the admirable bibliography attached. The author is grateful also to Mrs. Beach and to Mrs. Ellice Hicks Beach for help in the history of the Withers of Oakley Hall, and to Mr. Gathorne Wood for those of Theddon Grange; to the Rev. F. T. Madge for researches in Winchester Cathedral Library, and to Miss Trice Martin for the same at the Record Office; to the many clergy who have readily supplied him with information from the Registers in their charge; to the Rev. C. S. Ward, of Wootton St. Lawrence, and the Rev. George Horner, of Wimbledon, who, with the Dean of Durham, Messrs. F. J. Baigent and W. H. Jacob, of Winchester, and Dr. Andrews, of Basingstoke, have from time to time given him valuable help and information on antiquarian and literary matters connected with this work; and not least is his gratitude due to Messrs. Warren, of Winchester, for the admirable way in which the book is printed and the facsimiles and illustrations prepared.

REGINALD F. BIGG-WITHER.

Wonston Rectory,
July, 1907.

CORRECTIONS.

Page 22, for "Richard Fawkener," read "Peter."
,, 27, for "Alethea Wither," read "Alethea Bethell."
,, 55, for "Thomas," read "William Heathcote."
,, 81, for "Mrs. Charles Smith," read "Mrs. Charles Wither."

On Picture of Mrs. William Beach, for "1662—1742," read "1718—178
,, ,, ,, Dorothy Wither, for "1783," read "1752."
, ,, ,, William Wither B. Beach, for "1900," read "1901."

CONTENTS.

APPENDICES.

(pp. 177—end.)

LIST OF PEDIGREES.

LIST OF ILLUSTRATIONS.

EPIGRAM BY GEORGE WITHER, THE POET, ON THE WITHER ARMS AND CREST.

"To his loving friend and Cousin German Mr. William Wither"
(of Manydown), A.D. 1620.

"If that the *Standards* of the House bewray
What *Fortunes* to the owners may betide;
Or if their Destinies, as some men say,
Be in the names of any signified,
'Tis so in thine; for that faire antique Shield
Borne by thy Predecessors long ago,
Depainted with a clear pure *Argent* field,
The innocence of thy line did shew.
Three sable Crescents with a Chevron gul'de
Tells that black *fates* obscured our houses light;
Because the Planet that our fortunes rul'd
Lost her own lustre, and was darkened quite:
    And, as indeed our Adversaries say,
    The very name of Wither shows decay.
And yet despair not, keep thy *White* sustained,
And then it skills not what thy *Crescents* be.
What though the Moon be now increased, now waned?
Learn thence to know thy life's inconstancy;
Be careful as thou hitherto hast been,
To shun th' Abuses *Man* is tax't for here:
And then thy soul that's now eclipsed with sin,
When *Moon* and *Sun* are darkened, shall look clear;
And what so'er thy English name may threat,
The *Harvest's son* the *Greeks* entitle thee.
Ere thou shalt want, thy *Hare* will bring thee meat,
And to kill care, herself thy make-sport be:
    Yea, yet (though *Ennui's* mists do make them dull)
    I hope to see the wanéd *Orbs* at full."

NOTE BY G. W.—For the better understanding of this Epigram, note that his *Arms* are in a Field Argent, a Chevron Gules, betwixt three Crescents Sable. His *name* according to the Greeks is *υἱθερος* (*υἱὸς*, son; *θέρος*, summer or harvest). His *Crest* a Hare with three Wheat Ears in her mouth.

I grow and wither both together.

THE NAME "WITHER."

IN the opinion of such learned authorities as Dr. Skeat of Cambridge, and Professor Napier and Dr. Sweet of Oxford, the origin and derivation of the name WITHER is unknown.

That given by the poet George Wither in his Epigram quoted above, must be deemed purely fanciful; hardly less so is the suggestion of Mr. Barber in his ***British Family Names***, namely, that Wither is a personal name with the root wið = "against," *c.f.*, the English "withstand," hence one who opposes or a "warrior"; nor once more can Professor Mayhew's view hold, namely, that in connection with the Icelandic viðr (pronounced Wither) a wood, the word is allied with the old English "widu" "wudu," our wood, and so that the name means a "woodman." That the Icelandic "Viþarr" is the correspondic Norse name is likely, and that it is allied to the Icelandic "viðr" is possible; but the old English name for wood, "widu," would rather give Wider.

What we clearly do know is that WITHER is a genuine old English name of great antiquity. It appears in various Anglo-Saxon documents, *e.g.*, in a charter of Æthelred, dated A.D. 1005, one of the witnesses signs his name as "Ego Wiðer minister," where ð is the symbol for "th."[1]

The name also occurs in the Domesday record (1086) as a tenant prior to that census.[2] It constantly appears in the "Hundred Rolls," and always without prefix, suggesting that its origin is personal. It does not seem to be the name of a place, though it occurs apparently as the first element of the place names "Witheridge" (Devon), "Witherby" (Leicestershire), "Withersdale," "Withersfield" (Suffolk), "Witherslack" (Westmoreland), "Witherstone" (Dorset).

The forms "Wyther" and "Wither" are used interchangeably, *e.g.*, "Sir Thomas Wyther (*circa* 1320), father of Thomas Wither,"[3] "Otho Wither, son of Richard Wyther," baptised 1568.[4] In 1613, "Wyther" and "Wither" are the same person.[5] After the first quarter of the seventeenth century the form "Wyther" is no longer found.

With the possessive sign "s" the name becomes "Wythers" or "Withers," denoting of course son of "Wyther" or "Wither." The forms with and without the "s" are also used interchangeably, *e.g.*, in the House of Commons (7th August, 1646) the poet George Wither is called in the same speech "Mr. Wither" and "Mr. Withers": see also the Parish Registers of Wootton St. Lawrence, Kingsclere,

[1] Kemble's Codex Dip., vol. iii, p. 346, l. 8.

[2] See App. I, p. 178.

[3] Harl. MS., Vol. xiii, p. 130.

[4] Wootton Registers.

[5] Foster's Alumni Oxonienses.

IV, pp. 225—245.

and Romsey,[6] "Foster's Alumni Oxonienses," and the "Feet of Fines" (*passim*). At the present day the tendency of strangers to the name is to add the "s." It thus seems probable that all persons bearing the name Withers in England and America are descended from some original Wither or Wyther.

Sporadic forms of the name are "Wether" and "Wethar," both on several of the Manydown Court and Compotus Rolls. "Wethers" and "Whethers" are found in Foster's Alumni Oxonienses; "Whither" and "Whithers" in several Parish Registers; "Wethur" in the Subsidy Rolls; "Wythere" in the Basingstoke Rental Rolls; "Weethers" in the Alton Registers; and "Wother" in those of Basing. In the Magdalen College, Oxford, Register, "John Wythyrs" is Fellow in 1485. In the Eton College Registers "William Whither" is elected Fellow in 1477 and is sometimes mentioned as "Master Wyther." There are still other variations of the name.

CHAPTER I.

WITHER OF LANCASHIRE.

(1189—1389.)

Pedigree I.

WITHER OF LANCASHIRE.

(1189—1389.)

Sir Robert Wyther, Kgt., of Pendleton Hall, Lancashire and of Halton, Cheshire. Seneschal to Roger de Lucy, Constable of Chester (1179-1189). = Joan, dgt. of Sir Adam de *Bostock*, Kgt. (of Davenham, Co. Cheshire).

Reginald Wyther, son and heir, of Pendleton Hall. = Isabel, dgt. of Sir Thos. *Winstanleye*, Kgt. (of Winstanleye, Lancashire).

Thomas Wyther, son and heir. = Ursula, dgt. of *Hugh Cotgreave*, Esq. (Lord of Hargreave, Co. Cheshire), living 10 and 16 Edw. I (1282-1288).

Sir William Wyther, Kgt., Judge, Exor. of Edmund, 1st Earl of Lancaster, living 1279-1307. = Agnes, widow of Wm. de *Ipstanes*.

Sir Thomas Wyther, Kgt. Killed Sir Robert Holland, Kgt., 1328, d. 1329. = Agnes.

Thomas Wyther, son and heir. Steward to the Abbot of Walley, Lancaster. =

Thomas Wyther, of Vale Royal, Cheshire.	*Richard Wyther*, of Hunstanton, in Wynbury, Co. Chester.	*Robert Wyther*. Came to Manydown, Hampshire.
↓	↓	↓
Issue, see Chap. II.	Issue, see Chap. II. Wither of Essex, London, Somersetshire.	Issue, Wither of Hampshire.

CHAPTER I.

WITHER OF LANCASHIRE.

(1189—1389.)

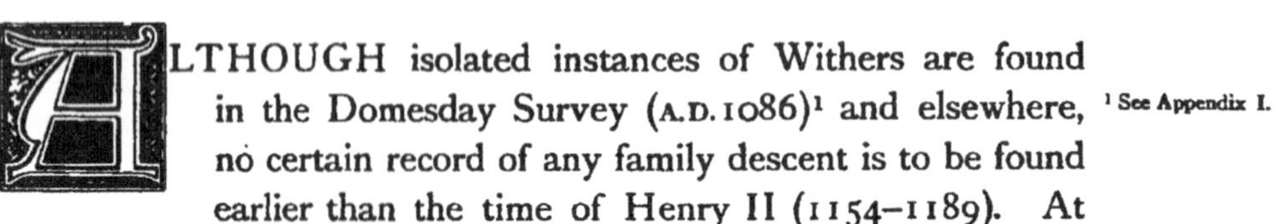

ALTHOUGH isolated instances of Withers are found in the Domesday Survey (A.D. 1086)[1] and elsewhere, no certain record of any family descent is to be found earlier than the time of Henry II (1154–1189). At this period we have definite information. The Pedigree of the *Cotgreave* family, executed by Randles Holme (one of a family of heralds), of Chester, in 1672, from documents compiled by William Camden in 1598, affords (if correct) a definite and distinct starting point for all Wither Pedigrees.

COTGREAVE PEDIGREE, 1189–1288.

It gives three generations of Withers, their marriages, and their armorial bearings: the Wither Arms of that Pedigree being identical with those now and without question for more than 500 years borne by the Wither family, namely, "*Argent, a chevron gules between three crescents sable.*"

The Wither family as it can be traced is clearly (as it is by tradition) of Lancashire origin. The Pedigree opposite this Chapter is taken as to the first three names from the Cotgreave Pedigree, and the date fixed within the ten years (1179–1189), when Roger de Lucy was Constable of Chester, temp. Henry II. His Constableship lasted till 12 John (1211).

[1] See Appendix I.

The following is the statement of one of the documents attached to the Cotgreave Pedigree, attested by Lady Harriet Cotgreave 19 November, 1841 :—

"Hugh Cotgreave, Esq., living ye 10 & 16 Ed. I (1282–1288), Lord of Hargreave, Tarvin, & Guilder-Sutton in ye Countie Palatine of Chester, married Ellinor daughter of Robert del Holme, Lord of Tranmere, and had issue Ralph his heir and Ursula who married *Thomas Wyther* or Wither, Esq., son and heir of *Reginald Wyther*, Esq., of Pendleton, Lancashire, by his wife Isabel, daughter of Sir Thomas Winstanleye, of Winstanleye in ye last named shire, which Reginald was son and heir of *Sir Robert Wyther*, Knt., of Pendleton, Lancashire, and Halton, Cheshire, Seneschal to Roger de Lucy, Constable of Chester and Baron of Halton, temp. Henry II (1179–1189). Ye above named Sir Robert married Joan dgt. of Sir Adam de Bostock, Knt., in ye last named countie."

The Arms emblazoned on the Cotgreave Pedigree are as follows :—

1st Shield.

Quarterly, 1st, argent, a chevron, gules between 3 crescents sable; for *Wyther*.

2nd, azure a chief, 3 chevronells in base, or; for *Fitz Hugh*, Baron of Malpas.

3rd, quarterly or and gules, a bend sable; for *Malban*, Baron of Nantwich.

4th, azure, a lion rampant, argent; for Eustace *Crewe de Montalt*, Lord of Hawarden, Flintshire.

Impaling, gules, a fess indented, ermine between 3 bugle horns, or, stringed argent; for *Cotgreave*.

2nd Shield.

Wyther, quartering the arms as above. Impaling, or, 2 bars azure, in chief 3 crosses patée gules; for *Winstanleye*.

3rd Shield.

Wyther, quartering the arms as before. Impaling, sable, a fess humetté argent; for *Bostock*.

The issue of Thomas Wyther and Ursula Cotgreave is uncertain. Three generations from Sir Robert Wyther (1189) would, according to the ordinary reckoning, bring us to A.D. 1279, thus the son of Robert and Ursula may well have been that

Sir Willm. Wyther (1279–1307).

Sir William Wyther, knight and judge, of whom we hear repeatedly between 1279–1307 through the Patent and Close Rolls of the time of Edward I, and of whom it is said in Foss' *Lives of the Judges*[1]: "His descendants removed from Lancashire to Manydown in Hampshire, where the family settled in the reign of Edward III."

SIR WILLIAM WYTHER was evidently in the confidence of Edmund, first Earl of Lancaster, brother of King Edward I, by whom Sir William Wyther was appointed (1287), at the request of the Earl, itinerant justice for pleas in Edmund's forest property in Lancashire, Derbyshire, Staffordshire, and Yorkshire.[2 3 4] He had also other judicial powers, as when, *e.g.*, he was appointed in 1306 one of the Commissioners to decide a cause in North Wales between the Earl of Arundel and Richard de la Chambre.[5] He was also one of the executors of Edmund's will.[6] His descendants (as will be seen) remained closely connected with the Lancaster family. Sir W. Wyther married (1294) Agnes, widow of William de Ipstanes,[7 8] but there is no authenticated pedigree of his issue.

Sir Thomas Wyther (1323–1328).

We next hear (1323) of a *Sir Thomas Wyther*, knight, who, as he inherited property, *i.e.*, the manor of Kimbolton, and land in Calton and Onemastmathfeld, county Hereford, from William de Ipstanes,[9] is probably the son of Sir William Wyther the judge. He also married an Agnes, to whom the property passed in 1329, "as Thomas is now dead."[10] All evidence points to the probability that this Sir Thomas Wyther is the man from whom begins the Elizabethan Pedigree made in 1576, confirmed by the College of Arms and various Heralds Visitations. The original of this

Elizabethan Pedigree, 1576.

[1] Vol. 3, p. 176, Ed. 1.

[2] Patent Roll 15, Ed. I, m. 15.

[3] Close Roll. 15 Ed. I, m. 6, d.

[4] Plac. de Q. War. Hil. 21, Ed. I.

[5] Parliaments Rolls, Vol. 1 p. 206.

[6] Debanco Roll, No. 123, m. 101, d.

[7] Close Roll, 23 Ed. I, m. 4.

[8] Appendix V, "Ipstanes Family."

[9] Feet of Fines, Stafford, Case 209, File 12, No. 52, 17 Ed. 2.

[10] Inq. p. m. 3 Ed. III, and Nos. 64. Close Roll, 3 Ed. III, m. 11.

pedigree with its crabbed Elizabethan writing has long been in the possession of the Withers of Manydown. It begins as follows:—

"Sir Thomas Wyther, kgt., in the countie of Lancaster, who was servantt and counsulor to Henry, 1st duke of Lancaster, and also to Thomas, Erle of Lancaster, etc., and from whom are descended these gentlemen underwritten. Colected anno 1576. Hee killed one Syr Robarte de Hollande, kgt., and was Bannyshed for a tyme out of England, etc. After called home, etc."

This incident as related by Dugdale[1] occurred in 1328 (the year before Sir Thomas Wyther's death), and redounded to the credit rather than otherwise of Sir Thomas Wyther:—

"*Baron de Holland, who was in the wars in Scotland, owed his advancement to his becoming Secretary to Thomas Earl of Lancaster. In 1st Ed. II (1307) he (Lord H.) obtained large territorial grants from the Crown. In 8th Ed. II he was first summoned to Parliament as Baron. Upon the insurrection of his old master, Thomas Earl of Lancaster, 15 Ed. II (1321), having promised that nobleman all aid in his favour, and failing to fulfil his engagement, Lancaster was forced to fly northwards, and was finally taken prisoner at Boroughbridge* [he was attainted and put to death, 1322], *when Lord Holand rendered himself to the King at Derby . . . . . for which duplicity he became so odious to the people that . . . . being taken prisoner in a wood near Henley Park towards Windsor, he was beheaded on the nones (7th) October, Anno 1328, and his head sent to Henry Earl of Lancaster* [brother of the late Earl Thomas], *then at Waltham Cross, in the co. of Essex, by Sir Thomas Wyther, a Kgt., and some other private friends.*"

The only difficulty in the above statement is that Henry 4th Earl of Lancaster was not created Duke until 6th March, 1351, but he was living in 1328, and it is evident that Sir Thomas Wyther was in the confidence of two generations of the Lancaster family, as his father Sir William had been in the confidence of and exor. of Edmund the 1st Earl. (See note below on the Lancaster Family.)

According to the Elizabethan Pedigree (1576) above mentioned and to the Essex Visitation (1634) Sir Thomas Wyther, knight, who was dead in 1329, was succeeded by his son and heir *Thomas Wyther*, Esq., county Lancaster, who married and had issue (three sons):—

THOMAS WITHER (1329-1389).

(1) *Thomas*, of Whalley, Lancashire.
(2) *Richard*, of Hunstanton, parish of Wynburg, Cheshire.
(3) *Robert*, who came to Manydown, Hampshire, and was the progenitor of the Withers of Manydown, Oakley Hall, and of Bentworth and Theddon Grange.

With Thomas Wyther and his three sons Thomas, Richard, and Robert, we hear the last of the Withers of Lancashire. It will not be difficult, with the aid of the Elizabethan Pedigree and various Heralds Visitations and Inquisitions Post Mortem, to trace the descendants of the three brothers who settled in various parts of England, especially in Essex, London, Somersetshire, and Hampshire. With the latter this book is especially concerned, but the London, Essex, and Somersetshire Withers, who seem to have sprung from the two elder brothers, Thomas and Richard, also demand notice, and a short chapter must be devoted to them before we tell the tale of the Withers of Hampshire.

In order not to overload this statement of the Wither origins I have relegated to the appendix a number of scattered references (taken from ancient documents in the Record Office and elsewhere) to individuals of the name of Wither or Wyther who had property in, or were connected with, various parts of England other than Lancashire and Hampshire prior to the reign of Henry IV (1412), from which time there is continued evidence of the settlement of the descendants of Robert Wither at Manydown and in Hampshire. I note here briefly that the student of a family history must observe with great interest that a continuous series of references in ancient charters of the time of Henry III, Edwards I and II, and Richard III, *i.e.*, of the thirteenth and fourteenth centuries, confirm privileges "which their ancestors had had" to various members of the family Wyther in the *Forest of Dene* (Gloucestershire), and especially in the manor of *St. Briavel's.*[1] There are also many early references to Wither families in Staffordshire and Herefordshire, from some of which pedigrees could be made. I have resisted the temptation to link on these disconnected pedigrees with the main line of the Withers of Hampshire as descended from the Wythers of Lancashire, though the Wythers of Ilum, "sometimes called Ipstonesland," Staffordshire,[2] are almost certainly (through the Ipstanes family) connected with the Sir William Wyther, the executor of Edmund, first Earl of Lancaster, and with Sir Thomas Wyther, the counsellor or chancellor of his son and grandson, Thomas, the second Earl, and Henry, the first Duke of Lancaster. The title of this work is "Materials for a History of the Wither Family." I must leave it to my descendants, who may have more leisure and greater opportunities, to link together these and future researches and discoveries into a more connected history of the origins of the Wither family, and of their settlement in other parts of England than Hampshire.

[1] See Appendix I, and Rudder's Gloucestershire, p. 307.

[2] Eoderweek's Survey of Staffordshire, p. 464.

NOTE ON THE LANCASTER FAMILY.

1.—Edmund, 1st Earl, bro. of Ed. I; ob. 1297.

2.—Thos. Plantagenet, 2nd Earl, attainted and beheaded 1322.

3.—Henry Plantagenet, 3rd Earl, brother and heir restored in blood and honours 1324; ob. 1345.

4.—Henry Plantagenet, son and heir, created Duke 1351; ob. 1361.

CHAPTER II.

DESCENDANTS OF THE TWO ELDER SONS

OF

THOMAS WYTHER, ESQ.

LIVING CIRCA 1363,

OF PENDLETON HALL, NR. CLITHEROE, LANCASHIRE.

CHAPTER II.

DESCENDANTS OF THE TWO ELDER SONS OF THOMAS WYTHER, ESQ.

LIVING CIRCA 1363,

OF PENDLETON HALL, NR. CLITHEROE, LANCASHIRE.

THIS chapter is necessarily very fragmentary. The facts recorded are based mainly on the statements of the Elizabethan pedigree which faces the chapter, supplemented by (1) the Heralds' Visitations for Essex in 1558, 1634, and 1672; (2) Inquisitions post mortem and Chancery proceedings at various dates in the sixteenth century; and (3) Wills at Somerset House.

Thomas Wyther (living circa 1363), of Pendleton Hall, Lancashire, had three sons—(1) Thomas, (2) Richard, (3) Robert.

Robert, the youngest, came to Manydown, and his descendants and their history are fully recorded under Wyther of Hampshire. I proceed to state briefly what is known of the two elder sons and their descendants.

THOMAS WYTHER of Whalley, Lancashire.

Of *Thomas*, the eldest, there is this note on the Elizabethan pedigree :—

"*Thomas Wyther Esquyer: servant and steward to the Abbot of Whalley in the countie of Lancaster. Hee slew one Robert Worsley Kg^t and for that deed hee with his brethren fled into Cheshire and served the Abbot of the Vale Royall*[1] *in the countie of Cheshire.*"

Careful researches among the archives of the Worsley family have failed to discover any particulars or confirmation of this deed,

[1] Vale Royall, a Cistercian Abbey founded by Edw. I, 1278.

though there were several Sir Robert Worsleys in succession at the end of fourteenth and beginning of the fifteenth centuries. Nor has anything been discovered of Thomas Wyther's descendants, except their names to the fourth generation, where they apparently end in three monks: one was Abbot of Combermere, co. Cheshire; another, *Daniel*, was Prior of the Vale Royall; and a third, *Richard* was a monk of Chester. (See Pedigree.)

RICHARD WYTHER of Hunstanton

Richard Wyther, the second son of Thomas of Pendleton Hall, "came to Hunstanton in the parish of Wynbury in the Countie of Cheshire, and married the daughter of Lea or Lee in the same parish." (See Pedigree.)

His grandson, *Robert Wyther* of Wynbury, was "Bayley" or "Receptor" for the Earl of Shrewsbury (circa 1450), and married Emery, daughter of Whiteacre of Nantwich, Esquire. Their descendants seemed mainly to have engaged in business in London, and some of them settled in Essex and Somersetshire.

LAURENCE WYTHER of Ilbrewers, Somersetshire.

Quarterly, 1st and 4th *Wyther*; and azure three standing dishes two and one, *Standish*; 3rd argent on a bend sable three stags' heads caboshed, or, *Stanley*.

Robert Wyther's eldest son *Lawrence*, an alderman of London, made a good marriage with Elizabeth, daughter of George Standish, Esq. (son of Sir Robert Standish of Standish, co. Lancaster, Knight), by his marriage with S. Stanley, fourth brother of the Earl of Derby. He bought the manor and park of Ilbrewers, near Taunton, Somersetshire, with 1640 acres of land.[1] He died 1574.

[1] Inq. p.m. 16 Eliz., p. 1, No. 77.

The issue of this marriage was *Fabian* (died 1548), a noted goldsmith of London, who lent money to Queen Elizabeth, and wrote books on astrology which may be seen at the British Museum, and *George* (born 1525), who took Holy Orders and became Rector of Danbury, Essex, and Archdeacon of Colchester and D. D. 1562. The Archdeacon evidently had Protestant

GEORGE WYTHER (Archdeacon of Colchester), of Danbury, Essex.

tendencies, for he objected to wearing the "cornered cappe" ordered by Archbishop Parker, and was in consequence suspended from preaching; but yielded at the urgent request of the people of Bury [St. Edmonds][1]. In 1582, he had some correspondence with Burleigh (Queen Elizabeth's minister), in which he tenders his "thanks for the good friendship and favour which he and others his brethren the ministers of Essex had found at Burleigh's hands in their late suits."[2] He was the author of *A view of the Marginal Notes of the Popish Testament translated into English by the English fugitive residents at Rhemes, in France,* published 1588. By his letters[3] to the Prince Elector Palatine, he seems to have taken a leading part on the Puritan side in the ecclesiastic controversies of the early years of Queen Elizabeth's reign. He died November 17th, 1605, aged 80.

[1] The Petyt MSS. B.M., Fol. 820.

[2] Salisbury Collection of Letters, B.M., Nov. 12, 1582.

[3] Zurich letters, 2nd series, ii, 159—163, quoted by Canon McColl, Reformation Settlement, pp. 344, 396, 417.

Wither, impaling ermine on a fess sable; 3 mullets, or, *Lister*.

George Wither's descendants lived at Danbury, Essex, where he had "a mansion."[4]

His third son, George of Danbury, married Ann Lister, of the ancient family of Lister of Yorkshire, "of which was Sir Martin Lister, the celebrated physician, temp Charles I."[5]

[4] Chancery Proceedings, 23 Eliz. B.b. 32, No. 12, W.W. 16, No. 42.

[5] B.M. 6065, Plut. 12 $\frac{V}{13}$.

Thomas Wyther, younger brother of Robert Wyther of Wynbury, came to Glastonbury, Somersetshire, and had a son *William* of Bridgwater. Another brother, *John*, seems to have settled at Dunster, in that county. A tombstone in Dunster Church, dated 1487, bears the following inscription:—

JOHN WYTHER of Dunster.

> "Of yor charitie pray for the soules of
> John Wyther and Agnes his wif, and
> John Wyther their eldest son, whose bodys
> Resteth under this stone anno d'ni Mill'mo
> CCCCLCCCVII penultimo die Septe'bris
> Expectando generalem ressurrect'onem mortuor'
> et vita' eterna. Amen."

This inscription confirms the pedigree in the Herald's Visitation of London, 1633–35, which also bears the correct crest and arms of Wither.[1] From this branch of the family came in direct descent Sir William Wither, Lord Mayor of London (1707).

Another son of Robert Wyther of Wynbury, *Richard Wyther*, born at Newport, co. Salop, died in London 1521, was a citizen and salter in London. Pedigrees and wills show that at least five generations of London Withers were members of the Salters' Guild. The interesting will[2] of Richard Wyther, with its early sixteenth century arrangement of obits, shows that he was an important member of the "coĩaltie of salters," to whom he bequeathed "a standing cup with cover gilt hanging in the knop there of iii saltes weying xxix unc. Dĩ." He also bequeathed a considerable sum towards "the gildying of the Altar of Corpus Xti in the Salters chappell." The Secretary to the Salters' Company tells me that the "standing cup" and other gifts mentioned in the will, were lost in the fire which destroyed the old Salters' Hall.

For the purpose of the pedigree, I have consulted the wills of numerous London Withers engaged in "business" between 1492—1721, and have placed in the Appendix a list of some thirty of the principal ones, with references to the Somerset House calendars, for the benefit of those who wish to consult them further. Needless to say the family spread widely in London and were engaged in various trades, and at the present day there are at least three families engaged in business in London who bear the Wither arms, but add an *s* to the name. One of the old London Withers, William Wither, "citizen and merchant taylor," who died 1592, was a grandson of John Wither of Manydown, who died 1506; but most of them seem to have sprung from Richard Wither of Hunstanton in Wynbury.

The earliest will[1] examined, dated 30th August, 1492, proved 5th November, 1492, is that of Richard Wether (*sic*) of the "fellowship of haberdashers," and is of such an interesting character that I append large extracts from it. The bequests to the poor of Hereford in addition to those of London, look as if this Richard was a descendant of Sir William Wyther, the judge, and connected with the Withers of Staffordshire and Herefordshire.

[1] P. C. C. 114 Doggett, S.H. See Appendix III.

The latest[2] of the London wills I have consulted is that of Sir William Wither, Kgt., 1721, who was son of a linen draper in Cheapside. The pedigree at the head of this chapter shows his descent from John Wyther of Dunster. He bore the Wither arms. He was knighted at Kensington,[3] when Alderman of London, 20th October, 1699, and was made Lord Mayor in 1707. He died at his country house at Fulham (1721), leaving various gifts to the poor of Fulham (and other parishes) "as are or have been housekeepers of the Communion of the Church of England." Sir William Wither's uncle, John, who married Mary, daughter of Sir Thomas Morton, Kgt., was called "King of Ham. He was very like King Charles II." The Lord Mayor's descendants were living at Fulham in 1768.

[2] P.C.C. 39 Buckingham, S.H.

SIR WILLIAM WITHER Lord Mayor.

[3] Le Neve's Knights, p. 471.

WITHER OF HAMPSHIRE.

(A.D. 1389—1871.)

CHAPTER III.

WITHER OF MANYDOWN.

(A.D. 1389—1789.)

a.

Martha.
Mary.
Ann.
Grace.

27, d. 1649.
1628.
29.
p.)

er

WITHER OF HAMPSHIRE.

(A.D. 1389—1871.)

CHAPTER III.

WITHER OF MANYDOWN, 1389—1789.

1389—1484.

"*ROBERT WYTHER 3rd sonne of Thomas Wyther, Esquyre of Lancashire came to Hampshire to a place called Manydowne, where hee married a wyfe, and by her had yssue.*" This statement of the Elizabethan Pedigree (1575) is confirmed by an old tradition in the family, which again is based on a statement contained in a document once among Mr. Wither Bramston's papers at Oakley Hall, now destroyed—"that the above Robert was the nephew and godson of Prior Robert Rudborne (1384—1394), of the Convent of St. Swithun's, Winchester, who made him 'firmarius' of the desmesne lands of the manor of Manydown."

Nothing more is known of this Robert, unless he is the same as the Robert Wyther of Hatfield, who was "Keeper of the Victuals" at Carisbrooke Castle, I.W., in 1344.[1]

[1] Exchq. Roll, Q.R. $\frac{24}{3}$, 18 Edw., iii.

Notices of WITHER in Hampshire, XIV and XV centuries.

That there were Withers in Hampshire in the fourteenth and fifteenth centuries is clear from the Lay Subsidy and Exchequer Rolls, and from the Obedientiary Rolls of the Priory of St. Swithun, Winchester. *e.g.*, In 1338, John Wythere is mentioned as renting a house from the Monks of St. Swithun in Southgate Street, Winchester, and again in 1352.[2] In 1378 John Wether

[2] Kitchin, Obed. Roll, p. 101, 408-10.

and his wife and Richard Wyther and his wife are taxed in the villat. of Whitwell and Rookley, I.W.[1] In following year we find Hugh Wyther in the retinue of the Sieur de Audelegh at the muster at Southampton.[2] In 1402 we get nearer Manydown. John Chase, the zealous Chapter Clerk (1623—1646) of Winchester Cathedral in his notes on documents belonging to the Chapter, records under the head of Wotton Manor a feoffment of lands and buildings in Nately Scures and Newnham, near Basingstoke, made to William Wither, 3 Henry IV (1402).[3] In 1412 Richard Wyther acts as attorney in a suit brought at Basingstoke by Hugh Kingsmill; and in the earliest rental roll (1400—1428) the same name is found paying rent to Basingstoke Manor.[4] In 1431–36 John Wythere holds lands in Co. Southampton and tenements in burgage in Winchester.[5] In 1414 John Wyther and Amice, his wife, sell a messuage, rents, and homage in Winchester and Otterborne.[6] At the inquisition for alien subsidies taken at Winchester 1453, John Wither is one of the jurors.[7]

The above note of John Chase, showing that in 1402 a Wither was recorded as possessing property under the Manor of Wootton, is most interesting and significant as bearing on our history. It is to be remembered that Wootton and not Manydown is the name of the Manor until 1430. "Unluckily," says Dean Kitchin in his interesting and detailed history of the great Manor of Manydown, compiled for the Hampshire Record Society in 1895, "we have no Roll extant between 1423 and 1430, so that the exact year of the change, and perhaps also the reason for it, is not to be discovered. All we know is that in 1423 the Manor is Wottone; while in 1430 it is Manidoune."[8] The Court and Compotus Rolls of the Manor for the fifteenth century have been carefully searched, but the inspection does not reveal the name Wither in connection with either Wootton or Manydown until the first year of Richard III (1484). In the Court Roll of the Manor of that year and in 1485, ***Thomas Wither*** is first mentioned, and in 1487 he appears as "firmarius."[1] From that date the record is continuous and complete.

[1] Kitchin, Manor of Manydown, p. 3.

I will now summarize, as much as is consistent with a family history, the long story of the Withers of Manydown.

Wither, impaling or, a lion rampant, double-headed azure, *Mason*.

THOMAS WITHER, 1484—1506.

(I.)—*Thomas Wither*, of Manydown, married Joan, daughter of Richard Mason, a family that for centuries held land at Sydmanton, one of the eleven tythings of Kingsclere, the ancient chieftown of the "hundred" of that name, seven miles north-west of Basingstoke.

Thomas Wither rendered the "Compotus" of the manor[2] in 1491, 1501, and in 1506, in which year he died and was buried at Wootton. In his will he speaks of "Septem pueris meis." Three only are known: ***John***, the eldest, who succeeded at Manydown; ***Richard***, of Sydmanton; and *Thomas*, "of Erlstone,"[3] in Burghclere parish. To his widow, Joan Wither, and her son, John, was granted in 1514 by Prior Silkstead the lease of "the scite of the Manor of Manydown and of the Rectory of Wootton." A facsimile and translation of this lease (the earliest we have) is appended in Chapter VII. Widow Joan Wither rendered the Compotus of the Manor as "firmaria" in 1507, 1516, 1522, and 1533. She died in 1528, and was buried at Wootton. Her will mentions her sons John and Richard, probably the only ones that survived.

[2] Kitchin, Manor of Manydown, p. 207.

[3] Hants Field Club proc., Vol. iii, p. 2., Erlstone Manor House.

At this point in the history there is a great deal of information in various "wills," in the "inquisitiones post mortem," and in the "Feet of Fines," Co. Southampton, concerning the descendants of Richard the second son of Thomas of Manydown and of Nicholas the third son.

Richard Wither, sometimes spoken of as of Sydmanton (his mother's native place), sometimes as of Wherwell, had six sons and two daughters, who settled in the parishes of Kingsclere and Burghclere. They are traceable for at least four generations. (See Pedigree IV.)

John, the eldest of the six, bought (1561) 1600 acres of land and six messuages in the parish of Kingsclere from the Edwards family.[1] John Wither's son *Henry*, who died 1602, bought some 2700 acres in addition and twenty messuages from the Fawkener family,[2] one of whom (Richard Fawkener) had married Henry's aunt Joan in 1575. This considerable property was situated in Erlstone (Burghclere parish) and in Sydmanton and Itchinswell (Kingsclere), and included the properties called Beenhams Court, Apshanger, and Strattons (all well known places in Kingsclere parish), which he left to his three daughters,—Frances, Anne, and Beatrice[3].

Wither, impaling sable 3 falcons argent, beaked legged and belled or, *Fawkener*.

Richard Wither's youngest son *Nicholas* settled at North Oakley (also in the parish of Kingsclere, near Hannington), the Manor of which he bought in 1586, together with 680 acres of land from Thomas Ayliffe.[4]

Another *Nicholas Wither*, son of John and Richard Wither's brother Thomas of Erlstone, was one of the witnesses of the will of Morphet Kingsmill, last Abbess of Wherwell (1570). He was then the occupant of the Manor of Middleton in the parish which now goes by the descriptive name of ***Longparish***, which Manor he held under the Abbess and Convent of Wherwell,

[1] Feet of Fines, Co. Southton., 3 and 17 Eliz.

[2] Fawkener Family, see chap. viii.

[3] Inq. post mortem, Co. Southton.

[4] Feet of Fines, Co. Southton., 28 Eliz.

Pedigree IV.

WITHER OF KINGSCLERE (SYDMANTON, ITCHINSWELL, AND NORTH OAKLEY).

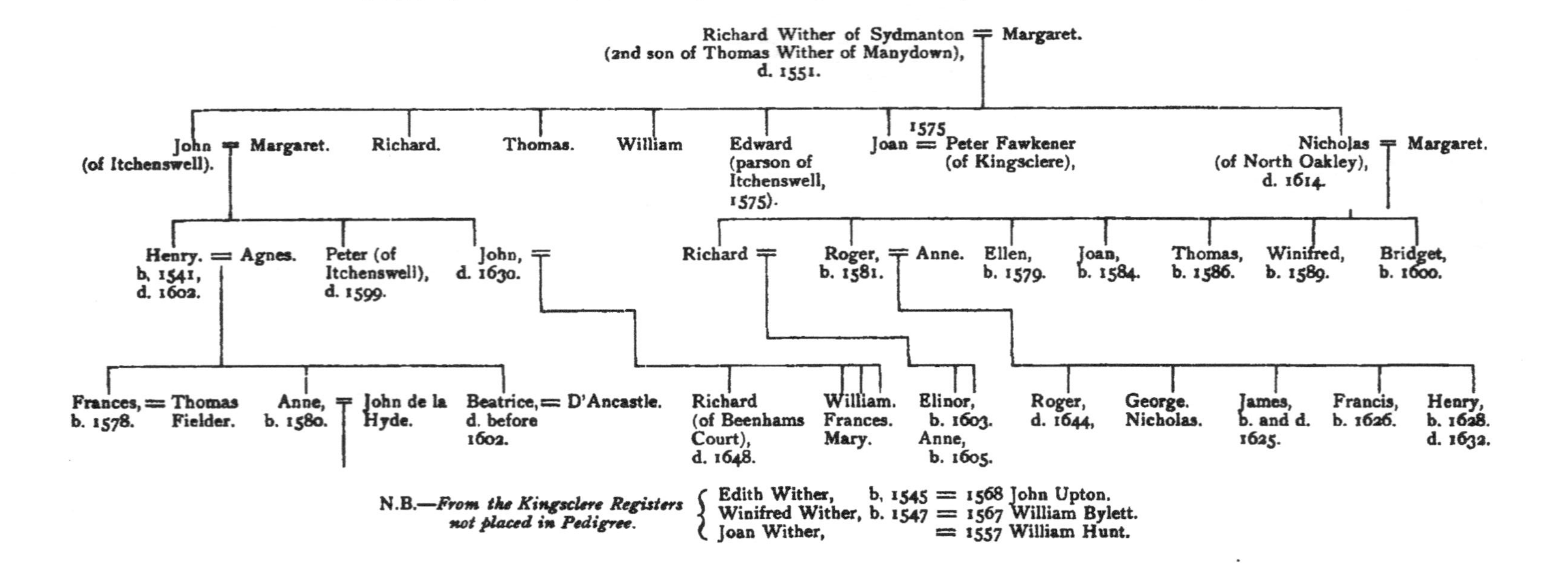

N.B.—*From the Kingsclere Registers not placed in Pedigree.*

- Edith Wither, b. 1545 = 1568 John Upton.
- Winifred Wither, b. 1547 = 1567 William Bylett.
- Joan Wither, = 1557 William Hunt.

and after the suppression of the monastery (1543) he held it under Sir Thomas West, Lord de la Warr, for his life, the life of his wife Jane, and that of their eldest son Nicholas.[1] He died a very old man in 1637. His son Nicholas bought subsequently from Lord de la Warr and from Sir Mathew Carew some 2000 acres of land and other property in Longparish,[2] where his descendants lived for four generations and are recorded in the Longparish Registers. (See Pedigree V.)

[1] See Clutterbuck's Wherwell Abbey.

[2] Feet of Fines, Co. Southton, 5, 7, 16, James I.

The members of these collateral branches of the family,—some of whom added *s* to the name, and some of whom seem to have held the position of yeoman farmers—seem by their various "wills" to have kept up their connection with their Hampshire neighbours and relatives, the Withers of Manydown, to whom I now return.

JOHN WITHER, 1506—1532.

Wither, impaling, quarterly, gules and sable, a lion rampant, between three crosses, pattée, or. All within a bordure argent charged with 8 torteaux, *Ayliffe*.

(2.)—*John Wither* of Manydown, eldest son of Thomas, married *Agnes Ayliffe*, a member of a very old Hampshire family[3] that then owned Skeyres or Skures, now Ewhurst Park, three miles north of Manydown. He rendered the "Compotus" of the Manor in 1530 and 1533, after his mother's death. He died in 1536. His "will" is so typical of ancient wills, and so interesting from its local character and as a family record, that I give it here in its entirety with its ancient spelling, and also the abstract of that of his widow, who died in 1544.

[3] Ayliffe family. See chap. viii.

WILL OF JOHN WITHER.

"In dei nomine the yere of our Lorde God, a thousand five hundred and 35, 23 day of Marche. *I, John Wether* of the p'she of *Laurens Wotton*, in the dioces of Winchester, being of good mynde and remembrance, make my last will and testa-

Pedigree V.

WITHER OF LONGPARISH.

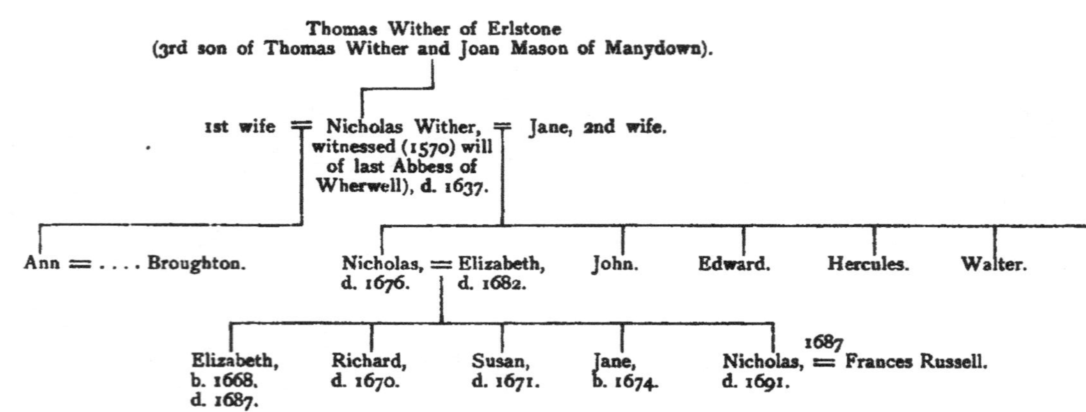

N.B.—*From the Longparish Registers and from Harleian Pub., vols. 23 and 24, pp. 99, 101, not placed in Pedigree.*

- Nicholas Wither the elder of Andover, buried at Longparish, March 29, 1664.
- Nicholas Wither of Andover, ætat. 25 = Mrs. Sarah Foyle of Abbotts Ann, February 15, 1664/5.
- Nicholas Wither of Longparish, ætat. 26 = Elizabeth Hussard of Upton, June 14, 1667.

ment in this manner of wise or manner of forme.—Furst I bequeath my soule to Almighty God, to our blessed lady and to all the blessed company in heven, my body to be buried in the church of St. Laurence Wotton before the 'rode lought' (sic). Also I bequeath to the said parish church 6 ewes. Also I bequeath to the cathedral church of St. Swythun, 2d. It: I bequeath to the high aulter of St. Laurence church 10*s*. It: I bequeath to the church of Wortyng, to the church of Ocle, to the church of Dean, to the church of Avington, to the church of Ewhirst, to the church of Baghurst, to the church of Tadley, to the church of Sherborn St. John to the church of Sherborn Allhallows, to every oon of them oon ewe. It: I bequeath to John my son, oon heifer. It: I bequeath to Richard my son, £6. 13s. 4d sterling, and myne '*endenture of yeres*' which I have upon the farm of ***Manydowne*** to be delyvred to the said Richard, my son, ymediately after Agnes my wif is married. Also I bequeath to the said Richard my son oon yeron bownd carte and plowe, and 6 horses, with their harnys and all apparel to them. It: I bequeath to the said Richards, my son, fourty ewes, a pott, a pan, a cofer, 2 broches, and a bedd with all the apparel to the said bedd, and I will that all theis bequests and legacies bequeathed to my said son Richard, that and he depart from this present lif without heirs male, then I will that all the said bequests and legacies, so to him bequeathed, retorne and goo to John my eldest son, and so from him to the next heir male of my name, and I will that the heirs of my son or of any other of my said children that shall enjoy such bequest as with the indentures of the said farm of ***Manydowne***, shall yerely keep a yerely mynde with ten masses, at the church of St. Laurence Wotton, for my soule, my father and mother's soule, and all xpen soules. It: I bequeath to George, my son, £6 sterlings, and 20 shepe. It: I bequeath to Thomas, my son, £5 sterlings. It: I bequeath to William, my son, £5 sterlings, to Agnes, my daughter, to Elynor, my daughter, to Ann, my daughter, to Alice, my daughter, to Margaret, my daughter, to every oon of them, £5 sterlings. And also I will that if it shall please God that any of my said children as George, Thomas, William, Agnes, Elinor, Ann, Alice, and Margaret, shall depart from this present lif or they come to lawful aige, then I will the bequest to hym or hir so departed shall be distributed and parted amongis them that bee a live. I bequeath to every oon of my god-children 2d. I bequeath to every oon of my servants oon lambe, the residue of my goods, my debtis and legacies paid, I give and bequeath to Agnes my wif, whom I make and ordyne my executrix, to dispose for the welth of my soule, my father and mother's soules and all xpen souls, after hir descrecon and mynd. And Richard Alyff, and Richard Whether I ordeyn and make to be my overseers. Theis bering witness, Sir Umfry Ornary, Vicar of Wotton, John Pottyng, pson of Okle, and John Ellams, with others moo."

Proved 4 July, 1536.

ABSTRACT OF WILL OF AGNES WITHER

(Née Aylitfe) Widow of above.

To be buried at Wooton by side of late husband. Bequeaths to the high altar of Wootton 3*s*. & 4*d*. To the Church of Wootton 4 sheep. To the Church of Kingsclere "to be a benefactour" 2 sheep. To the Church of Hannington "to be a benefactour" 2 sheep. To the Church of Sherborne S. John 2 sheep. To the Church of Sherborne Monachorum (Monk Sherborne) one sheep. To my 5 children that be unmarried, viz: Thomas, William, Anne, Alice, and Margaret £4 each besides the £6 by their father's will. To Thomas and William 20 sheep. To John Wither 10 sheep. To children's children a sheep. A 'trental of masses' at her funeral, the same at her 'months mynde' and at her 'yerely mynde.' "I give and bequeath my wedding ring to the maintenance of the chalice of the Church of Wotton aforesaid." Daughter Agnes Goodyer, Daughters-in-law Olyffe Wether (married John), Avelyn Wether (married George). Residuary legatee and exor, son Richard.

Overseers { Sir Rovland Feron, parson of Hannington.
Richard Wether (uncle) of Horewell (Wherwell).

Witnesses { Sir William Denet, parson of Wortyng.
Sir William Unwood, curate of Wotton. John Wether (son).
Thomas Ayliff (nephew), Richard Burnell, John Hake and George Wether (son).

Proved 1544.

It is evident from the above will of John Wither, and by subsequent dealings with the Manor that the "endenture of yeres which I have upon the farm of Manydowne" was not left to his eldest son *John*, but to *Richard* the second son, though this is the only instance in the long history of the Wither tenure of Manydown when it did not go to the eldest son. The tenure of Manydown was a peculiar one, something like, though not precisely, a copyhold. There was absolute fixity of tenure, but "fines" were paid to the lords (the Prior and Convent of St. Swithun's) on the death of the tenant, and at other periods according to the leases. As will be seen in the course of this history, the Withers of Manydown gradually became possessed in fee simple of considerable property (amounting in 1790 to about 6000 acres) around the comparatively small demesne lands (1557 acres) of the Manor which were not enfranchised until 1863.

I will now record what is known of Richard Wither's brothers and sisters, remembering that Richard (not John) succeeded his father John at Manydown.

(1.)—*John* seems to have retired to Ramsdell (three miles north). He married "Olyfe," who died 1563, and was buried at Wootton, for Ramsdell was not ecclesiastically separated from Wootton until 1868. Presumably he married again, for the Wootton registers record the names of six children of "John Wither of Ramsdell" between 1564—1580. He died and was buried at Wootton, November 8th, 1582.

(2.)—*George* married Avelyn Shanke, who died 1584. He settled at Dummer (four miles south of Manydown), and became the progenitor of the Withers of Hall Place (Oakley Hall). *See* chap. V.

(3.)—*William* married Jone Webb, and had a son Nathaniel who was living in 1633.

(4.)—*Agnes* married — Goodyer, and

(5.)—*Ann* married (1568) Nicholas Whitland.

I cannot trace what became of the other four children.

(3.)—*Richard Wither* of Manydown married *Margaret*, daughter of William Poynter, a family long settled at Whitchurch, Hants, that came originally from Somersetshire. Richard Wither is recorded in two old pedigrees as having married twice, making his eldest son, who succeeded at Manydown, the only child of an unnamed first wife. The only support I can find for this is the reference in the will of Richard Wither's widow, Margaret, who died 1582, to "John Wether my son in law."

Wither impaling sable, 2 piles, the points ending in crosses formées, 2 in base and 1 in chief, or, *Poynter*.

Richard Wither and Margaret his wife had eight sons, John, Richard, James, Arthur, George, Otho, William and Ferdinando; and five daughters, Margaret, Elizabeth, Barbara, Elinor, and Joan.

John succeeded at Manydown.

George, born 1562, became the father of the poet, George Wither, and settled at Bentworth, where his descendants lived until 1730. (See Chapter VI.)

Otho, born 1568, survived his mother and married, but died s.p.

Ferdinando, born 1574, married — Page of Harrow-on-the-Hill. He was admitted to Gray Inn 16th May, 1611. He inherited from his mother lands in the parish of Merton, Surrey. He was living 1638.

Wither impaling gules, a fess engraved ermine between three doves, or, beaked and membered of the field, all within a bordure engraved of the 2nd, *Page*.

The other sons died young.

The eldest daughter *Margaret* predeceased her father in 1560; the record of her burial is the first entry in the Wootton registers.

The other four daughters inherited from their mother copyholds in Woodmancote, near Micheldever, Hants.

Richard Wither died at Manydown, and was buried at Wootton, 23rd July, 1577.

JOHN WITHER, 1577—1620.

(4.) *John Wither* of Manydown, eldest son of Richard, married Joan, daughter of John Love, a family long settled at Basing Park, near Alton, Hants.[1] Joan's brother, Nicholas Love, became Head Master and Warden of Winchester College. I have been unable to discover either the will of John Wither, who died in 1620, or that of his widow, who died 1639; but their burials and the baptisms of their ten children (see pedigree) are recorded

Wither, impaling 3 bars, gules in chief, as many lions' heads, erased, of the last, *Love*.

[1] Family of Love. See Chap. viii.

in the Wootton Registers, and accord with the old pedigrees and with the Heralds Visitation of Hants in 1634, and with the Inquisitiones Post Mortem, 1620. Of the children,—

(1.)—*William*, born 1584. Succeeded to Manydown (see post).

Sable 2 bars argent in chief 3 plates, *Hungerford* impaling *Wither*.

(2.)—*Elizabeth*, born 1589, married, 1605, Edmund Hungerford, of N. Standish, Wiltshire, a scion of the Hungerfords of Farley Court, Somersetshire.

(3 and 4.)—*John*, born 1597, and *James*, born 1599, both went to Winchester College as scholars. The latter became a Fellow of New College, Oxford, where he died, 1627, aged 28, "pulmonis vitio." There is a tablet to his memory in New College cloisters. They left gifts to Wootton Church. (See Appendix IV.)

(5.)—*Richard*, born 1600, married Thomazine, daughter and co-heir of James Mason of Canterbury. He settled at Stoke-next-Guildford, where he had three sons and four daughters, one of whom, Grace, was married at Wootton in 1651. He was living in 1662, for in that year he gave his pedigree and names of his children to the Heralds Office.

During the life of John Wither there was some dealing with Manydown which I do not understand. There are two deeds extant of 22nd and 23rd Elizabeth (1580—1) which recite that the "farm of Manydown" and the rectorial tythe of Wootton, "formerly occupied by Richard Wither by demise," are leased by Dean Humphrey to Queen Elizabeth, and by her assigned to Michael Stanhope, gentleman of Grays Town, for sixty-five years, but I also possess a deed of indenture of 35th Elizabeth (1593) in which "John Wither of Manydown" buys from the Woodward of the Manor Singett and Roundgrove copses. Moreover, the usual renewal of the lease of Manydown and the rectorial tithe of Wootton to his son William in 1618 is granted for fifty years, and makes no allusion to the above transaction. It is difficult to see what the 1581 deeds mean unless, perchance, John Wither had in some way offended the Queen, who entered upon the Dean and Chapter lease and assigned it to another.

In 43 Elizabeth (1601) John Wither was appointed collector of the tenths and fifteenths in Hampshire and the Isle of Wight, The deed of quietus for the same, dated 1 James (1603), is among the family archives.

In 1613 an interesting family arrangement was made by deed[1] between John Wither and his eldest son William, by which the father gives up all his rights, titles, etc., in Manydown and the rectorial tythe of Wootton to his son, who was to keep him and his mother in certain reserved rooms at Manydown, paying him £40 a year and keeping for him two servants, a horse, three couple of beagles, and one greyhound for his pleasure, or to pay him 200 marks yearly if he chose to live elsewhere. William to educate his younger brothers, John, James, and Richard, and to pay them £300 each on their attaining the age of twenty-six years.

[1] See deed to James.

There is nothing to show that John Wither ever moved from Manydown, where he died 30th May, 1620. His monument and that of his wife, who died in 1639, is the earliest of the many Wither memorials in Wootton Church.

WILLIAM WITHER (?) 1620—1653.

(5.)—With *William Wither* (i) of Manydown, eldest son of John, born 1584, begins the series of five William Withers who "reigned" in succession at Manydown from 1620 to 1789.

Risley.

Wither, impaling argent a fess azure between three crescents gules, *Risley*.

He married *Susanna*, daughter of Paul Risley, of Chetwood (Bucks), Esq., by Dorothy his wife, daughter of Sir Richard Temple, of Stow, Knight.[1] Provision for the marriage was made by a sum of £1200 from Susan Risley's father, and her father-in-law and husband settled upon her for life as a jointure the manor and advowson of *Bighton*, near Alton, Hants, with 400 acres of land and other property in Bighton which John Wither had bought from Henry, Earl of Southampton in 1598.[2] The issue of this marriage was thirteen children (see pedigree), a numerous family, which equalled that of his grandparents, of whom however but few survived their parents.

ines, co. 40 Eliz.

Of the four sons :—

(1.)—*John*, the elder, born 1610, died s.p. 1634.

(2.)—*Paul*, predeceased his father, s.p.

(3.)—*William*, born 1623, succeeded at Manydown. (See Post.)

(4.)—*Robert*, born 1626, became Fellow and Steward of New College, Oxford. He married and settled at East Oakley, where his father left him property. He died 1679, leaving a son George.

Of the nine daughters :—

Susan, the eldest, married Richard Hill, of Bradley (co. Hereford).

Dorothy, married William Collins, Esq., J.P., of Corhampton, Hants.

Ann, married, 1646, Dr. John Pottenger, Head Master of Winchester College. Their eldest son, John, married his relative, Philadelphia Ernle, and became Comptroller of the Pipe Rolls (*temp.* Car. II). He has left charming memoirs. After the death of her husband she went to live with her sister Ann at Corhampton, where she died. There are slabs in the chancel of Corhampton Church to the memory of both sisters.

Mary, born 1631, married Michael Ernle, of Brimslade Park, Wilts, who settled on her the Manor of East Kennett, and lands in Calne, Wilts.

The other five daughters died unmarried.

William Wither in his lifetime added considerably to the family property at Manydown. In 1619 he bought from the *Uvedale* family the manor and tything of *Woodgarston* (two miles north of Manydown), comprising the manor house with chapel, the ancient Romano-British fort and 415 acres of land,[1] and in the same year he bought from the *Rumbold* family the moiety of the manor of *Worting* and the advowson of the Church, with 800 acres of land, ten messuages, three cottages, four lofts, and ten gardens in the parish of Worting.[2] He also bought land in 1650 at Hartley Wintney and Bishopstoke. But by far the most important acquisition was the *purchase in 1649 of the fee simple of Manydown* from the "Contractors" of the Long Parliament. In that fateful year an act was passed "abolishing Deans, Deans and Chapters, Canons, Prebends, and other officers belonging to any Cathedral or Collegiate Church in England and Wales," and their corporate lands passed into the hands of Commissioners for Sale.

[1] See Manor of Woodgarston, by Rev. R. F. Bigg-Wither.

[2] Feet of Fines, and numerous family deeds.

William Wither, whose interest in the old Cathedral Manor was paramount, naturally entered into negotiations with the "Contractors," and agreed to "purchase the Manor of Manydown with the Manor House and all and every the lands, rights, and hereditaments thereto belonging" for the sum of £6550. 14*s*. 4*d*. To this the whole of the "customary and immediate" tenants of the Manor gave their assent and consent to accept Mr. William Wither as their landlord in the terms of the interesting deed, of which a *facsimile* is opposite.

A detailed survey of the Manor made in connection with this transaction is published in Dean Kitchin's *Manor of Manydown*,[1] by which it appears that the demesnes, lands, and woods of the Manor in the occupation of William Wither amounted to 1212 acres, besides the submanor of *Hanington* then leased by Mr. Thomas Druett, and *Fabians and Marvins*[2] [Tangier Park and estate] then leased by Sir Richard Kingsmill, and a number of smaller holdings in Upper and Lower Wootton.

At the restoration in 1662, the Dean and Chapter of Winchester re-entered upon their rights in the Manor; but Mr. William Wither's son and heir, then at Manydown, was not restored one farthing of the large sum his father had expended on the purchase. He and his successors, however, retained the Manydown Manor house and the demesne lands of the Manor under the Dean and Chapter on long leases, renewable in the usual way every seven years, at a small annual rent and a moderate fine.

In 1862, when negotiations for the enfranchisement of Manydown were being carried on, my father (Lovelace Bigg-Wither) wrote to Lord Eversley (one of the Ecclesiastical Commissioners) citing the above facts, and pleaded (without effect) that they should be taken into consideration in assessing the sum to be paid for the enfranchisement.

The last twenty years of William Wither's tenure of Manydown coincided with the troubled times of King Charles I and the Commonwealth, in which a large majority of the Hampshire squires sided with the Parliament. I am disposed to think William Wither was at first, like his first cousin George

rest of the hono:ble Contracto:rs
lonings to the Dounes and

of Wontleton, Doe humbly certifie unto ye hono:bles
[illegible] and Consideration made thereof of
[illegible] of Mannor aforesaid Esquire beinge
said Mannor wth the appurtenances. And
[illegible] given unto us as Tenants by the late
his purchase become our Landlord in as
[illegible], And wee doe most humbly desire
reasonable Rates, and wth as much favour
[illegible] sett our hands and seales the day and

Richard Mogatt Edward Bigg
Rich: Wardlam Rich: Tikes

Wither the Poet, a loyal "King's man." It is not probable that the loyal city of Winchester would have elected him a freeman of that ancient city as they did on 1st April, 1631, if at that time he had been a Parliamentarian; but in 1642 we find him, among many other leading men in Hampshire, a member of the Parliamentary Committee of Public Safety, and he was appointed one of the Commissioners that year to seize warlike stores for the Parliament; and, I fear, he was the Wither member of the committee of three appointed in 1649 to see to the demolition of Winchester Castle.[1] That he had influence with the Parliamentary leaders is evident from the endorsement of an old letter referring to the visit of the "Committee of Religion" to Winchester College, which says: "*Dr. Pottinger* (Head Master), *by his interest in Mr. Withars* (*sic*) *of Manydowne, whose daughter he had married, was hardly acquitted, and Dr. Harris* (Warden) *with much more difficulty.*"

[1] Domestic State Papers, A.D. 1649. Vol. ii, N. 105, p. 320.

His wife, Susan Risley, predeceased him many years on 21st November, 1632. He was buried according to his will near her in the north aisle of old Wootton Church, 26th August, 1653.

Wm. Wither (ii). 1653—1671.

(6.)—*William Wither* (ii) of Manydown was born 1623. He married in 1646 Joan, daughter and co-heir of Thomas Geale of Alton, and cousin and co-heir of Barbara Loker of Andwell, near Basingstoke. By their marriage the old Priory estate at Andwell (held under a beneficial lease renewable on payment of a fine) came into the family. The old Priory House, with the ancient chapel and a picturesque trout stream, became the residence of Thomas Wither's second son and his descendants for 162 years, until the property was sold by Lovelace Bigg-Wither in 1808.

Quarterly 1st and 4th *Wither*, 2nd and 3rd *Mason*, bearing on a shield of pretence quarterly 1st and 4th argent 2 bars sable in chief 3 lions' heads erased of the same langued gules, *Geale*. 2nd and 3rd sable a boar's head over 2 upright spear-heads argent, *Loker*.

Just before William Wither's father died, *viz.*, in March, 1653, the lordships of the hundreds of Chuteley and Holshott were purchased from the Tilney family of Tilney Hall. This purchase was confirmed with the consent of the next Parliament by deed dated 3rd October, 1654. Apparently William Wither (ii) was considered a safe supporter of the existing Government, for a letter dated 18th January, 1659, addressed to a Captain Dunche from Richard Cromwell, then Protector, says: "I think we can justifie Whitchurch as well as Wallop. If you choose one you may choose two, and Dr. Walker may be the other; or rather Withers of Manningdowne, whoe is an active man, and one that Wallop hath disobleiged." However, after the Restoration, *viz.*, in 1663, William Wither was appointed High Sheriff of the county, 9th February, 1662–3; presumably, therefore, he was then considered thoroughly Royalist. His "Quietus" as High Sheriff is a specially interesting example of the kind of document in which the accounts of the county were presented to the King and a formal acquittance given at the end of the term. It is in the form of a "Pipe Roll" 12 ft. 8 in. long, in beautiful script. It is accompanied by a short vellum roll with the accounts of the Constabulary, and of that unpopular tax abolished I William and Mary (1689)—the "hearth tax." On 24th July, 1666, William Wither received his commission as major of militia in the Kingsclere division of Hants. On 1st September, 1667, Mr. Wither and his eldest son William were both admitted as freemen of the city of Winchester,[1] an honour which their father and grandfather had had before them. There were six children born to William Wither and Joan Geale,—

(1.)—***William***, born 1648, succeeded to Manydown.

(2.)—***Thomas***, born 1652, inherited the Andwell property and copyholds in Yateley parish, and the freehold property which his grandfather had acquired at Hartley

[1] See Freemen of Winchester (W. H. Jacob).

Wintney. He married Mary, daughter and heiress of Dr. Thomas Fulkes, Librarian of the Bodleian, Oxford. He left five sons and one daughter. His grandson, William, succeeded to Manydown in 1732. His will and that of his mother-in-law are appended.

(3.)—*Alethea*, born 1655, married in 1682, Mr. Thomas Bethell, merchant, of London. Their nephew, Thomas Bethell, married in 1718 Dorothy Bigg. Alethea Wither died and was buried at Wootton, 13th January, 1708.

(4.)—*Dorothy*, born 1661, married in 1684 Lovelace Bigg, Esq., of Chilton Folliat, Wilts. The grandson of this marriage was the Lovelace Bigg who succeeded to the Wither estates and to Manydown in 1789, on the death of the last of the Withers, when he assumed by royal license their name and arms.—See chap. iv.

Bigg, perpale ermine and azure, a lion passant, guard, or, within a bordure engraved of the third. Charged with 8 fleur-de-lis. or, impaling *Wither*.

(5 and 6.)—*Barbara* and *Joan* died s.p.

William Wither in his will laments that he is not able to provide for his younger children, "owing to debts left me by my father" (there is a list of portions to his uncles and aunts amounting to £4500, which I suppose are the debts referred to), and he adds "debts augmented by the late unhappy times."

William Wither died "variotis fugata," and was buried at Wootton, 29th November, 1671, aged 48. His widow died March 22nd, 1691, aged 71.

WM. WITHER (iii). 1671—1679.

(7.)—*William Wither* (iii), of Manydown, born 1648, was educated at Winchester and Oxford, and entered at Lincoln's Inn. His monument in Wootton Church tells us that he travelled through a great part of France and Italy in the suite of the Viscount Falconberg, Ambassador of Charles II to the Doge and Republic of Venice. Returned home, he was made, "because he deserved it," counsellor-at-law, justice of the peace, senator in parliament. This last notice refers to his election in 1678 as M.P. for Andover. It was, perhaps, because of his father's friendship with the Protector's family that Lord Falconberg, who had married Cromwell's daughter Mary, selected young Mr. Wither to accompany him on his Italian embassy.

He married, soon after his succession to Manydown, in 1671, his young relative and neighbour, Mary, daughter of George Wither, whose elder brother Gilbert was now the squire at Hall place (Oakley Hall). Mary Wither, whose parents were both dead, was not seventeen, but the marriage took place with the full consent of her uncle and guardian, Mr. Gilbert Wither, by special license, at Steventon Church, November 12th, 1673. The good (almost brilliant) promise of the early life of the young squire at Manydown was not fulfilled. Struck down by an attack of smallpox, he died 25th April, 1679, at the early age of thirty-one, leaving a widow and two little children—Mary, born 1675, and William in 1678. His brother, Thomas of Andwell, who was present at his death, has left a touching account of his affectionate thoughtfulness for his young wife on his deathbed, and for all who had tended him in any way. He appointed as trustees for the estates his uncle Robert, of East Oakley, and his sister Mary's husband, Michael Ernle, whom we find in many family documents of this period as a trustee and adviser. His widow continued to live at Manydown as guardian of the children until her death, twenty years later, in January, 1700, in her forty-fifth year. Her daughter Mary, for

Wither impaling *Wither*.

WILLIAM WITHER OF MANYDOWN.

Born 27th February, 1678; died 25th September, 1732; married Elizabeth Nicol.

From his Monument in Wootton Church.

whose maintenance there had been set apart by her father's will "the new built tenement called Battledown Lodge, with its appurtenances and farm lands now leased to my tenant Robert Garrett"—soon followed her mother. She died the next year (1701), and was buried in the same grave in Wootton Church.

Wm. Wither (iv). 1679—1733.

(8).—*William Wither* (iv) of Manydown, born 2nd February, 1678, and therefore hardly fourteen months old when his father died, had a long minority. He went to Winchester, Oxford, and Lincoln's Inn, as his father and so many of his ancestors before him, and then settled down at Manydown, occupying himself with his estates, and,—notwithstanding the many years of ill-health, which his monument records,—indefatigable in magisterial work, "non solum in hâc viciniâ, sed et per agrum Hantoniensem. Semper amatus, semper honoratus." He was High Sheriff of the County in 1706. Opposite is the portrait from his monument in Wootton Church.

Wither, impaling sable a pheon argent, *Nicol*.

He married, 14th January, 1703, Elizabeth Nicol, daughter of Richard Nicol, Esq., of Racton, in Sussex. His wife brought in £4500.

A nephew of hers, Charles Gounter Nicol, created in 1732 K.B., married from Manydown in Wootton Church, Elizabeth, daughter of William Blunden, Esq., of Basingstoke. Her niece married Sir Henry Maynard, of Walthamstow, Essex, who became one of the trustees of her husband's will. Sir Henry's son William, represented as a boy reclining on the ground, gazing at a parrot, is, together with Sir Charles Gounter's and Lady Nicol's pictures, among the most treasured of the family portraits now in the possession of the Misses Bigg-Wither at Brighton.

As an illustration of the life at Manydown in the days of William Wither and Elizabeth Nicol his wife, will be found in chap. vii, under "Manydown House," a ménu of the dinner provided for the tenants and those who attended the Court Leet of the Manor yearly on All Saints' Day or Goose day.

William Wither (iv) died September 25th, 1733, aged 55. His widow survived him only two years. They had no children; and now for the first time in the long history of the Withers of Manydown the estates went to a collateral, namely, to his cousin, William Wither, of Andwell, grandson of Thomas Wither, second son of William Wither and Joan Geale (see pedigree). His will is important, as bearing upon the future fortunes of the family, both Wither and Bigg. He devised all his freehold estates in Wootton, Monk Sherborne, Oakley, Pamber, Basing and Andover, and the leasehold estates of Manydown, Andwell, and Up Nately (subject to his wife's life interest), to trustees (Sir Henry Maynard and Edward Ernle) for William Wither of Andwell for life, and then to his first, second, and third sons (if any), and to their heirs male, and next to William's brothers, Thomas and Charles, in like manner, and in default of these to Thomas Bigg (eldest surviving son of Lovelace Bigg and Dorothy Wither) for life, and then to Thomas Bigg's brothers, Henry and Walter, and their heirs male. He further charged his estates with annuities and legacies to William Wither's brothers, and to the sisters of Thomas Bigg, Mary Blackstone, Dorothy Bethell, and Anne Banister. His will and that of his widow (to whom he left all his personal estate, and who had her own fortune) is annexed in appendix 3.

WM. WITHER (v). 1733—1789.

(9).—*William Wither* (v), the last Wither of Manydown, was born at Andwell in 1703. He and his two younger brothers, *Thomas* and *Charles*, were entered as scholars of Winchester College. Thomas left young and went into business in London. Charles went to Oxford and entered Holy Orders: both married but died without children long before their elder brother. Their

William (afterwards Sir W.) Maynard, Bart.

Aged 6 years, 1727.

only surviving sister Elizabeth never married, and died in 1735. Thus there was no one to carry on the direct line of Wither at Manydown if William Wither remained a bachelor, which he did to the end of his long life.

On the death of his cousin, William Wither (iv) of Manydown in 1733, he not only removed from Andwell to Manydown himself, but, as a note in the Up Nately registers says, under date anno 1734, "The body of Mr. Wither of Andwell and of his wife "and children (*i.e.*, his father and mother and two little sisters), "were removed from the chancel of Nately Chapel and interred in "ye parish Church of Wootton St. Lawrence in ye burying place "of ye ancestors of William Wither of Manydown, Esqre."

This is a touching evidence of the affection of the last of the Withers for Manydown and Wootton. He no doubt hoped that the name would be perpetuated there, and could hardly realize that for fifty-six years more he alone would bear the name at Manydown, and be the last to bear it.

There is a story that he was engaged to be married, and that he built a fine new coach in which to bring home his bride to Manydown; but, alas, the lady jilted him. The panels of the coach with the arms painted on them still exist.

Besides the estates entailed under William Wither's (iv) will above mentioned, he had various freehold and copyhold properties in Worting, Yately, and Up Nately in Hampshire, and in Chetwoode, Burton, Hartshorne, Linborough, and Gawcot in Buckinghamshire, all of which he left to "his cousin" Edward Lane, who lived with him.

He died at Manydown, 31st October, 1789, aged eighty-six, and was buried in the family vault in the chancel of Wootton Church, on November 5th.

His monument says :—

"In Him were united
The Hospitable Virtues of his Ancestors
With every characteristic quality
Which once distinguished
The Old English Gentleman.
On his death, all the male issue
Of an ancient and well respected family
Who had resided at Manydown
During the space of four centuries
Became extinct.

In grateful remembrance of their worthy relation, this monument was erected by Lovelace Bigg-Wither, heir general of the line of Wither, and Edward Lane, Esquire, sole executor."

In the above history I have endeavoured to trace in some detail the life of nine Wither residents at Manydown in succession from Thomas Wither in 1484 to William Wither in 1789, a period of 305 years. Records of the previous 95 years have only at present disclosed isolated notices of Withers at Wootton, as, *e.g.*, in 1402. I must leave to others, who may obtain fuller information, the task of filling up the gaps in the period indicated on William Withers' monument.

CHAPTER IV.

BIGG-WITHER OF MANYDOWN AND TANGIER.

(1789—1871.)

CHAPTER IV.

BIGG-WITHER OF MANYDOWN AND TANGIER.

(1789—1871.)

BY the will of the fourth William Wither of Manydown, who died without issue in 1732 (see Chapter III), the Manydown and other family estates were left, first to his cousin, William Wither of Andwell, and to his heirs male; then in default of these to the male descendants of his aunt, *Dorothy Wither*, who married (1684)[1] *Lovelace Bigg*, of Chilton Folliat, Wilts, son of Richard Bigg, of Haines Hill, in the parish of Hurst, Wilts, by his second wife, Mary Wade, niece of Sir Walter Long, Knt., of Draycott, the parliamentarian (Richard Bigg's first wife was the Lady Phœbe Ley, daughter of James, first Earl of Marlborough).

As the Manydown estates eventually came to Lovelace Bigg, grandson of the above-mentioned Lovelace Bigg and Dorothy Wither, born 1741, Lovelace Bigg's parentage and life before 1789, when he succeeded to the Wither estates and added their name, must now be noticed.

His father was the *Rev. Walter Bigg*, tenth child of Lovelace Bigg and Dorothy Wither, Fellow of Winchester College and Rector of the family living of Worting, two miles from Manydown, to which he succeeded in 1731 on the resignation of his brother Henry, Warden of Winchester College.

[1] The family name *Lovelace* seems to have come through John Bigg "the Denton hermit's" connection with Symon Mayne who married Coiluberry Lovelace of Hurley, Berks, circa 1649.

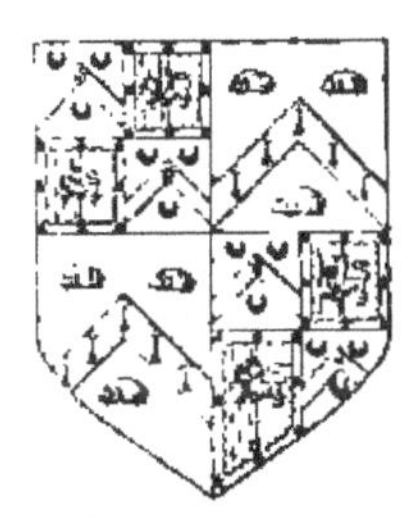

Bigg-Wither, quartering azure a chevron ermine between three hedgehogs or, *Harris*, (the coat assumed by Lovelace Bigg-Wither and his heir after 1790).

Walter Bigg married (1734) *Jane Harris*, daughter and heiress of Dr. John Harris, Fellow of Winchester College and Rector of Chiddingfold and Ash, Surrey, by his wife Jane, daughter of Dr. Edward Young, Dean of Salisbury, and sister of the poet Young, author of *Night Thoughts*.

The marriage of Walter Bigg, Rector of Worting, was commemorated by the following quaint epithalamium, written and addressed to him by William Spearing, Parish Clerk of Worting :—

"I rejoice my good Master, that now you are wedded,
And the beauteous Miss Jenny have happily bedded,
The beauteous Miss Jenny! who, gladly I hear,
Is as kind and good-humoured, as beauteous and fair.

My good Master and Mistress much Joy to you both,
Still may you observe your mutual Oath
'*To love and to cherish!*' and as for '*obey*,'
May you each be obedient and equally sway.

A New House the fair Bride at Worting will find,
Compleat and commodious, and pat to her mind;
An elegant Box, a more pleasing retreat
Than the Princess of Orange will have for her seat!

The good Warden,[1] for you who relinquished this place,
May depend that you here will beget a fine Race;
In whom the great Name of the *Biggs* may still live,
And the Heirs, of whose Heirs, may this Building survive.

The beneficent Lady of Fam'd Manydown[2]
Your first Child, I presume, will claim as her own.
Her spiritual Child; and will see it brought up;
And will give it much more than a Coral or Cup.

The good Wives of the Parish, obsequious all,
Will attend your Commands as oft as you call;
As oft as Occasion requires they'll march forth!
Of your beautiful Babes to assist at the Birth!

[1] Henry Bigg, elder brother of Walter, Warden of Winchester College (1731—40).

[2] The widow of William Wither of Manydown (*née* Nicol).

JANE HARRIS.
Mother of LOVELACE BIGG-[WITHER].
Died 1759.

And the diligent Clerk will always, I trow,
His Master obey, and his Mistress too;
And when'er at the Font these dear Babes shall be blest
With a hearty *Amen* will second the Priest." W. S.

LOVELACE BIGG, 1741—1789.

The sole issue of this marriage was Lovelace Bigg [Wither], who was privately baptized (14th August, 1741) in London, in the house of his uncle and godfather, Thomas Bigg, in Lincoln's Inn Fields, and in the presence of his aunts, Elizabeth Bigg and Dorothy Bethell. Great care was taken with his education. He was in due course entered as a Scholar at Winchester College, and on October 24th, 1758, was matriculated at Queen's College, Oxford. On May 12th, 1759, he was admitted Probationary Fellow of New College, and became in 1761 Full Fellow till his marriage in 1764. His mother, Jane Harris, died in 1759. His father's letters to him while at Oxford are full of earnest good advice, and show that Lovelace worked at French and Italian, as well as the usual Oxford studies. A letter dated March, 1761, refers to his father's easier circumstances through the death of his brother, Thomas Bigg, and his father's inheritance of the estates at Chilton Folliat, in Wilts, and at Woolston, in Berkshire. His father says :—

"*It will enable me after another year to be more liberal in your education, though in my judgment you cannot follow a better plan than that which has already been chalked out for you, which will make you a man of knowledge and a man of business, one who will know how to employ his time and his fortune, or to gain greater; one who may be of service to his country, either in public or private life.*"

He adds :—

"*As for myself, I esteem Worting as a child of my own, and, I believe, shall never leave it. However at present my sister Elizabeth will live at Chilton. It seemed to be my brother's desire that she should if she liked it, and indeed I could not with credit or even convenience desert both my livings* [Worting and Baghurst] *while I was capable of doing my duty.*"

Argent, two bars gules, in chief three cocks of the second, *Blackstone.*

In 1763, Lovelace Bigg [Wither] left Oxford for the Middle Temple, and studied for the Bar. On 20th September, 1764, he married Rachel Clitherow, sister-in-law of his cousin, William (afterwards Sir William) Blackstone. She died in childbed on 22nd July following, when the author of the famous *Commentaries* wrote to him the following letter of condolence :—

" *Wallingford,*

" *25th July, 1765.*

" *I feel it difficult to begin a letter to you, lest while I wish to alleviate I should increase your concern upon the present melancholy occasion. The best topic of consolation upon the footing of reason and religion, must be drawn from those very qualities in her you have lost, which renders that loss the more sensible. I shall therefore waive so delicate a subject, and leave it to that good sense, which God has blessed you with, to length of time, and your avocations of business, to blunt the edge of your present distress. But after all, dear Sir, there is nothing that the proudest wisdom can boast, there is nothing that can afford us any solid relief in deep affliction, but the doctrines of Christianity, in which we have been so happily educated, and the sure expectations of a future state. These are not suggestions of a mind unaffected with your misfortunes. I feel for you as a Friend, aud a relation, and more especially as a husband; but I write to you as a man, and as a Christian. . . . . If there be anything which is in my power to do for you, pray give me your directions without ceremony, and I will endeavour to see them executed. . . . . My wife and sister are as well as can be expected, considering the tenderness of their spirits, which makes affliction of every kind sit heavy upon them. Time, I hope, will relieve them, and from former experience I believe it will. Providence has happily ordered it, that violent sensations are not lasting. If they were, the frame of humanity could never sustain the shock. They desire to join with me in every affectionate wish, and every mark of regard, towards both yourself and your Father. Poor man, I sympathise with him likewise in lamenting the slender foundation upon which we build our prospects in this life. But he is able to administer comfort both to you and to himself. . . . .*

" *I am, your most sincerely affectionate and obedient servant,*

" *W. BLACKSTONE.*"

Sir William Blackstone, Knight, LL.D.
The eminent Commentator on the laws of England.
One of the Judges of the Court of King's Bench.
Born 1723; died 1780.

On 21st August, 1766, Lovelace Bigg [Wither] married his second wife, *Margaret Blachford*, daughter of Bridges Blachford, Esq., the head of a very old Isle of Wight family that owned Osborne, from whom the estate was bought by Queen Victoria in 1845.

Bigg, impaling barry wavy of six or and gules on a chief azure three pheons of the first, *Blachford*.

His wife brought in £3000, and he settled upon her a jointure of £300 out of estates in Wiltshire and from house property in Pangbourne (Berkshire), inherited from his uncle, Thomas Bigg, of Haines Hill, Hurst (Wilts).

In the summer and autumn of 1767, he and his wife, with her brother, Robert Pope Blachford and his wife (*née* Winifred Barrington), made a driving tour through England to the north, which Lovelace Bigg describes in a series of interesting and well written letters to his father at Worting. The tour took them "*through Buckinghamshire, the edge of Oxfordshire, and the greater part of Warwickshire.*" "*At Stowe,*" he says, "*Lord Temple has added much to his uncle's plan.*" Thence through Shropshire, Staffordshire, and Derbyshire. At Manchester, the Duke of Bridgwater's canal, thirty miles long, seems to have impressed him greatly as a "*vast undertaking, especially considered as the work of one man. He has two objects* (1) *to convey his coal to Manchester,* (2) *to extend his cut to the river near Liverpool. He sells coal to the poor at 3½d. a hundred.*" The travellers admired the Peak district, and Lovelace Bigg calls Matlock "*a little public place in a romantic scene.*" "*Chattesworth* (sic) *is shamefully neglected, having only the outside of a princely house.*" "*Buxton wells are, I presume, of great service in many cases, otherwise they would not be frequented. The place is paltry, it rains everyday all the year round, and is very cold.*" They stayed at York, saw Castle Howard, and made the acquaintance of Lord Rockingham, who "*appears quite as a king in his own country, is independent of party, and much respected.*" Thence they went *viâ* Harrogate and Ripon to Scarborough, where the ladies remained for the bathing, while Mr. Bigg and Mr. Blachford continued their journey north to Carlisle and Edinburgh, where they stayed some time.

Writing on the eve of the return home from Scarborough, October 20th, 1767, Lovelace Bigg says:—

> "*The Duke of York's death* (George III's eldest brother) *has occasioned some delay to our return. Wishing to join in the general mourning as soon as we can, we sent to town for a trunk we had packed up lest such an accident should happen, which meets us at York, when all our coloured things go to London by waggon, and we, properly arrayed in sables, proceed southward, making Worksop, Nottingham, Burleigh House* (which he later describes as a 'superb pile'), *Cambridge, Lord Byron's at Newstead Abbey, and Belvoir Castle on our way.*"

The tour ended where it began, namely at Boswell Court, Lovelace Bigg's house in Middlesex.

On 18th June, 1772, the Rev. Walter Bigg died, aged seventy-one, and was buried at Worting, leaving to his only son, Lovelace, £20,100 invested capital, and leasehold and freehold estates in Sherfield, Andwell, and Kingsclere, Hants, and Chilton Folliat (house and 300 acres), Wiltshire, together with an estate of 740 acres in Woolston, Berkshire, these two latter being subject to life interests of £450 per annum to his aunts, the widow of Thomas Bigg, and Mrs. Barton, widow of Warden Henry Bigg.

Lovelace Bigg also inherited in right of his mother (Jane Harris) Wymering Manor and house, with ten acres of land.

After his father's death, Lovelace Bigg went to live at Chilton Folliat. He became Chairman of Quarter Sessions,

DOROTHY BIGG, *æt.* 4. WILLIAM BIGG, *æt.* 5.

Born 1689; married Thos. Bethell. Born 1688; died 1715.

Children of Lovelace Bigg and Dorothy Wither.

Wiltshire, and many of his addresses to the grand juries at Marlborough and Devizes (1784—1788) on Prison Administration, the Poor and Game Laws, and Lunacy Acts, are extant. They show remarkable ability, clearness of view, eloquence, and common sense.

He was most generous to the poor as well as to his relatives. One instance of this will especially interest the family, and may be recorded here. His uncle, Warden Henry Bigg, left a house in Bond Street to his father, Walter Bigg, and then on certain contingencies to their nephew, Charles Blackstone (younger brother of the Judge). The contingencies failed; but Lovelace Bigg, on inheriting his father's property, felt that Charles Blackstone had been unfortunate, and he sent him £1000 and £100 for his daughter, Mrs. Williams, which gifts Mr. Blackstone acknowledged in the following letter, dated 30th December, 1788:

"*I find myself totally at a loss how to express my own and all my family's sense of the magnitude of the benefaction dictated by your benevolent mind, and which I this morning received in a promissory note carrying interest at five per cent., and a draft for £100 for Mrs. Williams. Your kind manner of conferring the favor also enhances the value of the gift. I, who was no stranger to Warden Bigg's will, having copied it at the time of his death, knew very well that the contingent legacy of the house to me was totally void, and for this reason I always understood that my late uncle, your father, procured for me the living of Weeke, by quitting Baghurst, by way of making me amends for my not being benefitted by the contingency aforesaid. But you, dear Sir, have most kindly (notwithstanding what your father had done) made yourself still a debtor, in equity, to me and my family, and in a princely sum. Assure yourself we accept it with heartfelt joy and gratitude; but we can never thank you sufficiently. . . . . My dear daughter is quite overcome with your goodness of heart, as indeed we are all, and she desires me to send her best and warmest thanks. May God's blessing, my dear Sir, ever attend you and your family, to whom we unite in best wishes and regards.*

"*Your highly obliged and affectionate humble servant,*

"*C. BLACKSTONE.*"

The last of the Withers of Manydown died October 31st, 1789, s.p., and the "heir general" was Lovelace Bigg (see p. 42). He at once assumed by Royal Licence the surname and arms of Wither. The letters patent under the Great Seal of England granting this are dated 2nd December, 1789, and the College of Arms, by virtue of this authority, "exemplified and confirmed to Lovelace Bigg, now Lovelace Bigg-Wither, the arms as annexed, namely:—

'Quarterly, first and fourth. Argent, a chevron, gules between three crescents sable; for *Wither*. Second and third, perpale ermine and azure, a lion passant, gules ducally crowned gold within a bordure, engrailed of the third, charged with eight fleur-de-lys, or; for *Bigg*.' And for the *crest* of *Wither*, 'a demi hare erect, azure, in the mouth three ears of ripe corn,' to be borne and used for ever hereafter by him, the said Lovelace Bigg-Wither, Esquire, and his issue male.

'Recorded in the Herald's Office, London, pursuant to a warrant from the most noble Charles Duke of Norfolk, Earl Marshal of England, and examined therewith, this 12th of December, 1789.

'Signed { George Harrison, Norroy and Register.
Benjamin Pingo, York Herald.'"

Lovelace Bigg-Wither, 1789—1813.

(1.)—*Lovelace Bigg-Wither* now took up his residence at Manydown. In 1790, he put a new front on to the house, and built a large dining room and drawing room over it.

In 1791, he sold his house and other property at Pangbourne for £20,000, and with the sum increased the Manydown property by the Monk Sherborne portion of Woodgarston Farm, Battledown and Worting Wood Farms, and White Hart Farm, Worting, Lechmere Green in Bramley and Pamber, Potlane Farm, Basing, and Blackgrove Farm, Up Nately, and by other property in West Sherborne, in all 1163 acres, as well as by additional lands at Wymering and Widley, amounting to 427 acres.

Lovelace Bigg-Wither's second wife, Margaret Blachford, died at Chilton Folliat, 27th December, 1784, leaving two sons and seven daughters.

LOVELACE BIGG-WITHER.

Aged 23 years.

From a miniature by Conway.

LOVELACE BIGG-WITHER.

Born August 4th, 1741; died February 24th, 1813; aged 71 years.

From a miniature.

The eldest son, *Lovelace Wither* Bigg, born 1780, died a scholar of Winchester College, 3rd March, 1794. *Harris*, the second son, named after his grandmother (Jane Harris), born 1781, succeeded to Manydown. One daughter, *Mary Ann*, born 1783, died an infant. The other six—*Margaret*, born 1768; *Jane*, born 1770; *Dorothy*, born 1771; *Elizabeth*, born 1773; *Catherine*, born 1775; *Alethea*, born 1777—came with their father and brother to Manydown, and eight young people between the ages of nine and twenty-one must have helped to make the old place, which had had a bachelor tenant for fifty-six years, a little more lively than of late.

The family circle was, however, soon broken into by marriage and death:—

Margaret, the eldest, married December 3rd, 1792, the Rev. Charles Blackstone, nephew of the Judge and Vicar of Andover.

Dorothy, died September 3rd, 1793, and her brother, *Lovelace Wither*, March 3rd, 1794, aged fourteen.

Jane, married, 15th January, 1795, John Awdry, Esq., of Notton, Wilts, father of Sir John Wither Awdry, Knt.

Elizabeth, married, January 11th, 1798, the Rev. William Heathcote, Rector of Worting, father of Sir William Heathcote, of Hursley Park, fifth Baronet.

Many glimpses of the life at Manydown between 1796—1799 are to be found in the letters of Jane Austen, whose father was Rector of Steventon, two and a half miles distant. The authoress was evidently very much at home with the party at Manydown, where she frequently stayed, and was especially intimate with Catherine and Alethea Bigg, who were about her own age.[1]

[1] Jane Austen was born at Steventon Rectory, December 16th, 1775.

Writing to her sister Cassandra of a ball (January 8th, 1799) given by Lady Dorchester, who then lived at Kempshott, Jane Austen says:—

[1] "*Catherine* [Bigg] *has the honour of giving her name to a set, which will be composed of two Withers, two Heathcotes, a Blackford, and no Bigg except herself.*"

[1] Letters of Jane Austen, ed. by Edward Lord Brabourne, pp. 195, 201, 202.

The following letter, dated Monday, January 21st, 1799, is especially interesting to the family:—

"*Our ball on Thursday was a very poor one, only eight couple and but twenty-three people in the room; but it was not the ball's fault, for we were deprived of two or three families by the sudden illness of Mr. Wither, who was seized that morning at Winchester with a return of his former alarming complaint. An express was sent off from thence to the family: Catherine Bigg and Miss Blachford were dining with Mrs. Russell. Poor Catherine's distress must have been very great. She was prevailed on to wait till the Heathcotes could come from Worting, and then with those two and Harris proceeded directly to Winchester. In such a disorder his danger, I suppose, must always be great; but from this attack he is now rapidly recovering, and will be well enough to return to Manydown, I fancy, in a few days. It was a fine thing for conversation at the ball; but it deprived us not only of the Biggs, but of Mrs. Russell too, and of the Boltons and John Harwood, who were dining there likewise, and of Mr. Lane, who kept away as related to the family. Poor man! I mean Mr. Wither, his life is so useful, his character so respectable and worthy, that I really believe there was a good deal of sincerity in the general concern expressed on his account.*"

Jane Austen's appreciation of Lovelace Bigg-Wither's "*useful life*" is confirmed by the fact that he was elected Chairman of Quarter Sessions in Hampshire, after he came to Manydown, as he had been in Wiltshire, when he lived at Chilton Folliat; and his ability and long experience made him a most useful magistrate on the County Bench. He was commissioned Deputy-Lieutenant for Wiltshire in 1770, for Berkshire 1785, for Hampshire 1793. In 1800 he spent much time in drawing up rules for organizing "an association to assist the labouring poor in the neighbourhood of Basingstoke," and in establishing a poorhouse for Wootton district.

The small party at Manydown, which, after the marriage in January, 1798, of Elizabeth Bigg with the Rev. Thomas Heathcote, consisted only of the old Squire and his two unmarried daughters, Catherine and Alethea, was considerably augmented in 1802. In March of that year the Rector of Worting died, and the widow with her baby boy, afterwards Sir William Heathcote, fifth Baronet of Hursley, came back to live at Manydown. Here she remained till her father died in 1813. Manydown House, which I have described in Chapter VII, became for the next ten years very much of a home centre, both for the married daughters and their children, and the widowed daughters and their children. "*There was something about it* (says Miss Awdry in her *Life of Sir William Heathcote*) *and its patriarchal owner which appealed strongly to his many grandchildren.*" Mrs. Blackstone, the eldest daughter, who had also been left a widow with a son and little daughter Margaret, lived close by at Worting. and were almost daily at Manydown, little William Heathcote and his cousin, Margaret Blackstone, only two years older, being devoted playmates. Mrs. Awdry, the second daughter, with some of her children, were often there from Notton. The two children had other sharers in their games and occupations. Young Edward Austen from Steventon, nephew of the authoress (Jane Austen), afterwards Rev. Austen Leigh, Vicar of Bray, and Caroline Wiggett, the adopted daughter of William Wiggett Chute, of the Vyne, were frequent visitors of the children, and then there were the two much loved Aunts, Kitty and Alethea. When in 1808 "Sweet little Aunt Kitty," (who the children wanted to stay on with them in the happy home at Manydown,) married the Rev. Herbert Hill, little William Heathcote and Margaret Blackstone, as recorded in the latter's *Memoirs*, "Would not go to the wedding and turned their backs upon the carriage with the happy pair as it passed them in Wootton Lane;" and

William Heathcote wrote in his poetry book, "*Sweet creature parted from all her friends but one,*" to which line Edward Austen, in recognition of the bridegroom's merits, added "*Who in kindness is excelled by none.*"

The two portraits opposite show Lovelace Bigg-Wither, a handsome young man with powdered hair and pigtail, and in his old age, venerable and kindly looking. Beloved by his children and grandchildren, and universally respected by all, he died February 24th, 1813, aged seventy-one.

Sir William Heathcote, who admired as well as loved his grandfather, writing in 1829, when he was twenty-five years old, says of him :—

"*In the spring of 1813 my excellent grandfather Mr. Wither, died, a man whose talents and virtues were honoured in their generation, and whose image is indelibly impressed upon my memory as the kindest of parents and most venerable of men.*"

The inscription on the tablet to his memory in Wootton Church cannot, as might sometimes be the case, be accused of overstating his merits. It says he was :—

"*Universally respected, beloved and lamented.*
As a magistrate
He was eminent, active, learned, and judicious.
As a private gentleman
He was not less distinguished
By those social and relative virtues which adorn
The Friend, the Parent, and the Christian.
His good deeds
Will long be recorded on earth
And hereafter be had in everlasting remembrance."

A summary of his will is annexed. (See appendix 3.)

HARRIS BIGG-WITHER. 1813—1833.

(2.)—Lovelace Wither Bigg, the eldest son, having died in 1794, *Harris*, the surviving son, born at Chilton Folliat,

18th May, 1781, succeeded at Manydown. A letter of his father to Mr. James Blackstone, dated July 7th, 1799, shows great anxiety about Harris' future education, especially as he suffered from a defect of speech. He had for some time been at a private tutor's (Mr. Wallington). He was eventually sent to Worcester College, Oxford.

He married, 2nd November, 1804, at East Dean, Sussex, *Anne Howe Frith*, only daughter of Beddington Bramley Frith, of Carisbrooke, I.W., Esq., Lieutenant-Colonel of the North Hants Militia, by his wife, Jane Howe, heiress of Brook House, I.W., and went to live at Manor House, Wymering, near Cosham. By the marriage settlement £400, secured on the Wymering property, was settled on his wife for life, and £4000 to sons and £10,000 to daughters. These sums, by power of appointment, were divided in equal shares to the four younger sons and five daughters, with addition of £1500 each to two younger sons.

During his father's lifetime a family arrangement was much debated, whereby the estates at Woolston (Berkshire) should be charged instead of Wymering with the jointure of Mrs. Harris Bigg-Wither, and with the portions of the children. Eventually, however, in 1828, the Woolston property, with its fine old sixteenth century house full of tapestry and old oak, which Henry VIII had given to Jane Seymour, was sold to Captain G. Butler for £25,500, and the portions of the sisters were paid off.

The issue of the marriage of Harris Bigg-Wither and Anne Howe Frith was five sons and five daughters. The seven eldest were born at Wymering, and four of the five sons took Holy Orders :—

(1.)—*Lovelace*, born 17th September, 1805, succeeded.

(2.)—*Harris Jervoise*, born 31st October, 1806, for forty-seven years Rector of Worting, Hants; died December 1st, 1887. (For descendants, see Pedigree VIII.)

(3.)—*William Henry Walter*, born 9th November, 1809, was Fellow of New College, Oxford, and after thirty-six years as Curate of Otterbourne, Hants, became Rector of Hardwicke, Bucks; died April 2nd, 1899.

(4.)—*Walter John Percival*, born 15th February, 1811, was Vicar of Herriard and of Wootton St. Lawrence; died March 15th, 1876.

(5.)—*Charles*, born 27th April, 1822, went to Nelson, New Zealand, and became J.P. and Member of Parliament for that country; died November, 1896. (See Pedigree VIII.)

The five daughters (all unmarried) were:—

(1.)—*Margaret*, born 1808, died 1883.

(2.)—*Jane Dorothy*, born 1812, died 1858.

(3.)—*Anne Frances*, born 1814, died 1874.

(4.)—*Elizabeth Mary Bramston*, born 1817, died 1879.

(5.)—*Marianne*, born 1819, died 1900.

On his father's death in 1813, Harris Bigg-Wither came to Manydown. Here he lived, as his forefathers, the life of a country squire, diligent in magisterial work, kind to the poor, and beloved by his family. Owing to his stammering, he was a man of few words, and rather avoided society. He was, however, very hospitable in his own house, but quick-tempered. A story is told of him, that on the occasion of a visit of the members of the Winchester Cathedral Chapter to the demesne lands of the Chapter of Manydown, after some dispute as to his right to cut down timber in the Park, Mr. Bigg-Wither invited the Reverend

THE REV. LOVELACE BIGG-WITHER,
of Manydown and Tangier Parks.
Born 1805; died 1874.

Canons, who were all his personal friends, to dinner, and gave directions to his butler that after dinner, the customary bowl of punch was to be made up of a bottle of each of the excellent wines that had been served during dinner. The mixture, as can be imagined, was not appetising, and after all had tasted with wry faces, he said to his guests: "Gentlemen, my punch is like you. In your individual capacity you are all very good fellows, but in your corporate capacity you are very disagreeable."

In 1831, Harris Bigg-Wither let Manydown to Sir Richard Rycroft (Bart.) and went to live at Tangier Park House, which adjoins Manydown, about three-quarters of a mile to the north on higher ground. The house, park, and farm (175 acres), which he had long desired to buy from the Sclater family, was at first rented and afterwards bought by his son Lovelace. Here at Tangier he died suddenly from apoplexy, March 25th, 1833, in the fifty-second year of his age.

His widow first went with her daughters to live at Farnham. Eventually she settled at Winchester, where she died November 13th, 1866, aged eighty-three years.

THE REV. LOVELACE BIGG-WITHER. 1833—1874.

(3.)—*Lovelace*, the eldest son of Harris Bigg-Wither, was born at Wymering (17th September, 1805), and was sent to school first at Twyford, under the Rev. G. Clarke, then to Winchester, where he was entered as a "Commoner" under Dr. Gabell; from thence he went to Oriel College, Oxford. Here he gained a Second Class in "Greats," Michaelmas Term, 1826. In the same class list with him were Lord Henry George Cavendish-Bentinck, Bishop Samuel Wilberforce, and Archdeacon Denison. On leaving Oxford he went to London, and studied for a time for the Bar. He however took Holy Orders, was Curate of Winslade, and became Vicar of Herriard (1831—1834).

Bigg-Wither, impaling sable, three fishes haurient, or, *Orde*.

Lovelace Bigg-Wither married, 23rd July, 1829, Emma Jemima, fifth daughter of the Rev. John Orde (Rector of Winslade, Hants, and of Wensley, Yorkshire), by his wife the Hon. Frances Carleton, daughter of Guy, first Baron Dorchester, and the Lady Maria Howard, daughter of Thomas second Earl of Effiingham. After the marriage he lived at Hook, where his eldest child was born.

Soon after the death of his father in 1833 he resigned his parochial duties for the care of the Manydown property, and came to live at Tangier Park, which estate (175 acres) he bought that year, together with Sheerdown Farm (160 acres) and 60 acres at Ramsdell, for £5300 from Miss Penelope Sclater, aunt of William Lutley Sclater, Esq., of Hoddington.

The issue of the marriage of Lovelace Bigg-Wither and Miss Orde was eleven sons and three daughters, namely:—

(1.)—Frances Anne Maria Carleton, born at Hook, July 16th, 1831.

(2.)—George Howard, born at Hackwood, July 27th, 1832; died January 24th, 1872.

(3.)—Rosamond Purefoy, born at Winslade, October 3rd, 1833.

(4.)—Arthur FitzWalter, born at Tangier, May 14th, 1835; entered Army; died August 10th, 1887.

(5.)—Guy Carleton, born May 22nd, 1836; Lieutenant Royal Navy; lost at sea, September, 1860.

(6.)—Edward Julian, born September 7th, 1837; Major 28th Regiment.

(7.)—Francis Orde, born September 5th, 1838; Army Doctor; died in India, March 27th, 1870.

(8.)—Lancelot Frith, born October 16th, 1839; died in India, September 19th, 1890.

(9.)—Emma Sophia, born November 30th, 1840.

(10.)—Reginald Fitz Hugh, born January 9th, 1842; in Holy Orders; Rector of Worting, 1879—98; Rural Dean of Basingstoke, 1890—93; Rector of Wonston, 1898.

Pedigree VII.

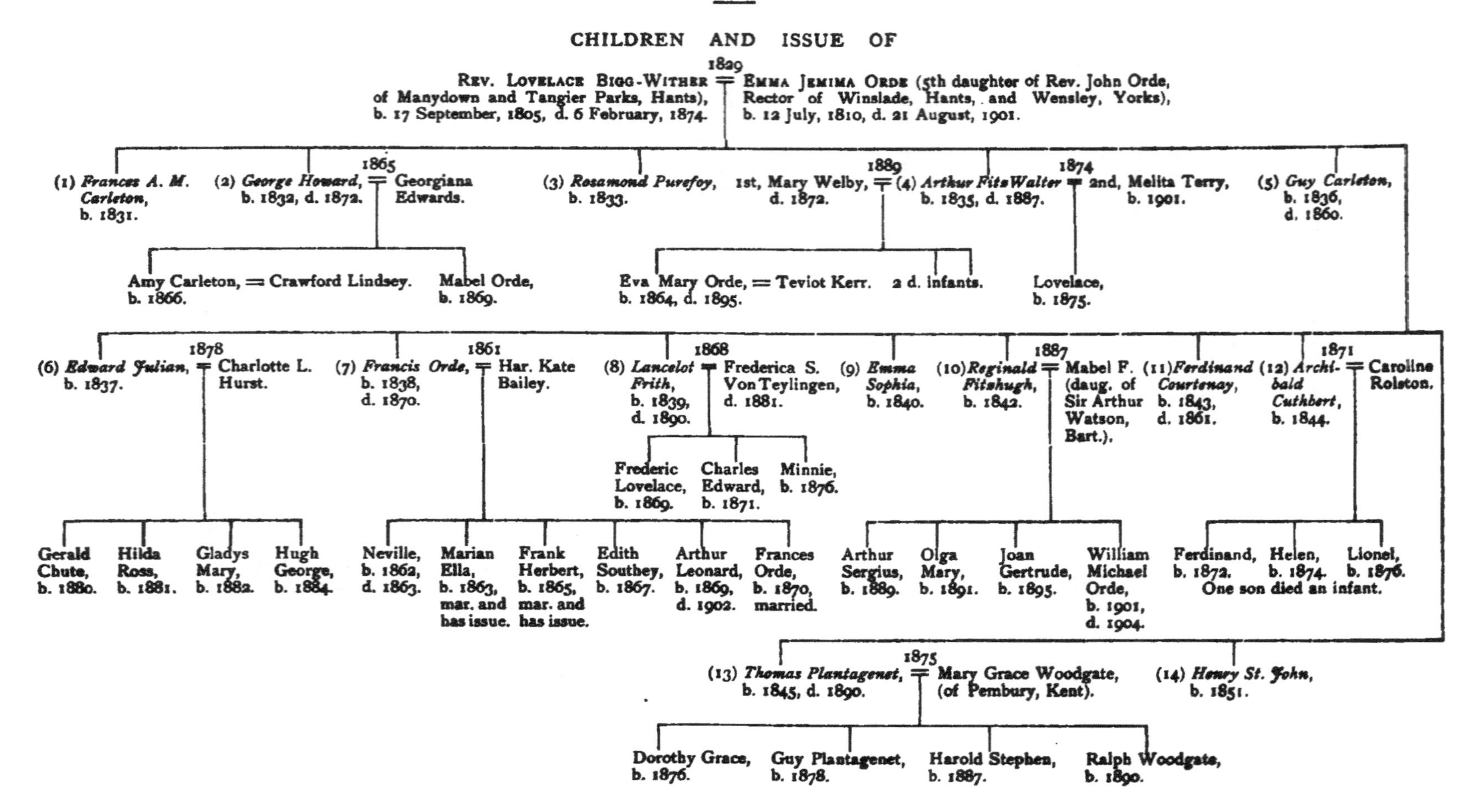

(11.)—Ferdinand Courtenay, born April 19th, 1843; Royal Navy; died Vancouver's Island, November 12th, 1861.

(12.)—Archibald Cuthbert, born September 25th, 1844; Lieutenant-Colonel and Indian Civil Service, D. P. W.

(13.)—Thomas Plantagenet, born October 8th, 1845; Ass. C. E., author of *Pioneering in South Brazil*; died at sea, July 19th, 1890.

(14.)—Henry St. John, born November 6th, 1851.

The marriages of the sons and their issue are recorded on Pedigree VII.

The members of this numerous family as children delighted in the beautiful grounds of Tangier Park House, which included a large bowling green and a "wilderness" or wood of about eight acres, intersected by numerous grass walks, bordered by laurels and other shrubs, radiating from a centre, in which was an old sun dial.

Even before coming into the family estates, Lovelace Bigg-Wither took an active part in the movement for the establishment of small allotment holdings for the agricultural labourers. In 1832 he published a letter addressed to the farmers of Wootton, Worting, Monk Sherborne, and other parishes in North Hampshire connected with the estates, commending the movement as a means, among other things, of reducing the poor rates. He also, together with his father, let about 120 acres to cottagers on the estates in small lots at *3d.* a pole, and printed an address to the allotment holders (numbering 170) on a broad sheet to be hung up in their cottages, pointing out the good effect he hoped it would have on them in promoting "respectability and comfort," and "the decent pride of honest independence." This action of his produced much correspondence with well-known men in all parts of England, *e.g.*, Mr. Gladstone, Mr. W. Duthey (of Northamptonshire), and the poet Southey. The latter, writing from Keswick (20th August, 1832), says:—

"I was surprised as well as pleased to see in what manner your pamphlet was noticed in the 'Times.' You have been doing (according to my judgment) in the best possible way, the only thing which can be done for bettering the condition of the agricultural labourer, and removing one of those great evils which have cankered the root of England's prosperity."

In later years other landlords sought from him information about allotments and followed his example, notably (in 1845) his neighbour, Mr. (afterwards Sir) Wyndham S. Portal.

But the improvement of the condition of the agricultural poor was not the only good work which occupied Mr. Lovelace Bigg-Wither's thoughts at this period of his life. He was also much interested in the establishment of Mechanics' Institutes in towns, and in lectures connected therewith.

In the autumn of 1841, he delivered the address at the opening of the second session of the Mechanics' Institute at Basingstoke, which was printed at the request of the society. It is an eloquent exposition of the value of these institutions for all classes, especially those engaged in business and trade. He says, in concluding his address:—

"Perhaps it is the dream of a sanguine imagination, but I fancy I see in the general and spontaneous rise of these institutions, in which men of all parties and of all varieties of opinion are joining, the dawning of another day for England, in which the sunshine light of truth will gradually draw off and dissipate into the clear air all those heavy and unwholesome mists of ignorance, which still in part overshadow and blight the land."

In politics, Mr. Bigg-Wither was a Whig of the old-fashioned sort, and he took an active part in supporting Sir Henry Mildmay and the Hon. Dudley Carleton for North Hants, in the elections of 1852 and 1857. Being in Holy Orders and without "cure," he was much sought after to help neighbouring clergy, which he occasionally did; but his duties as a landowner, and as a county magistrate, not to mention the cares connected with the education of his eleven sons, did not allow much time for giving such assistance. He however, when at home, regularly assisted on Sunday his brother Walter, Vicar of Wootton.

He was actively interested in elementary education, and built the schools at Wootton and Worting.

Mr. Bigg-Wither had received, as has been shown, a liberal education, and became an unusually well-informed man on almost all subjects, scientific as well as literary; but his preference was for poetry. During many long winter evenings he used to read out loud to the family selections from the great English poets, and his children have cause to be grateful to him for making them acquainted in their youth with the masterpieces of such men as Milton, Wordsworth, Southey, Longfellow, and Tennyson. He himself wrote many poems on family and national events, and in 1869 published a nearly literal translation of Homer's Odyssey in "accentuated dramatic verse," which was well received in literary circles. He also translated into verse the whole of the Iliad, but did not publish it.

Meanwhile, as years went on, the financial needs connected especially with the education and starting in life of his numerous sons, brought great anxiety and necessitated the sale of portions of the estate. Wymering House had been sold in 1835 for £5000, and the rest of the Wymering estate in 1859 to Mr. Thistlethwaite for £14,827. By this means Lovelace Bigg-Wither was able to pay off the portions of his sisters; but the needs of his own large family required more drastic measures, and it gradually became evident that the old estates must go. Thus in 1865, Hillside House, Worting, where Mrs. H. Blackstone and Mrs. Hill had lived, was sold to Mr. George Lamb, and in 1868, Worting Inn Farm (195 acres) also to Mr. Lamb, and Sherdown Farm (160 acres) to Mr. W. S. Portal.

Meanwhile, negotiations had been entered into as referred to on page 34 for the enfranchisement, with a view to sale of the leasehold portions of the Manydown and Tangier Park estates and the redemption of the Rectorial Tythe of Wootton. This was completed by deed dated 31st December, 1863, for £28,096, paid to the Ecclesiastical Commissioners. This large sum raised by mortgage on the estates further crippled Mr. Bigg-Wither's resources, and eventually, after much natural hesitation, in 1871, almost the whole of the old estates and of that which remained of the property bought by his grandfather, amounting to 2800 acres, together with Manydown and Tangier Houses, was sold to Mr. (afterwards Sir) Edward Bates, of Liverpool, for the sum of £102,840, including timber. Of this sum, £41,900 was retained by the trustees of the marriage settlement, and £28,096 had to meet the mortgages for the enfranchisement.

Thus came to an end the Manydown and Hampshire territorial possessions of a family that had lived upon them (as has been recorded in detail) for at least 413 years, *i.e.*, from 1484—1871.

After the sale Mr. Bigg-Wither went to live in Montpelier Road, Brighton, where he bought four houses,—relieved indeed of pressing and future financial anxieties, but with a heart aching for the old place, so much so that he bought in 1873, for £4987, some land called the Apletree Farm, adjoining Manydown and Tangier, "that he might feel himself," as he said, "still an owner of land in the old place." To pay for this was the last cheque that he signed. He died, at Brighton, from heart failure after rheumatic fever, February 6th, 1874, aged sixty-eight years, and was buried at Worting. His widow survived him thirty-three years, and died at Brighton, August 21st, 1901, aged ninety-two.

Pedigree VIII.

DESCENDANTS OF HARRIS JERVOISE AND CHARLES,
SECOND AND FOURTH SONS OF HARRIS BIGG-WITHER OF MANYDOWN.

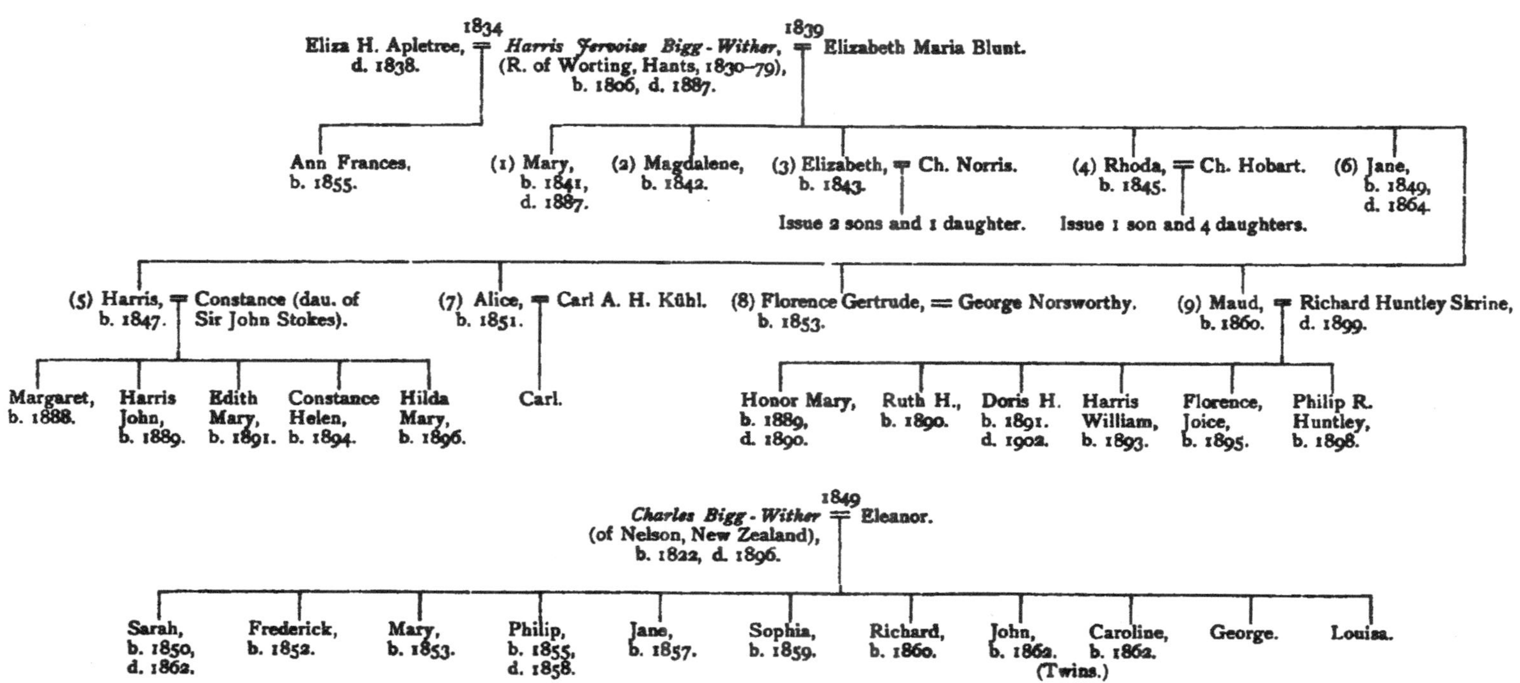

Oakley Hall.

CHAPTER V.

WITHER OF HALL (OAKLEY HALL).

(1620—1731.)

ITHER OF MANYDOWN.

ark),

orge, = Avelyn Shank.
1520, d. 1584.
86.

ier, = Agnes Page.

3 sons. { Thomas, b. 1545. John, b. 1549. Reginald, b. 1551, d. 1609.

Joan, = Walter Knight.
1581.

Agnes, = Chr. Cox.
b. 1596.

Elizabeth,
b. 1599.

Ann, = Henry Pinke (of Kempshott).
d. 1703,
buried at
Winslade.

Vither (of Manydown). (For issue, see Wither of Manydown.)

hy
2.

Andrew (of Gray's Inn), b. 1665, d. 1752, buried at Keevil.

Mary, b. 1666, d. 1677.

Maria, b. 1669, d. 1711.

Henry, b. 1667, killed in Flanders, 1694.

Wavell,

William, b. 1685, d. 1687.

Henrietta Maria, = Dr. W. King, D.L.
b. 1687, d. before 1731.

Issue 2 children.

a Maria, = (1748) Edmund Bramston (2nd husband) d. 1763.
d. 1790.

Wither Bramston, = (1783) Mary Chute (of the Vyne), d. 1822.
b. 1753, d. 1832,
s. p.

ta Brown,

Jane, = Ed. St. John,
d. 1882. d. 1886.

, Esq.,
Mals-
1905.

Henrietta Maria = Col. J. Wallington, C.B.

Issue.

William Wyndham (now Sir W. W. Portal, 1906),
Spencer John,
Bertram, and 4 daughters all married.

CHAPTER V.

WITHER OF HALL (OAKLEY HALL).

(1620—1731.)

GEORGE WITHER of Dummer, born circa 1520; died 1586.

(1.)—*GEORGE WYTHER*, the fourth son of John Wither of Manydown, who died A.D. 1536, and of Anne or Agnes Wither his wife, seems to have settled in the parish of Dummer, four miles south of Manydown.

He married Avelyn Shanke and had four sons—Gilbert, Thomas, John, and Reignold or Reginald.

From him are directly descended the Withers of Hall, though the Manor and the Manor house were not bought until 1620 by his grandson, (See Pedigree at the head of this Chapter). He is described in his will, proved 16th January, 1587, as of Dummer. He must have been a man of some property, for he bequeaths "all my lands lying in Lawrence Wootton and East Oakley and my lands called Staples, alias Gowldings Crofte, lying in Kempshott in the parish of Winslade to my son Gilbard Wethers and to the heirs of his body lawfully begotten." His "overseers" are his "cousins," John Wither of Manydown and Richard Ayliff of Ewhurst. He directs his body to be buried in the churchyard of Dummer, next his wife, who predeceased him two years in 1584. His burial is recorded in the Dummer registers, October 22nd, 1586.

GILBERT WITHER of Dummer, (1586—1599).

(2.)—*Gilbert Wyther*, George Wyther's eldest son, baptised at Dummer, 21st November, 1543, is called in the Dummer and Oakley registers, in both of which his burial is recorded, "Mr. Gilberte Wyther of Dummer."

He married in 1578 Agnes Page, and had four sons—George, Reginald, Henry, and William, and four daughters. (See Pedigree IX.)

In 1589–90 we find him buying property in Oakley parish from the Fiennes family.[1] The inquisition post mortem held at Alton in 1600 states the amount of that property to be 460 acres, with various houses and a messuage with appurtenances called Rastalles or Rastowelles.[2] His will, dated 1599, shows that he had property also in the adjoining parish of Dean.

[1] Feet of Fines, co. Southton.

[2] Inq. p. m., 42 Eliz.

All his land he left to his eldest son George, besides £100 each to his seven other children. Provision is made in his will that his heirs should not enter for twelve years after his decease upon the lands and tenements now in the testator's tenure or occupation, namely, "Bullsbushes park and barne, Northdowne, Evenger's Copse, and Barton Allins"; names which will be familiar to those interested in the present Oakley Hall property.

The inventory of Gilbert Wyther's goods attached to his will is valued at £936. 4*s*. 8*d*. (about £6500 of the present value), a considerable increase on that of his father's, which only amounted to £30. 17*s*. 4*d*.

Gilbert Wyther directs that his body be buried "in the body of the Parish Church of Church Oakley before the seat belonging unto the farm house of Rastowelles, and that my exors do provide a stone of marble of a foot square to be laid over my burial place graven with the date and year of my decease."

He died at Dummer, but was buried at Oakley 1st July, 1599.

A few years ago I discovered in an old furniture shop in Basingstoke a brass plate with the following inscription:—

HERE LYETH THE BODYE
OF GYLBARD WYTHER
WHOE DECEASED THE
XXXth DAY OF JUNE AN[o] 1599.

CHARLES WITHER, THE ELDER.

Born 1663; died 1697.

From a pastel, at Oakley Manor.

The plate is now (1907) in the parish chest of Oakley Church, to be refixed in the Church, from whence it was probably taken when the Church was rebuilt in 1869.

GEORGE WITHER of Hall, (1599—1666.)

(3.)—*George Wither*, born 1583, eldest son of Gilbert, is the first of the family known as "of Hall." He added to his father's property by buying, in 1616, 165 acres of land from the Rumbold family in Dean, and in 1619 he added another 460 acres in Oakley, bought from the Ayliffes, from whom he acquired the next year the manor of Hall and the manor house. The deed to that effect is among the Oakley Hall archives. He also, between 1629–52, bought land at Kingsclere Woodlands, Tadley, Hannington, and Bramley, and in 1656 the manors of the three Wallops, with about 1800 acres of land and considerable house property, as well as the advowson of the Church of Upper Wallop, on the Wiltshire border of the county.[1] Little more is known of him, except that he was one of the "Cursitor Barons" of the Court of Chancery. His legal training and practice is quaintly referred to on the monument to his memory in Dean Church.[2]

[1] Feet of Fines, co. Southton., 1629, 1630, 1640, 1652, 1656, 1658.

[2] Appendix III.

His wife's burial is recorded in the Dean Registers as "Mrs. Agnes Wither, the wife of George Wither of Hall, buried in the Chancel of Dean, 29th October, 1659."

George Wither died without issue in 1666, and the property went to his nephew Gilbert, son of his brother Henry:—

(2.)—*Reginald*, the second son, died without issue in 1616.

(3.)—*Henry*, the third son, is described as of St. Olave's, Southwark. He married and had two sons—*Gilbert*, who succeeded his uncle at Hall, and *George*, whose only daughter Mary married her cousin, William Wither, of Manydown. His daughter Ann married Henry Pinke, of Kempshott.

(4.)—*William*, the fourth son, born at Dummer in 1593, took Holy Orders and became Rector of Dummer in 1624. He was a Fellow of Winchester College, where there is a monument to his memory in the Cloisters.[1] He died in 1656.

[1] Appendix III.

GILBERT WITHER (1666—1676).

(4.)—*Gilbert Wither*, of Hall, eldest son of Henry Wither, of Southwark, born 1623, succeeded his uncle at Hall Place in 1666. He was educated at Winchester, and became Fellow of New College, Oxford, in 1647. He entered Holy Orders and became Rector of North Waltham and Dean. He married, 4th September, 1654, Elizabeth, daughter of Thomas Hall, of Basingstoke, by his wife Elizabeth daughter of Walter Pinke, of Kempshott Park, near Basingstoke, a family that owned Kempshott for most of the seventeenth and eighteenth centuries.[2]

[2] Family of Pinke, chap. viii.

The issue of the marriage of Gilbert Wither and Elizabeth Hall was numerous—seven sons and four daughters. The Dean registers[3] show that three sons and two daughters were buried there in the autumn and winter of 1677–8. Presumably there was some fever which carried off five of the family between the ages of sixteen and twenty-two. Two were buried in one grave.

[3] Appendix III.

Of the other children :—

Charles, the sixth son, born 1663, succeeded at Hall Place.

Andrew, the seventh son, born 1665, became a Bencher of Gray's Inn. Many extant deeds show that he acted as legal adviser of the family. He died an old man in 1752, and is buried at Keevil in Gloucestershire.

Henry, the youngest of the family, born 1667, entered the army. There are several interesting letters of his addressed to Mr. Thomas Jervoise, of Herriard, dated 1693–4, relating to incidents in the Campaign of Flanders, where he lost his life.

Mrs. Wither (*Née* Dorothy Smith),
Wife of Charles Wither, of Hall.
Died 1782.

From a picture by Sir Godfrey Kneller, at Oakley Hall.

Anne, the eldest daughter, born in 1662, married, 9th October, 1679, William Beach, Esq., of Fiddleton, Wiltshire, who bought the charming Jacobean house at Keevil, which has descended to Major Archibald Hicks Beach, of Oakley Hall. Their grandson William married another Anne Wither of Hall in 1746.

Mr. Gilbert Wither added Wyfolds and the advowson of Tadley to the property, and in 1671 bought the Manor of Inhurst, afterwards (1791) sold to Lovelace Bigg-Wither, of Manydown. He died in 1676. His widow married Dr. Watson, D.L., Dean of Battle, and had issue. She died 1694, aged sixty-one.

CHARLES WITHER, the elder, (1676—1697).

(5.)—*Charles Wither*, of Hall, fifth son of the Rev. Gilbert Wither, was born at North Waltham in 1663. He became a scholar at Winchester College, and married in 1682 Dorothy, daughter of Sir William Smith, Bart. There is a beautiful picture of her by Godfrey Kneller at Oakley Hall. She long outlived her husband, of whom little is known, except that he was High Sheriff of the County in 1686, and died August, 1697.

Mrs. Wither was buried June 3rd, 1732. The position of the vault in old Dean Church, where they were both interred, is minutely described in the Dean registers.[1] Two children only survived—Charles, who succeeded, and Henrietta Maria, who married Dr. William King, D.L. She died in the lifetime of her brother Charles.

[1] Appendix III.

There was a provision in Charles Wither's will, which caused a big lawsuit in the family. He left his only daughter, Henrietta Maria, who married Dr. King, £2500 on attaining twenty-one or marriage. He also left her an additional £3500 if his son Charles should die without male issue. This happened in 1731, and Dr. King, as administrator of his late wife's estate, thereupon sued in Chancery Andrew Wither (the brother and surviving exor of

Charles Wither, the elder), Frances (the widow and executrix of Charles Wither, the younger), and Dorothy, Anne, and Henrietta Maria (daughters of Charles Wither, the younger), for payment of this £3500. The result of the Chancery suit was that the Lord Chancellor pronounced judgment, 11th July, 1735, to the effect that the £3500 in question "is a subsisting charge on the said testator's real estate." Andrew Wither and the widow and daughters of Charles Wither, the younger, appealed to the House of Lords, mainly on the ground that Henrietta Maria King died in the lifetime of her brother Charles Wither, and that therefore the contingency above-mentioned never vested in her. The House of Lords however confirmed the decree of the Court of Chancery, with costs, 15th March, 1735-6.

CHARLES WITHER, the younger, (1697—1731).

(6.)—*Charles Wither*, "the younger," as he is called to distinguish him from his father, was baptised 8th August, 1684. He became a well-known and distinguished man, and I am able to give some details of his work and family life. He married in 1707 Frances Wavell, a member of the ancient Yorkshire family of Wyvell or Wavell, and cousin of Henrietta Wavell who married in 1728 Henry Wither, of Theddon Grange. They had five children; two (Frances and Charles) died in infancy; three daughters survived:—

(1.)—*Dorothy*, who died unmarried in 1752, the day after her mother's death.

(2.)—*Henrietta Maria*, who married (1st) Mr. Thynne Worsley, (2ndly) Mr. Edmund Bramston. She succeeded her father at Hall. (See post.)

(3.)—*Ann*, who married in 1746 her cousin, Mr. William Beach, of Fiddleton and Netheravon, Wilts, by which marriage Oakley Hall came to the Beach family in 1832.

Charles Wither has left two interesting journals. The first, written 1702, describes a ride from Oxford to Newcastle and

CHARLES WITHER, THE YOUNGER.

Born 1684; died 1731.

Commissioner of Woods and Forests.

Carlisle with his tutor, and back to Oxford; the second, describing a journey in Holland in 1706–7, before his marriage. He was High Sheriff of the County in 1708, when he was only twenty-five years old, and was M.P. for Christchurch from 1726–31. He was made Commissioner of Woods and Forests in 1720, an office, which as his letters and journals shew, entailed an immense amount of work. In a letter to his daughter Ann (afterwards Mrs. Beach) he says: "*I am up every morning at four and abroad till ten at night.*" And writing in French, September 8th, 1730, he says:—

"*Je suis si occupé dans les affaires de mon office, que c'est avec difficulté que je trouve du temps à manger, et encore moins en proportion à dormir. Je me reveille ordinairement avant qu'il fait jour, et sort sans dejeuner. Je reviens au logis environ midi, et à deux heures après diner je suis obligé de retourner à travail. Enfin je me suis tant fatigué que vous aurez de la peine à me connaitre quoique je me porte passablement bien.*"

"Your sisters have not yet been at Court; but go to-morrow, and Henny (Henrietta Maria, afterwards married to Mr. E. Bramston) hunts in her new habit, which is Garter blue gogram, laced with gold lace: they go to-night to a ball at Windsor with Miss Crossby, Miss Fielding, and Lady Fanny Montague, and I wish I could add with my dearest little Nancy . . . . . I beg of you stick to your spinnet and writing of music."

Anne evidently had a taste for music, for in his next letter, dated from Cranburn Little Lodge, near Windsor, her father says:

"The Princesses asked after you, and have made me promise to get a harpsicord here, and bring you hither next year for they long to hear you play, so pray tell Mr. Keeble for his credit I hope he will make you play Handell's lessons by that time, for the Princesses like them mightily . . . . Mr. Keeble has given me so satisfactory an account of your industry that I am more pleased than you can imagine."

Little Miss Anne Wither (she was only thirteen), remaining at home in Hampshire, was looked to by her father for information as to all his country affairs at Hall, and to supplement the more formal reports of his bailiff and chief groom. He says:—

"My dearest little girl is mistress of the Family and entrusted with the power of everything . . . . I beg you will tell me all about the fox-hunting . . . . I will write to Ned about the horses and dogs, and to Webb about my 'œconomie de Campagne' and the farms. You will oblige me by begging them both to follow carefully my orders . . . . I beg you will be very careful of all my business, and next letter you write let me know whether the Harvest people are diligent or lazy, and who does the business best and who worst, for I am sure by this time you are a good judge."

In October, 1731, he writes announcing the return home of the family :—

"I would have Dick the postillion come hither with the four horses on Wednesday; pray let him set out early in the morning on Wednesday, that he may be here betimes for the horses to have some rest. Let Webb go to James the Waggoner and tell him to provide to bring my goods and the maids by his waggon next Saturday. Tell Ned I would have the hounds kept fresh for me, for I think I have not been so well these twenty years as I am now, and shall hunt stoutly."

He came home, and died on 20th November following.

In the *Gentleman's Magazine* for that date is the following notice :—

"Death.—November, 1731, Charles Wither, of Hall, in Hampshire Esq. Surveyor of His Majesty's Woods and Forests and M.P. for Christchurch, Twyneham. He was, according to his own appointment, carried to his Interment at twelve o'clock at night by six of his Servants, one walking before with a candle and lanthorn, no Friends or Relations following."

There is an interesting letter from his widow to the same daughter Anne, dated June, 1742 :—

"My dearest Nancy,—Whatever mistakes may be in my will, I beg you and your Sisters as my last request, to take no advantage from it. I am sorry it is not in my power to acknowledge your goodness to me by giving you a better Legacy, which if I had I must have been unjust to your dear Sister Wither (Dorothy Wither, the eldest daughter), *who I beg you will never leave till marriage part you, which if you do, my spirit will never rest. I hope your Sister Worsley* (*i.e.*, the second daughter, Henrietta Maria, whose first husband was Thynne Worsley, son of Sir Robert Worsley, Bart.) *will be kind to you both: you have laid great obligation on her. I pray God to continue the good understanding that I leave among you. I thank you for*

MRS. EDMUND BRAMSTON

(*Née* Henrietta Maria Wither).

Born 1743; died 1790.

your kindness to me, and I hope that God Almighty will return it to you and your Sisters in this world and the next. Pray be mindful of your duty to God and your neighbour. Pray God bless you with a long and happy life. Farewell, my dearest soul, farewell for ever. *ff. Wither.*"

She died, after a long illness, September 28th, 1752, at Hall. Her eldest daughter, Dorothy, who had shown great devotion in the care of her mother, died the day after. They were buried the same day. The inscription on her monument in Dean Church, written by her sister (Mrs. Edmund Bramston), says:

"Perhaps it was one part of its reward
That Providence spared her the pain
She had always most dreaded.
For after having anxiously watched over her Mother
Through a long illness
When the lamp of life was just going out
She fell sick herself,
And expired the next day after her beloved Parent,
On whose life she had placed yᵉ chief happiness of her own."

MRS. EDM. BRAMSTON, (1748—1790).

(7.)—*Henrietta Maria Wither*, born 1713, married (1741) Mr. Thynne Worsley, son of Sir Robert Worsley (Bart.), of Appuldercombe, I.W. He died within a month of his marriage, 17th February, 1741. Mrs. Worsley married again (1748) Edmund Bramston, of an old Essex family.[1] He was gentleman usher to the Dowager Princess of Wales.

Quarterly, 1st and 4th or, on a fess sable, *Bramston*; 2nd and 3rd or, three fleurs-de-lis, gules, *Mondeford*; bearing on a shield of pretence, *Wither*.

The issue of this second marriage was *Wither Bramston*, born 1753, who succeeded; (2) *Augusta*, born 1749, died unmarried 1819; (3) *Henrietta*, born 1751, died unmarried 1771. Mr. Edmund Bramston died 20th June, 1763. His widow continued to live at the Hall until her death in 1790.

The life at Oakley Hall in the days of Mrs. Bramston is illustrated in different ways by the following *ménu* for the annual tenants' dinner, and the description of a ball at Hawkwood Park:

[1] Bramston Family, chap. viii.

"*Dinner for Tenants on New Year's Day.*

"1st Table—		2nd Table—
Boiled Turkey.		Boiled Turkey.
Chine.		Boiled Rump of Beef.
Goose and Apple Sauce.		Goose and Apple Sauce.
Sir Loin Beef.		Carrots, Turnips, Greens.
Turkey.		Minced Pye.
Greens and Pickles.		Plumb Pudding.
Minced Pye.		
Plumb Pudding.		

"This bill of fare has been dress'd at Hall Place on New Year's Day from time immemorial.

"HENRIETTA MARIA BRAMSTON.
"Jan. 1, 1770."

Masquerade Ball at Hawkwood.

Letter from Mrs. Bramston (*née* Henrietta Maria Wither) to her son, Wither Bramston, aged sixteen:—

"Hall Place, June 4th, 1769.

"I think it an age since I wrote to my dear Wither; but I have never ceased to think of him . . . . Last Wednesday we went to the masquerade at Hackwood. There was a great deal of company from London, and every house in Basingstoke was full. The Duchess of Bolton was a Tartarian Princess; she had a crown of diamonds upon her head of great value, and was a fine figure. The Duke was in a handsome Domino, and so was the Duke of Gloucester (brother of George III). The Duke of Cumberland was not there; but both the Queen's brothers were. There were a great many rich dresses and some very humorous masques, amongst which was an old witch, who danced with a man who sold gingerbread, a Methodist preacher, a Pope, a Devil, and a Cardinal. There was a pretty little Cupid, who I believe did some mischief with his bow and arrows. Miss Conolly was a Vestal, her sister Leonora in the Padlock, and Lady Mary Powlett wore the same dress. *Augusta* (Wither Bramston's elder sister) represented Fortuna. She had a silver gauze jacket and a petticoat, with a blue veil fixed to her head with diamonds, then tyed to her shoulder with silver tassels, and fixed to her hip across her back and twisted in festoons round her coat. She carried a gilt wheel in her hand. *Henny* (Wither Bramston's younger sister Henrietta) was a Dancer. She wore a jacket and petticoat of pink lustring, trimmed with silver gauze, with a little hat of the same on one side of her head, and flowers on the other; she danced, but Augusta refused several masques that asked her. Your

Colonel Beach.

Born 1783; died 1856.

From a water colour by Fred Tatham.

Colonel Beach's three children.

Mr. W. W. B. Beach (afterwards M.P.), Lady Portal, and Lady Wallington.

From a water colour by Fred Tatham.

sisters were greatly entertained, indeed it was a fine sight. At twelve the rooms were opened for supper, which was all cold except soups and peas. Nigri furnished the dessert, which was very elegant. The Spring Wood was beautifully illuminated, and the company was intended to walk in it, but the weather prevented. Mr. Osborn had Sir George Pocock's Nabob's dress, which is very fine, and Lady Cork borrowed all the rich jewels which were Lady Pocock's. My dress was a Venetian Domino trimmed with gold gauze, with a white high crowned hat, trimmed with the same. We did not get home till past four o'clock. . . . . . I have wrote so many letters this post that my hand and pen is quite tired. I would not however neglect writing to my dearest Wither, to assure him that I am, most truly,

"His ever affectionate mother,

"HENRIETTA MARIA BRAMSTON."

1st and 4th, or on a fess sable, three plates argent, *Bramston*; 2nd and 3rd *Wither*; impaling, gules, three swords barways, the points towards the dexter, proper pomels and hilts or, *Chute*.

WITHER BRAMSTON (1790—1832).

(8.)—*Wither Bramston*, born 1753, was thirty-six years old when his mother died, aged seventy-six (1790). He married (1783) Mary Chute, daughter of Thomas Lobb Chute, of the Vyne. He rebuilt Oakley Hall on the site of the old house in 1795, and entirely rebuilt Dean Church at his own expense in 1818.

At his death without issue in 1832, the Oakley Hall property went to the descendants of his aunt, Mrs. Beach (*née* Anne Wither), whose daughter, Henrietta Maria, married in 1779 Mr. *Michael Hicks*, of Keevil, Wilts, who assumed on the death of his wife's father in 1790, by royal license, the surname and arms of Beach. Their second son, *William Hicks Beach*, M.P., Colonel of the N. Gloucestershire Militia, succeeded to the Oakley Hall property on the death of Mr. Wither Bramston in 1832. He had three children—William Wither Bramston, Mary Jane, and Henrietta Maria.

Quarterly, 1st and 4th vairé, argent and gules on a canton azure, a pile or, *Beach*; 2nd gules, a fess wavy between three fleurs-de-lis or, *Hicks*; 3rd, a chevron gules between three crescents sable, *Wither*.

COLONEL BEACH (1832—1856).

Colonel Beach died in 1856, and was succeeded at Oakley by his only son (born 1826).

WILLIAM WITHER BRAMSTON BEACH (1856—1900).

(9.)—*The Rt. Honble. William Wither Bramston Beach* married (1857) Caroline Chichester, daughter of Col. Cleveland, of Tapley Park, N. Devon. He made considerable alterations and additions to Oakley Hall in 1860. He was Master of the Vine Hounds for many years; a great Mason, being Provincial Grand Master of Hampshire and the Isle of Wight; and a prominent Conservative, representing the Basingstoke and Andover Division of Hampshire for forty-four years. He became "Father of the House of Commons." He died as the result of an accident coming from the House of Commons in 1901, leaving a widow, two sons and a daughter. His elder sister, *Mary Jane*, married Mr. (afterwards Sir) Wyndham S. Portal, of Malshanger, Hants. His second sister, *Henrietta Maria*, married Colonel (afterwards Sir) John Wallington. His eldest son, *Archibald William Hicks*, late Captain King's Royal Rifles, married Violet, the only daughter of the Hon. Slingsby Bethell, C.B., and has issue. The second son, *Ellice Michael Hicks*, is in H. M. Diplomatic Service. *Margaret*, the daughter, married G. W. Nicholson, Esq., M.P., of Basing Park, Alton.

William Wither Bramston Beach, M.P.

Born 1826; died 1900.

List of Pictures connected with the Wither Family, at Oakley Hall and Oakley Manor.

1. Sir Henry Hobart (Lord Chief Justice, temp. James I), by *Zucchero.*
2. Lady Hobart (Dorothy, daughter of Sir Robert Bell, of Beaupré), by *C. Jansen.*
3. Sir William Smith, Bart., by *Sir Peter Lely.*
4. Lady Smith, by *Sir Peter Lely.*
5. Charles Wither, the elder, with his wife Dorothy (daughter of Sir William Smith).

5*a*. Mrs. Charles Smith, by *Sir Godfrey Kneller.*

6. Charles Wither, the younger, with his Wife Frances (daughter of Thomas Wavell, Esq.).
7. Dorothy Wither (daughter of Charles Wither, the younger).
8. Nancy Wither (daughter of Charles Wither, the younger).
9. Mrs. William Beach (*née* Nancy Wither).
10. Henrietta Maria Wither (Mrs. Edmund Bramston).
11. Thynne Worsley (First Husband of Henrietta Maria Wither).
12. Edmund Bramston (Second Husband of Henrietta Maria Wither).
13. Sir John Bramston (Lord Chief Justice, temp. James I).
14. Mrs. Wither Bramston (*née* Mary Chute).
15. Colonel Beach (water colour), by *Fred Tatham.*
16. Colonel Beach's Three Children (water colour), by *Fred Tatham.*
17. Mrs. Gilbert Wither (*née* Elizabeth Hall), pastel.
18. Mrs. Gilbert Wither (as a widow), pastel.
19. Andrew Wither, pastel.
20. Maria Wither (daughter of Rev. Gilbert Wither), pastel.
21. Charles Wither (the elder), pastel.
22. Charles Wither (the younger), pastel.
23. Charles Wither (the younger) with his Wife, pastel.

24—26. Miniatures in black and white of (1) Augusta Wither, (2) Henrietta Maria Wither, (3) Mary Chute.

CHAPTER VI.

WITHER OF BENTWORTH AND THEDDON GRANGE.

GEORGE WITHER THE POET.)

(1562—1730.)

Pedigree I.

WITHER OF BENTWORTH AND OF THEDDON GRANGE.

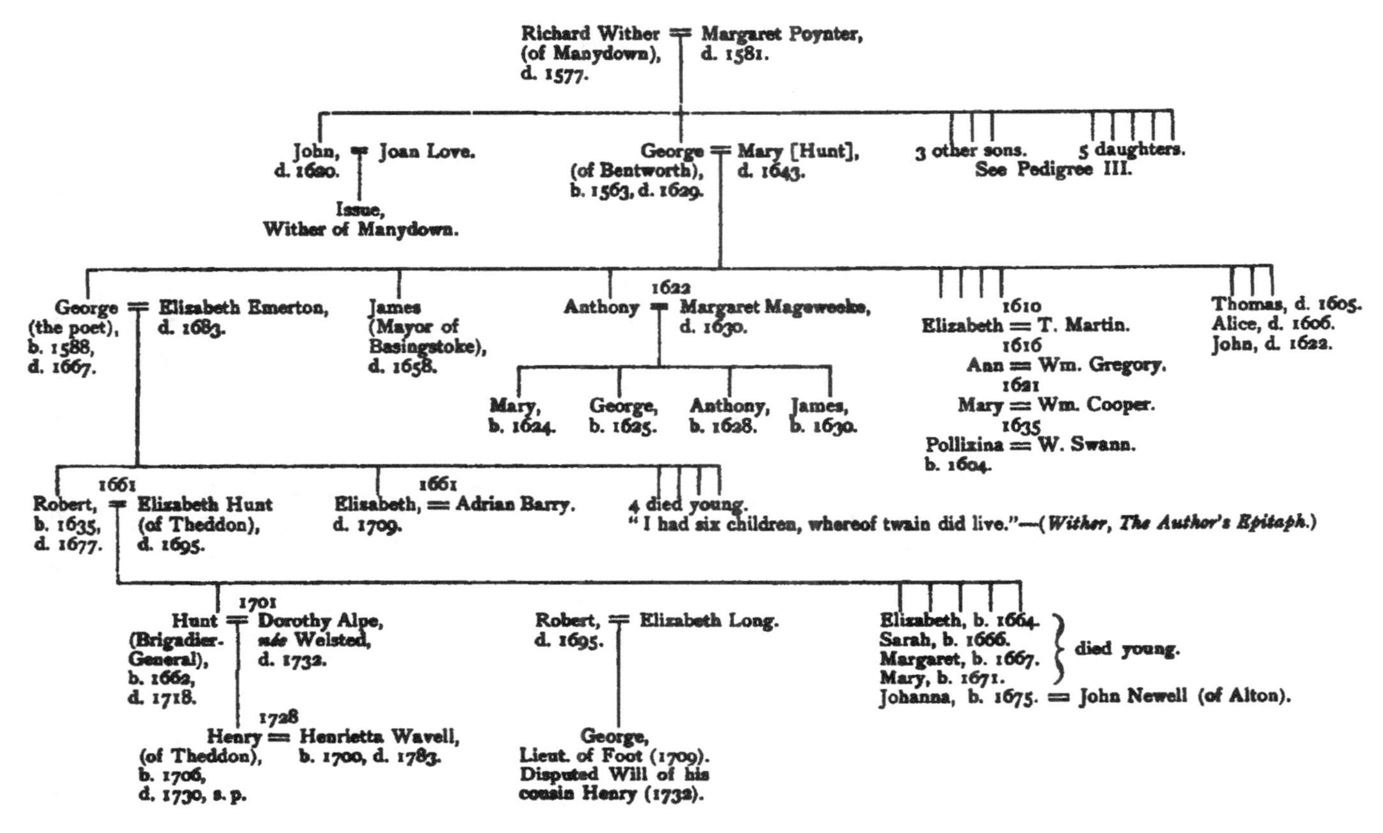

CHAPTER VI.

WITHER OF BENTWORTH AND THEDDON GRANGE.

(1562—1730.)

RICHARD WITHER, *of Manydown*, who was buried at Wootton, 23rd July, 1577, and was succeeded by his eldest son John, had several other children by his wife, Margaret Poynter, of whom *George*, the next in age, baptised 14th July, 1562, went to live and died at Bentworth, a village near Alton, Hants, where he acquired considerable property, and most probably a wife. He was father of the celebrated poet and satirist, *George Wither*, born at Bentworth, 11th June, 1588. The poet's mother is said in most biographies of G. W., and in many old pedigrees, to have been Ann Searle or Serle. This is an error, based probably on the following entry in the Wootton Registers: "*A.D. 1604, Georgius Wither et Annæ Serle, Feb. 11, nupt.*"; and would make the poet to have been born fifteen years before his father's marriage. There were about this time several George Withers in existence (the poet says sixteen), and another of them (George, of Winchester) married Ann, daughter of Gilbert Searle, in 1641. The question of the parentage of the poet, which has puzzled many, has been set at rest by the discovery in 1902, in the Probate Court of Winchester, of the will of George Wither the Elder.[1] In that will the testator speaks of his "wife Mary." Moreover, the Feet of Fines, co. Southampton, 5th Charles I (1629), records that "George Wither, Senior, Gentleman, and Mary, his wife," sold some ninety-six acres of land in

GEORGE WITHER, of Bentworth. (1562—1629.)

[1] See Appendix III.

"Bentworthe"; a subsequent sale in 1658 speaks of "Mary, widow of George Wither, of Bentworth." A fourth proof that the poet's mother was "Mary," not "Ann," is afforded by her will.[1] What her surname was is not certain, but the suggestion made by Mr. F. Sidgwick in the excellent Introduction to his book on the earlier poetry of G. W. is most likely correct, namely, that the poet's mother "Mary" belonged to the family of *Hunt*,[2] who then owned "Fidding," or *Theddon Grange*, close to Bentworth, a family that gave another daughter (Elizabeth) to the poet's son *Robert*, so bearing out the statement in G. W.'s poem—"A Sacrifice of Praise and Prayer."

[1] See Appendix II.

[2] Chapter VIII.

> "*The families from whom I was designed*
> *To take my being, Thou hast now twice joined*
> *And their two surnames, being joined together*
> *Denominate my grandson, Hunt L'Wither.*"

As in the parallel case of George Wither, of Dummer (the fourth son of John Wither, of Manydown, and the progenitor of the Withers of Oakley Hall), there is nothing to show why George Wither (the elder), of Bentworth, chose that place for his home, unless it was to be near his wife's family at Theddon. All we know for certain is that his five sons, *George*, *John*, *Thomas*, *James*, and *Anthony*, and his five daughters, *Elizabeth*, *Mary*, *Anne*, *Alice*, and *Polyxena* (see Pedigree), were born at Bentworth; that he died and was buried there (17th November, 1629), and that his widow "Mary" was buried there (29th April, 1643).[3]

[3] See Bentworth Registers, Appendix III.

At Bentworth, on 11th June, 1588, while the great Armada was on its way to England, a son was born to George and Mary Wither. This was the well-known poet and writer. A family history is perhaps hardly the place for a literary appreciation of his works, nor for a further full account of his eventful and long life; but this history would be more incomplete than it is if I did not here introduce a short account, based mainly on published biographies, of this remarkable man, with some remarks on his writings.

GEORGE WITHER, the Poet (1588—1667).

The student of a family history notes that the poet derived some education from Ralph Starkey the Archivist, who had married a niece of his aunt, Mrs. Richard Wither (*née* Poynter) of Manydown; but his chief education as a boy was at the (then) noted school of Mr. John Greaves (father of two noted men of learning) in the neighbouring parish of Colmer. His early life under the parental roof at Bentworth was one of ease and indeed of luxury. He alludes in one of his poems to the time:—

> "*When daily I on change of dainties fed,*
> *Lodged night by night upon an easy bed*
> *In lordly chambers, and had wherewithal*
> *Attendants forwarder than I to call,*
> *Who brought me all things needful; when at hand*
> *Hounds, hawks and horses were at my command.*"[1]

[1] "Britain's Remembrancer," 3rd Canto.

He entered Magdalen College, Oxford, when he was fifteen. Of his career at Oxford (1604–6) he himself gives an account at the beginning of his "*Abuses Stript and Whipt.*" But before he could "acquire the lowest degree" some cause, perhaps a change in his parents' fortune, brought it about that—

> "*I home returned somewhat discontent,*
> *And to our Bentworth's beechy shadows went.*
> . . . .
> *But finding that mere countrie business*
> *Was not my calling, . . . I soon forsook again*
> *The shady grove and the sweet open plaine.*"[2]

[2] Introduction to "Abuses Stript and Whipt."

So in 1606, when he was "thrice five years and three," he went to London and entered at "one of the Inns of Chancery," where for the next five years we hear very little of him. It is probable that "*Fidelia*" and "*Fair Virtue,*" including the "matchless lyric"—

> "*Shall I, wasting in despair,*
> *Die because a woman's fair?*"

were written and in private circulation at this time, though not published until long afterwards.

In 1611 came his first publication, "*Abuses Stript and Whipt*," a satirical criticism of the Government, which at once suppressed it. The death of Henry, the popular Prince of Wales, 6th November, 1612, and the marriage the next year of the Princess Elizabeth, "the noblest nymph of Thame," called forth the "*Obsequies*" and the "*Epithalamia*" in which Wither's muse was almost at its best.

The republication in 1613 of the "*Abuses Stript and Whipt*," with the appended "*Scourge*," containing an attack upon the Lord Chancellor (Cecil), brought about his committal to the Marshalsea, from which he was liberated after eighteen months imprisonment by order of James I, and doubtless through the intercession of his powerful patroness the Princess Elizabeth (afterwards Queen of Bohemia), who had "vouchsafed her word to clear me from all dangers" when it first appeared.[1] While in prison he wrote the charming pastoral poem the "*Shepherds Hunting*," the best known of all his works.

the King."

When liberated, Wither was at once admitted (8th July, 1615) to Lincoln's Inn, "At request of John Jeffreys, Arm., now reader and bencher."

In 1621 he published "*Withers Motto*"—"Nec habeo, nec careo, nec curo"—a poem which at once gained extraordinary popularity, and went through several editions; but again a hidden satire was discovered by some enemy in high position,[2] and he was (27th June, 1621) ordered to the Marshalsea once more, on the charge of libel, which he easily refuted, and he was released without trial.

tate Papers, cxxi, p. 130.

Soon after this, his finances being in a bad way, the poet obtained from the King a patent dated 17th February, 1622–3,

What I WAS is passed by:
What I AM away doth flie:
What I SHAL BEE none do see:
Yet in that my Beauties bee.

Published by W. Richardson, Castle Street, Leicester Fields

Geo: Wither

For description of the various portraits of George Wither, see p. 104.

giving him, "his exors and assigns," for fifty-one years the monopoly and copyright of "*Hymns and Songs of the Church*," a work in which he had put into lyric verse the Bible songs; and a further patent was granted him prohibiting the binding up of the authorized Psalm book in metre without a copy of Wither's "*Hymns and Songs*."[1] These patents at once brought him into collision with the privileges of the Stationers' Company,[2] and a dispute arose which lasted until 1633, when the patent was withdrawn, and Wither had no longer any difficulty about printing and publishing his numerous works.

[1] Domestic State Papers, B. M., vol. cxxxviii, pp. 268, 274–5.

[2] See "Scholars' Purgatorie."

All this time George Wither had been living in London; but between 1636—39 he seems to have retired to a house, which he calls "his rustic habitation," under Beacon Hill, near Farnham. Some (perhaps most) of the family property at Bentworth had been sold at this time, namely, nearly 100 acres, just before his father's death, November, 1629. In 1630 he sold a messuage and land in Bentworth to William Gregory and his wife Ann (the poet's sister). The deed relating to this is in the possession of an old man named F. Vickery, at Bentworth, and is signed by the poet, his two brothers, James and Anthony, and by his sister Pollixina, dated May 22nd, 1630. In 1637 he and his mother sold another 100 acres, with house and grounds, at Bentworth.[3]

[3] Feet of Fines, Co. Southton., Mar., 1629; Ditto, Mar., 1637.

In 1639 the poet exchanged for a time the pen for the sword, and we find him in that year Captain of Horse and Quarter-Master-General in the expedition of Charles I against the Scotch Covenanters, and—though he found time in 1641 to publish his "*Halelujah, or Britain's Second Remembrancer*," which contains the best of his religious poetry—the outbreak of the Civil War in 1642 again claims him as a soldier, this time on the Parliamentary side. He is said by Anthony-à-Wood to have "sold his estate and raised a troop of horse for the Parliament." I can find no authority for the first of these statements, though it is evident by his subsequent petitions to Parliament that he incurred great expenses and was reduced almost to poverty in furthering the Parliamentary cause.[1] That he did raise a troop of horse in his own neighbourhood, "according to my fortune and my place," is proved,[2] and he placed on his colours the legend "*Pro rege, lege, grege*," a motto which aptly defines his attitude towards the political questions of the time. He was a constitutionalist before his time.

[1] See pet., Sept. 19th, 1649, Domestic State Papers.

[2] "Campo Musæ."

On 14th October, 1642, Wither was appointed by the Parliamentary Committee Captain and Commander of Farnham Castle, for "defence of King, Parliament, and Kingdom." This was after its first capture by Sir William Waller. He withdrew after a brief occupation, and as the reasons for his doing so have been so misjudged,[3] and the story of events has been so confused, I give at length the circumstances as related by Mr. H. E. Malden in his recent *History of Surrey*, pp. 229—231, and in the volume of the *Victoria History of Surrey*, p. 407—519:—

[3] Onslow Papers, Hist. MSS. 149, p. 477.

"*On October 14th, 1642, George Wither, who had been put in command of forces raised for the Parliament in Surrey, was given a commission from the two Houses as Governor of Farnham Castle. Acc*[d] *to his own account he began actively to put the place in repair, to fortify it as best as he could, to collect stores, and dig a well. . . . Wither had no artillery, only two newly-raised squadrons, but half armed, a few irresolute volunteers whom he could not depend upon, about sixty muskets, some powder, matches, and balls.*[1] *He was persuaded also that Sir Rd Onslow, under whose orders he was acting, was not only jealous of him, but not to be depended upon in the cause. . . . He chafed under Onslow's orders; he was in perpetual irritation at not receiving vast supplies of men and munitions, which neither Sir Rd nor anyone else had it in his power to send him.*

"*The Royalists were in the neighbourhood, an attack appeared imminent, and he probably rightly judged that he could not resist it. What happened is obscure. In his pamphlet 'Se Defendendo'* (published 1643), *Wither says that he was ordered to come to London with a troop of horse, leaving an officer in charge at Farnham. This was when the King's army was advancing upon London after the Battle of Edgehill. A general story against him was that he had run away and deserted his garrison, and in another pamphlet called 'Justitiarius Justificatus'* (published 1645), *directed against Sir R. Onslow, who was then endeavouring to have Wither removed from the Commission of the Peace for Surrey,—he gives a different reason. In it he writes that Sir R. O. persuaded him to leave Farnham on the ground that his appointment was only temporary, and that he could do better service with a more assured position as Captain of a troop of horse in the field. . . . . . Wither certainly did not go without the intention of returning. On November 8th he got from Parliament an order for a supply of 'culverins,' or heavy guns, from the Tower.*[2] *The next day, however, the advance of Rupert's horse into North Surrey caused Parliament to rescind the order, for it was not feasible to get the train of artillery safely through the country. Wither asked leave to exchange the culverins for 'drakes,' or light artillery, which he thought he might convoy safely through byways. He was refused leave, however, and told that the fortress must be evacuated. Then he, perhaps, really did distinguish himself by an act of daring and skill. Alone on a swift horse, risking the encounter of Rupert's plunderers, he rode down to his own house. There he impressed all the carts and horses he could find at once, took them to Farnham, through the park, avoiding the Royalist town, and conveyed away safely all the men and what supplies there were in the Castle.*"[3]

On the very day of Wither's withdrawal of the forces from Farnham Castle his house, four miles off, was entered by Royalist troops and plundered, whereby he lost, he says, "above two thousand pounds," and also, it seems, several MSS. of unpublished

[1] Thig's Pamphlets, B. M., 14,713.

[2] Journal of the House of Commons.

[3] "Se Defendendo."

poems, etc. He himself was captured (though whether at this time or subsequently is not clear) and brought before the King at Oxford, when, according to the well-known story,[1] Sir John Denham pleaded successfully for his life on the ground that "So long as Wither lived he, Denham, would not be accounted the worst poet in England." It is difficult to trace his movements at this critical time of the great Civil War; but "Major Wither" was present at the Siege of Gloucester in 1643, and at the Battle of Naseby in 1645. In 1646 he was fined £500 for his violent attack in the pamphlet "*Justitiarius Justificatus*" (before referred to) on the Parliamentary General Sir R. Onslow, whom he had charged with sending money privately to the King, and who "had retorted by depriving him of his command of the Militia in East and Mid Surrey, and caused his removal from the Commission of the Peace."[2]

[1] See Lord Nugent, and Aubrey's Lives.

[2] Sidney Lee, Dic. Nat. Biography. Hist. MSS. Onslow Papers.

After the death of the King (January, 1649) and the establishment of the Commonwealth, Wither bombarded the Government afresh with petitions for sums due to him for "payment of his troops in the late wars," and for the plunder of his property by the Royalists. The summary of one of these petitions, dated 19th September, 1649, is so piteous and graphic that it is worth inserting here:—[3]

[3] Introd. to 7th Report of Hist. MSS., p. 73.

> "*George Wither complains that by want of his arrears of pay his family is reduced from eighteen household servants to one; his diet from several dishes at a meal to many meals out of one dish, and otherwise to no meal in the whole day. He is now feeding upon his household stuff in the hope that when it is consumed God will take him and his out of this unmerciful world.*"

The result of this forcible pleading was that the Houses of Parliament acknowledged that about £4000 was due to him, and an order was made out allowing him £150 annually out of Sir J. Denham's lands in Surrey. It is doubtful whether he ever got this money or any part of it; but it is difficult to reconcile the statements made by his biographers and his own pleas of poverty with the fact that on 28th September, 1648, he bought the manors of Bentley (Surrey) and Alverstoke, near Gosport, for £1185. 4*s.* 5¼*d.*,[1] and by his widow's will he seems to have still had property at Bentworth and elsewhere.

[1] Woodward, History of Hampshire, vol. iii, p. 352.

During the last days of the Commonwealth he lived out of London at a village called Hambledon, in Hampshire, until Cromwell gave him the Statute Office, or the "clerkship of recognizances," the benefit of which he lost (as he himself naively says) by declaring unto him (Cromwell) those truths which he was not willing to hear of.[2]

[2] Dom. State Papers, vol. cxxiii, 506, and Sidgwick Introduction, p. xxxviii.

He probably left Hambledon for London about 1654, in which year he sold 330 acres of his estate there to Sir Cheney Culpeper, Knight, to take up his new duties for the Court of Chancery. He subsequently (1658) sold fifty acres more at Hambledon;[3] but the manor was retained, and devised to his son Robert by his widow's will, with other property at Bentworth.

[3] Feet of Fines, co. Southton., Hilary Term, 1654-1658.

When the Restoration (1660) was assured, he welcomed the King in the following words:—

"I'le serve you faithfully in what I may,
And you, as King, love, honour, and obey."[4]

[4] "Verses to the King's Majesty."

But he expressed his apprehension as to the government of the country in "*Salt upon Salt*," "*Speculum Speculativum*," and other publications of his busy and rash pen, with a frankness which attracted the attention of the new Government. His house in the Savoy was searched, his papers examined, and a then unpublished poem called "*Vox Vulgi*" was made the excuse for his arrest (22nd May, 1661–2). He was committed to Newgate, then to the Tower, to await impeachment.[5] Here he whiled away his time by writing "*Crums found in a Prisoner's Basket*" and "*A Prisoner's Plea.*" No further proceedings against him were taken, and he

[5] Dom. State Papers, B.M., vol. xl, no. 54.

was released (27th July, 1663). The remaining years of his life were passed quietly at his house in London in writing untiringly, in collecting from previous writings, and in publishing "*Echoes from the Sixth Trumpet*," and in moralizing on the great plague of 1665.

He died in his house in the precincts of the Savoy, 2nd May, 1667, within a few weeks of his eightieth birthday. He was buried "within the east door" at the church of the Savoy Hospital in the Strand, "in streaming London's central roar." I have not been able to find his "will," if he ever made one.

"I am mainly indebted to Mr. F. Sidgwick's excellent Introduction to "*The Poetry of George Wither*," and to Mr. Sidney Lee's article in the "*Dictionary of National Biography*," for the above account of the poet's life. These living authors have doubtless made use of earlier biographies, the best of which are those of W. Winstanley (1687), Alex. Dalrymple (1785), Anthony à Wood, "*Athenæ Oxonienses*" (1721), J. Aubrey, "*Brief Lives*" (1898), and R. A. Wilmott's "*Lives of Sacred Poets*" (1834).

I have been able to make a few corrections and additions to these biographies from family records in my possession, and from the "Feet of Fines," co. Southampton.

I would commend to all interested in George Wither as a poet Charles Lamb's critical and appreciative essay (1818), in which he says:—

> "*The praises of poetry have been often sung in ancient and modern times; strange powers have been ascribed to it of influence over animate and inanimate auditors; but, before Wither, no one had celebrated its power at home—the wealth and the strength which this divine gift confers upon its possessor.*"

And again,—

> "*Whether encaged or roaming at liberty Wither never seems to have abated a jot of that free spirit which sets its mark upon his writings. The prison notes of Wither are finer than the wood notes of most of his poetical brethren.*"

Lamb, writing to the poet Southey, 8th November, 1798, and comparing Wither with his contemporary Quarles, says:—

"I perfectly accord with your opinion of old Wither; Quarles is a wittier writer, but Wither lays more hold of the heart. Quarles thinks of his audience when he lectures. Wither soliloquizes with a full heart. . . . Wither is like an old friend, whose warm heartedness and admirable qualities make us wish he possessed more genius, but at the same time makes us willing to dispense with that want. I always love Wither, and sometimes admire Quarles. . . . The extract you send from the "Shepherd's Hunting" places Wither in a starry height far above Quarles."

George Wither's best poems are written in the seven syllable line metre, of which he has shown himself a consummate master, *e.g.*:—

"Her true beauty leaves behind
Apprehensions in my mind
Of more sweetness than all art
Or inventions can impart.
Thoughts too deep to be expressed,
And too strong to be suppressed."[1]

[1] "Fair Virtue, or the Mistress of Philarete."

This is not the place for a further exposition of George Wither as a poet, nor for a full appreciation of his political character; but a descendant of the older branch of the family, and one who bears his name, may be allowed to refute briefly from his writings two charges—(1) that he was a "Roundhead," (2) that he was a "Puritan."

(1) That he was a Royalist at heart is evident from his Coronation Hymn (published 1641):—

"Him honour so and him so crown,
Him so invest and him so arm,
Him so anoint, him so enthrone.
And by Thy word him so inform,
That to Thy glory he may reign
To his content and for our peace."[2]

[2] "Halelujah," Hymn 84.

Of which the *Times*, September 11th, 1903, said "in no Coronation ode or hymn of the hundreds published on the occasion of Edward VII Coronation could we find anything to beat Wither's lines."

(2) No puritan could have written as follows on the Holy Eucharist :—

> "*But in this holy Eucharist*
> *By faith and grace divine*
> *We know we feed on Thee, O Christ,*
> *Receiving bread and wine.*
> *Thy real presence we avow,*
> *But so that we confess*
> *Mere carnal reason knows not how*
> *That presence to express.*"[1]

[1] Hymn 53.

How could the High Anglican doctrine be more clearly stated?

It is a pleasure to know that (as Mr. Sidney Lee says) "It is now universally recognised that George Wither was a poet of exquisite grace;" but it must also be acknowledged that "it was only for a season in his long career."

I have appended to this chapter what I believe to be the most complete list existing of his voluminous writings, based mainly on the bibliography contained in Sir Samuel Egerton Brydges' *British Bibliographer* (1810), compiled by Thomas Park. For this I am entirely indebted to the kindness and labour of Mr. Frank Sidgwick, of the firm of A. H. Bullen, publisher, 47, Great Russell Street, Bloomsbury, editor of the *Poetry of George Wither* (1902).

A short time before his death George Wither had expressed a desire to return "to the place of his nativity," but was dissuaded by his friends. His widow, however, to whom during his life he had shown the greatest affection and loyalty, returned to Bentworth, and continued till her death to live on a small estate called Gatwicke, which she had bought from her son Robert, who had it from his father-in-law, John Hunt, of Theddon Grange. Aubrey says that Mrs. George Wither "was a great wit, and could write in verse too." She died in 1683, and it is evident from her "will"[1] that a considerable portion of her husband's property had been saved in the wreck of his fortunes.

[1] Appendix 3.

Only two of the poet's six children survived him, Elizabeth and Robert:—

"I had six children, whereof twain did live."[2]

[2] Wither, "The Author's Epitaph."

(1.)—*Elizabeth*, who married Adrian Barry, of London, and of Thame, co. Oxford. Elizabeth Barry edited, between 1668 and 1688, several of her father's posthumous works. She died 1709.

ROBERT WITHER (1635—1667).

(2.)—*Robert Wither*, born 1635, made a good marriage with his relative Elizabeth, eldest daughter and co-heir with her sister Mary of John Hunt, of Theddon Grange, a fine house, situated within two miles of Bentworth. Here he took up his residence and lived till his death. He was buried at Bentworth 25th April, 1677. His widow survived him thirteen years, and was buried at Alton 3rd April, 1695. The eldest son of Robert Wither and Elizabeth Hunt was called *Hunt* after his mother's family, and was baptized at Alton, in which parish Theddon Grange is situated, 15th September, 1662.

Wither, impaling or, on a bend sable between 2 water bougets azure, 3 leopards' faces or, *Hunt*.

HUNT WITHER (1662—1718).

Hunt Wither married in 1701 a remarkable woman, and he had an unusual career. His wife Dorothy Alpe is simply called in the affidavit he made in 1709 before the College of Arms, "daughter and sole heir of Robert Welstead of London," but her domestic history is sufficiently curious to deserve a more extended notice from the simple fact that Hunt Wither was her fourth husband in less than eight years. She married (1st) Henry Perrin, who died 1694; (2nd) Richard Wilson, whose will was proved December, 1697; (3rd) Edward Alpe, who died 1700. All three were London physicians. By each of her four husbands she had one child.

Hunt Wither became Colonel of Foot in the British Army, and in 1707 was commissioned Brigadier-General in the service of Charles III, King of Spain. Many interesting papers concerning his troop and his campaign in Spain are among the Oakley Hall archives, his exor. being Andrew Wither, of Gray's Inn, brother of Charles Wither, of Hall. On the death of his father in 1718 he came to live at Theddon, and was much interested in the development of the Theddon estate.

Brigadier Hunt-Wither was buried at Shalden, 29th June, 1718, the advowson of which Church was then in the possession of the Lords of Theddon, and according to Colonel Chester a memorial was erected to his memory in Shalden Churchyard, which however no longer exists.

His widow survived him fourteen years, her daughter, Dorothy Bonham (*née* Perin), administering to her estate 8th May, 1732, when she is described as of Old Alresford, Hants.

HENRY WITHER (1705—1730).

Here her son *Henry*, by General Wither, was baptized, February 13th, 1705-6. He married in 1728 *Henrietta Wavell*, and died at Theddon, without issue, 3rd April, 1730. His will, which is curious was unsuccessfully disputed by his cousin and heir at law, *George Wither*, son of his only uncle Robert, who had died in the West Indies in 1695. By this will he left (subject to the life interest of his widow) all his estates in Theddon and Bentworth to *Henry Bonham*, and, failing issue, to his brother, *Richard Bonham*, sons of Thomas Bonham, of Old Alresford, who had married Dorothy Perin, Henry Wither's stepdaughter. He directed that the Bonhams were to take the "name of Wither instead of Bonham," "and my further will is

ANDREW WITHER,

Brother of CHARLES WITHER, of Hall, and of MRS. WILLIAM BEACH.

Born 1665; died 1752.

From a pastel, at Oakley Manor.

that before my funeral my body is to be opened by John Leech, Surgeon, and my heart taken out." . . . . "To be carried to burial by six of my labouring men, and that the side of my coffin be taken out, and laid by the side of my coffin in or near the place where my ancestors on my mother's side (Dorothy Welsted) have been buried in Long Sutton, Hants." A huge deed on eight sheets of vellum, dated 1732, now in possession of the present owner of Thedden Grange (Mr. J. Gathorne Wood), embodies the will, and records the interrogatories and depositions of the witnesses before two Masters in Chancery, "in a cause wherein Henry and Richard Bonham, infants, by Thomas Bonham their father and next friend are Plaintiffs against George Wither, gentleman, defendant." The Pedigree following shows what became of the Bonhams.

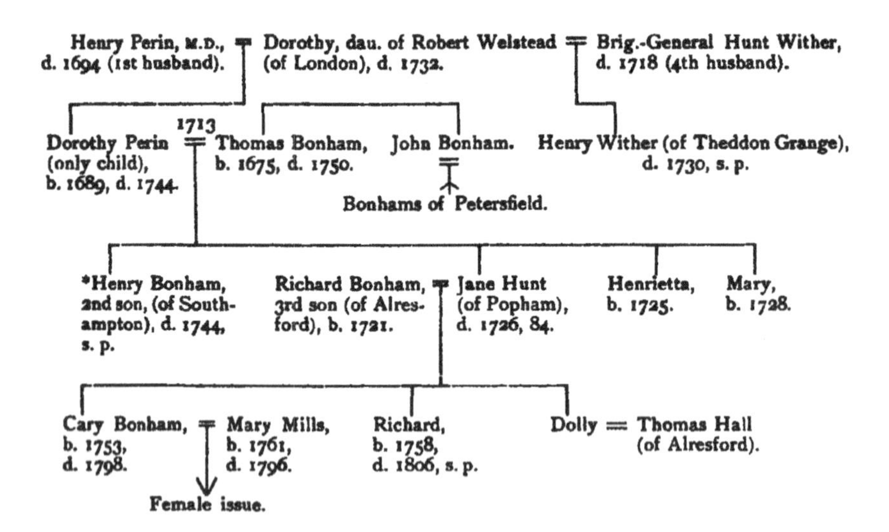

* The seal on Henry Bonham's Will bears the Arms of *Wither* quartering *Hunt*.

A tombstone lately (1895) uncovered in St. Lawrence Church, Winchester, records the burial of "Henrietta Wither (relict of Henry Wither, Esq., of Theddon in this County), who died March 23rd, 1783, aged 84."

With Henry Wither the connection of the Withers with Bentworth and Theddon ceases.

CHRONOLOGICAL BIBLIOGRAPHY OF THE WORKS OF GEORGE WITHER.

Date.	*Title.*	*Size.*	*Description.*
[?]	A New Song of a young man's opinion of the difference between good and bad women [From Hazlitt. Probably it is not Wither's earliest appearance in print, as Hazlitt thinks.]	Folio	Broadside, undated.
1611	Abuses Stript and Whipt. No copy known. First published 1613; also 1614, 1615, 1617	8vo.	[First edition probably called in.]
1612	Prince Henry's Obsequies. Also 1617	4to.	Funeral poem.
1612–3	Epithalamia, or Nuptial Poems	4to.	[Marriage of the Count Palatine with Princess Elizabeth.]
1614	[At end of W. Browne's *Shepherd's Pipe*; Other Eclogues (the second by G. W.); An Other Eclogue by Mr. George Wither]	8vo.	Both reprinted in the *Shepherd's Hunting*.
1614	A Satire written [some copies "dedicated"] to the King. Also 1615, 1616.	8vo.	Verse.
1615	The Shepherd's Hunting	8vo.	Verse: pastorals.
1615	Fidelia (private edition); published 1617; also 1619 ...	12mo.	Verse.
1619	A Preparation to the Psalter	Folio	Prose.
1620	Exercises upon the First Psalm	8vo.	Prose and Verse.
1620	The Works of Master George Wither [containing *Satire to the King*, *Epithalamia*, *Shepherd's Pipe*, *Shepherd's Hunting*, and *Fidelia*]	8vo.	Surreptitious or pirated edition, disclaimed by G. W.
1621	Songs of the Old Testament, translated into English measures	12mo.	Prose and Verse.
1621	Wither's Motto, "*Nec habeo, nec careo, nec curo.*" Also 1633	8vo.	Verse.
1622	Fair-Virtue, or the Mistress of Philarete	8vo.	Verse.
1622	Juvenilia [re-issued 1626; new edition, 12mo., 1633] ...	8vo.	Complete copies contain all G.W.'s poetry written to date.
1623	Hymns and Songs of the Church. Also 1625, etc.	8vo., 12mo., and 4to.	Sacred Verses.
1625	The Scholar's Purgatory	8vo.	Prose.
1628	Britain's Remembrancer	12mo.	Poem on the Plague.
1632	The Psalms of David translated into Lyric Verse ...	8vo.	
1635	A Collection of Emblems, ancient and modern ...	Folio	Verse.
1636	The Nature of Man [from Nemesius]	12mo.	Prose translation.
1641	Halelujah, or Britain's Second Remembrancer ...	12mo.	Sacred verses.
1641	A Prophecy written long since for this year 1641 ...	8vo.	Reprint of 8th Canto of *Britain's Remembrancer*.
1643	Mercurius Rusticus	4to.	Prose.

Date.	*Title.*	*Size.*	*Description.*
1643	Campo-Musae; or Field Musings of Capt. George Wither	8vo.	Verse.
1643	Se Defendendo	4to.	Prose.
1644	The Two Incomparable Generalissimos of the World ...	Folio	Broadside.
1644	The Speech without Door	4to.	Prose tract.
1644–5	Letters of Advice	4to.	Prose.
1645	Some Advertisements for the new Election of Burgesses	4to.	
1645	The Great Assizes holden in Parnassus by Apollo ...	4to.	Verse. Probably not G. W.'s.
1645	Vox Pacifica	8vo.	Verse.
1646	What Peace to the Wicked?	4to.	Verse tract.
1646	Justitiarius Justificatus	4to.	Prose tract.
1646	Opobalsamum Anglicanum	4to.	Verse.
1646	The Speech without Door defended without Reason ...	4to.	Tract.
1646	The Doubtful Almanack	4to.	Tract.
1647	Major Wither's Disclaimer	4to.	Prose, disavowing above.
1647	Amygdala Britannica	4to.	Verse tract.
1647	Carmen Expostulatorium	4to.	Verse.
1648	Majesty in Misery. Also 1681	Folio	Broadside.
1648	Prosopopoeia Britannica	8vo.	Verse.
1648	A Single Si Quis, and a Quadruple Quaere	4to.	Verse.
1648	The True State of the Cause betwixt King and Parliament	(?)	
1648	The Prophetical Trumpeter	8vo.	
1648	The Tired Petitioner	Folio	Broadside.
1648	Verses presented to several Members of the House of Commons	(?)	Verse.
1649	Carmen Eucharisticon	4to.	Verse tract.
1649	A Thankful Retribution	(?)	Verse.
1649	Vaticinium Votivum	8vo.	
1650	Respublica Anglicana	4to.	Prose tract.
1651	Three Grains of Spiritual Frankincense	12mo.	
1651	A Letter to the Honourable Sir John Danvers, Knight	4to.	
1651	The British Appeals	8vo.	Verse.
1652	A Timely Caution	4to.	Verse tract.
1652–3	The Dark Lantern	8vo.	Verse.
1653	Westrow Revived	8vo.	Funeral poem.
1653–4	The Modern Statesman	12mo.	
1654	To the Parliament . . . . of England, Scotland, and Ireland	Folio	Prose tract.
1655	Vaticinium Causuale	4to.	Verse tract.
1655	The Protector. Also 1656	8vo.	Verse.
1656	Boni Ominis Votum	4to.	Verse tract.

Date.	*Title.*	*Size.*	*Description.*
1657	A Sudden Flash	8vo.	Verse.
1657	The Character of Man [from Nemesius]	8vo.	Translation.
1657	A Cause Allegorically stated	(?)	
1657	An Address to the Members of Parliament	(?)	Verse.
1657	A Private Address to the said Oliver	(?)	Prose and verse.
1657	Another Address given to Richard Cromwell's own hands	(?)	
1657	A Declaration in the Person of Oliver Cromwell ...	(?)	
1657	The Humble Declaration and Petition	(?)	
1658	A Private Address for the Third Day of September, 1658	(?)	
1658–9	The Sinner's Confession...	(?)	
1659	The Petition and Narrative	4to.	Prose and verse.
1659	Salt upon Salt	8vo.	Verse.
1659	Epistolium-Vagum-Prosa-Metricum	4to.	Prose and verse.
1659	A Cordial Confection	4to.	Prose tract.
1660	Fides Anglicana	8vo.	Prose.
1660	Furor Poeticus (i.e.) Propheticus	8vo.	Verse tract.
1660	Speculum Speculativum	8vo.	Verse.
1661	The Prisoner's Plea	8vo.	Prose.
1661	Vox Vulgi: not printed till 1879, by W. D. Macray, in Pt. II of *Anecdota Bodleiana.*		
1661	A Triple Paradox...	8vo.	Verse.
1661	Joco-Serio	8vo.	Verse tract.
1661	An Improvement of Imprisonment	8vo.	Verse.
1662	A Proclamation . . . to all the Inhabitants of the Isles of Great Britain	8vo.	Prose and verse tract.
1662	Parallelogrammaton	8vo.	Prose.
1662	Verses intended to the King's Majesty	8vo.	Verse tract.
1664	Tuba Pacifica	8vo.	Verse tract.
1665	Three Private Meditations	8vo.	Verse.
1665	Meditations upon the Lord's Prayer	8vo.	Prose.
1665	A Memorandum to London. . . . Thereto is . . . added a Warning-piece to London	8vo.	Verse.
1666	Sighs for the Pitchers	8vo.	Verse tract.
1666	Echoes from the Sixth Trumpet [reissued 1668 as *Nil Ultra*, and again in 1669 as *Fragmenta Prophetica*]	8vo.	Prose and verse.
1666	Vaticinia Poetica	8vo.	
1668	Vox et Lacrimae Anglorum	8vo.	Verse, posthumous.
1684	Gemitus de Carcere Nantes	4to.	Posthumous.
1688	The Grateful Acknowledgment	4to.	Selections from *Prosopopoeia Britannica.*
1688	Divine Poems: by way of paraphrase on the Ten Commandments [re-issued 1728]	8vo.	Verse: edited by his daughter Eliz. Barry.

THE PORTRAITS OF GEORGE WITHER.

There are at least five engraved portraits of George Wither the poet.

(1.) The portrait facing page 87 (and according to Granger the best) is by John Payne. It is prefixed to the folio edition of the *Emblems*, 1634–5.

(2.) That by William Holle, originally prefixed to *Abuses Stript and Whipt*, is an oval portrait and round it the words: "I grow and wither both together. G. W. an° ætatis suæ 21, 1611."

(3.) That by Roger Daniel (rare), re-engraved by James Brook Pulham in 1827. Above is the poet's motto, "Nec habeo, nec careo, nec curo," and the date, 1623. Round the oval portrait is the legend: "Viva effigies clarissimi Poetæ Georgii Wither"; below, six lines of his verse.

(4.) The Delaram portrait, which in treatment somewhat resembles No. 1, is prefixed to the *Preparation to the Psalter*, 1619.

(5.) Is in the *Fragmenta Poetica*, 1669. It represents the poet as an old man, in armour, crowned with bays, facing to the right. Legend: "Vera effigies Georgei Wither, armiger, qui obiit an° 1667, ætat. suæ 79." Six lines of his verse below.

A portrait in oils by Cornelius Jansen, which belonged to J. M. Gutch (the friend of Charles Lamb), was sold at Sotheby's in 1858. (See *Athenæum*, No. 1588.)

CHAPTER VII.

HISTORY OF THE PRINCIPAL ESTATES

HELD BY

WITHER, BIGG, AND BIGG-WITHER.

SUMMARY OF CONTENTS.

CHAPTER VII.

HISTORY OF THE PRINCIPAL ESTATES

HELD BY

WITHER, BIGG, AND BIGG-WITHER.

IN the following notes on the history of some of the estates held by the family in Hampshire and other counties, I have tried to combine matter which may be of interest not only to members of the family, but to students of history, especially of the history of Hampshire.

1.—MANYDOWN.

The earliest known mention of Manydown is found in Bishop Sandale's Register,[1] where it is recorded that he sealed an "inspeximus" at Manydown, 27th August, A.D. 1318. Dean Kitchin, in his Introduction to the Manydown and Wootton Court and Compotus Rolls, published 1895 for the Hampshire Record Society, has given a full account of the history of the Manydown Manor. Its salient points I reproduce here, as well as some additional information.

[1] Ed. by F. J. Baigent, p. lii and liii Introd.

The Manor, at least from 1265 (the date of the earliest Roll), belonged to the Prior and Convent of St. Swithun, Winchester, and included the sub-manors of Hannington and Baghurst. The 131 Court Rolls and 18 Compotus Rolls (1300—1634) which were among the Wither archives, (probably obtained when William Wither bought the Manor in 1649,) are now added to the existing collection of Manydown Rolls in the Cathedral archives, which is thus one of the most complete groups of MSS. of the kind in existence, numbering as it does, 74 Compotus and 190 Court Rolls.

In the early Rolls the Manor was not called Manydown, but Wottone. But in addition to the mention of Manydown (A.D. 1318) in Bishop Sandale's Register, the Compotus Roll of 1328 indicates that there was a Manor house there in that year, for it records that the men of Wottone cut, made, and carried the hay in the Manidoune garden for their lord—" In toto gardino de Manidoune falcando spargendo et levando, ijs." ; and where a garden was, there was (says Dean Kitchin) certainly a dwelling-house.[1] It is probable that by this time the monks had already begun to live at Manydown, though for nearly a century longer the Manor is still called Wottone on the marginal headings of the Rolls. It is not until 1430 that the name Manidoune is substituted for Wottone.

[1] Manydown Manor, p. 3 Introd.

It is also evident from the Rolls that there were two Manor houses, one at Wootton and one at Manydown, distant about a mile apart. Dean Kitchin thinks that the change in the name of the Manor coincided with the probability as shown by the extensive repairs necessary in 1338, 1369, and 1378, that "the more ancient house at Wootton had at the end of the fourteenth century fallen into decay or was otherwise less convenient and pleasant for the somewhat frequent visits of the Prior, Receiver, and other Monastic authorities." This view is supported by the fact that in 1380 the garden of the house at Wootton was rented by William Aylmer, then Vicar of Wootton. It is probable that the old Manor house, or part of its site, had become the home of the Vicars of Wootton after 1299, in which year the Rectory of

Manydown in 1790.

Wootton was "appropriated" to the Prior and Convent of St. Swithun, and the parish henceforth served by Vicars only.[1]

[1] Manydown Manor, pp. 4, 5, 22 Introd.

MANYDOWN HOUSE.

Little of the ancient house at Manydown remains. The present house is in its main features late sixteenth or early seventeenth century. The house is described in a survey made in 1649, the year when William Wither bought the Manor from the Contractors of the Long Parliament. It then consisted of:—

"A faire Hall, a Parlor Wainscotted, a Kitchen, a Buttery, two Cellars, a Larder, one Scullery, a Bakehouse, two Malting-houses, a Kilnehouse, a Wellhouse, Eleaven Chambres within the dwelling-house (whereof five Wainscotted), a Gatehouse Chamber, a Chamber for Husbandmen to lodge in, a Cheese Chamber, two Stables, three Barnes and other necessary Outhouseing, an Orchard, two Gardens, a Courte, a hop Garden, and a large yard, containing in the whole by Estimation eight acres."

In the present house, which retains at least the ancient ground plan, are incorporated traces of the original house, and some pillars in the cellars may be of the thirteenth or fourteenth century. One of the most remarkable of the relics of the old time is *the well* and raising gear, which has been carried up above the middle of the first floor, so that when once raised the water could run into any of the ground or first floor rooms by gravitation. The house is built round a square court, which is still called the "Cheyney"[2] Court, on one side of which is the old court room, where the lord of the Manor or his representatives (for nearly 400 years the Withers of Manydown) held the "Court leet" and the "Customary Court," where the affairs of the tenants were transacted.

The south front of Manydown house was rebuilt in 1790, when Lovelace Bigg-Wither also added the present dining-room and the large drawing-room over it. An excellent billiard room

[2] The derivation of the word is unknown, but it is interesting that the legal affairs of the tenants of the Prior and Convent, and afterwards of the Dean and Chapter, were held in a room called the "Cheyney" Court, at the south-west angle of the Close of Winchester Cathedral.

in good taste has taken the place of some old rooms adjoining the old court room, by which the present owner, Mr. Sydney Bates, has also added greatly to the amenities of the seventeenth century house.

In the fourteenth and fifteenth centuries the park at Manydown was much larger than at present. It extended from Wootton on the east to Hannington and Freemantle Farm on the north-west, and included what is now Tangier Park. It was noted for its good sport and fine timber. In it, the Rolls tells us, were wild animals, "feræ," probably red deer. Here the Prior's friends and even the Lord Prior himself hunted, aye, and royalty, too. In 1324 Hugh le Despenser (Edward II's favourite) came there with twelve horses to hunt with Prior Richard of Enford. In 1361 and again in 1363 the huntsmen of Edward III were there in force. The Prior's huntsmen were also spoken of in the Rolls of 1364, 1377, and 1392. In 1430 one Robert Peverille was amerced for poaching in the Lord's park at Manydown. He "cum canibus suis intravit in parcum domini et ibidem occidit unam feram nomine '*pryket*'" (deer).[1]

The *timber* in Manydown Park was evidently big and valuable, and was largely used by William of Wykeham when he reconstructed the nave and roof of Winchester Cathedral. The Compotus Roll of 1392 records that ninety-one cartloads, "carectæ," of timber were sent from Wootton in that year, and again in 1398 timber was twice sent for the works at the Cathedral Church. Half a century later, in 1459, three huge oaks, felled at Manydown, were sent to the Priory of St. Swithun's for the roof of the great hall of the Priory, which is still the main part of the Dean of Winchester's residence in the Close.[2] The present area of the park is about 213 acres, exclusive of Tangier Park adjoining. The acreage of the whole estate is now 4362 acres.

A full detailed account of the lands of the Manor of Manydown, and of their value in 1650 and again in 1808, is to be found in Dean Kitchin's book, pp. 178—197.

MANYDOWN INVENTORIES (1653, 1671, 1679).

On the death, in 1653, of William Wither of Manydown, the subjoined interesting inventory of his household goods and of the demesne farm was made. It is inscribed in clear script on a vellum roll 9ft. 7¾ in. long by 4¾ in. wide. The total value of the goods are estimated at £843. 10*s.* 8*d.*, equivalent in modern value to about £6000. On the death of William Wither's son in 1671 the total value was estimated at more than double that sum, namely, at £1690. 18*s.* 4*d.* In a third inventory roll, namely, that made on the death of William Wither's grandson in 1679, the value is estimated at £1401. 11*s.* 8*d*, The difference being mainly due (as it appears) to the value of standing corn, which, when the first inventory was made in the month of March, 1653, was of course not much. It is interesting however to note that as time went on a little more luxury appears in the furniture of the rooms, the goods in the "Greate Chamber" being valued in 1653 at £17. 1*s.*; in 1671, at £26. 18*s.* 8*d.* The value of the silver plate in 1653 was only £11; in 1671, £80; in 1679, £100, equivalent to about £700 of modern value.

INVENTORY, 1653. On parchment roll, 9ft. 7¾ in. by 4¾ in.

A true and perfect Inventory of all and singular the goodes and chattells of *William Wither of Maindowne* the elder, in the County of Southt., Esquire (Deceased), taken before *George Wither of Hall*, in the said Countie of Southt., Gent., *Richard Wither of Stoake*, in the County of Surrey, Gent., and Martin Miller of West Sherborne, in the County of Southt. aforesaid, Yeoman. The eight day of October in the yeare of our Lord God one thousand six hundred fifty and three (1653).

IN THE PARLOR.

Imprimis, two Tables, one sideboard, one couch, nine leather chairs, Ten leather stooles, Three carpets, Two curtaines, One curtaine rod, One paire of Andirons, One ffire panne and Tongs, and one paire of Bellowes ... ... vij*l.* v*s.*

In the Hall.

Item, ffour Tables, one sideboard, three fformes, three chaires, one paire of Andirons, one ffire fforke, one paire of Tables, one clock and case, one ci stoole and six cushions ... xj*l*.

In the Buttery.

Item, one Table, one fforme, Three joyn'd stooles, two Bynns, Two Table basketts, one pewter Sisterne, cupps and glasses ijs. viij*d*.

In the Kitchen.

Item, one Table, one fforme, one joyn'd stoole, five brasse potts, five brasse kettles, three brasse skilletts, Two iron potts, one iron dripping pann and six spitts, one iron kettle, two iron racks, one fire pann and tongs, one Jack, one gridiron, three paire of potthangers, two paire of brass candlesticks, one paire of pewter candlesticks, four dozen of pewter and one pie plate ... . xiij*l*. xixs. iij*d*.

In the Bakehouse and Brewhouse.

Item, one Jacke and one paire of iron Racks, one mault mill and brewing vessell ... ... vs.

In the Mealehouse.

Item, one malding kywer, ffour tubbs, one stone mortar and pestle, and one brass mortar and pestle ... ... i*l*. xiijs. iiij*d*.

In the Milkehouse.

Item, one cheese presse, one dozen and halfe of boles and kywers, two brasse panns, one chorne, six cheesfattes, two cheese tubbs, and one washbowle ... ... iiij*l*.

In the Wash-house.

Item, two Burking tubbs, two wash bowles and three kywers ... xxs.

In the Malthouse.

Item, one yeating fatte [vat], one iron beam and scales ... ... xxvs.

In the Skullery.

Item, one copper kettle, one frying panne, and two trays ... xxxs.

In the Larder.

Item, one salting troughe, two providing troughs, and two dressers i*l*. vjs. viij*d*.

In the Seller.

Item, three stands, nineteen hogsheads and barrells, one tunnell and one cand chest ... ... iij*l*. xs.

Oak Mantelpiece (Manydown),

with Initials of John Wither and date 1603, in the Justice Room.

IN HIS LODGING CHAMBER.

Item, in wearing apparrell		xxs.
Item, in ready money		xxs.
Item, one Beddstead, feather bedd, bowlster, two pillows, three blanketts, one Rugg, one couch, three chaires, two stools, one Table, one sideboarde, two carpetts, one paire of andiers, one firepanne and tongs, three hand-gunnes, one paire of pistols, and one Trunke	xvj*l*.	vjs. viij*d*.

IN THE DRYEING CHAMBER AND PASSAGE.

Item, five chests, four trunkes, one close-stoole, two tables, one paire of andiers, tongs, two flasketts, and one Still ...	iiij*l*.	vjs. viij*d*.

IN THE NURCERY CHAMBER.

Item, one great cubberd, one chaire, two stooles, two boxes, and one beddstead		xjs.
Item, one silver tankard and a dozen of silver spoons	vij*l*.	

IN THE PORCH CHAMBER.

Item, one Bedd Stead, one ffeather bedd, bowlster, and pillows, one counterpanne, two paire of blanketts, curtaines, and vallance, one paire of andirons, firepann, and tongs, one sideboarde cubberd, one pictor, one trundle bedstead, one paire of blanketts and one coverlidd	x*l*.	js. iiij*d*.

IN THE CANOPYE CHAMBER.

Item, one canopy beddstead, one featherbedd bowlster, two paire of blanketts, one great presse, one stoole and one looking glasse	vj*l*.	xvs.

AT THE STAIRE HEAD.

Item, one greate Presse		xxvjs. viij*d*.

IN THE GREAT CHAMBER.

Item, one Beddstead, Curtins, and Vallance, one counterpanne, Downebedd bowlster, two pillows, one trundle beddstead, six chaires, foure stools, one sideboard table, one linery cubberd, one paire of andirons, ffire shovell and tongs, three curtaines, three curtaine rodds, two carpetts, one paire of bellowes and one couch	xvij*l*.	js.

IN THE LITTLE CHAMBER.

Item, one beddstead bowlster, two pillowes, three blanketts, one ragge Curtaine and Vallence, one trundle bedd, fflock bedd and bowlster, two chaires, four stooles, one sidecubberd and cubberd clothe, one paire of andirons, ffire pann and tongs and one paire of Bellowes	vij*l*.	ijs.

IN THE PARLOR CHAMBER.

Item, one Table		vs.

IN THE OUTER GARRETT.

Item, one Beddstead, one fflock bedd, one bowlster, one Rugge, one blankett, one table, one livery cubbird and one joyned stoole	ij*l.*	vj*s.* viij*d.*

IN THE INNER GARRETT.

Item, one ffeather bedd, Beddstead Bowlster, one Rugge, one paire of Blanketts, Curtaine and Vallance, one Side table ...	viij*l.*	vj*s.* viij*d.*

IN THE HIGHE WARNSCOTE CHAMBER.

Item, one beddstead and one ffeather bedd bowlster, coverlidd, two blanketts, curtaines, and vallence, one trundle bedstead, one sideboard, one table, one leather chaire, two old carpets	v*l.*	

IN THE SERVING MEN'S CHAMBER.

Item, two Beddsteads, two flockbedds, two bowlsters, three paire of blanketts and two Coverlidds		L*s.*

AT THE STAIRE HEAD.

Item, one ironbound chest, one table and one close stoole ...		xiij*s.* iiij*d.*

IN HIS STUDYE.

Item, one Deske, one Table, one Chaire, one Kerskett Trencher, books, one iron chest and one stoole	iij*l.*	v*s.*

IN THE MAIDES CHAMBER.

Item, two beddsteads, two fflockbedds, two bowlsters, two pair of blanketts, one Rugge, one coverlidd, two ould chests, one iron beame and scales		L*s.*

IN THE HUSBANDMEN'S CHAMBER.

Item, five bedsteads and bedding	iij*l.*	vj*s.* viij*d.*

IN THE GATEHOUSE CHAMBER.

Item, one beddstead, two chaires, two stooles and one trundle beddstead		xx*s.*

IN THE CHAMBER OVER THE LONG HOUSE.

Item, one presse bedd, two chaires, woodden skreyes [screws], one dozen and half of wooden platters and shovolls ...	j*l.*	vj*s.* viij*d.*
Item, of Table Linnen and other linnen	xxvj*l.*	x*s.* x*d.*
Item, one coach and coach harness	xx*l.*	
Item, one Herriott, being a grey stoned horse, and one stray mare colt	v*l.*	

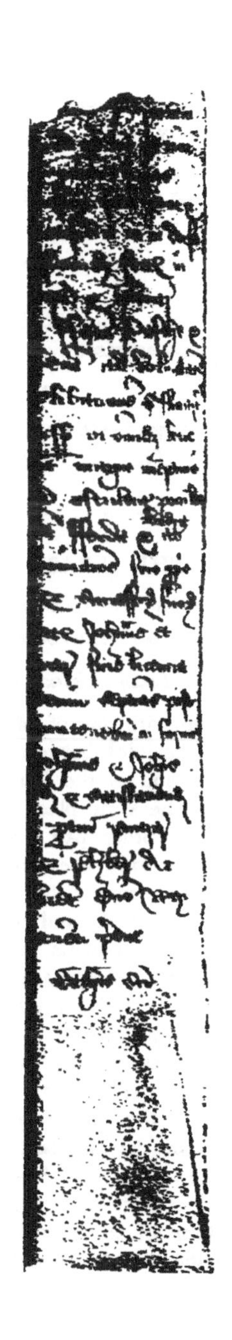

Item, of Sheepe, six hundred and forty	cxcij*l.*	
Item, of horse beasts, thirteen, and harnesse for ploughs and carts	liij*l.*	
Item, of rother beasts of all sorts, forty-five	xxxj*l.*	
Item, poultry of all sorts		xl*s.*
Item, tythe corne taken up before the death of the deceased ...	x*l.*	
Item, corn of all sorts growing upon the Demesne	cc*l.*	
Item, carts, ploughs, harrows, winnering fannes and other instruments	xxj*l.*	
Item, for other utensils and necessaries of household stuffs and husbandry not before particularly apprized	iij*l.*	
Sumne total	dccccxxj*l.*	x*s.* viij*d.*

This inventory was exhibited ye firste day of March in the year of our Lord 1653, English style, by Mr. Thomas Tender, Notary Public.

TRANSLATION OF THE LEASE OF MANYDOWN

GRANTED IN 1514 TO JOAN OR JOHANNA, WIDOW OF THOMAS WITHER OF MANYDOWN, AND HER SON JOHN.

[*Facsimile of Latin original opposite.*]

"This indenture made on the 6th day of March in the year of our Lord 1514. Whereas [illegible] between Thomas Sylkestede, by the mercy of God, prior of the house and of the Cathedral Church of St. Swithun at Winton, and of the Convent of the same place on the one part and Johanna Wether [illegible] Southton on the other part: Witnesseth that the aforesaid Prior and Convent with one consent gave over and to farm let to the aforesaid Johanna and John the site of their manor of Manydown [illegible] viz: all the demesne lands, meadows, grazing lands, and pastures belonging to the same site, and the stpa (? stipendia) of the tenants there not rated in money, and also the Rectorial tithe of Wootton belonging or pertaining to the Rectory. Whereas, moreover, the aforesaid Prior and Convent gave over, freed and demised to the aforesaid Johanna and John 96 wethers at 18*d.* a head, 9 rams at 14*d.* a head, and other animals and utensils as are specified at the back of this indenture. To have and to hold the site of the aforesaid manor, the lands, meadows, grazing lands and pastures, and also the Rectory with [illegible] together with the attachments for trespasses made in the aforesaid cornfields, meadows, grazing lands and pastures to the above mentioned Johanna and John and to their assigns from the feast of St. Michael the Archangel next coming after the date of the present to the end of a term of 30 years from thence next following and complete to render annually to the said Prior and his successors £16. 13*s.* 4*d.*

sterling to be paid in two principal terms, viz: at the feast of Easter, and St. Michael the Archangel in equal portions: Whereas the aforesaid Johanna or John will have [illegible] one cloth garment of the aforesaid Prior and of his successors or 6*s.* 8*d.* instead of the said garment at the will of the said Prior and of his successors. Whereas also the said Johanna and John or their assigns will have annually during the said term sufficient 'housebote, haybote, fyrebote, and ploughbote' in the woods of the lord there by official weight (*per deliberationem officiariorum*) of the same lord Prior and of his successors: Whereas the said Johanna and John or their assigns will maintain all the houses, thatched earth walls (*stramine coopertos muros terreos*), ditches, hedges and fences of the same manor, and to them by these presents demised, in all good and sufficient repair, and will maintain at their own charges and expenses through the whole of the aforesaid term. The aforesaid shall leave '*magno meremio opere*,' stones, tiles or slates only excepted: Whereas also the same Johanna and John or their assigns shall find for the Seneschal, Treasurer, and Clerk of the Prior and for others coming with them twice a year food, drink, bed and '*lectennia*' required by them, and convenient stabling, hay and provender for their horses sufficient for holding the terminal courts, and also pay the Sacristan of the said Prior all '*feoda et vadia*' of old custom: Whereas also the aforesaid Johanna and John or their assigns at the end of the said term shall well and advantageously store in granaries on the site of the said manor all the corn and hay of the manor as well that sown at their own cost as that '*de Rectoria existentia*,' and shall leave all hay, corn and straw stored by them at the end of the term on the same site to the use and convenience of the said Prior and his successors: Whereas also the said Johanna or John or their assigns have their '*status*' on the site of the said manor, and will inhabit the mansion of the said manor during the aforesaid term: Whereas it is not allowed to the aforesaid Johanna and John nor to their assigns either to demise, let or assign the status or aforesaid term which they have in the aforesaid manor or in the said Rectory, or in any of its parcels without leave of the said Prior or his successors on pain of forfeit of their term: Whereas, if it shall happen that the said rent of £16. 13*s.* 4*d.* be in arrear in part or wholly for 12 weeks after the date of the aforesaid feasts . . . . or if the aforesaid Johanna and John shall not repair the house and close pertaining to the said manor, in the manner specified above; or if it shall happen that the aforesaid Johanna and John shall die before the said term, that then if the assigns of the said Johanna and John within two months next following their death shall not find two or three good and sufficient persons bound to the said Lord Prior and his successors in a sum of £50 to fulfil, complete and satisfy all and each of the said covenants and payments in this present indenture—that then it shall be lawful for the said Prior and his successors to re-enter upon the lands, tenements, and other premises of the site of the said manor, and to seize, recover, and rehold all stores and utensils specified at the back of this indenture . . . . Whereas lastly the said Prior and his successors will render and pay to the King tenths and subsidies on the manor and Rectory during the term aforesaid. In testimony whereof

Johanna and John on the one part have set this seal, and the common seal of the said Prior and Convent is set on the other. Given in the Chapter House of the Cathedral Church of St. Swithun, Winchester, the above mentioned month and year.

On the back of the lease is the following in English:—

"Also hit is covenantyd and agreyd bytwene the wythyn wrytyn Persons and grauntyd by the wythyn namyd Johanne and John by these present Indentures That when eny maste yere [*i.e.*, a year in which acorns, etc., are plentiful] shall fortune that then the sayd Johanne and John or their Assygnes shall inclose iij acras grownde or more at their pleasure in the Parcke of Manydone and leve reasonable maste wythyn the sayd closure. And so the sayd maste ther to remayne and grewe for the conteneuans of the woode wythyn the sayde Parcke. Takyn for the labour the wynefalleys (windfalls) yf eny shall fortune wythyn eny such closure wythyn the sayde Parcke during the sayd tyme of Inclosure. Also the sayd Johanne and John hathe reservation beyonde the wythyn wrytyn [illegible] the pay of makynge thes present Indentures of the wythyn named Lord Prior that ys to wyte: xxv quarters wheat, iiij quarters barley, xxi ottys (oats), iiii horsse, the price of a pece xiij^{s} iiij^{d}; ii du (?) bestys, the price of a pece vi^{s} viij^{d}; iiij oxsyn . . . x^{s}; xij kyne . . . v^{s}; vi Bullocks . . . iiij^{s} vj^{d}; vi yerelinges . . . x^{s}; vij Calvys . . . iij^{s}; 1 Bore and vi Pyggs . . . xx^{d}; vii geese and i cocke and v henes. . . . He or she or ther Assygns to deliver hyt agayne at ende of ther terme or other to the valewe [illegible] wythyn wryttyn to sayde Prior, hys successors, or assygnes."

Endorsements:—

"Indentura . . . pro ffirmario de Manydowne Johanna Whethar vidua pro scitu manerii de Manydon."

"v° Hen. viii Prior Silkstede, the scite of Manydown and Rectori de Wootten to Johan Wether, wid., and John Wether sum of 30 lib."

List of existing Leases of Manydown with Dates and Names.

A.D. 1514.—Prior Sylksted to Joan Wither (widow) and her son John for 30 years.
„ 1534.—Prior Broke to John Wither for 50 years.
„ 1544.—Dean Kingsmill to Richard Wither for 50 years.
„ 1577.— „ „ to John Wither.
„ 1618.—Dean Young to William Wither I and son William for 50 years.
„ 1627.—Dean Young to William Wither I for lives of three sons, John, Paul, and William.
„ 1634.—Dean Young to William Wither I, for lives of William, Robert, and Gilbert Wither.
„ 1674.—Dean Clark to William Wither II's trustees for 21 years.
„ 1677.— „ „ to William Wither III's „ „

A.D. 1679.—Dean Meggott	to William Wither III's trustees	for 21 years.		
„ 1685.— „ „	to William Wither IV	„	„	
„ 1730.—Dean Naylor	to William Wither IV	„	„	
„ 1737.— „ „	to William Wither V	„	„	
„ 1744.—Dean Pearce	to William Wither V	„	„	
„ 1751.—Dean Cheyney	to William Wither V	„	„	
„ 1772.—Dean Ogle	to William Wither V	„	„	
„ 1779.— „ „	to William Wither V	„	„	
„ 1786.— „ „	to William Wither V	„	„	
„ 1814.—Dean Rennell	to Harris Bigg-Wither	„	„	
„ 1828 — „ „	to Harris Bigg-Wither	„	„	
„ 1835.— „ „	Rev. Lovelace Bigg-Wither, Fine on renewal, £2096. 8s. 6d.	„	„	

„ [1863.—Manydown Manor enfranchised and Rectorial Tythe of Wootton redeemed by Rev. L. Bigg-Wither.]

Ménu.

An old *ménu* (dated 1732) of "Court Provisions" at Manydown on All Saints' "Goose Day" and the following day in the days of William Wither and Elizabeth his wife (*née* Nicol) in the handwriting of the latter:—

The First Course.

A hash of a calves head at ye upper end.
A chine of beef at ye bottom.
A tongue and udder and marrow bones on ye one side.
Mince pies on ye one side of ye tongue.
A goose on ye other side of ye tongue.
A loyn of pork on ye other side of ye Table.
A goose on ye one side of ye Pork.
A bake Pudden on ye one side of ye Pork.
A sallet in ye middle.

The Second Course.

A dish of chickens at ye upper end.
A chine at ye bottom.
A loyn of veal on ye one side of ye Table.
3 Rabbits on ye one side of ye Veal.
Artichoaks and pease on ye other side of ye Veal.
3 Rosted Ducks on ye other side of ye Table.
Partridges on ye one side of the Ducks.
A dish of pickles on ye other side of the Ducks.
The sallet to stand.

Tangier in 1839.

The Third Course.

A dish of tarts at y^e upper end.
A gammon of Bacon and tongues at y^e bottom.
Sturgeon on y^e one side.
A pigeon pye on y^e other side.
and five salvers.

Guests the 1st Day.

The Rev. and Mrs. Fenton.
Mr. Wm. Garret, Mr. Robert Garret, Mr. Taplin, Mr. Bigs, Mr. Vince, Mr. Hays, Mr. Thos. Penton, Mr. Andrew Poynder — and wives.
Goody Page of Wootton.
Goody Page of Worting.
Goody Pearce.
Thomas Warteridge.

26 ye first day.

Guests the 2nd Day.

William Penton, Edward Penton, Goodman Luke, Goodman Winkworth, Goodman Hunt, Paul Hobs, Goodman Tilbury — and wives,
Thomas' wife.
Goody Micham.
Goody Savage.
Goody Walldren.
Philip Burgess.
Thomas Stephens.
William Allen.

28 ye second day.

The dinner on the second day was the same with slight variations. On each night there was also a bountiful supper of two courses.

2.—TANGIER PARK.

The property now known as "Tangier Park," consisting of about 143 acres lying north of Manydown Park, was, previous to the Restoration (1660), known as "Fabians." It came into the possession of the Prior and Convent of St. Swithun's, Winchester, early in fifteenth century, and was attached to their great Manor of Manydown. The earliest lease from the Convent in existence is dated 16 Henry VI (1440) to one Robert Dynley, Armg. It was however in their possession as early as 1413, as shown by the Wootton Compotus Roll of that year.[1] In 1427 the Prior of St. Swithun was fined in his own Manorial Court for blocking up the "bridle path running between the land formerly belonging to John Fabian and the park of Manydown,"[2] *i.e.*, the path running from the present Tangier Lodge along the avenue to the gate overlooking Malshanger.

The Fabian family[3] seem to have been great people in Wootton and Oakley in the fourteenth and fifteenth centuries, and John Fabian, who in 1411 still held the property, which in 1413 had passed to the Convent, was (as many existing documents show) a person of considerable importance between 1389—1447.[4]

There are no leases of "Fabians" extant between 1440—1570; but from the latter date the history of the property is continuous. It was a copyhold held on lives, renewable by fines.

Throughout the first part of the seventeenth century it was held by the Kingsmills of Woodcote and Sydmonton until the Restoration, when it passed to Sir Thomas Hooke, who is traditionally said to have built the present house, on which is the date 1662, and to have called it Tangier, after the African town of that name, which formed part of the dowry of Charles II's Queen, Catherine of Braganza. In the Chapter lease to Sir Thomas Hooke in 1670, the property is still described as "Fabians." Tangier Park, as it was afterwards called, passed by purchase from the Hooke family in 1710 to Mr. Henry Limbrey, and then by marriage to the Sclaters. In 1833 it was bought by Rev. Lovelace Bigg-Wither, who lived there until 1871, when, after enfranchising it, he sold it together with Manydown to Mr. (afterwards Sir) Edward Bates.

---

[1] Kitchin, Manor of Manydown, p. 204.

[2] Ditto, p. 64.

[3] See Winchester Chapter Records.

[4] Millard's Basingstoke, pp. 215, 221, 223, 225, 254, 238, 260.

3.—THE MANOR AND ADVOWSON OF WORTING.

Connected with the Wither Family from 1593—1898.

The manor and parish of Worting, which seem to have been nearly co-extensive, comprising about 1100 acres, is situated two miles west of Basingstoke.

In 1016 Worting was a Royal Manor. In that year it was granted by King Edmund Ironside to the Abbey of St. Peter's, Winchester, called the New Minster, afterwards Hyde Abbey,[1] among whose possessions it remained until the Dissolution (1538).

In 1541 Henry VIII granted the Manor to Sir William Paulet, afterwards first Marquis of Winchester.[2]

In 1571 the manor and advowson passed, first to Richard Pyncke (one of the Pinks of Bighton and Kempsholt), then to Thomas d'Abridgecourt, a family that owned Strathfieldsaye, then in 1579 to James Rumbold of Preston Candover, all three members of old Hampshire families.[3]

In 1593 John Wither of Manydown bought lands in Worting, and in 1619 his son and heir, the first William Wither of Manydown, bought a moiety of the manor and the advowson from the Rumbold family, and afterwards acquired the other moiety. The lands belonging to the manor in 1620 amounted to 1065 acres.

In 1797 Lovelace Bigg-Wither of Manydown bought Worting House and land from the Edwards family, and built "Scraps" Farm and the adjoining cottages.

After Lovelace Bigg-Wither's death in 1813, his son Harris sold Worting House and forty-seven acres to Lord Spencer

[1] Cottonian MS. in the British Museum.

[2] Comp. Minis. H. VIII, Roll 32, Aug. Office.

[3] Family deeds.

Chichester (second son of the first Marquis of Donegal), who was connected with the Royal household at the neighbouring Kempsholt Park, where George IV lived when Regent (1811—1820). From Lord Spencer Chichester's creditors the property was bought by Lady Jones, daughter of Bishop Shipley of St. Asaph's, from whom it descended to the present owner, Lieut.-General Warren.

In 1836 the Warren family bought an additional fifty acres from the Rev. Lovelace Bigg-Wither, who sold in 1866 Scraps farm to the same family, and in 1868, the Worting Inn and farm (195 acres) to Mr. George Lamb, and in 1871 the Worting Wood farm and other property in Worting (amounting to 720 acres) to Mr. Edward Bates.

Hillside House, Worting, with fourteen acres, was left by the last William Wither of Manydown to Edward Lane, from whose executors it was bought in 1827 by Harris Bigg-Wither of Manydown. Its first tenant after the purchase was his aunt, Mrs. Herbert Hill, widow of the late Rector. Mrs. Harry Blackstone, sister-in-law of the Judge, had previously lived there. This property was sold in 1865 to Mr. George Lamb.

The following members of the family have been Rectors:—

1724.—*Henry Bigg*, afterwards Warden of Winchester College.
1731.—*Walter Bigg*, father of Lovelace Bigg-Wither.
1800.—*William Heathcote*, father of Sir William Heathcote, Fifth Baronet of Hursley.
1802.—*Charles Blackstone*, fourth son of Sir William Blackstone, the Judge.
1815.—*Herbert Hill*, who married Katherine Bigg.
1820.—*Frederic C. Blackstone*, son of Charles Blackstone and Margaret Bigg.

1832.—*Harris J. Bigg-Wither*, second son of Harris Bigg-Wither of Manydown.

1879.—*Reginald F. Bigg-Wither*, seventh son of Lovelace Bigg-Wither of Manydown and Tangier Parks, collated, 1898, to Wonston Rectory, Hants.

The old Worting Church was entirely destroyed by a fire which sacked the village and burnt "a good Christian woman," 9th May, 1655; and the Church that existed in 1848 was pulled down, rebuilt from the foundations and enlarged in that year.

The Rectory House was destroyed in the great fire of 1655. The present house was built in 1732, and enlarged in 1880.

The Schools were built in 1855 by the Rev. Lovelace Bigg-Wither; they were enlarged in 1886, and again in 1901.

The great lime tree by the railway arch was planted in 1740 by the Rev. Walter Bigg, Rector of Worting, to mark the boundaries of the parishes of Basingstoke and Worting.

4.—ANDWELL ESTATE (NEAR BASINGSTOKE).

HELD BY THE WITHER FAMILY FOR 167 YEARS, *i.e.*, FROM 1641—1808.

The Priory of Andwell was a cell to the Abbey of Tyrone. Its possessions were acquired by William of Wykeham in the year 1391, and he annexed them to Winchester College in the same year, at which date their annual value was £10.

The Mill and miller of Andwell with a virgate of land pertaining to the mill, and other lands in the immediate neighbourhood appear to have been given to the Priory by Roger de Port in the eleventh century. This fact appears from a charter of St. Thomas a'Beckett confirming the monks of Andwell in their possessions, which is preserved in Winchester College.

The Priory house, a substantial flint building, was pulled down about forty years ago by the then lessee, who sold the materials for the repair of the roads and built the present farm house with money found by the College.

The chapel exists, and is used as a store or granary.

The estate was until recently held under the College on a beneficial lease, renewable every seven years on payment of a fine. The lease appears to have come into the Wither family by purchase about 16 Car. I, A.D. 1641. The following persons appear to have been the lessees at the successive renewals while the lease was in the family :—

Date of lease.	*Name and description of lessee.*
6 May, 1646.—	[1] William Wither of Andwell, gentⁿ.
6 May, 1652.—	William Wither of Andwell, gentⁿ., and Joan his wife.
2 Nov., 1657.—	William Wither of Manydown, gentⁿ., and Joan his wife.
2 Nov., 1664.—	William Wither of Manydown, gentⁿ., and Joan his wife.
1 Nov., 1671.—	William Wither of Manydown, Esq., and Joan his wife.
1 Nov., 1677.—	Robert Wither, of the University of Oxford, Esq., and Michael Ernle of Brimslad, Co. Wilts, Esq.
1 Nov., 1683.—	Thomas Wither of Andwell, Esq., and Michael Ernle of Brimslad, Co. Wilts, Esq.
1 Nov., 1685.—	The same.
3 Nov., 1700.—	William Wither of Manydown, Esq.
1 Nov., 1708.—	Lovelace Bigg of Chilton Foliat, Co. Wilts, Esq., and Jacob Renoldson of Bristol, merchant.
1 Nov., 1715.—	The same.
1 Nov., 1722.—	The same.
1 Nov., 1729.—	William Wither of Manydown, Esq.
1 Nov., 1736.—	Thomas Bigg of Lincolns Inn Fields, surgeon.
1 Nov., 1743.—	The same.
1 Nov., 1750.—	Thomas Bigg of Chilton Foliat, Wilts, Esq.
1 Nov., 1757.—	The same.

[1] This William Wither, who succeeded to Manydown in 1653, married Joan Geale of Alton, cousin and co-heir of Barbara Locker of Andwell.—See chap. iii.

1 Nov., 1764.—Walter Bigg of Worting, clerk, executor and residuary legatee of Thomas Bigg, late of Chilton Foliatt.
1 Nov., 1771.—The same.
2 Nov., 1778.—Lovelace Bigg of Chilton Foliatt, Wilts, Esq.
1 Nov., 1785.—The same.
1 Nov., 1792.—Lovelace Bigg-Wither of Manydown, Esq.
1 Nov., 1799.—The same.
1 Nov., 1806.—The same.

In the year 1808 Mr. Lovelace Bigg-Wither obtained the permission of the College to alienate the lease, which passed out of the family in that year by sale to William Trimmer, of Ashley Farm, near Andover.

The rent was £6. 15*s.* 1*d.*, 515 gallons of wheat and 344 gallons of malt.

5.—THE MANOR OF WOODGARSTON.

OWNED BY WITHER OF MANYDOWN FROM 1619—1871.

Woodgarston or Wodegarstone is a tything and manor in the parish of Monk Sherborne, in the Hundred of Basingstoke, situated about five miles to the north-west of that town, on the road to Kingsclere. The place is chiefly remarkable for the small circular hill fort of about 120 yards in circumference, with a deep surrounding ditch. Situated in a commanding position, over 500 feet above the level of the sea, near the two great Roman roads leading from Silchester to Old Sarum and from Silchester to Winchester, it was probably used as a Roman station; but its origin is doubtless British. The name contains the Celtic word "caer" or "gaer," Anglice "fort," and "ton" is the old word for manor. Thus Woodgarston would signify the fortified enclosure in the wood—the manor of Woodgarston. It comprises about 415 acres, made up of 275 acres round the old fort and five other detached portions, forming a chain of irregular islands in the parish of Wootton. St. Lawrence, extending from near Ramsdell Church on the north to the South-Western Railway on the south. This manor has a most interesting and complete history from the time of the Conquest,[1] when, according to the Domesday Survey (1086), it formed part of the possessions of the great Norman baron, Hugh de Port, and was held by him, together with the Manor of Nateley, of the Lords of Basing, and their barony, by the military service of one knight's fee.[2]

[1] Manor of Woodgarston, by the Rev. R. F. Bigg-Wither.

[2] Millard's Basingstoke, p. 59.

In the reign of Henry I the two manors, Woodgarston and Nateley, were granted by John de Port to *Matthew de Scures*; hence the name of the parish Nateley Scures. Matthew, with the assent and consent of Roger de Scures, his heir, granted Woodgarston to his son Matthew for one-fifth of a knight's fee. The deed making this grant is undated, but has been fixed by Mr. A. W. Kirkaldy, Oxford, and other experts, at between 1160 and 1170 A.D.

Among the ancient deeds relating to this manor of Woodgarston, now in the possession of Mr. Sydney Bates, is one of 10th Henry III (1226) concerning the services in the chapel attached to the manor house. It seems that the Prior of the Benedictine House of Monk Sherborne, about three miles distant, was under obligation to serve the chapel, which he failed to do. James de Scures referred the matter to the Pope. The deed recites letters from Honorius III appointing a commission consisting of the Priors of Carisbrooke, I.W., and of Southwick, near Porchester, and "Master Luke, of Sarum," to enquire into and settle the business. Their award was, and it was agreed, that the Prior and monks of Sherborne were bound to provide for the "celebration of the Divine Office" on three days a week and on certain festivals. Further that when the Scures family were at home, the chaplain, after the service, should have a meal provided for him in the house, and that in consideration of his services certain messuages on the manor should be granted by the Lord to the Prior and convent. It is a remarkable instance of the all-embracing jurisdiction of the Papacy in the Middle Ages, that a dispute about the obligation to serve a small chapel in an out-of-the-way place like Woodgarston, in distant England, should come under the far-reaching ken of Pope Honorius III at his residence at Reate, in Italy, in 1226.

The court-yard of the manor house, now used by farm labourers, is still bricked and paved, and the ruins of the chapel are remembered by more than one old resident.

There are three interesting deeds of the reign of Edward III dated 1331, 1332, and 1340, leasing the manor to Roger de Fyfhide and to Edith his widow. The Fyfhides for centuries held five hides of land (hence the name) at Fyfield near Andover. These leases mention the furniture of the chapel, and give the names of old farm instruments.

In 1381 *John de Uvedale* married Sibilla, the heiress of the Scures family, and Woodgarston passed to the ancient Hampshire family of Uvedale, in which family it remained until after the death of Sir William Uvedale in 1615. In 1619 it passed by purchase to *William Wither* of Manydown, and remained in the Wither and Bigg-Wither family until 1871, when it was sold with the rest of the Manydown property to Mr. (afterwards) Sir Edward Bates, Bart.

6.—WYMERING MANOR AND ESTATE.

Wymering, which came to the Bigg-Withers on the death in 1768 of Rev. Richard Harris, brother of Jane Harris, who was the mother of Lovelace Bigg, is of special interest to the family as the home of the Rev. Charles Blackstone (Vicar of Wymering 1774—1804) and of Harris Bigg-Wither from his marriage (1804) to the death of his father, Lovelace Bigg-Wither, in 1813. Here Harris Bigg-Wither's six elder children were born.

The history of the manor has been sketched by Mrs. Andrew Davies in her *History of Cosham* (pub. 1906). At the time of the Domesday Survey (1086) it was held by William the Conqueror in demesne as it had been by King Edward the Confessor, in connection with Portchester Castle. In the thirteenth century the manor was granted first to Fulkes de Wymering and afterwards to William de Fortibus, and was held of the King by military service at Portchester. In 1285 Edward I granted the manor to *John le Botelier*, in whose family it remained for a century; it then passed to the *Waytes*, from whom it passed in 1570 by marriage to the *Brunings*, a well-known Roman Catholic family. On the death of Edward Bruning, aged 98, in 1707 the manor changed hands several times until in 1761 the *Rev. Richard Harris* (great-grandson of Warden Harris), Vicar of Wymering and Rector of Wydley, bought a moiety of the manor from Sir Edward Worsley, and in 1768 the rest of the manor from William Smith.

The Rev. Richard Harris died without issue and intestate in 1768, and the manor went to his nephew and heir at law, Lovelace Bigg, who in 1783 added to the property 127 acres by purchase from Lord Dormer.

In 1835 the old manor house and sixty-eight acres was sold by the Rev. Lovelace Bigg-Wither for £5000 to Mr. John Martin, who had long been tenant, and the rest of the property, comprising about 336 acres with house, was sold in 1858 to Rev. G. Nugee and Mr. Thos. Thistlethwayte for £14,827. 14*s*. 8*d*.

7.—THE MANOR AND ADVOWSON OF BIGHTON, HANTS.

BOUGHT BY JOHN WITHER OF MANYDOWN IN 1598.

In A.D. 959, King Edwy granted ten mansœ in the parish of Bighton to *Hyde Abbey*[1] (the monastery of St. Peter by Winchester as it was then termed). At the time of the Domesday Survey (A.D. 1086) the manor of Bighton was held by Hyde Abbey and was assessed at seven hides. It remained the property of the Abbey until the dissolution of the monasteries.

After the surrender of the Abbey of Hyde (1538), King Henry VIII granted the manor of Bighton to his physician, Dr. Augustine de Augustinis, to hold for his life.[2] Later the King granted it to him and his heirs for ever to hold of the King and his successors for an annual payment of £2. 18*s* 5½*d*.[3] Three months later Augustine and Agnes his wife sold the manor and advowson to *Thomas Wriothesley*.[4]

In 1598, Henry Wriothesley, Third Earl of Southampton, sold to *John Wither of Manydown* the manor and advowson of Bighton together with 1 messuage, 21 cottages, and 400 acres of land for £680 sterling.[5] In 1609 the property was charged with a jointure for Susanna Risley, the wife of William Wither, eldest son of John, and was settled on their heirs.[6] There is an interesting letter now in the possession of Mr. Montagu G. Knight, of Chawton House, dated March 2nd, 1619 from William Wither of Manydown to his "good cosen" John Knight concerning the appointment to the living of Bighton then vacant.

In 1635 (after the death of his wife), William Wither and his eldest surviving son Paul, sold the Bighton property for £600 to *Robert Eyre, Esq*.[7]

Between 1692—1726, Sir Robert Worsley held the manor. The Tilney family held it, 1726—35. The property reverted to

[1] Birch (Cart. Sax. iii, 151.)

[2] Letters and Papers (Hen. VIII), xvi, 718.

[3] Pat. 37 Hen. VIII, fol. 3, m. 39.

[4] Feet of Fines, Co. Southton, March 37 Hen. VIII.

[5] Feet of Fines, Co. Southton, 40 Eliz.

[6] Inq. p. M. 18 Jas. I, part 2, No. 25.

[7] Feet of Fines, Co. Southton, 11 Charl. I.

the Eyres in 1743, but in 1795 it passed again away from them. In 1822 the Duke of Buckingham was lord of the manor.

8.—HAINSHILL, CHILTON FOLLIAT, AND WOOLSTON.

THESE THREE ESTATES CAME TO THE FAMILY THROUGH THE BIGGS.

(1) *Hainshill*—in the parish of Hurst, an isolated part of Wiltshire, six miles east of Reading and four miles north of Wokingham—was the home of Sir Francis Windebank, Secretary of State to Charles I. Here his friend Archbishop Laud visited him several times between 1624 and 1629, as recorded in Laud's diary. In 1640 these two celebrated Royalists and Churchmen were imprisoned, and the house and estate confiscated by the Long Parliament. It was bought by Richard Bigg, son of Alderman Bigg, who died 1632, and was settled on Richard Bigg's first wife, the Lady Phebe Ley, daughter of James, first Earl of Marlborough. Here was born in 1661, by his second wife, his son Lovelace Bigg of Chilton Folliat, who married Dorothy Wither. The estate descended through his half-brother John Bigg (son of Lady Phebe Ley) to Lovelace Bigg, and was acquired in 1787 by Mr. Charles Garth, father of the present owner, Thomas Colleton Garth, the well-known master of the Garth hounds.

On the north wall of Hurst Church is a tablet with the following inscription:—

Near this place lyeth buried the body of the Lady Phebe,
One of the daughters of James Ley, Earle of Marlborough,
Late wife of Richard Bigg of Hurst in the county of Wilts, Esquire,
Who had issue by him 4 sons—James, John, Daniel, Richard.
She died the 13th day of February, 1659.

JAMES LEY, First Earl of Marlborough.

(First Creation, 1625.)

Father of Lady Phœbe Ley, First Wife of Richard Bigg, of Haines Hill.

The parish of Hurst is greatly benefitted by the will of the last mentioned of her four sons. Richard Bigg, who was a Fellow of New College, Oxford, and died 31st July, 1677, aged twenty-seven, left the rents of three houses in the parish of St. Giles in the Fields, London, to the poor of the parish to be distributed annually in bread laid on the black marble slab of the Bigg monument in Hurst Church. His will, which is curious and interesting, (see Appendix III,) was annually read in Church until 1886, from which date Richard Bigg's bequest has been administered in accordance with the provisions of a scheme approved by the Parish and by the Charity Commissioners. £30 is administered in bread during the year. The rest is spent in increasing the allowances of the inmates of the Almshouses at Hurst and Twyford. Any surplus is used to help the poor of Hurst in sickness or distress.

(2) *Chilton Folliat*, an estate of 300 acres with good house, was bought about 1650 by Richard Bigg, son of Richard Bigg who bought Hains Hill (see above). It was settled by his son Lovelace Bigg on his wife Dorothy Wither in 1686. Here Lovelace Bigg's eight younger children were born (including Warden Bigg and Rev. Walter Bigg). It was the home for twenty years of Lovelace Bigg [Wither] until he succeeded to the Manydown Estates in 1789, when he sold it. Here all but his eldest child were born. Here his grandson, Eroll Blackstone, was curate in 1839—49. In Chilton Folliat Church is the following monumental inscription :—

Here lies the Body
Of that truly worthy Gentleman
Lovelace Bigg, Esquire, of this Parish
Who was the son of Richard Bigg, Esquire, of Hainshill
In the parish of Hurst, and county of Wilts,
And married Dorothy youngest daughter
Of William Wither, Esquire, of Manydown Hants,
By whom he had six sons and six daughters.

[*Here follow fourteen lines of laudatory inscription omitted.*]

He departed out of this life
On the 6th day of February, 1724
In the 64 year of his age,
He married to his second wife Rachel
Daughter of Thomas Fettiplace, Esq., of Farnham in Berks
In the same vault are interr'd the Remains of

Her Mother Mary Bigg	who died	1711	aged	84
His Wife Dorothy		1717		55
His Son William		1715		27
His Daughter Sarah		1716		20

In Memory of whom this was Erected
By His Son and Heir, Henry Bigg, D.D.,
Warden of Winchester College.

On the monument there are three shields:—

1st, *Bigg* quartering *Wade*.
2nd, *Bigg* impaling *Wither*.
3rd, *Bigg* impaling *Fettiplace*.

(3) *Woolston*—near Farringdon, in the present parish of Uffington, Berkshire—was formerly part of the possessions of the Cistercian Abbey of Beaulieu, near Southampton. The property comprised about 740 acres of valuable grazing and arable land, and included a very fine old manor house full of tapestry and magnificent oak panelling. At the Dissolution (1538) Henry VIII gave the manor to one of the Seymours. Later the property was divided, and was owned in the seventeenth and beginning of the eighteenth centuries by the families of Sanders and Hughes, from whom it was purchased in 1754 as to one moiety by Thomas Bigg, who left it to his brother, Rev. Walter Bigg, from whom it came to his son Lovelace, who in 1776 bought the rest of the property together with the manorial rights. The whole was sold by Harris Bigg-Wither of Manydown in 1828 for £25,500, to Captain G. Butler, who sold Woolston Manor Farm (445 acres) in 1864 to Lord Craven. His son, Mr. William Butler, retains the rest.

CHAPTER VIII.

A.—FAMILIES CONNECTED WITH WITHER AND BIGG-WITHER.

B.—FAMILIES OF THE NAME WITHERS BEARING THE SAME ARMS AS WITHER OF MANYDOWN.

SUMMARY OF CONTENTS.

CHAPTER VIII.

FAMILIES ALLIED WITH WITHER OF MANYDOWN.

1.—MASON OF SYDMANTON.

MASON.

JOAN or Johanna Mason married Thomas Wither, of Manydown, who died and was buried at Wootton St. Lawrence, A.D. 1506 (see page 21). The name *Mason* abounds in the Elizabethan Purveyance taken for the hundred of Kingsclere, A.D. 1575. In this document Thomas Mason of the Sydmanton tything is styled of "Colletts" and "Aynolds." There are also Edmund and John Mason of the same place; George and James Mason, of Erlstone, parish of Burghclere; and Christian Mason, of Freefolk. In 1540 the Rev. Canon Mason was appointed to the Prebend of St. Lawrence the Greater, in the Monastery of Romsey, Hants, to which was attached the Church of Tymbesbury, two miles distant.[1]

[1] See Liveing's "Annals of Romsey Abbey."

The Masons of Hanningford, Co. Huntingdon; the Masons of Sion, Co. Middlesex; and the Masons of Yorkshire bear the same *Arms*, namely, "Or, a lion rampant double-headed, azure."

2.—FAWKENER OR FAUCONER OR FAULKNER.

FAWKENER.

Peter Fauconer, of Kingsclere, married (1575) Jane, daughter of Richard Wither, of Sydmanton (see Pedigree IV, p. 23).

The Fawkeners are a very old Hampshire family. The name of Ralph le Fauconer occurs in a grant of 47 Henry III (1263), relating to Wyke or Week manor, St. Mary Bourne, Hants. In 1552 Richard Fauconer was seated at Hurstborne Priors, Hants. He married Elinor, daughter of George Pembridge, and had issue, Sir Richard Fauconer, who died without issue, and three daughters, the youngest of whom, Alice, married Richard Kingsmill, of Sydmanton.

At the end of the fifteenth century we find another Richard Fauconer at Kingsclere. His great grandson, Peter, married Jane Wither, of Sydmanton. Below is the pedigree :—

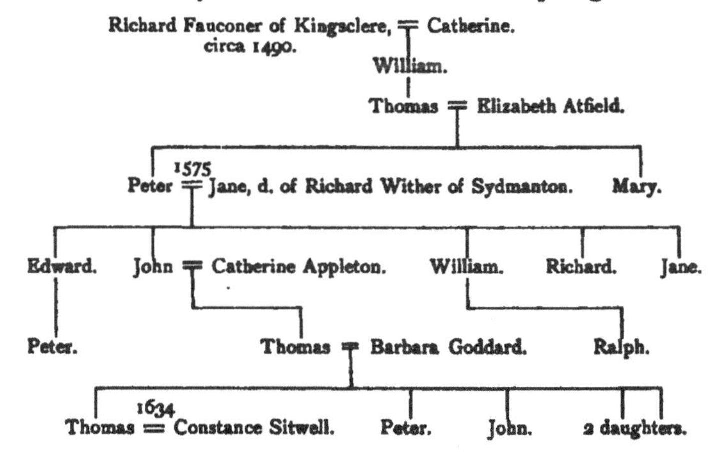

N.B.—Most of the valuable church plate at Kingsclere was given by John Fawkener in 1694.

Arms.—"Sable, three falcons close, or, beaked, legged and belled, or."

3.—AYLIFFE OR AYLIFF.

AYLIFFE.

Ann or Agnes Ayliffe married John Wither, of Manydown, who died A.D. 1536 (see p. 24). The Ayliffes are another old Hampshire family, that in the fifteenth, sixteenth, and seventeenth centuries owned considerable property in North Hampshire, especially at Scures, (or, as it is now called "Ewhurst Park,") at Hannington, and at Dean. In 1501 the manor of Scures, or Skeyres, or Ewhurst, was granted by Magdalen College, Oxford, to William Warham, afterwards Archbishop of Canterbury. From him it passed to John Ayliffe, of Scures.

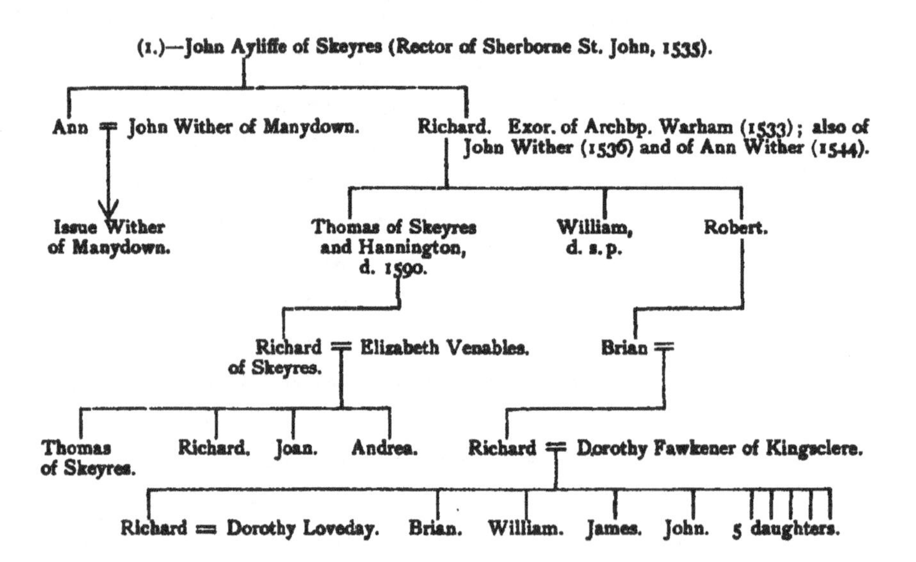

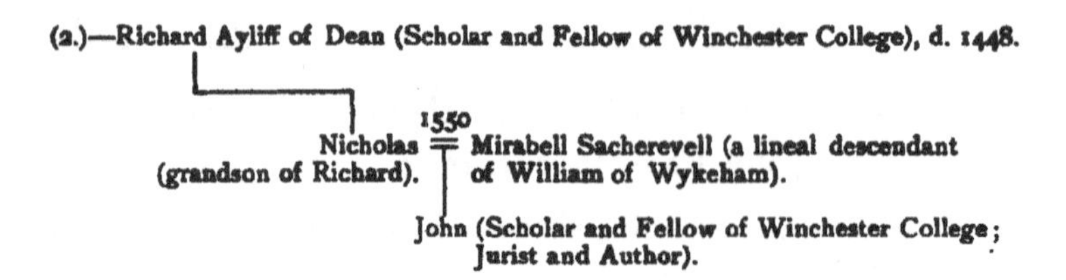

N.B.—Hall Place (Oakley Hall), in the parish of Dean, was bought from the Ayliff family by George Wither of "Hall," in 1619.

Arms.—"Quarterly gules and sable, a lion rampant between three crosses pattées, or: all within a bordure argent charged with eight torteaux."

4.—LOVE.

LOVE.

John Wither, of Manydown (1577—1620), married Joan, daughter of John *Love*, of Basing Park, near Alton, Hants. The family appears to have been seated at Basing Park early in sixteenth century.

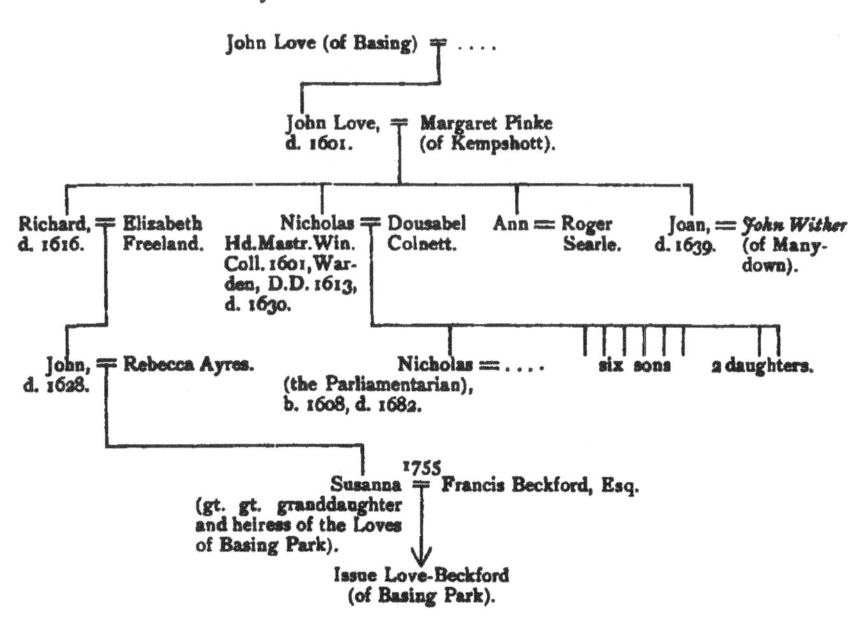

5.—PINKE.

PINKE.

The family of ***Pinke*** or Pink, from whence sprang Dr. Robert Pinke, Warden of New College (1617), is also an old Hampshire family, originally seated at Bighton, near Alresford. Henry, son of John Pinke, of Bighton, bought the manor of Kempshott, in the parish of Winslade, from Sir Benjamin Tichborne in 1590, and the family lived at Kempshott until the middle of the eighteenth century, and a branch at North Waltham.

There have been at least two marriage connections between the Withers and the Pinkes. Margaret, the sister of Henry Pink, of Kempshott, married John Love, of Basing (see above), and their daughter, Joane, married John Wither, of Manydown, in 1583. Again in 1650, Ann, the sister of Gilbert Wither, of Hall (Oakley), married Henry Pinke, of Kempshott. The last of the line of Pinke, of North Waltham was Dorothy Wither Pinke, who died 1825.

6.—RISLEY.

RISLEY.

William Wither, of Manydown (1620—1653) married ***Susanna***, daughter of Paul ***Risley***, Esq., of Chetwode (Bucks), by his wife Dorothy, daughter of Sir John Temple, of Stowe, Knight.

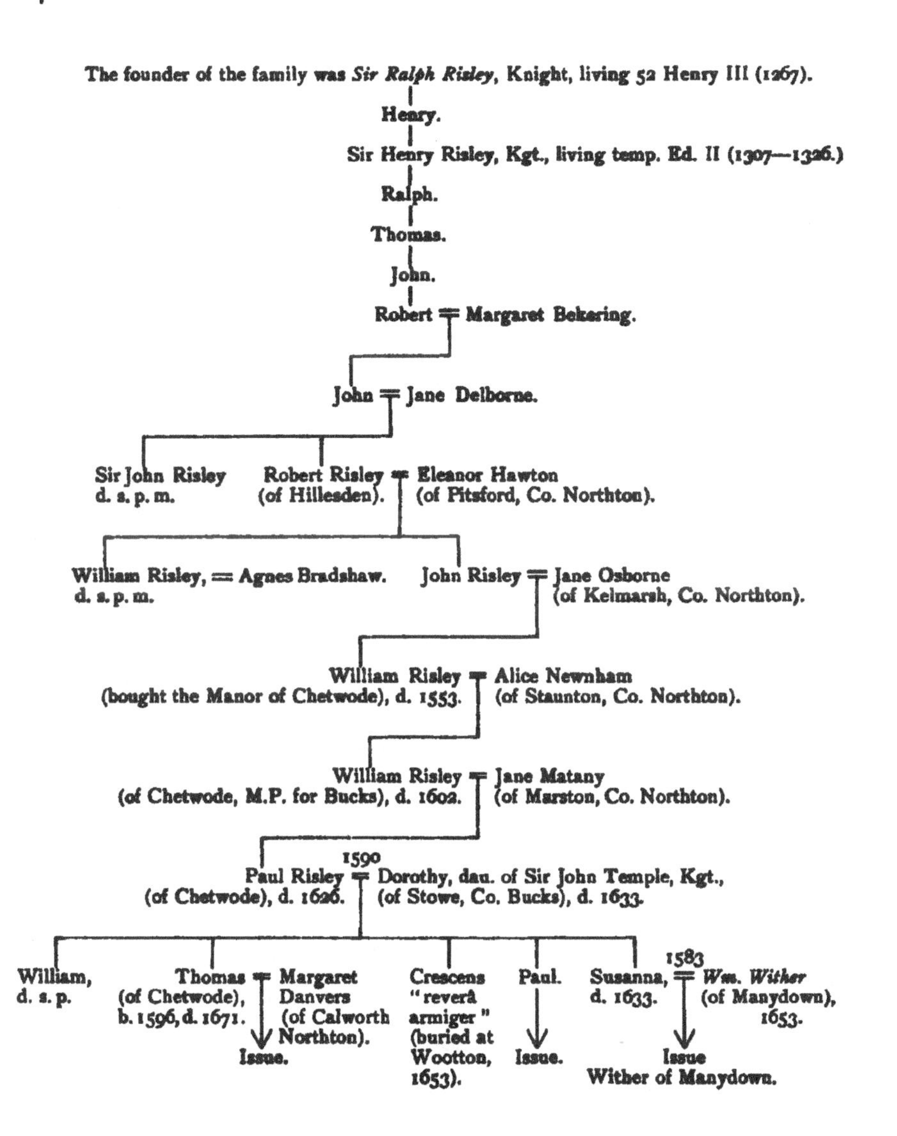

Arms of Risley.—"Argent a fess azure between three crescents gules."

7.—POTTENGER AND ERNLE.

POTTENGER ERNLE.

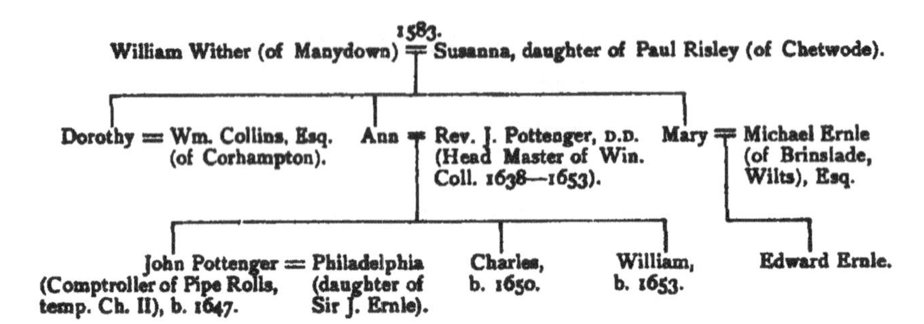

The family of Ernle derives its name from the village of Ernley or Ernle, in the rape of Chichester, Co. Sussex, where Richard de Ernle was seated, temp. Henry III. His second son, John de Ernle, Knight of the Shire for Sussex (1331), married Isabel, daughter and heir of his uncle, William de Ernle, and widow of Fulco Paulin. He acquired with her in dower the manor of Ernle, etc.

From these ancestors was lineally descended Sir John Ernle, Chancellor of the Exchequer, temp. Charles I, and father of Mrs. John Pottenger above mentioned.

Michael Ernle and his son Edward were successively trustees of three Withers of Manydown. The dates and the *hours* of the births and baptisms of the three sons of Dr. Pottenger and Ann Wither are accurately recorded in the Baptismal Registers of St. Michael's, Winchester, together with the names of the children's sponsors or, as they were called in those Puritan times "witnesses."

8.—BRAMSTON.

BRAMSTON.

This family has lived at *Skreens*, near Maldon, Co. Essex, since the beginning of the seventeenth century. It traces its origin from William Bramston, who was Sheriff of London, 18 Richard II (1394). The more modern founder of the family was:—

Sir John Bramston, Kgt. (Lord Chief Justice in 1635), born at Malden, d. 1645. = Bridget, daughter of Thomas, M.D., son of Sir Edmund *Moundeford* Kgt., (of Feltwell, Co. Norfolk), whose mother was the 20th daughter of Sir William Lock, Lord Mayor of London.

Children:

- Sir John Bramston, of Skreens, made Knight of the Bath at coronatn. of Charles II, M.P. for Essex, d. 1699. = Alice Abdy, d. 1647.
  - Antony (of Skreens), d. 1722. = Catherine, dau. of Sir Th. Nutt.
    - John, predeceased his father, 1718.
    - Thomas (of Skreens). = Elizabeth Berney (2nd wife).
      - Thomas Berney (of Skreens, M.P. for Essex), b. 1732, d. 1812. = Mary Gardiner.
        - Thomas Gardiner (of Skreens, M.P. for Essex), d. 1831. = Maria Anne Blaauw.
          - Thomas William (of Skreens). = Eliza, 5th dau. and coheiress of Sir Eliab Harvey, G.C.B., of Rolls Court, Chigwell.
            - Thomas Harvey Bramston (of Skreens), present head of the family. No male issue.
            - Sir John Bramston (late of the Colonial Office).
          - Rev. John Bramston (Dean of Winchester), d. 1893. = Clarissa Trant.
            - Rev. John Trant Bramston (Master Winchester Coll.), b. 1844. = Jane, dau. of Archdeacon Ady (of Colchester).
              - John A. T. Bramston, b. 1880, d. 1906.
              - Margaret Clarissa, b. 1878. = R. D. Beloe (Master Win. Coll.).
        - Rev. John Bramston-Stane (added name of Stane).
    - 8 daughters.
  - (1) Mary = Sir And. Jenour, Bart.
  - (2) Elizabeth = her cousin Moundeford.
- Sir Moundeford Bramston, Knighted at the Restoration. = Alice, daughter of Sir George le Hunt.
  - John.
  - Moundeford = Eliz. Bramston, dau. of his uncle.
    - John = Isabella Masters.
      - Edmund E. Bramston (Gentleman Usher to the Dow. Princess of Wales), d. 1763. = (1748) Henrietta Maria, dau. of *Charles Wither*, of (Oakley) Hall, b. 1713, d. 1790.
        - *Wither Bramston* (of Oakley Hall), b. 1753, d. 1832, s. p. = Mary Chute.
        - Augusta, b. 1747, d. 1819, unmar.
        - Henrietta M., b. 1751, d. 1771, unmar.
  - 8 other children.
- Francis Bramston, Baron of the Exchequer, 1678.

The Bramston *Arms* are:—"Or, on a fess sable three plates argent."

The Mondeford *Arms* are:—"Or, three fleur-de-lis gules."

9.—HUNT, OF BENTWORTH AND THEDDON.

The Hampshire family of Hunt seems to have come from Exeter and Chudleigh, Co. Devon. They are traced in the Visitation of 1620 back to the year 1500. Early however in the seventeenth century they are found settled at Bentworth, Theddon, and Popham, Co. Southampton. A dispute arose between these three branches of the family as to the arms, or rather as to the differences, which was settled in 1628, and confirmed by the College of Arms as follows:—

HUNT.

"*Whereas difference and question hath been made between the Hunts of Bentworth Hall, the Hunts of Popham, and the Hunts of Ffidding* [Theddon], *in the parish of Alton, all within the county of Southampton, for the bearing a coat of arms unto which house they all challenge a property. And forasmuch as it plainly appeareth that the Hunts of Bentworth is the prime and principal house as is sufficiently proved. It is therefore condescended, concluded, and agreed between the said parties that the house of Bentworth shall bear the coat and crest without different; the house of Popham with a crescent; and the house of Ffidding with a mullet. And for the publishing of peace and law, the avoiding of questions and contentious trouble hereafter, the parties have hereunto interchangeably set their hands and seals.*

Heralds' College, ch. 19, p. 98.

"*(Signed) GEORGE HUNT, ROBERT HUNT.*

"*The 4 of November, 1628.*

"*This is a true copy of the agreement concerning the differences betwixt these gentlemen, copied out of the original instrument showed here in the Office of Arms the day of grace aforesaid.*

"*(Signed) RI. ST. GEORGE CLARENCEUX.*"

Arms.—"Azure on a bend between two water bougets or, three leopards' faces gules."

Crest.—"On a mount vert, against a halbert erect in pale gules, headed argent, a talbot sejant or, collared and tied to the halbert of the second."

Attached to the above document are the Pedigrees below, signed by John Hunt, of Theddon.

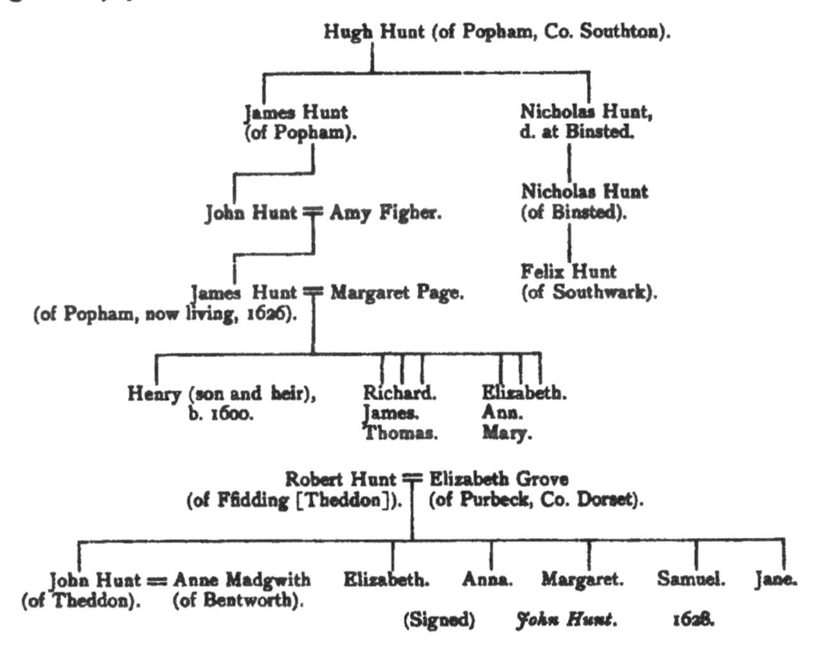

The above John Hunt had two daughters, Elizabeth and Mary, coheiresses, the elder of whom married Robert Wither, only surviving son of George Wither the poet, for whose descendants see Pedigree X, Chapter VI.

The Hunts have now disappeared from the neighbourhood, but the interesting old manor house once called "Bentworth Hall," afterwards "Hall Place," now the "Manor Farm," still remains with its stone shield blazoning the Hunt Arms.

10.—HARRIS.

HARRIS.

The Rev. Walter Bigg, father of Lovelace Bigg [Wither], married (1734) *Jane*, eldest daughter and eventual heiress of the Rev. John *Harris*, D.D., Rector of Chiddingfold and Ash, Co. Surrey.

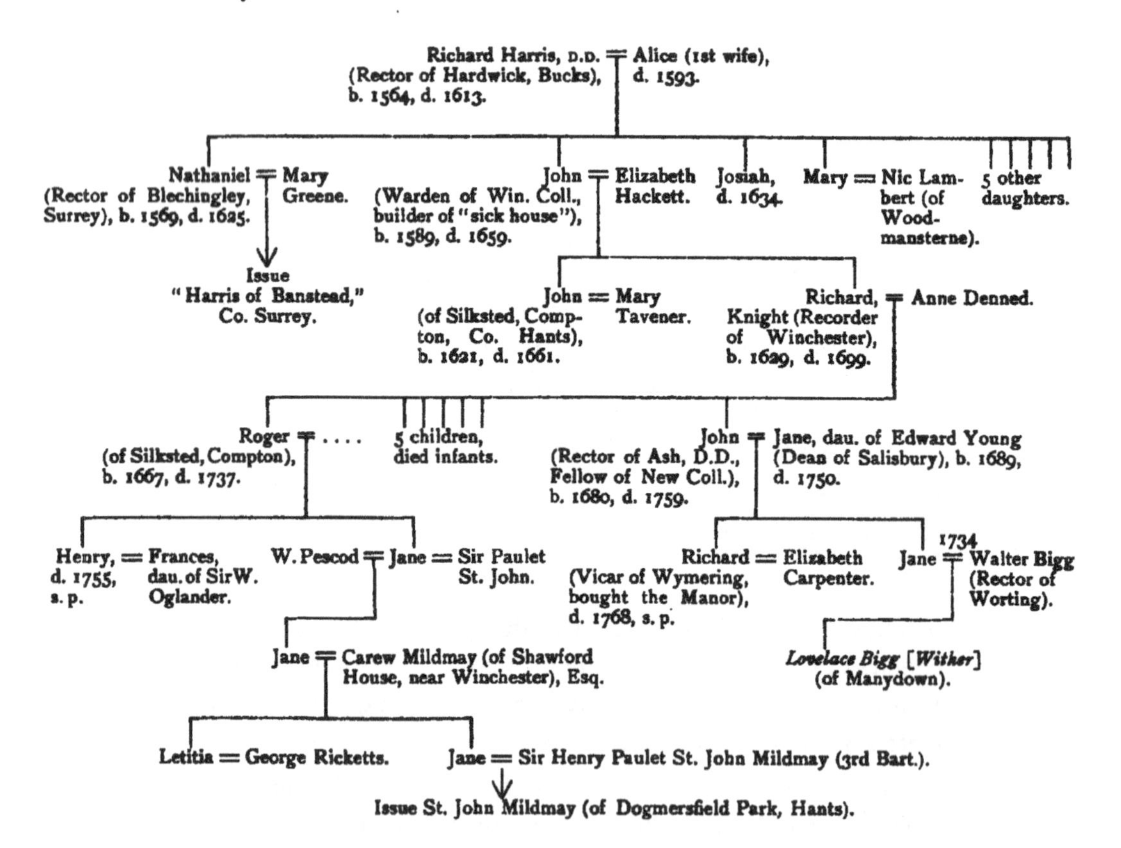

There are two good pictures extant of Jane Harris, the mother of Lovelace Bigg-Wither.

Harris of Banstead (Surrey). The Banstead Branch sprung from Nathaniel, eldest son of Dr. Richard Harris, is very numerous. It was further connected with Banstead through the marriage of Nathaniel's sister Mary with Nicholas Lambert, whose descendants had long resided at the neighbouring parish of Woodmansterne, and now live at Banstead.

Harris of Compton (Hants). The manor of Sylksted, in Compton Parish, was long the residence of the Harris family, and Compton Church is full of memorials of the family, some with very quaint epitaphs. (See *Hampshire Notes and Queries*, Vol. III, p. 63.)

The family is probably of French origin, for the hedgehog (French "herisson") in the Harris arms is in heraldry associated with De Hériz (Harris).

Arms.—"Azure a chevron ermine between three hedgehogs or."

11.—BLACHFORD, SIMEON, MACKENZIE, MANSFIELD.

Lovelace Bigg [Wither], of Manydown, married August 21st, 1766 (as his second wife), Margaret, eldest daughter of Brydges Blachford, Esq., of Osborne, Isle of Wight, and of Jane, his wife (*née* Pope).

Margaret Blachford.

Second Wife of Lovelace Bigg-[Wither].

Born 1739; died 1784.

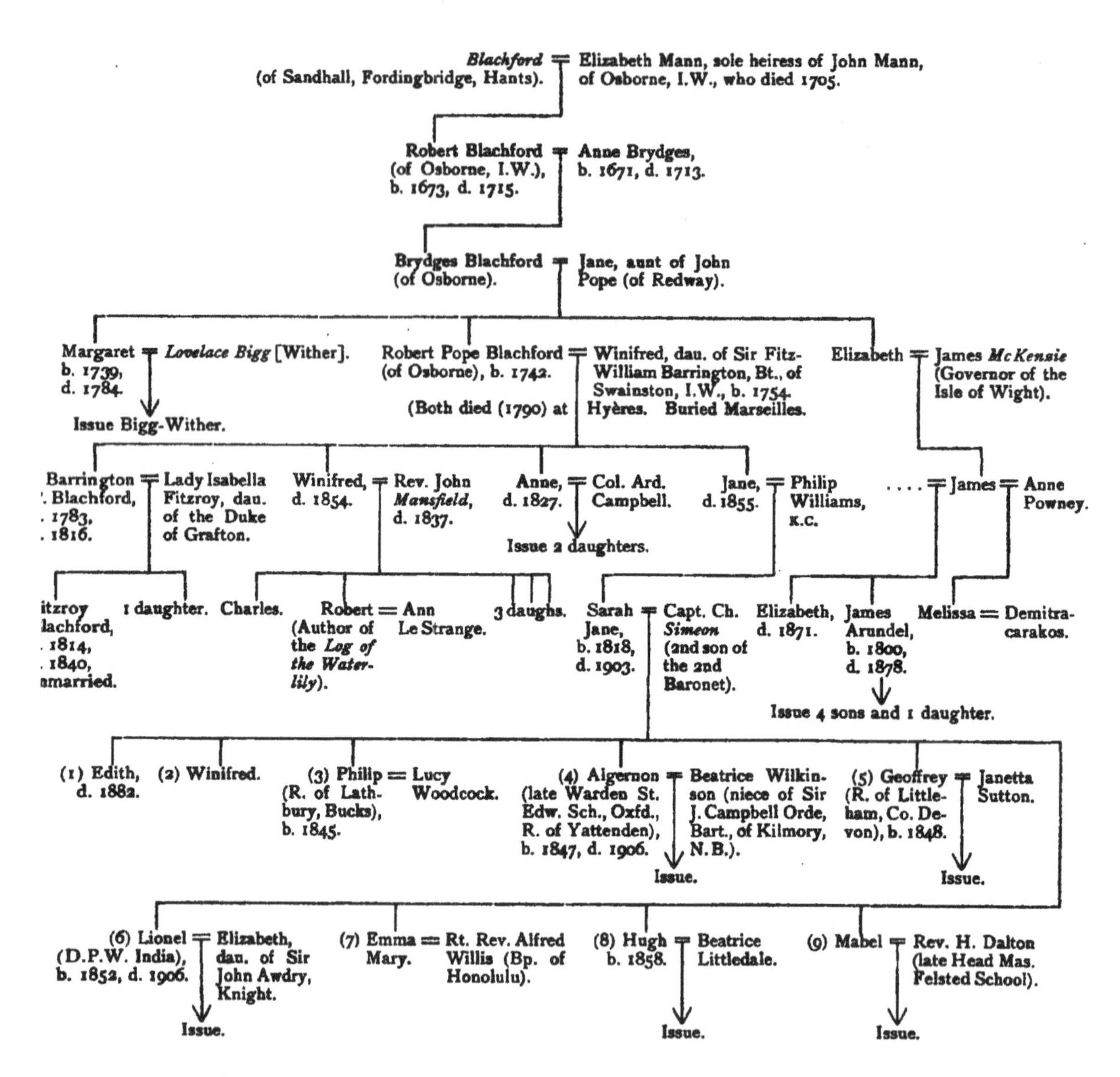

N.B.—The manor of Osborne, Isle of Wight, belonged to the old Isle of Wight families of *FitzAzor*, *Lisle*, *Chyke*, and

Boureman, in succession up to 1533. The *Lovybonds* held it from 1560 to 1630; the *Manns* until 1705, when it passed by marriage to the *Blachfords*, who held it until 1840. In 1845, the manor and house was purchased by Her late Majesty Queen Victoria, who greatly enlarged the old manor house, built by Robert Pope Blachford. The estate has now (1906) been presented to the nation by King Edward VII. (See *Hants Field Club Proceedings*, Vol. II, Part iii, for further particulars of the Blachfords, Manns, and Popes.)

Blachford *Arms.*—"Barry wavy of six or and gules on a chief azure three pheons of the first," borne by Blachford, Lord Mayor of London, 1750.

12.—BLACKSTONE,

OF CASTLE PRIORY AND CROWMARSH, WALLINGFORD, BERKS.

BLACKSTONE.

Sir William Blackstone, the learned Commentator on the Laws of England, was first cousin of Lovelace Bigg [Wither], of Manydown, through the marriage of his father with Mary Bigg, sister of the Rev. Walter Bigg, Rector of Worting.

The Crowmarsh and Castle Priory estates came to the Blackstones through the Biggs.

The family is now represented by William Blackstone Lee, J.P. (of Chantry, near Frome), great grandson of Sir William Blackstone by the marriage of his daughter Philippa with the Rev. Harry Lee, son of "Warden Lee," of Coton Hall, Salop.

Arms.—"Argent two bars gules in chief three cocks of the second."

BLACKSTONE PEDIGREE.

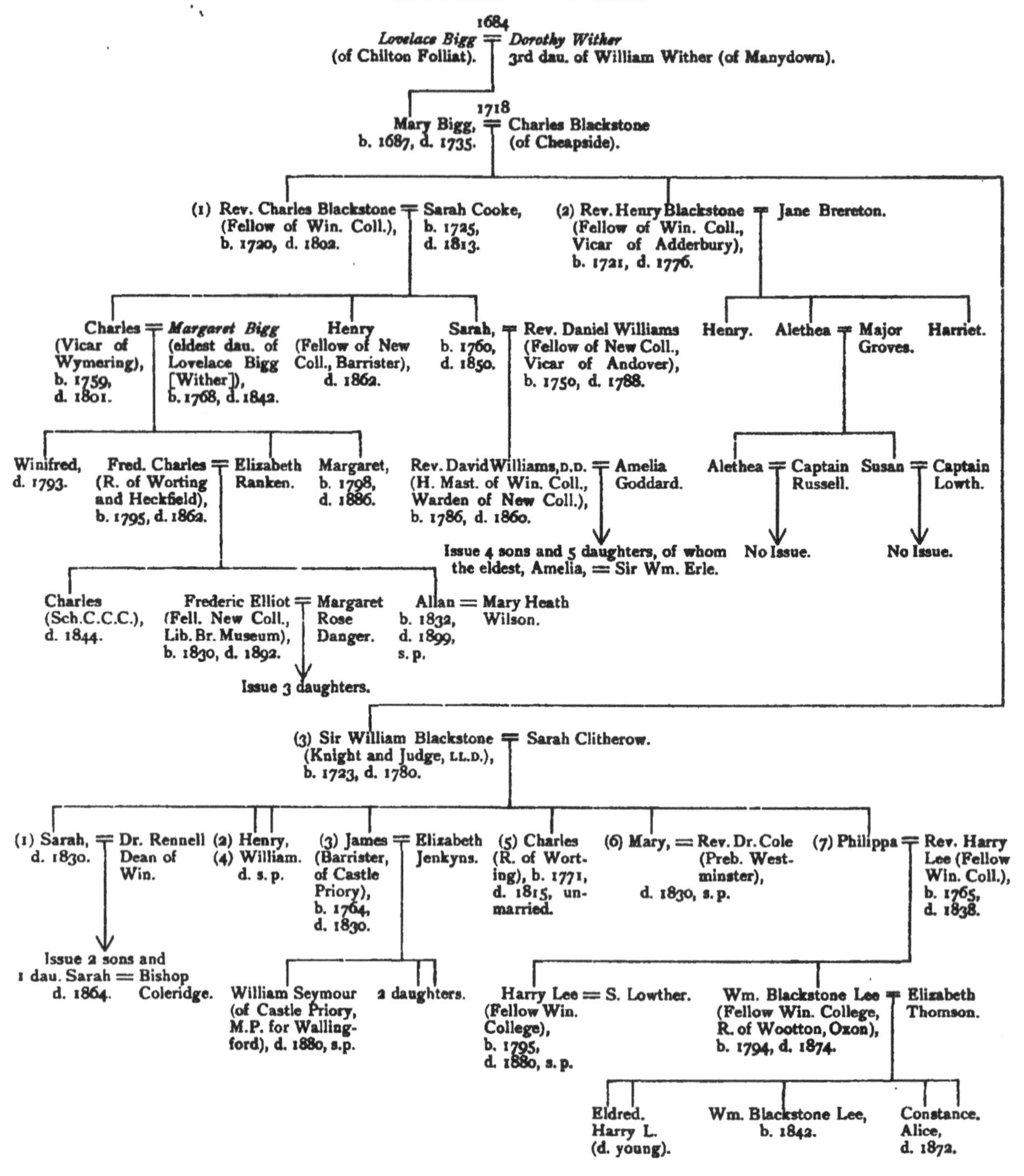

Awdry, Short, Stainforth.

13.—AWDRY, SHORT, STAINFORTH.

SHORT.

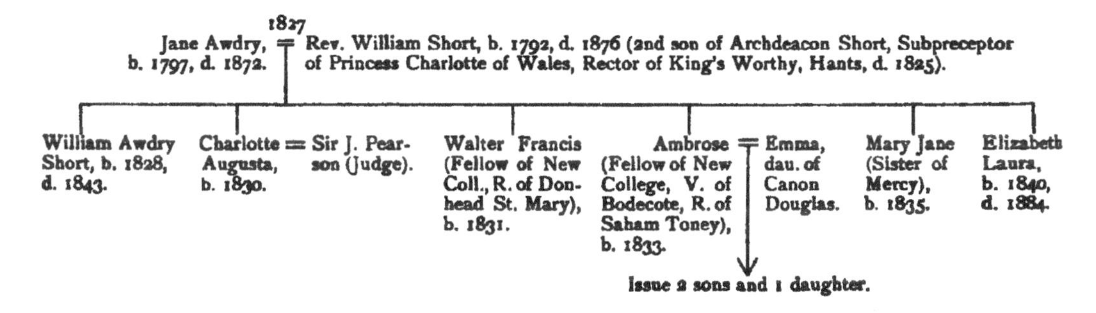

STAINFORTH.

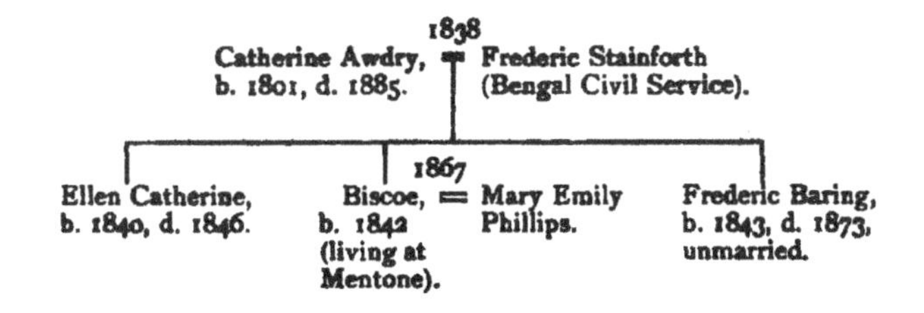

Jerem
b. 18
d. 18

14.—HEATHCOTE,

HEATHCOTE.

of Hursley.

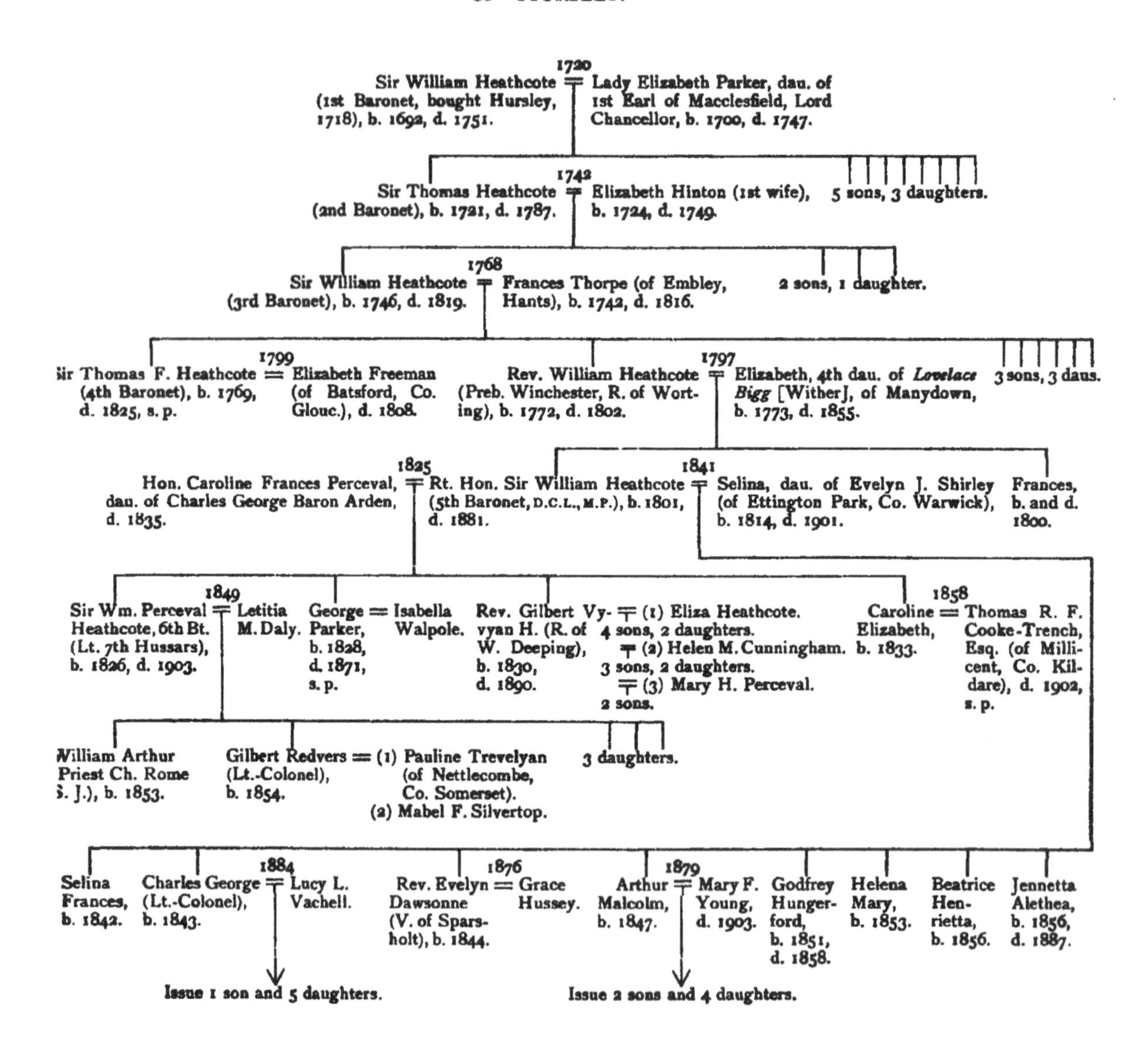

N.B.—The complete *History of the Family of Heathcote*, which numbers at least fourteen different branches, and has produced many distinguished men, has been fully written by the Rev. Evelyn D. Heathcote (late Vicar of Sparsholt). The work has been beautifully brought out by Messrs. Warren and Son, Winchester, and contains many illustrations and numerous coats of arms.

The estate and manor of Hursley, which was bought from the representatives of Richard Cromwell (the Protector) in 1718, was sold after the death, in 1881, of the late Right Hon. Sir William Heathcote, fifth Baronet, son of Elizabeth, fourth daughter of Lovelace Bigg-Wither.

Arms.—" Ermine, three pomeis, each charged with a cross, or."

15.—ORDE.

The family of Orde is of great antiquity, and long possessed considerable estates in Northumberland and Durham. The founder of the family was Simon de Orde, of East Orde, Co. Durham, who died 1362. From him descend through junior branches the Barons Bolton and the Baronets Orde. The senior branch is represented by the Ordes of Nunnykirk, Co. Northumberland; the junior branch by the Shafto-Ordes of Weetwood, Co. Northumberland.

Arms.—" Sable three fishes (salmon) haurient, in fesse argent."

ORDE PEDIGREE.

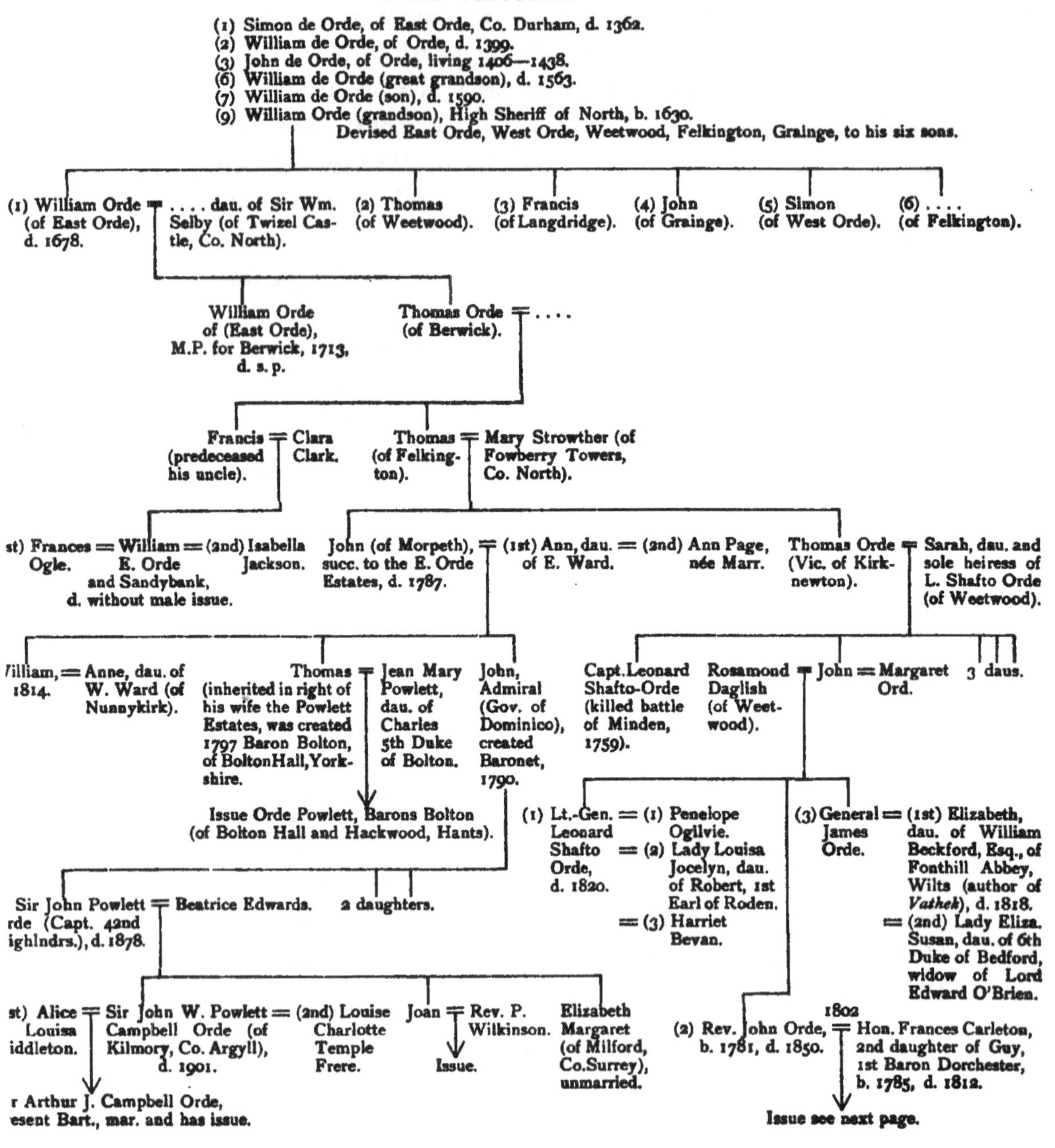

16.—MASSEY, CRAVEN, CUTHBERT, DOMVILLE.

1802
The *Rev. John Orde* = The *Hon. Frances Carleton* (2nd dau. of Guy, 1st Baron
b. 1771, d. 1850. Dorchester, and the Lady Maria Howard),
b. 1785, d. 1812.

MASSEY, CRAVEN, CUTHBERT, DOMVILLE.

The Rev. John Orde, of Lincoln College, Oxford, M.A., held at different times five livings. In 1796 he was instituted to Kingsclere Vicarage, Hants, on the presentation of the Hon. Thomas Orde-Powlett; in 1811 to the Rectory of Winslade, on the presentation of the Dowager Lady Bolton. He resigned the Vicarage of Kingsclere in 1817, having been instituted that year to Abbotstone Rectory with Itchen Stoke Vicarage on the presentation of Lord Bolton. These he resigned on his institution in 1829 to the Rectory of Wensley, Yorkshire.

He had by his first wife (the Hon. Frances Carleton) six daughters:—

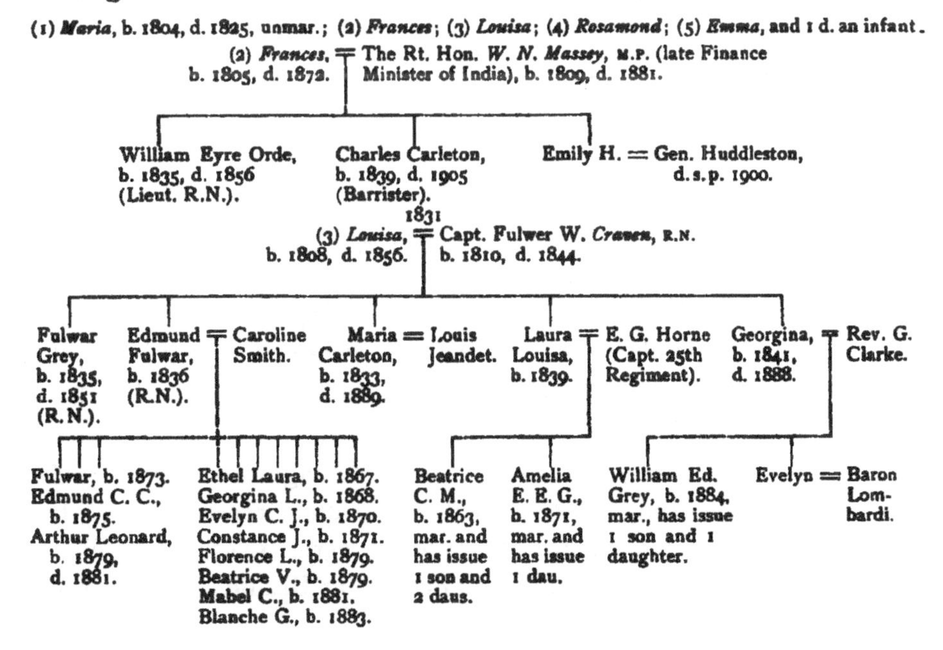

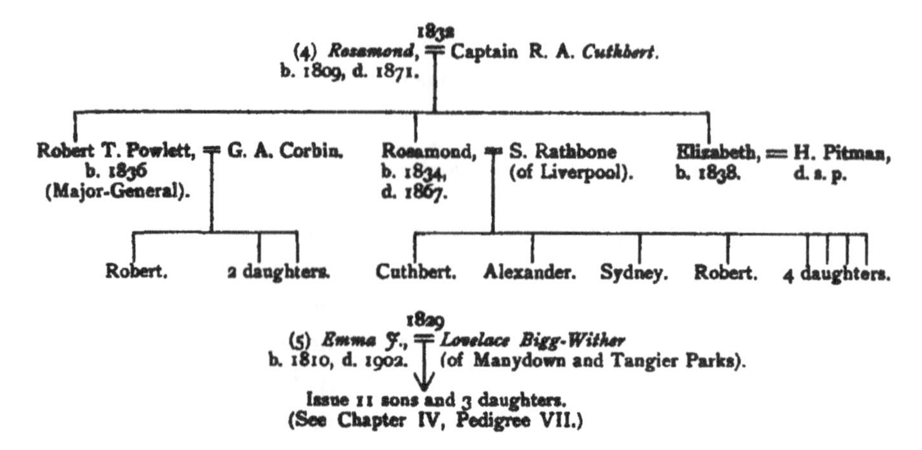

Mr. Orde married, secondly, Marianne Burley, and by her had a daughter Mary Ann, who married in 1848 the late Sir James Domville, third Baronet, who died 1887, leaving a son, Sir William Cecil H. Domville, Admiral R. N. Two other sons, John and Powlett, died young, and their daughter, Eleanor Ida, married Count Francesco Ranchibile.

17.—CARLETON.

CARLETON.

The family of Carleton, of Carleton Hall, near Penrith, came originally from Cumberland, where it was settled at the time of the Conquest, the representative of the family then being one Baldwin de Carleton.

The family has always been distinguished by its military services to king and country down to quite recent times. It was represented at Agincourt, October 25th, 1415, by William de Carleton and [Thomas] de Carleton[1]; at Beaujé, 1421, by Captain

[1] Sir Harry Nicholas, Rolls of Agincourt.

Carleton, "who, disdaining to fly, endeavoured to rally the English, but nought availed him, he fell with the rest, deeply beloved and sore lamented"[1]; at Vernieul, October 24th, 1424, under the Duke of Bedford, where "the only Englishmen of note slayne were Captain Dudley and Captain Carleton."[2]

Chronicles.

Chronicles.

The Church and the Law were also represented in the sixteenth century by George Carleton, Bishop of Chichester, and Hugh Viscount Carleton, Chief Justice of Common Pleas, Ireland.

There have been two distinct Baronies in the family, namely, *that of Carleton and Dorchester*. The first was granted to *Sir Dudley Carleton* (son of Anthony Carleton, of Brightwell, Co. Oxford, member of a younger branch), who was knighted by James I in 1610. He was Ambassador to the Republic of Venice; Secretary of State, *temp*. Charles I; and was created in 1628 Baron Carleton and Viscount Dorchester, Co. Oxford. He left no children, and was buried in Westminster Abbey, 1632.

From Launcelot Carleton, of Brampton Fort, Co. Cumberland (brother of Thomas Carleton, sixteenth in direct descent from Baldwin de Carleton), who settled at Rossfad, near Inniskillen, Ireland, *temp*. Charles I, descended the distinguished General, *Sir Guy Carleton*, K.B., born 1722. He was Colonel of 4th Dragoons, served in the Guards at the Battle of Fontenoy (1745), was Quartermaster-General under Wolfe during the Canadian Campaign of 1755, gallantly defended Quebec (1775) and saved Canada. He was created for his services Baron Dorchester of Dorchester, Co. Oxford, 1786.

Sir Guy Carleton married (1772) the Lady Maria Howard, daughter of Thomas Earl of Effingham, by whom he had nine sons and two daughters.

CHILDREN OF SIR GUY CARLETON, BARON DORCHESTER.

Sons :—

(1.)—*Guy*, born 1773.—Lieutenant 3rd Dragoon Guards, fought at Laincelles, was attacked by camp fever and sent home, where he died November, 1793; *ætat.* 20.

(2.)—*Thomas*, born 1774.—Brigade-Major 1st Dragoon Guards, was shot at the Battle of Catteau while assisting his dragoon orderly, 1794; *ætat.* 20.

(3.)—*Christopher*, born 1775.—Lieut.-Colonel 25th Dragoons. He died of wound fever on board the East Indiaman "Devonshire," in Madras Roads, 4th February, 1806. He married, 1797, Priscilla Belford, who was drowned with her daughter in the founding of a packet which struck the pierhead at Ostend, 29th October, 1815. Colonel Carleton's only son, *Arthur Henry*, born 1805, became second Baron Dorchester after his grandfather's death in 1808, and died unmarried 1826.

The fourth and fifth sons, *William*, born 1778, and *Launcelot*, born 1780, died the same day of scarlet fever, 23rd October, 1780.

(6.)—*George*, born 1781.—Lieutenant-Colonel, wounded at Badajoz, killed at the storming of Bergen op Zoom, 1814. Married Henrietta, daughter of Edward King, Esq., of Askham Hall, Co. Westmoreland, by whom he left three daughters and a son *Guy*, born 1811, who succeeded his cousin and became third Baron. Guy, Lord Dorchester, died 1875, leaving two daughters, Henrietta Ann, born 1846, and Maria Georgina, born 1847.

(7.)—*Charles*, born 1786.—Royal Navy, fell from a mast on H.M.S. "Phœbe," was killed, October 13th, 1799.

(8.)—*Dudley*, born 1790.—Lieutenant 4th Dragoons, served all through the Peninsular War, where he contracted pneumonia and died October, 1820.

(9.)—*Richard*, born 1792.—Took Holy Orders, and was Rector of the family living of Nateley Scures, Hants. He married Frances Louisa, daughter of E. Horton, Esq., of Catton Hall, Co. Derby, and died 1868, leaving a daughter, Maria Louisa, and a son, *Dudley Wilmot*, born 1822, who went all through the Crimean Campaign and became Lieutenant-Colonel of the Coldstream Guards. Colonel Dudley Carleton succeeded his cousin Guy in 1875 and became fourth Baron, and died without issue 1897.

Sir Guy Carleton, 1st Baron Dorchester, had also two daughters:—

(1.)—*Maria*, born 1779, who married William, second Baron Bolton, and died 1863, s.p.

(2.)—*Frances*, born 1785, who married the Rev. John Orde, Rector of Winslade, Hants, Vicar of Kingsclere and Rector of Wensley, and died 1812, leaving five daughters (see Orde family), of whom the youngest, Emma, born 1810, married 1829, Lovelace Bigg-Wither, of Manydown and Tangier Parks, and had fourteen children (see Bigg-Wither Pedigree VII), and died 1902, aged 92.

The Barony of Dorchester was revived in 1899, two years after the death of the fourth Baron, in the person of the eldest daughter of the third Lord Dorchester, the Hon. Henrietta Anne Carleton, of Greywell Hill, near Odiham, Hants. The following letter, dated from Downing Street, July 3rd, 1899, announced to her the Royal recognition of the military services of her ancestors, no less than twenty-nine of whom had served in the Army and Navy since the time of Charles I, of whom sixteen had fallen in active service, including three Carletons[1] at Marston Moor in 1644:—

[1] Bell's Martial Biographies, p. 187.

"*Madam,—I have great pleasure in informing you that Her Majesty has been pleased that the Barony of Dorchester should be conferred upon you and your heirs male in recognition of the distinguished military services rendered to Her and Her predecessors by so many members of your family on various occasions, and have the honour to be your obedient servant.*

SALISBURY."

Lady Dorchester has by her first husband, Francis Paynton Pigott Stainsby Conant, who took the name of Carleton in place of his last two names, and died in 1883,—one surviving son, the Hon. Dudley Massey Pigott-Carleton, born 1876, and one daughter. Lady Dorchester married again (1887), Major-General Richard Langford Leir, of Ditcheat, Co. Somerset, who added the name of Carleton.

Arms.—"Ermine on a bend sable three pheons argent."

Supporters.—"Two beavers proper, the dexter gorged with a mural, and the sinister with a naval crown or."

FAMILIES THAT ADD "S" TO THE NAME WITHER, BUT BEAR THE WITHER ARMS.

1.—WITHERS OF LIVERPOOL.

This family bear and have borne for some generations the same coat of arms as Wither of Manydown. Tradition in the family says that the George Withers who married Mary Lay, of Nottingham, and who died a young man in 1774 (see Pedigree below), came from the south of England, and that he "wilfully destroyed memoranda which gave any clue to his former residence." His son Joseph settled in business in Liverpool, and became the progenitor of a numerous family, of whom three at least had a distinguished career, namely :—

(1.)—*Richard Withers*, of the Uplands, West Derby, born 1815, died 1884, married three times and left numerous children (see Pedigree). He was for twenty-five years Chairman of the Liverpool Stock Exchange. He was also Deputy Chairman of the Manchester, Sheffield, and Lincolnshire Railway Company; a Director of the South-Eastern Railway Company and of the Bridgwater Navigation Company, and was a member of the Committee of the Railway Clearing House in London. He was Deputy-Lieutenant for Westmoreland and J. P. for the hundred of West Derby.

(2.)—*Colonel Joseph Withers*, a son of the above Richard by his first wife (born 1841, died 1899), of Brierly Close, Windermere, was High Sheriff for Westmoreland in 1894.

(3.)—*Harry Livingston Withers*, nephew of the above Richard, born 1864, died 1892, was a distinguished Scholar of Balliol College, Oxford, where he obtained a first in "Mods." and a first in "Greats." He became Principal of the Isleworth Training College, and afterwards "Sarah Fielden" Professor of Education in Owen's College, Manchester. Some of his writings with a biographical introduction have been published by J. H. Fowler, of Clifton College, where H. L. Withers was also for a time a master.

The present head of the family is Richard Eric Withers (born 1878), eldest son of Thomas Randle Withers, of the Lowlands, West Derby, Liverpool.

A branch of this family is living in Preston, Lancashire, and bear the Wither arms. A member of the family married, *circa* 1790, into the ancient Lancashire family of Bigland, of Bigland Hall, near Cartmel, and by a curious coincidence their descendants have been called "Big-Withers."

Their *Arms* are:—"Azure two ears of big-wheat, or."

The *Crest* is:—"A lion passant reguard; gules, holding in his fore paw an ear of big-wheat, as in the Arms."

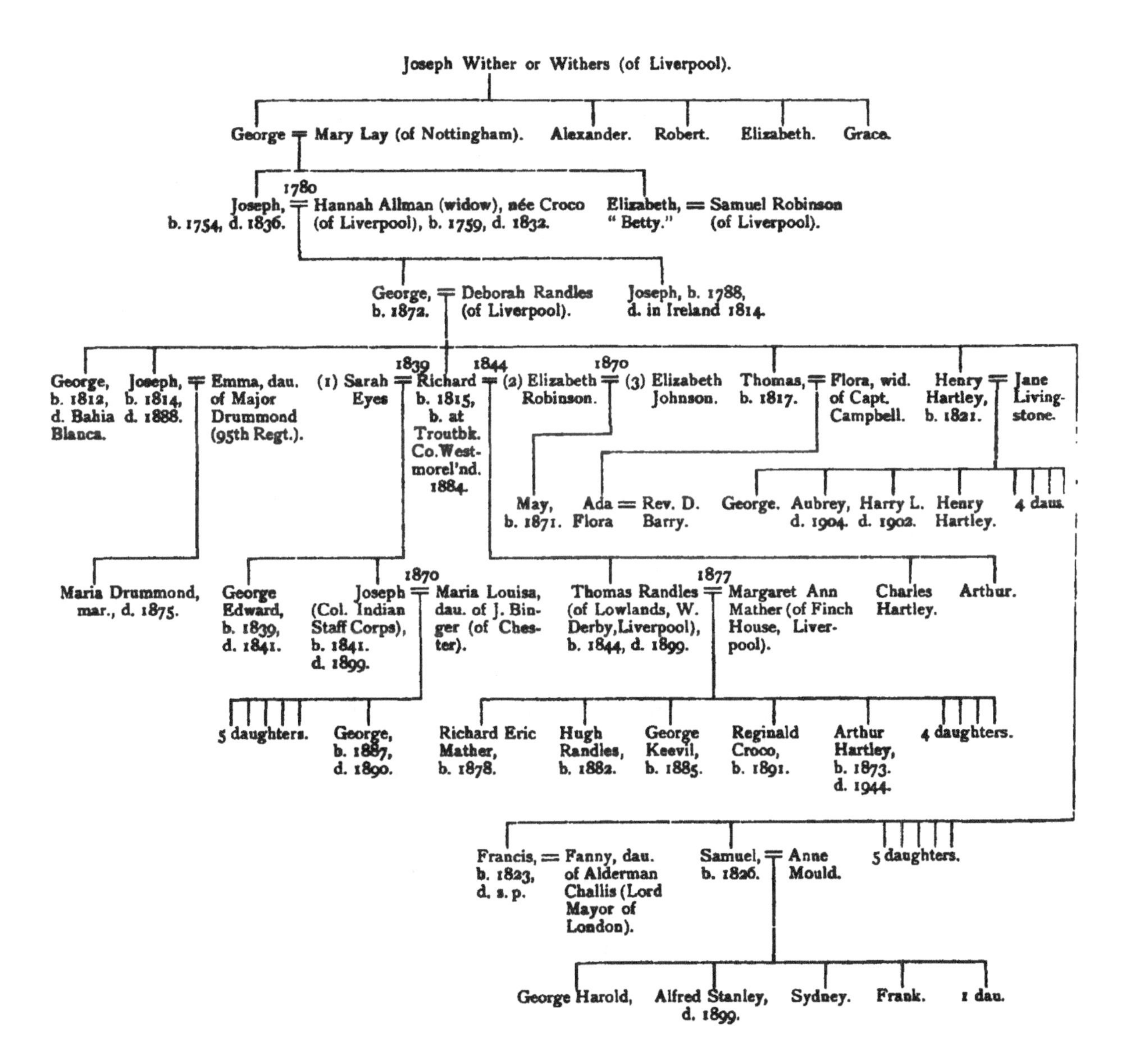
Joseph Wither or Withers (of Liverpool).
George = Mary Lay (of Nottingham).
Alexander.
Robert.
Elizabeth.
Grace.
1780
Joseph, b. 1754, d. 1836. = Hannah Allman (widow), née Croco (of Liverpool), b. 1759, d. 1832.
Elizabeth, "Betty." = Samuel Robinson (of Liverpool).
George, b. 1872. = Deborah Randles (of Liverpool).
Joseph, b. 1788, d. in Ireland 1814.
George, b. 1812, d. Bahia Blanca.
Joseph, b. 1814, d. 1888. = Emma, dau. of Major Drummond (95th Regt.).
1839 1844 1870
(1) Sarah Eyes = Richard b. 1815, b. at Troutbk. Co. Westmorel'nd. 1884. = (2) Elizabeth Robinson. = (3) Elizabeth Johnson.
Thomas, b. 1817. = Flora, wid. of Capt. Campbell.
Henry Hartley, b. 1821. = Jane Livingstone.
May, b. 1871.
Ada Flora = Rev. D. Barry.
George.
Aubrey, d. 1904.
Harry L. d. 1902.
Henry Hartley.
4 daus.
Maria Drummond, mar., d. 1875.
George Edward, b. 1839, d. 1841.
1870
Joseph (Col. Indian Staff Corps), b. 1841. d. 1899. = Maria Louisa, dau. of J. Binger (of Chester).
1877
Thomas Randles (of Lowlands, W. Derby, Liverpool), b. 1844, d. 1899. = Margaret Ann Mather (of Finch House, Liverpool).
Charles Hartley.
Arthur.
5 daughters.
George, b. 1887, d. 1890.
Richard Eric Mather, b. 1878.
Hugh Randles, b. 1882.
George Keevil, b. 1885.
Reginald Croco, b. 1891.
Arthur Hartley, b. 1873. d. 1944.
4 daughters.
Francis, b. 1823, d. s. p. = Fanny, dau. of Alderman Challis (Lord Mayor of London).
Samuel, b. 1826. = Anne Mould.
5 daughters.
George Harold,
Alfred Stanley, d. 1899.
Sydney.
Frank.
1 dau.

2.—WITHERS OF LONDON.

PEDIGREE of Thomas Withers = Gladys Mary, dau. of (Solicitor, 4, Arundel Street, Strand). Major Edward Bigg-Wither.

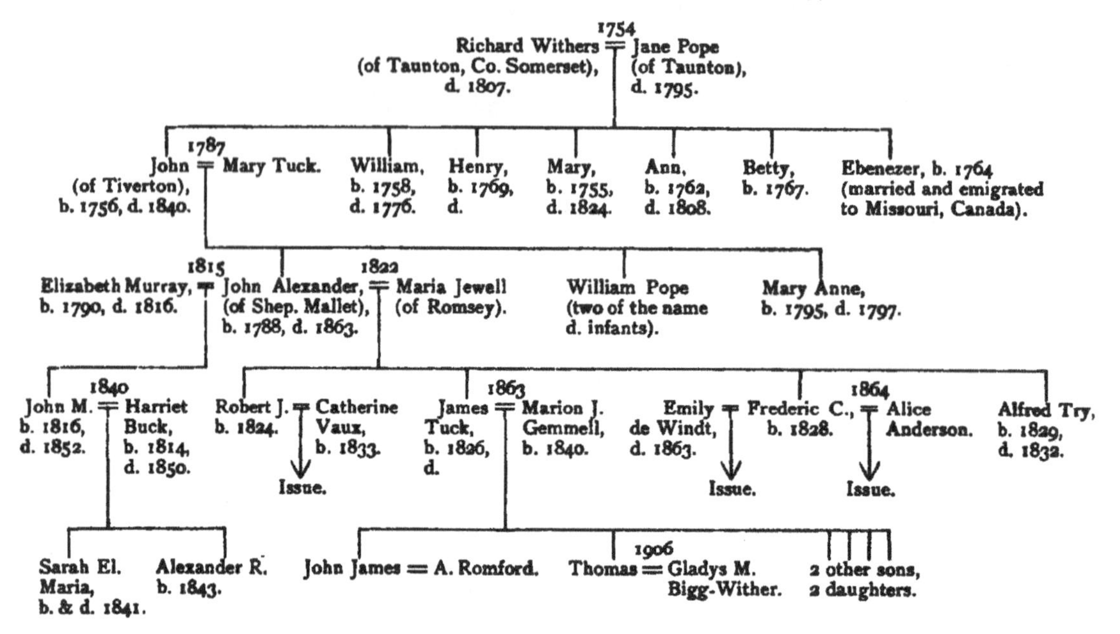

The Pedigree below was among the papers of James Tuck Withers (see above).

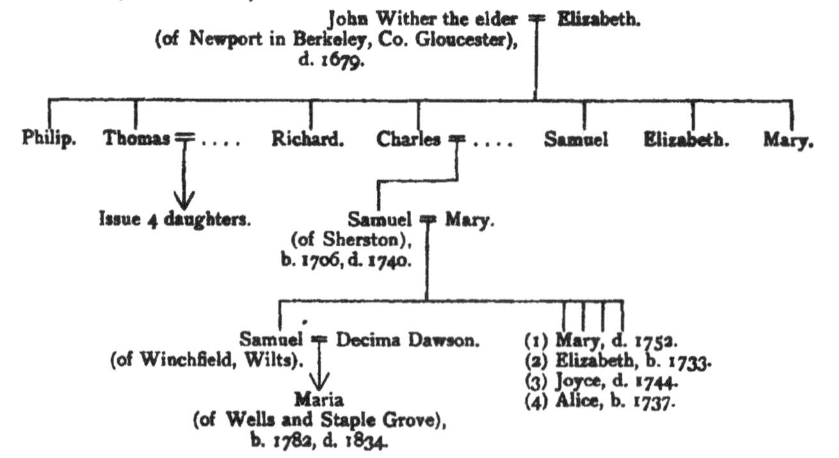

N.B.—There are at least two other families of Withers living, or engaged in business, in London, that bear the Wither arms, descended probably from Sir William Wither, or Withers, Lord Mayor of London, 1707. (See Pedigree II and Chapter II.)

3.—WITHER OR WITHERS OF UNITED STATES OF AMERICA.

WITHER of America.

There are a great number of Withers living in the United States, especially in Virginia, Kentucky, Illinois, Alabama, and Texas; and some of these families use the Wither arms and crest.

Origin.

The tradition amongst them is that in the reign of Charles I, two brothers of the name came from England with a grant of land in Fairfax, now Virginia. The tradition takes various forms, but all agree that these two Withers "presented Charles I with a pair of elk horns, in token of loyalty at a time when evidence of it was grateful to him and dangerous to those who offered it. The king in consequence made a grant of land in Stafford and Fairfaix, Co. Virginia."

In the list of passengers who came to Jamestown, Virginia, in the early part of seventeenth century are two Withers. I am informed by Mr. Henry C. Withers, of Carrolton, Illinois, and by Mr. Robert G. Withers, Attorney-at-Law, late of Cripple Creek, Colorado, now of Goldfield, Nevada, and by his cousin, Mr. H. C. Lay, of Telluride, Colorado, that "from these two brothers sprang the two families of Withers, known as those of *Fauquier* and *Dinwiddie* Counties respectively. To the first named belong *Senator Robert E. Withers* (of whom afterwards) and *Captain*

William Withers, and others of the name now in Virginia, Kentucky, and Illinois. The Dinwiddie branch became extinct in the male line in 1879; its representatives are now living mainly in Alabama, Texas, Colorado, and Arkansas."

For the following account of the Fauquier Withers, I am indebted to Mr. Henry Clay Withers, of Carrolton, whose great grandfather on his mother's side was John Bruce, who fought for Prince Charlie at Culloden in 1745, was deprived of his estates in Scotland, and fled with his wife to America.

Withers of Fauquier, Virginia.

The first known record in Virginia is of John Withers, the ancestor of Thomas Withers, of Green Meadows, Fauquier County, Virginia, who married and had issue:—

(1.)—*John Withers*, who moved to Garllatin, Tennessee.

(2.)—*Mathew Keene Withers*, second son, who married Miss Jennings, of Fauquier County, Virginia, lived and died there, leaving several descendants.

(3.)—*William Withers*; Captain in the Revolutionary War; wounded in the River Raisin Fight; married Patsey Ashby, and moved to Kentucky.

(4.)—*Enoch Keene Withers*, who married Janet Chinn, and died at Green Meadows, Fauquier County, Virginia, leaving *Robert Walter*, his third son, who married and moved to Campbell County, Virginia, and was the father of Hon. Robert E. Withers, Senator from Virginia in 1878.

(5 and 6.)—*James* and *Benjamin*, both of whom went to Kentucky.

The Hon. Robert E. Withers, above named, was a General in the Confederate Army during the Civil War; was severely wounded in the great Battle of Gettysburg, Pennsylvania, in General Picket's Division, which was nearly all destroyed. After the war he came into prominence in Virginia; was elected United States Senator from that State. Afterwards, he was United States Consul-General at Hong Kong, China, and later held the office of Grand Master Knights Templar Masons in the United States. He now resides at Wythesville, Virginia.

Captain William Withers, of Virginia, after the Revolutionary War, settled in Mercer County, Kentucky, and was succeeded by his son, Abijah Withers, of Garrard County, Kentucky, married, and had issue:—

William Withers, now of Mineral Wells, Texas; born 1819.

William Withers married Elizabeth Bruce, daughter of Hon. Horatio Bruce, a lawyer and legislator, of Garrard County, Kentucky, and has had issue:—

(1.)—*Henry Clay Withers*, Atty, Carrollton, Illinois.

(2.)—*Dr. Horatio B. Withers*, Mineral Wells, Texas.

(3.)—*Zackary T. Withers*, Joshua, Texas.

(4.)—*George M. Withers*, Mineral Wells, Texas.

(5.)—*Eliza*, married to Wallace Baker, Mineral Wells, Texas.

(6.)—*Clara*, married to M. W. Parker, Mineral Wells, Texas.

William Withers counts, as now living, thirty-five of his immediate descendants, children, grandchildren, and great grandchildren.

WITHERS of Dinwiddie, Virginia.

The immediate founder of the Dinwiddie branch of the Withers, namely, William Withers, Secretary to Governor Dinwiddie, of Virginia, in 1752, elicited some early facts about his Wither ancestry in a lawsuit, which he successfully maintained *v.* Augustine Washington in 1755. These facts have been put on record in "*Hening's Statutes at Large*," Volume VI, page 513, published at Richmond, Virginia, in 1809, by which it appears that *John Withers*, of the County of Stafford, Colony of Virginia,

Will of JOHN WITHERS, of Stafford, Virginia, 1693.

dying without male issue, left a certain tract of land, known as Chotank, and containing 533 acres, by his will dated 29th August, 1693, to his daughter Sarah, and after her death to Mr. *Thomas Withers*, of Lancaster, in Great Britain. Thomas Withers died, leaving two sons :—*Edmund*, who died without issue ; and William, who died, leaving issue, *Thomas*, who died, leaving issue, *William*, born in England, January 31st, 1731–2. This William Withers came to Virginia in 1748. There is extant a letter written by his grandson, the Rev. Edmund Withers, dated December 7th, 1878, in which he says :—

"*My grandfather came to Va. in 1748, to take possession of his portion of a grant of land made to his ancestors by Charles I. It lay in Fairfax Co., and when he came of age, he took possession of it and sold it to Mr. Lawrence Washington. It is still called Woodlawn. In 1752 my grandfather became Private Secretary to Governor Dinwiddie. The fathers were College mates at Trinity College, Cambridge.*"

Another of William Withers' grandsons, Mr. John Grammer, a much older man, with a personal knowledge of his grandfather, gave in 1886 the following interesting particulars of this William Withers :—

"From my recollection of my grandfather's (William Withers) conversations, and from information furnished by my mother, his daughter, I am enabled to make out the following account. The father of the above William Withers, who resided in the south of England, was drowned before the birth of his only child, and as it was thought by his family that he had married rather beneath his standing in society, his son was removed when quite young from the care of his mother and brought up in the family of the brother of his father, who was a clergyman having charge of a parish near Scarborough or Flamborough Head, in Yorkshire. Being thus separated from the circle of his immediate family connections, he knew but little of his relations and seldom spoke of his ancestry. He kept up a very affectionate correspondence with his mother until near the outbreak of the Revolutionary War, and from her letters, my mother (who had several of them) inferred that whatever might have been her rank in English society, she was at least a very sensible, intelligent, and pious woman.

"In 1748 or 1749 he was sent by his uncle to Virginia, and received from him as a parting present, a small Bible and a Book of Common Prayer, with an injunction to carry them in his pocket and never permit a day to pass without seriously consulting them, as if properly used they would prove the most valuable inheritance he could possibly receive; and he did carry them in his pocket until they were past using, and I have heard him say that he believed he had complied literally with his uncle's injunctions, having no recollection of ever permitting a day to pass from the time of his first leaving England without reading or having read to him a portion of God's Word.

"These books he had coarsely rebound with leather, and they were so worn when they came into my possession (about six years after his death), that nearly half the outer columns and many lines from the top and bottom of the pages were wanting.

"He came out to Virginia that he might take possession as soon as he might come of age of a tract of land which he inherited from his father, it being part of a grant which had been made by Charles I to one of his ancestors. This tract was in the County of Fairfax, and is a portion of the Woodlawn estate devised by General George Washington to Mrs. Lewis, it having been sold by my grandfather to Mr. Lawrence Washington, by whom it was devised as a part of Mount Vernon to his brother George.

"On his first arrival in Virginia, he landed at Mr. Anthony Walke's, on Nansemond River, in Nansemond County, and he lived as a clerk in Mr. Walke's store until 1752, when on the arrival of Robert Dinwiddie as Governor of the Colony, he was called to Williamsburg, where he resided in the Governor's family as his Private Secretary during the whole period of his administration of the Government. In January, 1758, he sailed with the Governor and his family for England. On the voyage Governor Dinwiddie died, which rendered it necessary for my grandfather to remain with Mrs. Dinwiddie in England more than a year to assist her in settling with the Government the accounts of her deceased husband's administration. Sometime during the year 1759 he returned to Virginia. In 1761 he married, and receiving with his wife a large number of negroes, but no land on which to employ them, and finding the climate of Williamsburg unfavourable to his health, he purchased a tract of land, Locust Grove, in Dinwiddie County, to which he removed in 1762, and on which he resided the remainder of his life.

"He was a man of medium stature, of good features, with a countenance which beamed with benevolence and vivacity, but of very dignified deportment and highly polished manners, with much more taste for literature than for agriculture, and whose reading (especially of his favorite poets, Milton and Young), even after he had lost all his teeth, was so musical, that it was a delight of my childhood to listen to him, even before I was able to understand the meaning of the words. In all his habits, he was remarkable for punctuality, regularity, and temperance, and equally so for the enlightened, cheerful, and devout tone of his piety. He had indeed so used his uncle's parting gift as to obtain from them the richest of all inheritances."

To Mr. Robert G. Withers, of Goldfield, Nevada, I am indebted for the following particulars of the marriage and descendants of Mr. William Withers, of Dinwiddie :—

William Withers (1), born in England, January 31st, 1731 (O.S.); married, October 19th, 1761, Priscilla Wright, of Nansemond, Co. Virginia; died February 26th, 1816, aged 85 years; buried at Locust Grove, Dinwiddie Co.

Priscilla Wright was born February 25th, 1734 (O.S.), in Nansemond Co., Virginia.

Children of William (1) and Priscilla Withers.

Priscilla Wright (2), born October 17th, 1762; married, May 1st, 1788, John Grammer; died June 11th, 1835.

William (2), born July 9th, 1764; died, unmarried, November 14th, 1779.

Thomas (2), born September 11th, 1766, at Locust Grove, was a planter or farmer; married (*a*) November 28th, 1793, Elizabeth Walker, who died March 26th, 1802, and (*b*) October 20th, 1803, Elizabeth Grammer; died January 19th, 1843, at Poplar Hill, Dinwiddie Co. [Issue below.]

Dorothy (2), born June 6th, 1768; married May 16th, 1799, Jones Mitchell; died April 28th, 1838.

John (2), born March 2nd, 1770; married Mary Herbert Jones and moved to Alabama; died April 16th, 1826. [Issue below.]

David Wright (2), born November 12th, 1773; died unmarried December 3rd, 1821.

Children of Thomas Withers (2) and his first wife, Elizabeth Walker.

William (3), born December 4th, 1794, at Poplar Hill; married . . . . 1817, Eliza Stith; died October 8th, 1824, leaving no children.

Ann Eliza (3), born December 20th, 1795; married (*a*) March 10th, 1814, General W. H. Brodnax, and (*b*) October 24th, 1834, Samuel Pryor; died May 23rd, 1867.

Robert Walker (3), born November 9th, 1798; married (*a*) May . . . 1822, Martha Wilkins, and (*b*) in 1833 Mary Dorothy Withers, daughter of John Withers (2); died September 19th, 1854, at Huntsville, Alabama. [Issue below.]

Children of Thomas Withers (2) and his second wife, Elizabeth Grammer.

John Grammer (3), born September 1st, 1804; died June 30th, 1805.

Mary Timberlake (3), born May, 1806; married December 17th, 1823, Roger B. Atkinson; died October 12th, 1858; issue five sons and six daughters.

Thomas (3), born July 30th, 1808; died unmarried April 6th, 1879.

Louisa Walker (3), born July 15th, 1810; married November 8th, 1832, Rev. Charles Dresser; died April 2nd, 1891; issue six sons and five daughters.

David Wright (3), born May 6th, 1812; died unmarried September 20th, 1843.

Bolling Walker (3), born January 17th, 1814; died May 31st, 1815.

Elizabeth (3), born July 30th, 1815; married November 28th, 1833, Rev. Thomas Adams; died August 25th, 1871.

Sarah Grammer (3), born February 22nd, 1817; died March 16th, 1831.

Edmund (3), born October 31st, 1818; in Holy Orders; educated at Trinity College, Hartford, Connecticut, and at the University of Virginia; married June 5th, 1845, Clara Colquhoun Gilliam, daughter of Robert Gilliam and Janet Colquhoun; he died February 24th, 1879. [Issue below.]

Richard Barton (3), born July 17th, 1820; died February 26th, 1821.

William (3), born December 21st, 1824; died April 12th, 1845.

Children of Robert Walker Withers (3) and Mary Dorothy Withers.

Robert Walker (4), born in 1834; married (*a*) April 25th, 1876, Mary G. Pickens, who died without children, and (*b*) Mrs. J. P. Burke, May 25th, 1882; lives at Huntsville, Alabama.

Thomas (4), born 1836; died 1842.

John (4), born 1838; died 1843.

William (4), born 1848; moved to Texas, and died leaving sons.

Mary Le Vert (4), born 1842; married November 25th, 1869, Major Charles A. Poellnitz.

Thomas (4), born 1843; died 1849.

Maria Louisa (4), born 1845; married December 20th, 1882, Richard Horace Brown, of New Orleans.

Ann Elizabeth (4), born 1847.

Helen (4), born 1849; married December 18th, 1872, William C. Pickens, who died August 16th, 1874, leaving one son, William, born October 13th, 1873.

Henry (4), born 1851.

Allen Jones (4), born 1853; died 1858.

Children of (Rev.) Edmund Withers (3) and Clara Colquhoun Gilliam.

Clara Colquhoun (4), born June 23rd, 1846; died August 23rd, 1846.

Thomas (4), born February 28th, 1849; married (*a*) Eliza Maury, daughter of Commodore Matthew F. Maury. She died without children, January . . . 1881; and (*b*) Jennie Barnes, married August 3rd, 1882. He graduated at Virginia Military Institute, and took special course in engineering with degree of C.E. and M.E.; now lives at Goldfield, Nevada. [Issue below.]

Edmund (4), born November 2nd, 1851; died January 11th, 1862.

Elizabeth Grammer (4), born December 27th, 1853; died January 17th, 1863.

Janet Colquhoun (4), born December 27th, 1853; married September 30th, 1879, William B. Harrison, Virginia. They now reside at Denver, Colorado. Two children, Clara Colquhoun, born September 11th, 1880, and Jane St. Clair, born August 5th, 1885, died December 22nd, 1888.

Clara Colquhoun (4), born October 18th, 1856; died October 23rd, 1875.

Robert Gilliam (4), born December 25th, 1858; married May 4th, 1887, Gretta Hayes, of Columbia, Mo., who was born June 13th, 1863. Graduated at Virginia Military Institute, and studied law at University of Virginia. Attorney and counsellor at law, and now lives at Goldfield, Nevada. [Issue below.]

Louisa (4), born October 1st, 1861; married June 25th, 1884, R. H. Cabell, of Virginia, and now lives in Virginia. Has two children, Richard H., born June 21st, 1885, and Clara W., born January 23rd, 1887.

Children of Thomas Withers (4) and Jennie Barnes.

Edmund (5), born September 7th, 1883, and died very soon.

Delos (5), born May 9th, 1885; died October 29th, 1888.

Thomas (5), born May 28th, 1886; past Midshipman U. S. Navy.

Jennie (5), born March 11th, 1888.

Colquhoun (5), born March 21st, 1892; died October 31st, 1901.

Noble (5), born September 7th, 1895.

Cleeman (5), born September 27th, 1897.

Children of Robert Gilliam Withers (4) and Gretta Hayes.

Robert Gilliam (5), born May 29th, 1899; died July 12th, 1899.

Clerimond (5), born July 12th, 1890.

Theodore Lyster (5), born May 25th, 1895.

Children of John Withers (2) and Mary Herbert Jones.
(Founders of the *Alabama* branch.)

John Wright (3), born 1796, and died young.

Susanna Claiborne (3), born July 23rd, 1798; married in 1817 Clement Comer Clay, Chief Justice of Alabama at age thirty, Governor of Alabama, Congressman, U. S. Senator; she died January 2nd, 1866. One of her sons was Clement Claiborne Clay, U.S. Senator, Senator of Confederate States, Member of Confederate Cabinet, and Commissioner of Confederate States to Canada. At the close of the Civil War, he and Jefferson Davis, President of the Southern Confederacy, were by the United States arrested as rebels and as the two foremost leaders of the rebellion, and were imprisoned for a number of months at Fortress Monroe, in Virginia. He was subsequently released without trial. He was born December 13th, 1817, married Virginia Tunstall, a beauty and wit, and died January 3rd, 1881.

William Frederick (3), born February 29th, 1800; married (*a*) in 1826 Catherine Hawkins, born September 22nd, 1804, by whom he had six children; and (*b*) Harriet Carter in 1846, by whom he had two children. He died in 1849 or 1850 in Texas. [Issue below.]

David Wright (3), born 1802; died unmarried June, 1833.

Priscilla Wright (3), born February 5th, 1804; married February 27th, 1828, William Mc Dowell, of Alabama, born October 21st, 1801; she died February, 1877.

Augustine Jones (3), born January 6th, 1806; married October 8th, 1834, Mary Woodson, of Alabama, born June 4th, 1815; he died at Huntsville, Alabama. [Issue below.]

Ann Eliza Ward (3), born March 8th, 1811; married November 14th, 1838, F. J. Le Vert, of Alabama, born July 11th, 1791, died November 30th, 1869; she died February 29th, 1880.

Mary Dorothy (3), born August 22nd, 1812; married, 1833, Robert W. Withers (3); died within the last few years.

Jones Mitchell (3), born January 12th, 1814; married January 12th, 1837, Rebecca Eloisa Forney, of Alabama, born July 20th, 1818. He was a cotton broker in Mobile, Alabama, and a Major-General in the Confederate Army. [Issue below.]

Maria Herbert (3), born 1817 or 1819; married February 2nd, 1860, Anastasius Meneos, a Greek and an Episcopal clergyman. She died in 1867 without children.

Children of William Frederick Withers (3) and his first wife, Catherine Hawkins.

John (4), lived and died at San Antonio, Texas, leaving children.

Susanna Claiborne Clay (4), born July 13th, 1829.

William Frederick (4), born July 29th, 1832.
Caleb Hawkins (4), born August 30th, 1835.
Mary McClelland (4), born May 4th, 1837.
Catherine Hawkins (4), born June 24th, 1839.
Clement Augustine (4), born February 5th, 1842.

Child of William Frederick Withers (3) and his second wife, Harriet Carter.

Thomas Champ (4), born April 13th, 1849.

Children of Augustine Jones Withers (3) and Mary Woodson.

Augustine Jones (4), born September 17th, 1836; died unmarried October 21st, 1861, in the Confederate Volunteer Service.
Philip Woodson (4), born December 10th, 1838; died April 8th, 1839.
Mary Woodson (4), born June 6th, 1840; married May 31st, 1873, Henry P. Huff.
Maria Florence (4), born July 15th, 1842; died August 2nd, 1844.
Susanna Clay (4), born January 26th, 1845; married September 4th, 1866, James Bradley White, born February 22nd, 1845.
Philip Woodson (4), born May 12th, 1847.
Lawson Clay (4), born January 7th, 1849.
Maria (4), born August 29th, 1851; married April 21st, 1873, Alexander White; died May 28th, 1878.
George Bailey (4), born October 22nd, 1853; died unmarried July, 1881.

Children of Jones Mitchell Withers (3) and Rebecca Eloisa Forney.

Harriet Brevard (4), born March 2nd, 1838; married Daniel Huger.
Mary Jones (4), born July 16th, 1839; died March 23rd, 1841.
Daniel Forney (4), born January 3rd, 1841.
Mary Jones (4), born August 29th, 1843.
Priscilla McDowell (4), born July 16th, 1845.
Jones Mitchell (4).

N.B.—The above genealogies do not carry out the issue of females; but it may be noted that Mary Timberlake Withers (daughter of Thomas Withers and Elizabeth Grammer), who married Roger B. Atkinson, had a daughter Elizabeth, who married the *Right Rev. Henry Champlin Lay*, Bishop of Arkansas, and later Bishop of Easton, Maryland. One of her children, Henry C. Lay, has given me much information concerning the American Withers.

It will interest English, and especially Hampshire readers of these notes to know that another child of Mary Timberlake Withers and Roger Atkinson, namely Thomas Withers, who died in 1872, was the father of Mary Withers Atkinson, who married J. Bonham-Carter, Esq., of Adhurst St. Mary, near Petersfield, whose sad death, January, 1906, followed so soon by that of his widow, Hampshire people deplore.

There are, of course, many others in America who bear the name Wither or Withers, whose families are not mentioned in the above genealogies, *e.g., Mr. Henry M. Withers*, Heist Buildings, Kansas City, Mo., who says that his first American ancestor was a General in Cromwell's Army, who came to Virginia at the time of the Restoration, and who was the father of five sons. Other members of the Wither or Withers family will no doubt pardon the compiler of this history if he has found it impossible to trace them all out; but he has little doubt that future researches will enable him to trace the connection with their English ancestors of the two Withers who came to Virginia in the time of Charles I. It is not unlikely that the story of the presentation of the elk's horns will resolve itself into the common custom of those earlier times of tenure of land by yearly or periodic service of some simple character, such as a flag or a rose or a sparrow hawk (see Appendix I). The land in Virginia may well have been granted by Charles I to two loyal Withers by the feudal service of a pair of elk horns.

APPENDIX I.

NOTICES OF WITHER

TAKEN FROM ANCIENT DOCUMENTS (1086—1413).

SUMMARY OF APPENDIX I.

Extracts from Ancient Documents, A.D. 1005—1413.

1.—Documents referred to.

2.—Wither of the Domesday Survey.

3.—Wither of Gloucestershire.

4.—Wither of Staffordshire.

5.—Wither of Herefordshire.

6.—Wither of various other Counties (excluding Hampshire).

APPENDIX I.

Extracts from Ancient Documents, A.D. 1005—1413.

BEFORE giving abstracts of various notices of persons of the name of *Wither* taken from ancient documents, mainly in the Record Office, between the reigns of Kings Ethelred II and Henry IV inclusive (979–1413), I desire briefly to explain the documents referred to under initials.

Inquisitiones post mortem.

(1.) *Inquisitiones post mortem*, or *Escheats*, of which there are two series: (*a*) the Chancery series begin in the early part of the reign of Henry III, A.D. 1216; (*b*) the Exchequer series begin Edward I, A.D. 1272. They were taken by virtue of writs from the Sovereign to the Escheator of each county or district, who was directed to summon a jury on oath to enquire what lands any person (especially the "tenants in capite") died seised of, and by what rents or services the same were held, who was the next heir, and of what age, that the king might be informed of his "escheat" or "wardship." They are the best evidences of descents of families and of property.

Subsidy Rolls.

(2.) *Subsidy Rolls* are records of the Court of Exchequer. They are of two kinds, lay and clerical. Some of these rolls begin as early as Henry III, but most counties have none before the middle of the reign of Edward I. They are of great value both to the genealogist and to the topographer, as they contain lists of the principal inhabitants of every parish, with the amount at which they were taxed, whether in land or goods, thus affording a clue to their position in life, and to the part of the country from which they came.

Hundred Rolls.

(3.) *Hundred Rolls*, taken under a commission dated 2 Edward I (1274) to enquire about abuses which had grown up during the reign of Henry III, concern rights of manor, free warren, chase, fishery, frank pledge, etc. They give the (*a*) county, (*b*) hundred, (*c*) manor, (*d*) lord of the manor, (*e*) free tenants, villein tenants, cottarii, socage tenants. A sequel to these rolls are the *Placita de quo Warranto*, or trials to test the justice of the claims mentioned in the Hundred Rolls.

Testa de Nevill.

(4.) *Testa de Nevill* contains an account of the "tenants in capite" from the time of King John, A.D. 1199.

Book of Aids.

(5.) *Book of Aids*, dated 20 Edward III (1327), gives an account of the knights' fees for nearly every county.

Charter Rolls

(6.) *Charter Rolls* begin with 1 John, A.D. 1199, and practically end with last year of Richard II, A.D. 1399. They include the "inquisitiones ad quod damnum," and contain grants of fairs, markets, licences in mortmain and various privileges.

Close Rolls.

(7.) *Close Rolls*, so called because they are registers of sealed or closed letters to individuals on various matters of the highest interest to the genealogist, *e.g.*, orders to the sheriffs, directions for collecting subsidies, assignments of dower, etc.

Patent Rolls.

(8.) *Patent Rolls*, in distinction to above, were "patent" or open to every one to read and take notice, extend from 3 John (1201), and contain innumerable grants of offices and lands, etc.

Fine Rolls.

(9.) *Fine Rolls*, which begin 6 John (1205), are records of the Court of Chancery of writs of seisin on heirs doing their fealty or homage for the lands of a deceased, custody of heirs, livery of seisin, of dower, licence to remarry, to leave England, etc., etc.

Feet of Fines.

(10.) *Feet of Fines*, which begin in the reign of Richard I (1189–1198) and cover an unbroken period of over six centuries, having no parallel in the records of any other country, are practically deeds of conveyance of land. A "fine" was so called, as Blackstone defines it, "because it put an end (finis) not only to the suit then commenced but to all other suits concerning the same matter." "Feet" refers to the title of the records, "Fines sive Pedes (feet) Finium." They are of the utmost value to the topographer and to the genealogist, and the earlier "fines" give minute accounts of the transfer of advowsons and manors at a date when deeds are excessively rare.

There are other public records, *e.g.*, the *Plea Rolls* and the *Coram Rege Rolls*, which are referred to in the undermentioned *Wither* extracts, which I need not explain: and for the character of these and other documents I take this opportunity of expressing my indebtedness to Mr. Walter Rye's *Records and Record Searching*, and to Mr. Thomas Astle, late "Keeper of the Records."

Kemble's Codex Diplom., Vol. iii, p. 346, l. 8.

In a charter of Æthelred, dated 1005, one of the witnesses signs his name as "Ego Wiðer minister." Here ð is the symbol for "th." [See Introduction: "the name Wither."]

From the Domesday Survey, A.D. 1086.

NORF.

*   *   *   *   *   *   *

Sir Henry Ellis' Index. (Folio 157.)

Træ Witt de Warenna. H de Ensforda. Stinetuna. Rardulfus ten⁹. quam tenuit *Wither*. i. lib. hõ. t. r. e. iii. car. træ. sep. ix. vill. xxxviiii. bor. 7 iii. s. sep̃. iii. cã in dnĩo. 7. viii cã. hoũ. 7 iiii. ac̃. p̃ti. silũ. c. por. 7 i. mol. sep̃. ii. r. 7. xx. añ. 7. xl. por. 7. cxx. oũ. 7 xxvii. cap̃. 7. iii. uasa apũ. i. ecclesia. xiiii. ac̃. Et. xiiii. soc̃. lxxx. ac̃. sẽp. iiii. car̃. silũ. x. por. 7. i. ac̃ p̃ti. 7. i. bor. duos ex h soc̃ tenebat R. qndo forisfec̃. & habebañ duo decim. ac. & ual. xx. đ. inť totũ. tc̃ ual. c. sol. m. vii. lib. & hť. leug̃ in long̃. 7 dim̃ in lato. 7 redđ. xi. đ. ingeldũ regis.

Translation.

NORFOLK.

The lands of William de Warenna. Hundred of Ensford. Stinetuna is held by Rardulf which *Wither* held. In the time of King Edward, 1 freeman 3 ploughlands then as now, 9 villeins, 38 bordars, 3 slaves, three ploughs on the demesne, 8 ploughs belonging to the men, 4 acres of pasture, woodlands for 100 swine, 1 mill then as now, 2 rounceys, 20 geese, 40 pigs, 120 sheep, 27 goats, 3 hives of bees, one church with 14 acres. Also 14 sokemen with 80 acres then as now, 4 ploughs, woodlands for 10 pigs, one acre of meadow, one bordar. Two of the sokemen Rardulf held when he made forfeiture, and they had 12 acres and were worth 20 pence, while the whole value of the land was worth 100 shillings, now 7 pounds, and it has one league in length and half in breadth, and pays 11 pence in tax to the King.

NORF.

Hac forda. turold̄. tenet. qd̄ tenuit *Wither*. i. lib̄. hō & i. car̄. t̄ræ. 7 dim̄· sep. vi. vill̄. 7. x. bor̄. 7. i. s. sēp. ii. cā in dn̄io. 7. iii. car̄ hōū. 7. iiii. ac̄. pti. silū. lx. por. Et. i. soc̄. xi. ac̄. t̄ræ. 7. dim̄. car̄. i. mol̄. qn. rec̄. iiii. r. m°. iii. 7. x. an. 7. xl. por. 7 lx. ou. m°. l. vi. uasa apu. 7. i. eccl̄a. ix. ac̄. 7. ii. ac̄. pti. sēp. ual̄. l. sol̄. 7 h̄t. v. quar̄ in long̃. 7 iii. in lato. 7 redd̄. iiii. d̄. qc̄qs ibi teneat. (Folio 157, *b.*)

Translation.

NORFOLK.

Hacforda is held by Turold which *Wither* held. 1 freeman 1½ ploughlands then as now, 6 villeins, 10 bordars, 1 slave, then as now 2 ploughs on the demesne, 3 ploughs belonging to the men, 4 acres of meadow, woodlands for 60 swine. Also one sokeman with 11 acres of land, ½ a plough [*i.e.*, 4 oxen], 1 mill when it was taken over, 4 rounceys [*i.e.* hack horses] now 3, 10 geese, 40 swine, 60 sheep now 50, 6 hives of bees, 1 church with 9 acres, 2 acres of meadow, then as now it was worth 50 shillings, it has 5 furlongs in length and 3 in breadth and pays fourpence for whoever he may hold there.

WITHER OF GLOUCESTERSHIRE.

A.D. 1220—1379.

A continuous series of references in ancient charters (temp. Henry III) confirm privileges, appoint to offices and record properties, "which their ancestors had had" in the forest of Dene (Gloucestershire) and in the manor and town of S. Briavels, near Coleford, and in other parts of the county, to individuals bearing the name of *Wither*, or *Wyther*, *e.g.*:

In 1220 *Richard Wither* and *Roger Wither* are to have their forges in the forest for dead and dry wood [no doubt for making charcoal], "as they had them in the time of K. John and Richard (I)." (Close Roll, 5 pt. i, m. 19.)

Close Roll, 10 Hen. III, m. 11, m. 28.

In 1225 this Richard is appointed with others "to keep the peace in the forest of Dene." In the same year *Hugh Wyther* is murdered.

Fine Roll ii, 33, 80, 85, 229.
Charter Roll, 35 Hen. iii, m. 2.
Forest Roll, Box 1, Roll 6.

Between 1249–1251 we find "*Philip Wyther*, the son of Hugh Wyther," "constabularius, wodewardus viridarius et custos foreste sub Comite Warrwice" [Earl Warwick]; but he and his brothers Alexander and Adam seem to have got into trouble about hunting rights. Hugh Wyther gave his son Philp a carucate of land in Newland.

Charter Roll, 36 Hen. III, m. 20.
Forest Roll, Box 1, Roll 6.
Inquis. post mortem, 54 Hen. III, File 38.
Charter Roll, 55 Hen. III, m. 7; *vide* also Rudder's History of Gloucestershire, pp. 307, 498, 527.

By the inquisition post mortem, A.D. 1270, after the death of *Walter Wyther*, who held of the king in chief, the manor and serjeantry of the balliwick of St. Briavels, with considerable land also in Caldewalde and in Hewelsfield, together with the manor of Sydneye, all in the forest of Dene, are shown by the Charter and Forest Rolls to have belonged to *Walter Wyther and his ancestors from the time of King John*. Walter Wyther died at his house at Sydneye, 30th September, 1270, when his heirs were declared to be his twin daughters, *Sibilla*, wife of Robert de Brunshope, and *Elizabeth*, wife of William Buter, and their son William, then aged six years.

Hund. Roll, Co. Gloucester, vol. i, p. 175.

In the next reign, 4 Edward I, 1275, we find *Roger Wyther* holding land of the King in chief in the hundred of Botlowe (Co. Gloucester).

Inq. a.q. dam., 2 Edw. II, No. 112.
Patent Roll, 3 Edw. II, m. 19.

In 1308 *Robert Wyther* holds the manor of Hulle and lands and rents in Berkeley, Pœhampton, and Bevynton (co. Gloucester), which he and his wife Sibyl convey in 1310 to the Abbot and Convent of Kingeswode (Forest of Dene).

Patent Rolls, 12 Edw. II, pt. ii, m. 19 *d*.
Patent Rolls, 15 Edw. II, pt. i, m. 15 *d*.
Patent Rolls, 19 Edw. II, pt. ii, m. 21 *d*.
Patent Rolls, 20 Edw. II, pt. ii, m. 28 *d*.

In 1319 *John Wyther*, of Launtony, is mentioned as hunting in the park of Painswick, belonging to the Earl of Pembroke, and in 1341 *William Wyther*, of Upton St. Leon, as hunting in the same place.

In 1345 *John Wyther*, of Herthull, is commissioned to arrest trespassers in the forest of Dene.

Forest Roll, Box 1, No. 10.

In 1374 *John Wyther* is one of the jurors (all of whom are Gloucester men) in an inquisition relating to the chase of Kingswode.

Fine Roll, 3 Rich. II, m. 30.

In 1379 *John Wyther, Co. Gloucester*, is one of the sureties for the custody of the Priory of Newwent.

Suggested Pedigree from above extracts.

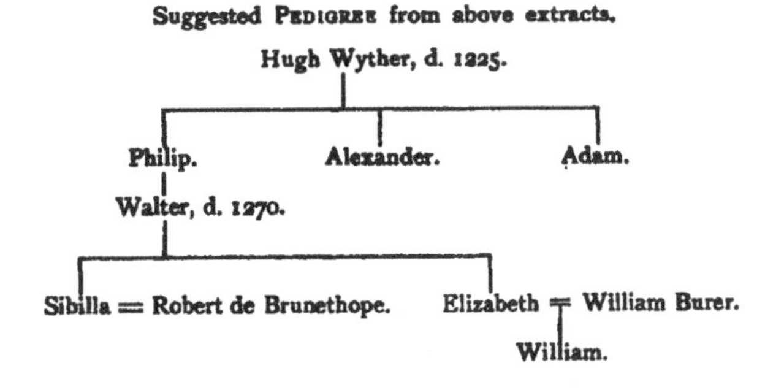

WITHER OF STAFFORDSHIRE.

A.D. 1250—1412.

Henry de Hulmes to the Abbot and Convent of Dieulacres, quitclaims his manor of Upper Hulme and a portion of the land called Pescloudes lying by the Roches "juxta rupem" in the parish of Leck (Co. Stafford) with warrant in consideration of 27 marks for gersom.

Dieulacresse Charters, Cheshire, No. cviii, undated, temp. Hen. III, circa 1250. See the Ancestor, Vol. vi.

Witnesses, *William Wyther*, and Robert de Cheltelton, *Knights*.

A.D. 1292.—Writ to the Escheator, South of Trent, to take into the King's hands the lands of William, son of *Roger Wyther*, tenant in chief.

Fine Rolls, 21 Edw. I, m. 18.

In January, 1293, Robert Bek granted land and rent in Maddeleye Alfo to *William Wyther* and Orabilla his wife, for their lives, the same to revert after their deaths to the said Robert and his heirs.

Feet of Fines, Stafford, 21 Edw. I.

In the same year [1293] John de Grendon and Joan his wife granted to *William Wyther*, and his heirs, a messuage and land in Ouere Matherfeud, for which he gave them a sparrow hawk.

Feet of Fines, Stafford, 21 Edw. I.

On the same date [Jan., 1293] Reginald son of Reginald de Legh granted a messuage and land in Calton to *William Wyther* and *Orabilla* his wife, for their lives, by rent of a rose, with reversion to himself and his heirs.

Feet of Fines, Stafford, 21 Edw. I.

On the 3rd of February, 1293, Ralph de Munjoye and Isold his wife granted to *William Wyther* land in Matherfeud, for which he gave them a sparrow hawk.

Feet of Fines, Stafford, 21 Edw. I.

On the 20th of January, A.D. 1295, Henry, son of Richard Inthelane of Matherfeld, and Julia his wife granted to *William Wyther* a messuage and land in Swynesscogh, for which he gave them seven marks of silver.

Feet of Fines, Stafford, 23 Edw. I.

Two years earlier, in Hilary Term, 21 Edw. I [A.D. 1293], we find *William Wyther* serving on a jury in a suit touching the manor of Great Wyrleye, Co. Stafford.

Placita de Quo Warranto, 21 Edw. I, Rot. 31.

In October, A.D. 1295, an order was given to acquit *William Wyther* of £21. 12*s.* 8*d.* which he owed to the Exchequer, as the King has pardoned him at the instance of his brother Edmund.

Close Roll, 23 Edw. I, m. 4.

On the same day *William Wyther* [Sir W. W. the judge] and *Agnes* his wife, late *the wife of William de Ipstanes* were acquitted of £21. 12*s.* 8*d.* due to the Exchequer for the arrears of the £10 by which Agnes made fine with the King to marry whom she pleased, provided he was a subject of the King, and of the 50 marks by which she made fine with the King for having the homage of John, son and heir of the said William de Ipstanes. Her dower as widow of William de Ipstanes was only granted to her, on her taking oath not to marry without the King's licence.

Close Roll, 23 Edw. I, m. 4.

Close Roll, 21 Edw. I, m. 10.

In November, A.D. 1303, commission of oyer and terminer was issued to *William Wyther* and others by jury of the counties of /Derby, Stafford, Leicester,

Patent Roll, 32 Edw. I, m. 29*d*.

Warwick and Wilts, touching persons who entered the free chases of Thomas Earl of Lancaster.

Feet of Fines, Stafford, 34 Edw. I.

In January, A.D. 1306, Reginald son of Reginald de Legh granted a messuage and land in Calton to *William Wyther* for £100.

Patent Roll, 13 Edw. II, m. 36 *d*.

In August, A.D. 1319, the Abbot of Burton upon Trent complained that *Walter Wither of Ilum* and Joan his wife, and *Philip*, *Hugh*, *William* and *John* his sons, *Nicholas Wyther* of Thorpe, and others, went by night to his manor of Ilum Co. Stafford, broke the gates and drove away cattle.

Feet of Fines, Stafford, 17 Edw. II.

A few years afterwards, January, A.D. 1324, *Hugh* son of *Walter Wyther*, and Ellen his wife rented four messuages and land in Ilum of Walter Wyther of Ilum and Joan his wife, and of the heirs of Joan, with remainder, if they die without heirs, to William brother of the said Hugh.

Originalia Roll, 17 Ed. II, Rot. 34.

The said Hugh and Ellen had a suit at York in the same year against Walter Wyther of Ilum and Joan his wife (1324) concerning messuages and lands in Ilum, probably those mentioned above.

Close Roll, 17 Edw. II, m. 3 *d*.

In July, A.D. 1324, *Sir Thomas Wither, knight*, William de Ipstanes, and others, acknowledge that they owe to John de Kynardeseye £20; to be levied, in default of payment, of their lands and chattels in counties Stafford and Derby.

Lay Sub. Roll, Stafford, 177/1.

In the beginning of the next reign, 1 Edward III [A.D. 1327–8], we find several persons of the name of Wyther living in the hundred of Totmonslow, co. Stafford, as in that year *John Wyther* of Roucestre, *Walter Wyther* and *Hugh Wyther* of Okouere and Ilom paid varying amounts towards the subsidy granted to the King. John de Ypstanes of Ipstanes, and John de Ipstanes of Casterne and Wetton also contributed to this subsidy. The two latter are mentioned as paying their share towards the subsidy collected in the same hundred six years later, 6 Edward III [A.D. 1332–3].

Lay Sub. Roll, Stafford, 177/2.

Coram Rege Roll, 272, 2 Edw. III, m. 11 *d*. (2nd Nos.).

In Easter Term, A.D. 1328, William, son of *William Wither*, John de Ipstanes, William de Ipstanes and Philip de Ipstanes were acquitted of the charge brought against them by Isabel, widow of Richard de Picheford, of having caused the death of her husband.

Close Roll, 3 Edw. III, m. 11.

In September, A.D. 1329, the King ordered the Sheriff of Stafford to restore to *Agnes, widow of Thomas Wyther*, a messuage and land in Calton and Onemastmathefeld which had been taken into the King's hands by reason of the disobedience of the said Thomas. He and his wife Agnes had acquired the premises in June 1324 from William de Ippestanes, and had continued their joint seisin until the tenements were taken into the King's hands.

Feet of Fines, Stafford, 17 Edw. II, Case 209, File 12, No. 52.

Patent Roll, 13 Edw. III, pt. ii, m. 7.

A few years later in October, A.D. 1339, two men named Broun were pardoned for causing the death of *Philip Withir* of Ylom, presumably the same Philip who with his father, Walter Wyther of Ilom, and brothers, was accused by the Abbot of Burton-upon-Trent of trespass.

In A.D. 1369 Sir Nicholas Beekes claimed lands in Calton, which he said descended to him from his great grandmother Lettice, who inherited them from her mother *Orabilla, wife of William Wyther.* William and Orabilla acquired lands in Calton in 1293.

De Banco Roll (433), Hilary, 43 Edw. III, m. 38 *d.*

In A.D. 1375 we find Simon le Warde and Elizabeth his wife claiming against Agnes Narwedale the eighteenth part of the manor of Alstonefeld, which Roger de Lytelebury gave *Sir William Wither*, grandfather of the said Elizabeth, and which, after the death of him and his *son Thomas*, ought to have descended to her, as daughter and heir of Thomas.

Feet of Fines, Stafford, 21 Edw. I, No. 37.

De Banco Roll, Mich., 49 Edw. III, m. 370 *d.*

In the next reign, Richard II, there is no Wither mentioned in connection with Staffordshire. Some years later in the reign of Henry IV, A.D. 1412, Thomas Blunt and Joan his wife claim lands in Ilum. Joan, who was the daughter of William Bygge, had been married before to *John Wyther*, "*Lord of Ilum*" [probably the same John who was son of Walter Wyther of Ilum, see above]. The lands in dispute had been settled on her in dower by a deed dated 9 Richard II [A.D. 1385–6]. *William Wyther*, son and heir of the said John, had taken possession of the lands by force, but was ordered to surrender them to Thomas Blount and Joan.

Assize Roll (814), 1–14 Henry IV, m. 8 [A.D. 1399—1411].

Notes of descents taken from above extracts.

(1.)—Sir William Wyther, Kgt. = Agnes, widow of William de Ipstanes.
1250—1307.

Sir Thomas Wyther, Kgt. = Agnes.
(Acquired the Manor of Kimbolton, Co. Hereford, 1323-4, of William de Ipstanes.
Slew Sir William de Holland, 1328. Was dead in 1329.)

Inq. p. m., 17 Edw. II.

Inq. p. m., 3 Edw. III (2nd Nos.), 64.

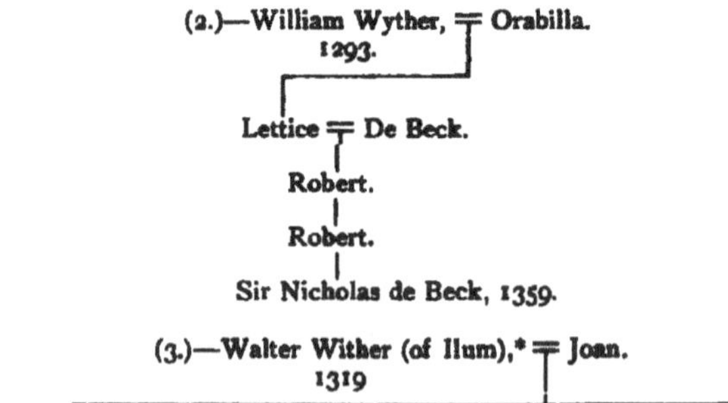

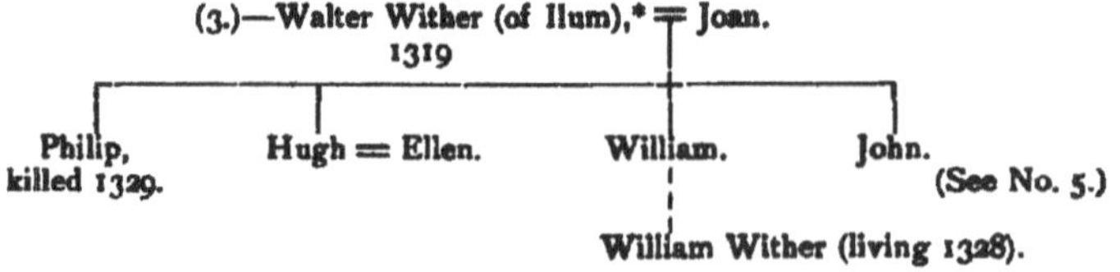

* NOTE.—"*Ilam*, or Ilum by Casterne, sometimes called Ipstones lands."

Erdeswick's Survey of Staffordshire, p. 484.

(4.)—Sir William de Wither, Kgt.
|
Thomas Wyther.
|
Elizabeth = Simon le Warde.
(living in 1375).

1385
(5.)—John Wyther, = Joan Bygge = Thomas Blount.
Lord of Ilum.
|
William Wyther.

THE FAMILY OF IPSTONES OR IPSTANES OF IPSTONES STAFFORDSHIRE.

Fine Roll, 21 Edw. I, m. 26.

8 Dec. 1292. Writ to the escheator south of Trent to take into the King's hands the lands of *William de Ipstanes*, deceased, who held of the heir of Nicholas late baron Stafford, deceased, who has died under age and is the King's ward.

Inq. p. m., 21 Edw. I, No. 134.

Inquisition taken at Stafford on Thursday before the feast of St. Thomas the Ap. 21 Ed. 1 [19 Dec. 1292]. The jurors say that *William de Ipstanes*, deceased, held the manors of Ipstanes and Foxwyst of Theobald de Verdun. He also held Scharpeclyff, Padewyck, Le Guypp, and le Wyte Halgh of Lord de Chetelton. Also the moiety of Casterne [where is Ilam] of John, Lord of Ockover. Also a fourth part of the manor of Blumenhal of the heirs of Baron Stafford.

John de Ipstanes, aged eight years at Easter 20 Ed. i [1292] is son and heir of the said William. His marriage belongs to the King.

Herald and Genealogist, Vol. vi, p. 43.

"Erdeswick, in his *Survey of Staffordshire* (ed. 1844, p. 139), noticing a place called 'Cresswell' in that county, says it was anciently possessed by a race of gentlemen of the same name, and that it afterwards came as he supposed by descent to *John de Withers*, who called himself *Ipstones*. That John de Withers, alias Ipstones, had issue Alice, wife of Ranulf Brereton. . . . In 1375–8 we meet with John de Ipstones Miles, 'alias *Sir John de Withers al' Ips.*,' who was living in Creswell temp. Edward III, his father having married the daughter and heir of Sir Henry Creswell. He was the father of William (1398–1400) whose daughter Alice carried the manor temp. Henry VII to Ranulph Brereton."

Erdeswick, Staffordshire, Ed. 1844, p. 139.

"This John de Ipstones, alias Sir John de Withers al Ips', was knight of the shire for Stafford, and was slain (1394) on his way up to Parliament."

It is evident from the above extracts from Erdeswick and from ancient documents that there was an intimate connection between the Wither and Ipstanes families in Staffordshire in the thirteenth and fourteenth centuries, and it is significant that Burke's *General Armory* describes the Ipstanes Arms as "*argent, a chevron between three crescents gules*," *i.e.*, the same as the Wither arms.

WITHER OF HEREFORDSHIRE.

(A.D. 1255—1385.)

The references to Herefordshire Withers are comparatively few. There are three undated deeds concerning land and rent in Hereford. To one of these, by which Adam Seym granted land to the monks of Dore, *William Wither* was a witness. In another he granted certain land in the town of Hereford, "where meat was sold," to Alice, late the wife of Roco, son of Mael.

Aug. Office, Misc. Books, Vol. lv, Register of Acornburye.
Ancient Deed, B. 4206.
Ancient Deed, B. 4111, fol. 57.

By the third undated deed, Denise, widow of Henry, son of Ralph, released to *William Wyther* all her right in a rent which her late husband sold to the said William, issuing from land in the street where meat was sold in Hereford. In the latter half of the reign of Henry III, A.D. 1255, *William Wyther*, citizen of Hereford, released to the Nuns of Cornbury two yearly rents issuing from land in Hereford, part lying in the butchers' market and part in Weibrugestret.

Ancient Deed, B. 4101, fol. 58.
Ancient Deed, B. 4061, fol. 61 *d*.

The next reference is of a considerably later date, when near the reign of Edward II, A.D. 1326, *Thomas Wither* of co. Hereford, with others, bailed Thomas de Everyngham out of Newgate prison.

Close Roll, 20 Edw. II, m. 7.

In the beginning of the next reign, 2 Edward III, A.D. 1328, *Thomas Wyther* and *Sybil*, his wife, sold to John Saym and Agnes, his wife, a messuage in Hereford.

Feet of Fines, Hereford, Hilary, 2 Edw. III.

In the following year, 1329, an inquisition states that *Thomas Wyther and Agnes, his wife*, had acquired the manor of Kynebalton of *William de Ippestanes*, and that they held the same from 1324 [17 Edward II] till 1329 [3 Edward III] when it was taken into the king's hands by reason of the disobedience of the said Thomas to the king. In the same year [1329] the king ordered the sheriff of Hereford to restore the manor of Kynebalton to the said Agnes, *Thomas Wyther being then dead*. [See Wyther of Staffordshire.]

Inq. p. m., 3 Edw. III (2nd Nos.), 64.
Close Roll, 3 Edw. III m. 11.

In June 1336 Robert Moryn and Isold, his wife, sold to *Richard Wyther* of Walinton a messuage and land, and the moiety of a mill in Upledene.

Feet of Fines, Hereford, Trinity, 10 Edw. III.

In the reign of Richard II, A.D. 1385, *Walter Wyther* and Alice, his wife, sold to Leonard Hakeluyte, John Burghulle, clerk, and John Forest, clerk, a messuage, land and rent in Longeford and Hompton.

Feet of Fines, Hereford, Easter, 9 Ric. II.

Extract from the will [A.D. 1413] of Leonard Hakeluyt, knight of Brugewat [Bridgewater]:—

P.C.C., 213 Marche, S.H.

"Item lego fabricie ecc̃ie paroch̃ de Lungwardyn in com̃ Hẽford̃ IX ti argenti debit̃ ecc̃ie pdicte ex legac̃ie de *Walter Wyther* et exc̃e suor̃." [See Feet of Fines of Richard II above.]

In 1427 *Robertus Wyther* is M.P. for Hereford.

Blue Book, 1st Mar., 1878.

In 1492 *Richard Wether* of London demises money to the poor and to poor prisoners in Hereford. [See complete will, Appendix III.]

P.P.C., 114 Doggett, S.H.

NOTICES OF WITHER

IN VARIOUS OTHER COUNTIES FROM THE TIME OF KING JOHN TO HENRY IV INCLUSIVE.

(A.D. 1199—1413.)

Ancient Deed, A. 6126, undated.

Grant by Lucy, relict of *John Wyther*, of Farlingtone, co. Hants, to Matilda, her daughter, of a message and land in Farlingtone, part of the land lying at Gengheham, part at "la Werepathe," and part in "la Hale," with common of pasture for certain beasts. [Hants.]

Ancient Deed, B. 926, undated.

Thomas, son of *Wither*, was a witness to an undated deed by which Hugh de Wdeuerton granted to Philip, prior of Chirbury, and the canons of that place, a messuage in exchange for the messuage in Chirbury which they had granted to him. [Salop.]

Ancient Deed, B. 1923, undated.

Walter Wither was a witness to the sale by Roger de Lenchwike to Roger de Persore, for twenty marks, of the mills of Lenchwike and of lands belonging to them in Werfurlong, Mulfurlong and Collesdene, rendering yearly to the cook of Evesham 25*s.* and forty sticks (sticas) of eels, or if so many were not taken, 1½*d.* for each stick. [Henry III.] [Worcester.]

JOHN.—A.D. 1199—1216.

Fine Roll, 6 John, m. 17.

In 1204 the Abbot of Sherborn gave one mark of silver that, if *Walter Wither*, son and heir of Walter Wyther who died in prison accused of homicide, was seized of his said father's land after his death, it should not be delivered to Richard, brother of Walter the younger, who has obtained the King's letters giving him seisin of the land. [Dorset.]

HENRY III.—A.D. 1216—1272.

Patent Roll, 8 Hen. III, m. 3.

In 1224 the King gave license to *Walter Wither*, who navigated the ship of Henry Langford, to come to England with his ship, and dwell there until Easter, 1225, and to return from thence.

Close Roll, 10 Hen. III, m. 28.

In December, 1225, a writ was issued to the Sheriff of Lincoln, at the instance of William, Earl of Albemarle, to set free on their each finding six sureties, Richard, son of Norman de Useby, and three others, named, accused of the murder of *Hugh Wyther*.

Patent Roll, 12 Hen. III, m. 3*d.*

In July, 1228, justices were appointed to take the assize of novel disseisin at Oxford on the morrow of the beheading of St. John the Baptist (30th August, 1228), which Walter de Parco arraigned against *William Wyther* of a tenement in Bensinton. [Oxfordshire.]

Coram Rege Roll, No. 33, Hilary, 13 Hen. III, m. 10*d.*

In 1229 William Wuleman claimed against *Richard Wyther* and Albreda, his wife, one toft in Marketrudham as his right. [Norfolk.]

In June, 1232, justices were appointed to take the assize of novel disseisin on the morrow of St. Mary Magdalene (23rd July), at Norwich, which Roger de Swating arraigned against *John Wither* and others of a tenement in Lecton. [Norfolk.]

Patent Roll, 16 Hen. III, m. 6*d*.

In 1249–50 *Ralph Wyther* claimed messuages of land in Shuldham against Adam, son of William de Shuldham, Simon de Lund and Agnes, his wife, and others, named. [Norfolk.]

Coram Rege Roll, No. 76, Mich., 34 Hen. III, m. 21.

In 1252 *Nicholas Wyther* was witness to a deed produced in a suit concerning land in Muncketon. [Yorkshire.]

Coram Rege Roll, No. 88, Mich., 35 Hen. III, m. 8.

EDWARD I.—A.D. 1272—1307.

In 1272 James de Shurle sued Clementine widow of Henry de Yrton for not allowing him to redeem the land of *Wm. Wyther* to whom Henry III had granted it, and claimed that the said Henry held his lands of Yrton of him. [Derby.]

Placita Coram Rege, Mich., 1 Ed. I, Roll 8.

In 1273 *Ralph Wyther* of Lenchurch contributed 2*s*., *Alfred Wyther* of Eldresfield 18*d*., and Wm. Wyther of La Pulle 3*s*. towards the subsidy. [Worcester.]

Worcester Lay Subsidy Rolls.

In 1275 *Sir William Wyther* (the judge) was a witness to a grant made by Wm. Bagod to the Bishop of Bath and Wells.

Close Rolls, 4 Edw. I, m. 18*d*.

In 1276 in a suit between Alexander de Cleseby and Emma widow of Hasculph de Cleseby, Felicia her daughter and others, the said Emma was attached by *Geoffrey Wyther* of Berford. [Yorks.]

Coram Rege Roll, No. 24, m. 27*d*., Trin., 4 Edw. I.

In 1278 there was a suit between the Prior of Alvingham and *Thos. Wyther*, and others, of a plea of trespass committed upon him by them. [Lincolnshire.]

Close Roll, 6 Edw. I, m. 4*d*.

In 1278 *Elyas Wyther*, for ½ an acre and one rod of land which he held, ought, with others, to make a bridge at Warem's. And for ½ an acre of meadow he ought, with others, to make a bridge at Lenewynesamery (Hertford) over the river Luye [? Lea]. [Herts.]

Placita de Quo Waranto, 6 Edw. I, Rot. 39.

In 1279 a commission was issued to *Wm. Wyther* [the judge] and others to deliver the gaol of Shrewsbury of Robt. de Whitinton and Wm. de la Chaumbre, imprisoned there for trespasses.

Patent Roll, 7 Edw. I, m. 11*d*.

In 7 Edward I (1278–9) *Wm. Wyther*, steward, *John Wyther* and *Simon Wyther* are among the villein tenants of the Abbot of Thorneye in his manor of Wodestone, Normancross hundred. [co. Hunts.]

Hundred Rolls (printed), Vol. ii, p. 643.

Ric. Wyther is one of his villein tenants in Fareshed hamlet, and *Wm. Wyther* is one of eighteen cottagers there, paying rent and doing service to him. [Hunts.]

Hundred Rolls (printed), Vol. ii, p. 645.

In the same year *Ric. Wyther* is one of ten "servi" in Hayle, in the hundred of Bampton, co. Oxon.

Hundred Rolls (printed), Vol. ii, p. 704.

Henry Wyther and *Roger Wyther* are villein tenants of the manor of Estcot, Chadlington hundred.

Hundred Rolls (printed), Vol. ii, p. 730.

Hundred Rolls (printed), Vol. ii, p. 753.
Hundred Rolls (printed), Vol. ii, p. 754.

Ric. Wither is one of the free sokemen of the manor of Bensinton, in the half hundred of Ewelme. Maud, his sister, holds 5½ acres of him in Wardburg. William Miles sold *Wm. Wyther* ½ acre of meadow. [Oxfordshire.]

Hundred Rolls (printed), Vol. ii, p. 412.
Hundred Rolls (printed), Vol. ii, p. 464.

In 8 Edward I [1279–80] *John Wyther* was one of the free tenants of Philip de Coleville, and *Agnes Wyther* was one of his thirty villein tenants. Both of them held ten acres of land in the hundred of Cestreton. [Cambs.] *John Wyther* holds 1½ rods of land in Impeton in the same hundred. [Cambridge.]

Rot. Wallie, 11 Edw. I, m. 4.

In 11 Edward I [1282] there is mention of foot soldiers "hominibus peditibus" in cos. Nottingham and Derby to be chosen by *Wm. Wyther*.

Feudal Aids (printed), Vol. ii, p. 15.

In 1285 *Adam Wyther* is one of the twelve jurors of the hundred of Pidleton.

Close Roll, 13 Edw. I, m. 3.

In 1285 [13 Edward I] *William Wyther*, imprisoned at St. Albans for the death of Edm. Punchardun, wherewith he is charged, has letters to the Sheriff of Bedford to send the King the names of twelve men who shall mainpern to have him before the justices at the first assize, so that he may be released in the meantime.

Close Roll, 15 Edw. I, m. 1 *d*.

In 1287 [15 Edward I] *Thos. Wither* and others came before the King, and sought to replevy their land in Chudingefeld, which was taken into the King's hands for their default against Eleanor, late the wife of Robert le Bel. [Surrey.]

Ancient Deed, A. 3864.

In 1287 Bartholomew, son of Thomas de Porta of Ipswich, granted to William, son of William le Fraunk of Belstede, a messuage in Belstede Parva, at a rent payable to *Henry Wyther* and his heirs. [Suffolk.]

Inq. a. q. dam., 15 Edw. I, File 11, No. 1.

In an inquisition taken June, 1287, on Walter de Cokeseye, who holds the manor of Goldicot, *Ralph Wither* is one of the jurors. [Worcestershire.]

Patent Roll, 15 Edw. I, m. 15.
Close Roll, 15 Edw. I, m. 6 *d*.

In February, 1287 [15 Edward I] *Wm. Wyther* [the judge] and Roger Brabazum were appointed, at the request of Edmund, the King's brother, justices in eyre of the forest in the county of Lancaster, for the period since the said Edmund had held the said forest by grant of Henry III, and in the same month a writ of summons of an eyre for pleas of the forest to be held at Lancaster before them was issued.

Patent Roll, 15 Edw. I, m. 3.

In October, 1287, a commission of oyer and terminer was issued to *William Wyther* (the judge) and Roger Brabazun, at the instance of Edmund the King's brother, touching trespasses in the said Edmund's parks and chases in Derbyshire and Staffordshire.

Patent Roll, 16 Edw. I, m. 15.
Close Roll, 16 Edw. I, m. 8*d*.

In February, 1288, *William Wyther* and Roger le Brabazun, at the request of the King's brother, were appointed justices in eyre of the forest in the County of York for the pleas, from the time of its grant to him by Henry III. And in the same month a writ of summons of an eyre for pleas of the Forest to be held at York was issued.

Patent Roll, 18 Edw. I, m. 16.
Parliamentary Roll, 18 Edw. I, Vol. i, p. 63.

In July, 1290, licence was granted to *Henry Wyther* for the alienation in mortmain to the Abbot and monks of Cumbe of 15 acres of land in Hapesford. [Cheshire.]

In November, 1290, restitution was made to *Wm. Wyther* of the custody, during the heir's minority, of the manor of Iysho (Co. Warwick) late of Nicholas, Baron of Stafford, tenant in chief; which was formerly demised by him to *William Wyther*, without licence, and therefore seized into the King's hands. [Warwick.]

Patent Roll, 18 Edw. I, m. 2.

In an inquisition taken June, 1293, concerning a grant of land to the Prior and Convent of Worcester *Ralph Wither* is one of the jurors.

Inq. ad q. d., 21 Edw. I, File 19, No. 13.

In 1292–3 21 Edw. I an inquisition was held in the hundred of Buddelegh, Co. Devon. *Alexander Wyther* was one of the jurors.

Testa de Nevill, p. 190.

In November, 1294, *Sir William Wyther* (the judge) was witness to the confirmation of a grant by Edmund the King's brother to Master Walter de Gloucestre, clerk of the manor of Kyngeshagh, Co. Nottingham.

Patent Roll, 22 Edw. I, m. 2.

In 1295 mention is made of *Wm. Wyther* and Roger Brabazon having been lately appointed by the King justices of the forest of Pykering, Co. York, which belonged to Edmund the King's brother of the grant of the late King Henry III.

Close Roll, 23 Edw. I, m. 7 and m. 1*d*.

In July, 1296, John de Betsyngton brought an appeal in the County of Dorset, against the Abbot of Bynedon, for the death of *Nicholas Wyther* his uncle. [Dorset.]

Patent Roll, 24 Edw. I, m. 12.

In 1296 (24 Ed. I) John Gayman brought an appeal in Co. Dorset against Wm. de Haliburn, Abbot of Bynindon and two of the monks, for the death of brother *Nicholas Wyther* of Bexinton, sometime monk of Binindon, his kinsman. [Dorset.]

Patent Roll, 24 Edw. I, m. 17*d*.

In 1297 the Bishop of Durham complained that his free warren at Rustington and Fordes, Co. Sussex, had been entered, and *Richard Wyther* his warrener had been assaulted. [Sussex.]

Patent Roll, 25 Edw. I, pt. 2, m. 4*d*.

In 1297 Mabel widow of Alan de Coupland claimed in dower lands in Whytington, against Blanche widow of Edmund the King's brother, Henry de Lacy Earl of Lincoln, *William Wyther and others, executors of the will of the said Edmund* (first Earl of Lancaster), and custodians of the lands and heir of John de Morthing. [Lancashire.]

De Banco Roll, No. 123, m. 102*d*., Mich., 25 and 26 Edw. I.

In 1298 John Russel, of Cambridge, was pardoned for the death of *Alan Wyther*, of Co. Cambridge.

Patent Roll, 26 Edw. I, m. 24.

In November, 1303, a commission of oyer and terminer was issued to *William Wyther* (the judge), and others, by jury of Cos. Derby, Stafford, Leicester, Warwick, and Wilts, touching persons who entered the free chaces of Thos. Earl of Lancaster.

Patent Roll, 32 Edw. I, m. 29 *d*.

In 1304 *Thomas* and *Geoffrey, sons of Richard Wyther*, of Rydley* (or Riddesley), were pardoned for the death of John, son of Nicholas Fecesause, in consideration of their services in Scotland.

Patent Roll, 32 Edw. I, m. 8.

* *Ridley* in Chester, Kent, Northumberland.

Patent Roll, 32 Edw. I, m. 6 *d.*

In 1304 (32 Edw. I) the Abbot of St. Edmunds complained that whereas he was lord of the town of St. Edmunds, and had certain rights there, ***Simon Wither*** and others usurped those rights. [Suffolk.]

Patent Roll, 35 Edw. I, m. 29 *d.*

In 1307 commission of oyer and terminer was issued to ***William Wyther*** (the judge), and others, on representation that Edm. Earl of Arundel took Ric. de la Chaumbre the elder to Oswaldestre and imprisoned him there. [The Marches of Wales.]

Parliamentary Roll, 35 Edw. I, vol. i, p. 206.

In 1306 ***Wm. Wyther*** (the judge) was appointed one of the Commissioners to hear and decide the suit between Edm. Earl of Arundel and Ric. de la Chaumbre, concerning trespassea done within the liberty of Oswaldestre in the Marches of Wales.

EDWARD II.—A.D. 1307—1327.

Close Roll, 2 Edw. II, m. 12.

In 1309 an order was made to release ***Roger Wyther***, of Evesham [Worcester], who fled to the church of Tippetre, from Colchester gaol, and to safely convey him to the said church, whither he had fled to be saved by the immunity of the church, on the information of R. Bishop of Lincoln.

Patent Roll, 5 Edw. II, pt. i, m. 25.

In July, 1311, ***John Wyther*** is nominated attorney for Wm. de Wasseburne, staying in Ireland.

Patent Roll, 8 Edw. II, pt. 1, m. 18 *d.*

In September, 1314, Ingelgram Berenger complained that ***Wm. Wither***, ***Henry Wither***, and others, broke his dykes and closes at Fordinton, Co. Dorset.

Inq. p. m. 7 Edw. II, No. 1 (Rot. origin., p. 204).

In March, 1314, an inquisition taken after the death of ***Roger Whither*** shewed that he held of the king in chief a burgage in the suburbs of the city of Exeter; and land in Whitheghen of Geoffrey de Albermarle. His son and heir was ***Adam***, who was aged eighteen years.

Close Roll, 10 Edw. II, m. 31.

In July, 1316, John Sweyn, in the king's prison at Exeter for the death of ***Wm. Wyther***, had letters to bail him until the first assize.

Patent Roll, 11 Edw. II, pt. 2, m. 18 *d.*

In May, 1318, John, son of John Toly, of Northereik, complained that ***Robt. Wyther*** and others assaulted him at Rudham, Co. Norfolk.

Patent Roll, 12 Edw. II, pt. 2, m. 13 *d.*

In May, 1319, John Bishop, of Ely, complained that ***Walter Wyther*** and others cut his grass at Brigham, Co. Norfolk, and carried it away.

Patent Roll, 12 Edw. II, pt. 2, m. 10 *d.*

In June, 1319, Hawisia, late the wife of William de Alta Ripa, appealed in the county court of Sussex against ***Wm. Wyther*** and others, for the death of her husband.

Patent Roll, 14 Edw. II, pt. 1, m. 10.

In November, 1320, Adam de London was pardoned for the death of ***Ranulph Wyther***. [No county.]

Patent Roll, 17 Edw. II, pt. 2, m. 8.

In June, 1324, a protection was granted to ***Wm. Wyther***, going with ***Thos. Wyther*** beyond the seas on the king's service. [No county.]

Patent Roll, 20 Edw. II, m. 7.

In November, 1326, ***Thos. Wyther*** was pardoned 100 marks, residue of 300 marks, whereby he made fine with the King to save his life and have his lands again.

EDWARD III.—A.D. 1327—1377.

In 1327 *John Wyther* and *Wm. Wyther*, of Eldesfelde, in the hundred of Pershore, Co. Worcester, paid respectively 16*d.* and 12*d.* towards the subsidy granted I Edw. III. [Worcestershire.]

Worcester Lay Subsidy Roll, $\frac{200}{1}$

In 1827 *Richard Wyther* was bailiff of the liberty of the Bishop of Ely. [Essex.]

Coram Rege Roll 269, 1 Edw. III, Trinity Term, m. 77.

In January, 1329, the Mayor and Sheriffs of London were ordered to attach by their bodies *Sir Thos. Wither* and others, and all who came in their train against the king at Bedeford, and to cause them to be kept safely till further orders. [Bedfordshire.]

Close Roll, 2 Edw. III, m. 2 *d.*

In February, 1329, a pardon was granted to the Abbot and Convent of St. Edmunds for acquiring lands in Bury St. Edmunds, amongst them a rent of 11*s.* from *Simon Wyther*. [Suffolk.]

Patent Roll, 3 Edw. III, pt. 1, m. 30.

In 4 Edward III, 1330–1, William, son of Hugh de Leyak, pleaded against Pagan de Waldon, and others, lands in Chaddesden, that *William Wyther* gave to Hugh, son of John de Leyak, of Chaddesden, and Orabilla, his wife, and their heirs; which lands ought to have descended after the death of the said Hugh and Orabilla to the said William as their son and heir. [Derbyshire.]

Assize Roll No. 165, m. 32.

In 1331–2 *Robertus Wyther* was M.P. for Cricklade [borders of Gloucestershire and Wiltshire].

Bluebook, 21st March, 1878.

In January, 1333, *Ric. Wyther* of Thorp [co. Leicester] complained that Hugh atte Welle of Walton, and others, assaulted him at Burton-on-the-Wold, co. Leicester, and carried away his goods. [Leicester.]

Patent Roll, 6 Edw. III, pt. 3, m. 2d.

In 1335 the Abbot of Ramsey complained that *Nicholas Wyther*, and others, came with armed force and banners flying as in war, and broke his houses at Ramsey, and did other damage. [Hunts.]

Patent Roll, 9 Edw. III, pt. 2, m. 32 *d.*

In 1337 *Walter*, son of *John Wyther*, of Wrangle, pleads against Walter, son of Richard Porter, of Wrangle, in a suit concerning some horses and oxen taken from him at Wrangle. [Lincoln.]

Coram Rege Roll No. 40, m. 63. Hilary, 11 Edw. III.

In 1338 Alan Fitz Hugh and others are defendants in a plea of trespass at the suit of *John Wyther* of Brunne. [Lincoln.]

Coram Rege Roll No. 47, m. 42 *d.*, Mich., 12 Edw. III.

In May, 1339, the Exemplification of the certificate of assignment of dower to Agnes, late the wife of John Heyroun of Enefeld, made before the escheator in the counties of Somerset, Dorset, Devon and Cornwall, on Monday before the feast of St. Gregory the Pope, 10 Ed. III [11 March, 1336], by the oath of *John Wyther* and others.

Patent Roll, 13 Edw. III, pt. 1, m. 15.

In October, 1339, *John Wyther* of Herthull was pardoned for the death of John Tomberel of Huwaldesfeld, in consideration of his service in going beyond the seas in the king's company and staying there until the present time.

Patent Roll, 13 Edw. III, pt. 2, m. 7.

The pardon is again recorded in April, 1340. [There is a Herthull in Yorkshire, Cheshire and Derbyshire.]

Patent Roll, 14 Edw. III, pt. 1, m. 19.

This John Wyther is commissioned in 1345 and 1346 to arrest trespassers in the King's forest of Dene co. Gloucester.

Patent Roll, 14 Edw. III, pt. 3, m. 35.

September, 1340. Exemplification of an inquisition taken at Conwaye, N. Wales, on Monday before St. Hilary, 13 Edw. III [10 Jan., 1340] by the oath of *Richard Wyther* and other jurors.

Patent Roll, 19 Edw. III, pt. 3, m. 10 *d.*

In November, 1845, the Abbot of Rameseye complained that whereas he had caused certain cattle doing damage to him at Rameseye to be taken by his servants; *Henry Wyther*, *Simon Wyther*, and others rescued the cattle, carried away his goods and assaulted his servants. In June, 1346, the Abbot made a similar complaint against them. [Hunts.]

Patent Roll, 20 Edw. III, pt. 2, m. 28 *d.*

Patent Roll, 19 Edw. III, pt. 3, m. 6 *d.*

In January, 1346, John Cary complained that *Walter Wyther* of Clouesworth [co. Somerset] and others assaulted him at Welles, co. Somerset, so that his life was despaired of. [Somerset.]

Inq. ad q. d., file 297, No. 13.

In January, 1351, an inquisition was taken at Ingham, co. Norfolk, when the jurors said that it was not to the prejudice of the king or any other, if *Sir Oliver Wyther* and Ralph Bygoth, parson of the church of Trunch, granted to the Prior and Convent of Hykelyngg the Manor of Pallyngg; which manor was held of John Bardolf by knt's service. [Norfolk].

Lay Subsidy Roll, Southants.

In 1352 (?) *John Whitthere* paid 2*s.* 8*d.* to the subsidy. [Southants.]

Blue Book, 1st March, 1878.

Willielmus Wyther, 1368, M.P. Dorchester.

Fine Roll, 39 Edw. III, m. 5.

In January, 1366, writs were issued for the arrest of four persons, each owing to the king 1000 *li*, in which they are bound by their writings made to *Walter Whithors* with the king's assent.

Charter Roll, 152, 43—45 Edw. III.

In November, 1369, the king granted free warren to *Walter Whithors* in all his lands of Benchesham [Surrey.]

Charter Rolls, 43 Edw. III.

In 1370 the free warren of Benchesham in the hundred of Croydon was granted to *Walter Wyther* by charter. [See Manning and Bray, Surrey.]

Fine Roll, 45 Edw. III, m. 17.

In October, 1371, the king having seized the Priory of Warham, on account of the French War, as an alien priory, grants the custody thereof to William de Barra, the Prior, at a yearly rent of 4 li., for which he finds two sureties, one of whom is *Wm. Wethir*, of co. Dorset.

Fine Roll, 48 Edw. III, m. 14.

In 1374 the king granted to *Walter Whithors*, his esquire, the custody of the castle of Haddele, except the water mill belonging thereto, for his life at ten marks yearly rent, without obligation to repair buildings within the said castle or lordship. The king had previously in September, 1354, granted him the custody of the said castle at the same rent. [Essex.]

Ancient Deeds, C. 2058.

In August, 1375, Ric. Cates, Wm. Taillour, *Simon Wyther*, and John de Hykelyng, chandler of Great Yarmouth, made a bond for £40 to Sir Edward de Wyndesouere, king of England. [No county.]

* In Cambridge, Gloucester, Hunts, Oxon, Salop, Stafford and Warwick.

RICHARD II.—A.D. 1377—1399.

In November, 1377, ***Wm. Wither of Dorchester*** was appointed collector in the county of Wilts, of the subsidy on cloth granted to the late king; with power to retain a moiety of all forfeited cloth. [Dorsetshire.]

Patent Roll, 1 Ric. II, pt. i, m. 17.

In November, 1377, ***Wm. Wyther*** and others were commissioned to arrest and deliver to the Prior of Bruton, Wm. Cary, a Canon of that Austin Priory, who is wandering about under a secular habit. [Somerset.]

Patent Roll, 1 Ric. II, pt. ii, m. 26d.

In January, 1380, John Stryk, of Chesterton,* was pardoned for not appearing to answer *Geoffery Wyther* touching a debt of £20.

Patent Roll, 3 Ric. II, pt. ii, m. 31.

In June, 1384, Robt. Smyth, of South Kilworth, was pardoned for the death of *Henry Wyther*, parson of South Kilworth, killed at South Kilworth on Ascension Day, 15th May, 1382. [Leicestershire.]

Patent Roll, 7 Ric. II, pt. ii, m. 5.

LICENSE [A.D. 1396] to ***William Wyther***, John Blount, Robert Gutton and Thomas Bertram, who are seised of eighteen messuages and twenty shillings rent in the town of *Dorchester*, co. Dorset, held of the King in burgage and worth 100*s.* yearly, to the use of the fraternity of the Blessed Mary in the Church of St. Peter in Dorchester, which messuages and rent were forfeited under the Statute of Mortmain, *to grant* the same to "Domina" Margaret Sharnesfeld. License also to the said Margaret, William, John, Robert and Thomas, and to others of the fraternity aforesaid, to *found a new fraternity* in honour of the Blessed Mary, the wardens of which shall bear the name of the wardens of the fraternity of the *Blessed Mary* in the Church of St. Peter in *Dorchester*; and of which the said Margaret shall be called the founder. License to the said wardens that they may receive the said messuages and rent from the said Margaret, and may hold the same to themselves and their successors for ever, notwithstanding the Statute of Mortmain, or that the said messuages and rent are held of the King in burgage.

Fine Roll, 20 Ric. II, m. 8.
Patent Roll, 20 Ric. II, pt. i, m. 29.

Wm. Swaghere = Isabella, died seised of lands in Kyngesweye and
died before his wife. | Brixham in her own right.

Elena, daughter and heir, died seised =

John, son and heir, feoffed ***John Whither***, who said he was feoffed by John Corbrigge, of Kingesweye, 8 Richard III, 1384. [Devonshire.]

Coram Rege Roll, No. 73, m. 30, Trin., 19 Ric. II.

In March, 1388, ***William Wyther*** was appointed one of the collectors of the subsidy in co. Derby.

Fine Roll, 11 Ric. II, m. 15.

In January, 1392, *Ralf Withors*, chevaler, was appointed one of the collectors of the subsidy in co. Berks. In February, 1392, two other persons were appointed in his place. [Berks.]

Fine Roll, 15 Ric. II, m. 17 and m. 12.

* In Cambridge, Gloucester, Hunts, Oxon, Salop, Stafford, and Harwich.

De Banco Rolls:—
Easter, 16 Ric. II, m. 328*d*.
Hilary, 17 Ric. II, m. 58.
Mich., 19 Ric. II, m. 558*d*.

In 1393, 1394, and 1395, Thos. de Cleseby, by *John Wyther*, his attorney, pleaded against John de Garton concerning a messuage in Richmond.

HENRY IV.—A.D. 1399—1413.

Mich., 10 Hen. IV, m. 465*d*.
Trinity, 12 Hen. IV, m. 192.
Trinity, 12 Hen. IV, m. 192*d*.
Trinity, 13 Hen. IV, m. 108.
Assize Roll, 2-12 Hen. IV, 2 m. 25.

. The same *John Wyther* acts as attorney in Yorkshire in 1404, 1408, and 1411, and also in Leicestershire in 1411 and 1412.

Patent Roll, 2 Hen. IV, pt. i, m. 40.

In October, 1400, Andrew Swyneford, chaplain, was presented to the Church of St. John, Devyses, with the Church of St. Mary in the same town annexed to it, in the diocese of Salisbury, void by the resignation of *John Wyther*. [Wiltshire.]

Neve's Fasti.

In November, 1400, John Wyther succeeded as Subdean of Salisbury.

NOTE.—Since the account of the Family of Ipstones (p. 184) was printed, my attention has been called to the following Pedigree of Ipstones and Brereton, published in the *History of the Ancient Parish of Leek*, Co. Stafford, by John Sleigh, p. 183.

Harliean MSS., 1535, 68 *b*, etc.

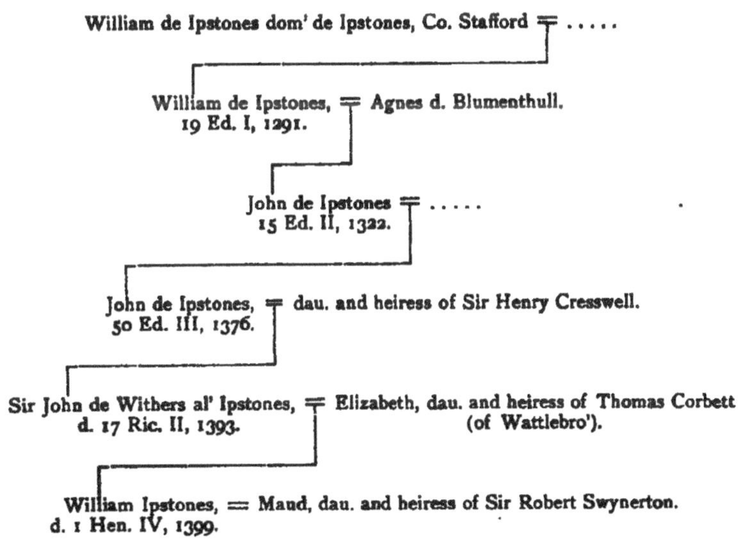

Vol. xii, pp. 80, 86, 96.

The *Staffordshire Collections*, edited by William Salt, Archaeological Society, contain many notices of Wyther and Wither not printed above: *e.g.*, Richard Wyther, bailiff of Richard de la Pole in Newburgh A.D. 1348, 1349.

APPENDIX II.

A.—EXTRACTS FROM DOMESTIC STATE PAPERS.

B.—EXTRACTS FROM HISTORICAL MANUSCRIPTS.

APPENDIX II.

A.—*Extracts from Domestic State Papers.*

(BRITISH MUSEUM.)

A.D. 1514—1534. *John Wither*, or Withers, Prebendary of Mapesbury, St. Paul's, London, and St. Martin's, Beverley, York; Rector of East Woodhay, Hants; died 1534; the friend and agent of Cardinal Wolsey.

1514.—No. 5334. Thos. [Wolsey] Bp. of Lincoln, Postulate of York. Indenture by which Anthony de Vivaldis, of Genoa, Will. Botry, mercer, and Tho. Raymond, grocer, of London, engage to pay for Wolsey's pallium and the expenses of his promotion in the Court of Rome, 2000 *l.* to be repaid by *John Withers, clk.*, and 5704 ducats by Ric. Pace and Will. Burbank, resident at Rome, to Lazarus de Grymaldis and Andrea Gentili, Genoese merchants, 18 Aug., 6 Hen. VIII. *Signed by Wolsey and Withers.* Seal attached. Latin.

1514.—No. 5396. Pace to Wolsey, Sep. 10 (Rome). Has received his letter, dated London, 25 Aug., expressing his desire that 1260 *l.* should be paid for expediting his bulls. Has not one "ducat of my late Lord's [Cardinal Bambridge] in my hands: nother the bank of Grimaldi's, nother none other had ony money of my said Lord's." All the stuff left at Burbank's departure does not amount to the sum required. The cloth that was sent out of England is not esteemed as the colors were not good. Has, however, done his best, and paid into Grimaldi's bank 4000 ducats of gold. To make up the sum will keep certain rich investments and altar cloth, which stuff did cost my late Lord 500 ducats of gold. Has ordered Burbank to present him with one other rich cloth of Arras, and written to *Wythers* to supply the sum wanting, and of his grace's desire that proper respect should be had "unto your places which be fallen into great decay."

1534.—Vol. VII, No. 105. Gilbert Burton, priest, to Lady Lisle. Mention of "*Mr. Withers'* house, a residentiary of St. Paul's." Editor's Note.—John Withers, prebendary of Mapesbury in St. Paul's, who died in 1534.

1534.—No. 1223. Sir J. Russell to Cromwell. Whereas it pleased you to write to my lord of York for the advowson of a prebend held by *Mr. Wythers* in the Collegiate Church of Beverley, for my chaplain, Manchester, and my lord replied that he never intended to give advowson of that or any other thing in his collation, but that you should have the next prebend not much above 40 *li.*, the same prebend is void by the death of *Wythers.* Though it is somewhat above 40 *l.*, I suppose it will fall within the limits of his promise. I beseech you therefore to remember my chaplain. Ampthill, 2 Oct. Signed.

1534.—No. 1252. Thomas Runcorn, priest, to Cromwell. My Lord my master [Bishop Gardiner] has conferred upon me the benefice of Estwodehay, vacant by the death of Master *Widders.* As he died intestate, much was embezzled. I sequestrated the goods, and took an inventory of the goods and debts which I send you. There was a little plate, now in the hands of a brother of Dr. Layton's, by the doctor's command, but by what authority I know not. He will not deliver it. The rest I send you. I would be glad to know your wishes.

* * * * * * *

1534.—No. 1660. *John Wethers*, Merchant Taylor, to Cromwell. The Dean of the Arches has commanded him in Cromwell's name to bring to the latter 250 mks. in ready money, and to give to Dr. Leegh the lease of his uncle, *Dr. Wether's* house,* which done he shall have ministration given him. Cannot raise this sum from his uncle's goods. Is contented that Cromwell shall have the lease to do his uncle's goods. Is contented that Cromwell shall have the lease to do his pleasure with if he will help him to obtain the stuff, plate and money "conveyed" by his servants. Supposes that John Dolman and his uncle's chamberlain, who robbed the house, have as much as 200 or 300 mks. They say some of the money belonged to Sir Robt. Garryte, priest, who was chief of their counsell in all their false doings. They have also conveyed away the will. Asks him to send letters to his uncle's debtors. The corn and cattle at his benefice of Woodhey was sold by Mr. Kyngsmell much under value. Payment of his debts is also demanded. Begs Cromwell to help him. Has got ready the 250 mks. and asks to whom he shall pay it.

1534.—No. 1661. [*John*] *Whythers.** "The value of plate and ready money, late Master *Whythers.*" Ready money, 8*s.* 1*d.* For the inventory of his goods at his parsonage of Wodhay, 17*l.* 5*s.* 7*d.* Plate, gilt, 87¾ oz. at 4*s.*, parcel-gilt, 10 oz. at 3*s.* 8*d.*, and white plate, 559 oz. at 3*s.* 6*d.* Total, 133*l.* 13*s.* 10*d.*

1535.—No. 234. List of obligations, bills, and papers in the custody of William Body, custodian of the Jewelhouse. "Bill of goods of *Dr. Wyther.*"

1535.—No. 235. "Plate embezzled by Bodye." * * * * "Beguiled Mr. Whalley by his own saying, at the weight of *Dr. Whythers'* plate," an ale pot, a goblet, a spoon, and a pair of pouch rings. * * * * A standing cup with a cover from *Mr. Whythers'* plate, * * * * a vestment and amice of *Mr. Withers.* "Saved in gold that was parted, and rascald of silver that was coined, 1½oz. Item, said to *John Whythers* that your mastership had the sapphire, the turquoise, the emerald to your use."

* John Wythers, prebendary of St. Paul's, who died in 1534.

1535.—No. 992. John Smyth, of Paules, to Cromwell. I have to advertise you of my brethren's presumptuous proposed answer to your letter for the next advowson of the vicarage of S. Giles, Cripplegate, granted unto you by consent of *Mr. Withers*, late deceased, long before his death, as Mr. Incent affirmed when he and I were with you touching our church, * * * * * * * * * * * * * 19 Dec.

Fabian Wither (goldsmith). See Pedigree II.

1537.—Vol. XII, No. 1150. Assay of silver. Jury between the King and Roger Rowlett and Martin Bowes, masters, and the King's coiners, taken in the Star Chamber at Westminster, 8 May, 29 Hen. VIII. List of names among which is "*Fabian Wether*," crossed out.

1538.—Vol. XIII, No. 1280. The King's Payments. *Fabyan Wythers* (goldsmith), servant, that gave pomegarnads 6*s*. 8*d*.

1539.—No. 403. Grants in February, 1539. Grant 20. *Fabyan Wythers*, goldsmith of London. Licence to export 40 quarters of wheat within the next three months. Westminster, 5 Feb., 30 Hen. VIII.

Vol. CXLIV, 19. *Dr. George Wither* [Archdeacon of Colchester] to Walsyngham. In favour of the strangers of the Dutch church in Colchester. Advantages of their residence in that town.

JAMES I.—A.D. 1603—1610.

1604.—Vol. VIII (p. 123). Presentation of Thos. Beresford on resignation of *Dr. Hen. Withers*, to the parsonage of Eynesford, Kent.

1623.—Vol. CXXXVII, No. 27. Chamberlain to Carleton. More feasting and dancing this Christmas than ever. The masque scenes were devised by Inigo Jones, and the masque written by Ben Jonson, but he runs a risk by impersonating *Geo. Withers*, the poet, as a whipper of the times, which is a dangerous jest. * * * London, 25 Jan.

CHARLES I.—A.D. 1625—1636.

1626.—Vol XVIII, No. 66. *William Wither* [of Manydown] to Sec. Conway, Lord Lieut. of Hants, promises that at all times of musters he will be ready to show one light horse with his rider completely armed.

1626.—Vol. XXX, No. 63. Letter from the Council to the Duke of Buckingham. In the form of letter to the Lord Lieutenants of the several counties, apprising them that it is the King's pleasure that if the persons employed to exercise the Trained Bands are willing to stay in England, their allowances from the several counties should be continued. This letter relates to *John Withers* and Emanuel Healing, who had been employed in that service in the Cinque Ports.

1628.—Vol. XCIII, No. 1. Commission out of the Court of Exchequer to Francis Windebank, *George Wither*, and two others, to examine witnesses on behalf of John Chamberlain, of Sonning, against Matthew Payne, Henry Soundy, and John Symonds. Westminster, 12 Feb.

Vol. XCIII, No. 52. Commission to *Anthony Wither* and others to find out all moneys collected by one and one half per cent., or tonnage of shipping, towards the expedition for suppressing the pirates of Algiers. Westminster, 16 Feb.

1628.—Vol. CXII, No. 76. Sec. Conway to Isabel Lady de la Warr, of Middleton (Longparish), Hants. Has received her letter in favour of *Mr. Withers* for a company. The regiment which her son commanded is disposed of to Sir Henry Whitehead, who must also have a company, but Conway will see if *Mr. Withers* may not have that company. If not, in honour of her request, he shall have another.*

1628.—Vol. CXVI, No. 42. Sec. Conway to Sir Henry Whitehead. When the Secretary was moved by Lady de la Warr to confer the company in the regiment, which was lately her son's, on *Capt. Withers*, he forebore to resolve until he had acquainted Sir Henry. Now sends the commission that *Capt. Withers* may receive it from his hands. 5 Sept.

1629.—Vol. CXLV, No. 57. Grant to *Henry Withers*, the King's servant, of the benefit of two recognizances forfeited by John Lyvesay, George Chauncey and John Munck, at Hertford Assizes, amounting to 80 *l.* in all. Westminster, 26 June.

1630.—Vol. CLXXIV, No. 97. Abstract of a commission [from the King] to *Anthony Wither* [brother of poet] and Samuel Lively to repair into the cos. of Gloucester, Wilts, Oxon, and Somerset, and the several places there where white cloth is usually made, and there to notify the commission, and inquire in a manner therein directed how the statutes for true cloth making are executed. Whitehall, 29 October.

1631.—There is a note of this commission in a list of various letters patent granted during 6 Ch. 1. Vol. clxxxvii, No. 46.

Vol. CCVI, No. 56. Statement of *Anthony Wither* concerning the opposition he received from Nathaniel Stephens, Justice of the Peace in co. Gloucester, in the performance of his commission to see to the true execution of the statutes for clothing.

No. 57.—Another similar statement of *Anthony Wither* concerning the similar opposition of Sir John Danvers.

1632.—Vol. CCXV, No. 56. *Anthony Wither*, one of the Commissioners for reforming cloth-making, to the Council. Report of his proceedings and the

* See Chap. III, pp. 22 and 24. Nicholas Wither, of Longparish. See also extracts below under years 1640—1641.

impediments cast in his way. At Bradford he was cast into the Avon by the servants of Thomas Horne, a tucker, at a place where the river was twenty feet deep, to the imminent danger of his life. Points out various defects in the statutes which should be amended.

N.B.—There are many other references in this and the following years of Ch. I concerning the commission for cloth-making and *Anthony Wither's* part therein.

1632-3.—Vol. CCXXIV, No. 21, and Vol. CCXXXVII, No. 5. Sir George Whitmore, *John Withers* and others to the Council. Report upon the present state of Bethlehem Hospital, Its history briefly sketched, and details given of diet, etc. Dr. Crooke was the master of the house.

1633.—Vol. CCXLVIII, No. 51. Sir Abraham Dawes to William Trumbull. Prays him to procure a pass for *Elizabeth Withers* to go into the Low Countries to her husband, who is an officer under Colonel Morgan. 25 October.

1634.—Vol. CCLXXIV, No. 14. Bishop Curle, of Winchester, to Sec. Windebank. Presents the suit of a nephew of his * * * who has spent much time and most of his fortunes in his Majesty's service, not without the report of spirit and knowledge in military affairs. [Endorsed by Windebank, "In favour of *Mr. Wither.*]

Vol. CCC, No. 60. A petition of John Mason, a maimed soldier, concerning his pension, in which *Withers*, treasurer for maimed soldiers, is mentioned.

Vol. CCCX, No. 6. Particulars of the yearly rent of the lands and tenements of Thomas Pennington, of Chigwell, Essex. Among others, "32 acres in the occupation of *Henry Withers* at 20*l.*"

1636.—Vol. CCCXX, No. 60. Petition of *William Withers*, clerk, rector of Thwaite, co. Suffolk, to Archbishop Laud and rest of Commissioners for Causes Ecclesiastical, concerning Robert Reeve, owner of great part of the parish, who refuses to pay his tithes and annoys the petitioners in other ways. May 9.

1640.—Vol. CCCCL, No. 84. John Ashburnham to Nicholas. Mention of *Nicholas Wither* in negotiations concerning the farm of Longparish. Westover, 14 April.

1641.—Vol. CCCCLXXIX, No. 5. Receipt by *Edward Wither* for 7*l.* 10*s.* received from Edward Nicholas by the hand of Henry Thornbourgh, to the use of Lady Cicely De la Warr for a half year's rent for the farm of Long Parish, Hants. 1 April.

1640.—Vol. CCCCLXVII, No. 113. Letters of Attorney from Edward Nicholas giving power to Richard Green to receive possession of Middleton Farm in Long Parish, for him from *Mr. Nicholas Withers.* 19 Sept.

1640-1.—Vol. CCCCLXXVI, No. 40. Richard Green to Edward Nicholas. Mention of Nicholas' farm at Longparish and of *Mr. Withers*, who "has been very earnest upon the discourse we had at London to help him to 500*l.* Sarum Close, 10 Jan.*

* See Chap. III, p. 22 and 24.

1649—1660.

1649.—Vol. II, No. 105 (p. 320). Council of State to Messrs. Betsworth, Moore and *Wither*. Authorizing them to put in execution a former order that Winchester Castle be made untenable. Whitehall, 26 Sept.

1650.—Vol. IX, No. 48 (8). The Commissioners of the Great Seal to commission *George Withers* and three others to be Justices of the Peace for county Hants. 6 May.

1651.—Vol. XVII, I. 110 (34). Militia Commissions granted by the Council of State. Jan. 13, 1651, co. Hants. Troop F. Captain *James Withers* [brother of the poet. Mayor of Basingstoke, 1650].

I. 119 (165). Commissions for Volunteers raised on alarm of invasion by Charles II.

Aug. 15, 1651. co. Hants. Troop H. Captain *James Wither*.

1652—1653.—Vol. XLV, 106. Letters and papers relating to the Navy, etc. Jan. 12. From Hum. Felsted to Adm. Com. * * Asks a warrant for *John Withers* as master of the Marigold.

1654–5.—Vol. XCIV, No. 91–8. Council. Day's Proceedings. 23 Feb. The petition and remonstrance of *George Wither* referred to Wolsey, Pickering, Jones, and four others, to consult with the trustees at Drury House and his Highness counsel learned and report.

1655.—Vol XCVI, No. 46–75. Notes of petitions referred to the Committee for petitions, on which no reports nor Council orders were given. *George Wither*, for payment of 300 *l.* out of Haberdasher's Hall, ordered by Parliament out of discoveries, he having brought in more than that by discoveries, being for interest of 700 *l.* formerly due. Noted, Money and submitted to Council, a report drawn at large. Report returned from Drury House. 17 Ap., 1655.

1655.—Vol. C, No. 55, 19. Council. Day's proceedings. 29 Aug. Order on report from the Committee on *George Wither's* petition, stating the case in full.

1658. — Vol. CLXXXI, No. 66. Council. Day's proceedings. 1 June. (13, 14.) List of Members proposed to be added to the Commissioners in co. Hants for ejecting scandalous ministers and their assistants, approved. *Wm. Wither*, of Manydown; *Geo. Wither*, of Winton.

1658.—Vol. CLXXXIII, No. 24, IV. Note of Committal of Jas. Potter, by *William Wither*, for disturbing Mr. Benthall, minister of Baghurst, Hants.

1659 — 1660. — Vol. CCXIX. Index entries of proceedings in Council. 16 Jan. *Richard Wither* to be serjeant-at-arms. [His name often occurs in this capacity in warrants of the Council of State, etc.]

CHARLES II.—A.D. 1663—1666.

1664.—Vol. XCVIII, No. 86. Privy seal dormant for 200*l.* to ***Eleanor Withers*** and Joan Halsnouth for particular services rendered to the King in his escape from Worcester. Minute. 20 May.

1664-5.—Vol. CXI, No. 71. *Capt. John Withers* to the Navy Commissioners. Sends the muster book of the Hind. Has brought several volunteers and pressed men from Aldborough, and is ready to fetch others from Scarborough. The Hind, Harwich, 30 Jan.

1666.—Vol. CLVIII, No. 111. Petition of *Elinor Withers* and Joan Halsnorth to the King for settlement of pensions of 50*l.* each, conferred on them for their services after the battle of Worcester; have received 100*l.* each, assigned to them as a gift. 14 June. (See No. 86 above.)

1666.—Vol. CLXI, No. 108. Order for a warrant for above annuities.

1689.—S. P. Dom. Petition Entry Book, 35, p. 79. Passes or Post-warrants. For *Sir William Wither* [the Lord Mayor] and five others to go to Holland. 17 May.

1690.—H. O. Military Entry Book, 3, p. 4. Warrant for a Commission for *William Withers*, senior, and many others to be deputy-lieutenants of the City of London. 1 March.

N.B.—There are numerous entries in the Domestic State Papers concerning George Wither the poet, some of which are referred to in the record of his life, Chapter V.

B.—*Extracts from Historical Manuscripts.*

(BRITISH MUSEUM.)

1558, Sept. 20.—Wells Cath. MSS. Marriage Licence without banns in favour of *Thomas Withers*, nuper Rector of Roade.

1643.—Vol. VII, p. 569. Petition of Frances Withers, wife of *Stephen Withers*, late Rector of Steering, Co. Essex. Her husband has been in prison for twelve months because he could not conscientiously obey some Parliamentary commands. Neither she nor her husband can procure the money required, and their corn (all they had to support them) has been seized in the barns. Prays relief.

1645.—VI Report L 7 VIII, 68. House of Lords. Draft order for payment of £103 to *Joanne Withers* (widow), due to Edward Withers, her late husband.

1647.—Application for an order for Dr. Aylett to institute and induct *William Withers* to the Rectory of Fakenham, Co. Suffolk. Annexed:—

(1) Certificate from the Assembly of Divines approving of Mr. Withers.

(2) Certificate from Thomas Soame and another that Mr. Withers, whom they have known for two years, has been a constant preacher of God's word, of civil and honest life, and a man of sufficient parts to officiate in the Rectory of Fakenham.

1648.—VII Report LIX, p. 282. Petition of *Antony Wither*. Complains that the Earl of Chesterfield is raising an additional building to a house in Covent Garden in such a way as will prove noisome to divers neighbours by depriving them of light and air, contrary to the covenant made with the Earl of Bedford. Prays that building may be stayed.

1648.—Vol. VII, p. 43. Application for an order for Dr. Aylett to institute and induct *Samuel Withers* to the Rectory of Wofton, *alias* Woughton upon Green, Co. Bucks. Annexed:—

Certificate that Withers, who has for twelve years past been incumbent of Honingham, Co. Norfolk, has always been of unblameable life, painful in his duties, of humble, meek, and Christian behaviour, studious of peace and of sound doctrine.

1663.—Vol. VII, p. 436 and following. Statement that *Samuel Withers*, Domestic Chaplain to Lord Byron, has been arrested contrary to privilege.

1668.—Dartmouth MSS., Admiralty. Samuel Pepys to Lord Dartmouth writes particulars concerning the Dutch Fleet and sends two letters from *Mr. Withers*, Clerk to the Fishermen's Company, giving an account of the fishermen sent down to the fleet, by which he thought that 552 men have been supplied to the fleet by the Company, besides those who have entered themselves as Volunteers.

1709.—Vol. X, p. 7. Letter of Henry Wither [of Theddon Grange] to Horace Walpole, dated at Alresford: "We got a 16th place on the Eton Foundation Election bill, which if it happens this year will be soon enough: if not, I hope we shall have a forward one the next, for our reputation in the School is very good."

APPENDIX III.

---

190 WILLS OF WITHER, BIGG, BIGG-WITHER.

CONTENTS OF APPENDIX III.

NOTE.—In addition to the above the Will of John Wether, of Manydown, (A.D. 1536,) is printed in full in the text, Chap. III, p. 26, with the abstract of that of his widow, *née* Ann or Agnes Ayliffe.

APPENDIX III.

LONDON WILLS.—PREROGATIVE COURT OF CANTERBURY.

(SOMERSET HOUSE.)

No.	Date.		P. C. C. No. and Volume.
1	1492	*Richard Wether*, of Hereford, Cit. of Lond. (in full below)	114, Doggett.
2	1506	*Thomas Wether*, of Manydown	6, Adeane.
3	1521	*Richard Wyther*, Cit. of London and Salter (in full below)	14, Manywaring.
4	1536	*John Wither*, Manydown (in full in text)	
5	1539	*Alicia Withers*, widow of Richard, Salter	29, Dingley.
6	1544	*Agnes Wether* (*née* Ayliffe), widow of 4, (abstract in text)	19, Prynning.
7	1544	*Nicholas Withers*, Citizen of London and Haberdasher	25, Spert.
8	1548	*Fabian Withers*, Citizen of London and Goldsmith ...	26, Propertwell.
9	1550	*Richard Wyther*, of West Molesley and Thames Ditton	
10	1553	*John Withers*, Citizen of London and Merchant Taylor	21, Tashe.
11	1561	*Richard Withers*, Citizen of London and Salter ...	3, Loftus.
12	1566	*William Wethere*, of Hadley, Co. Middlesex	21, Crymer.
13	1569	*Thomas Wyther*, Clerk, Parson of Hadley	
14	1569	*Thomas Withers*, Parson of Toddington, Co. Bedford ...	19, Sheffield.
15	1570	*John Wyther*, of Itchinswell, Parish of Kingsclere, Hants (abstract below)	20, Lyon.
16	1573	*Laurence Wyther*, Citizen of London and Salter, and of Ilbrewers, Somerset	10, Martyn.
17	1577	*John Withers*, Citizen of London and Salter	48, Daughtry.
18	1582	*Margery Wether* (*née* Margaret Poynter), of Manydown	31, Tirwhite.
19	1582	*Robert Wyther*, of the City of New Sarum	5, Rowe.
20	1587	*Richard Wyther*, (brother of above)	23, Spencer.
21	1589	*John Withers*, Cit. of Lond. and Merchant Taylor ...	80, Leicester.
22	1592	*John Withers*, Citizen of London and Salter	62, Harrington.
23	1593	*William Withers*, Citizen of Lond. and Merchant Taylor (son of John Wither of Manydown)	13, Nevell.
24	1595	*James Withers*, Citizen of London and Draper ...	36, Scott.
25	1597	*Jane Wyther* (widow of 23)	99, Cobham.
26	1601	*John Wether*, of Stechworth, Cambridgeshire	72, Woodhall.
27	1613	*Richard Withers*, of Frampton Cottrell, Gloucestershire	51, Capel.
28	1624	*Richard Withers*, Citizen of London (brother of George Wither, of Gray's Inn, gent.)	99, Byrde.

No.	Date.		P. C. C. No. and Volume.
29	1631	*John Wither*, of Penshurst, Kent	95, St. John.
30	1631	*Charles Wyther*, of Taunton, Somerset	138, St. John.
31	1632	*Henry Withers*, of Chigwell, Essex	72, Awdley.
32	1635	*Henry Withers*, Citizen of London and Salter ...	95, Sadler.
33	1639	*James Wither*, of Balliol College, Oxford	185, Harvey.
34	1640	*Henry Wither*, Hants Probate granted to Roger Wither	169, Admon.
35	1641	*John Withers*, of Marlborough, Wilts	21, Evelyn.
36	1645	*Henry Withers*, of Little Thonop and Chigwell, Essex ...	138, Rivers.
37	1647	*Joyce Wither*, of Newport, par. of Berkley, co. Glosc. ...	86, Fines.
38	1647	*Richard Wyther*, Somersetshire	253, Fines.
39	1648	*Oliver Wither*, of Basingstoke, Hants (brother of the poet)	22, Essex.
40	1649	*Alexander Wither*, of West Quantoxhead, co. Somerset ...	173, Fairfax.
41	1650	*Stephen Withers*, Dr. of Shedring, co. Essex	47, Pembroke.
42	1652	*Thomas Withers*, Abbey of Mondard, Leicester ...	94, Bowyer.
43	1654	*Humphrey Wither*, Citizen and merchant, London (cousin of above)	329, Alchin.
44	1657	*Antony Wither*, of Winchfield, Hants	253, Admon.
45	1657	*Henry Wyther*, of Trunch, Norfolk	529, Ruthen.
46	1658	*Roger Wither*, of Kingsclere (grandson of Nicholas Wither, of North Oakley)	188, Wotton.
47	1658	*James Wyther*, Mayor of Basingstoke (brother of poet)...	416, Wotton.
48	1658	*Charles Withers*, of North Stanbridge, Essex	540, Wotton.
49	1659	*John Withers*, Citizen of London and draper	16, Pell.
50	1662	*George Wither*, of Winchester (father of Mary Wither of Manydown), (abstract below)	56, Laud.
51	1668	*Richard Wither*, of Hadwick, Hurstbourne Priors, Hants	55, Hene.
52	1680	*Edward Wither*, of Stome Hill, Salop	101, Bath.
53	1682	*Eliza Wither*, of Bentworth (widow of the poet), (abstract below)	11, Drax.
54	1694	*Eliza Watson*, (widow of Gilbert Wither, of Hall) ...	258, Box.
55	1696	*Antony Wither*, of St. Martins-in-the-Fields, London (son of George Wither, of Stoke, Guildford)	85, Bond.
56	1699	*Eleanor Fulkes* (mother of Mary, wife of Thomas Wither, of Andwell)	132, Pett.
57	1700	*Thomas Wither*, of Andwell (abstract below)	31, Dyer.
58	1700	*Francis Wither*, of Hannington, Hants	91, Noel.
59	1703	*John Withers*, of Bristol	61, Degg.
60	1712	*Maria Wither* (sister of Charles Wither, of Hall) ...	40, Barnes.
61	1721	*Sir William Withers* (Lord Mayor of London)	39, Buckingham.
62	1745	*Frances Wither* (*née* Wavell, widow of Charles Wither, of Oakley Hall)	296, Bettesworth.
63	1752	*Andrew Wither*, of Gray's Inn (brother of Charles Wither, of Oakley Hall)	111, Bettesworth.

WILLS AT WINCHESTER PROBATE REGISTRY.

No.	Date.	
1	1528	*Johanna Wither* (*née* Mason), of Manydown.
2	1539	*John Wither*, of Burghclere.
3	1539	*Elizabeth Wither* (mother of above; will below).
4	1544	*Otho Wither*, of Basingstoke.
5	1545	*Roger Wither*, of Heckfield.
6	1547	*Thomas Wither*, of Kingsclere.
7	1551	*Richard Wither*, of Wherwell.
8	1559	*John Wyther*, of Hurstbourne Tarrant.
9	1560	*John Wither* (index; will missing).
10	1569	*Richard Wither*, of Westover, Wherwell.
11	1577	*Richard Wither*, of Manydown (married Margaret Poynter).
11*a*	1582	*John Wyther*, of Ramsdell.
12	1588	*James Wither*, of Leckford, near Andover.
13	1599	*Peter Wither*, of Itchinswell (son of Peter).
14	1599	*Gilbert Wither*, of Dummer (abstract below).
15	1602	*Henry Wither*, of Itchinswell.
16	1610	*David Wither*, of East Woodhay.
17	1614	*Edith Wither* (widow), of Sherborne St. John.
18	1620	*John Wither*, of Manydown (index; will missing).
19	1622	*George Wither*, of Leckford, near Andover.
20	1622	*Peter Wither*, of Itchinswell.
21	1630	*George Wither*, of Bentworth (father of the poet).
22	1637	*Nicholas Wither*, of Longparish.
23	1640	*Thomas Wither*, of Wherwell.
24	1642	*William Withers*, of Fullerton.
25	1647	*Robert Wither*, of Denemede, Hambledon.
26	1647	*Ellen Withers*, of Romsey.
27	1661	*George Wither*, of Uppen Lodge, Wherwell.
28	1667	*George Wither*, of Hall (Oakley Hall).
29	1676	*Gilbert Wither*, of Hall (Oakley Hall).
30	1676	*Thomas Withers*, of Andover.
31	1677	*William Withers*, of Wickham, Hants.
32	1681	*Francis Withers*, of Wherwell.
33	1683	*Nicolas Wither*, of Bramshot.
34	1687	*Thomas Wither*, of Dummer.
35	1694	*John Wither*, of Tangley.
36	1695	*George Wither*, of Hannington.
37	1698	*Charles Wither*, of Hall (Oakley Hall).
38	1708	*Thomas Withers*, of Longparish (admon.).
39	1711	*Barbara Wither*, of Bramshot.
40	1721	*George Wither*, of Romsey.

No.	Date.	
41	1732	*Dorothy Wither*, of Wyford, Pamber.
42	1752	*Richard Withers*, of Romsey.
43	1753	*Richard Withers*, of Romsey.
44	1754	*Elizabeth Wither*, of Upnateley (widow of William Wither of Andwell).
45	1756	*Peter Withers*, of Romsey.
46	1756	*John Withers*, of Romsey.
47	1762	*George Withers*, of White Nap, Romsey.
48	1772	*John Withers.*
49	1778	*Richard Withers*, of Romsey.
50	1782	*John Withers*, of Romsey (the elder).

In addition to the above wills of the P.C.C. at Somerset House, and of the Probate Registry at Winchester, the following wills are in the possession of the *Rev. R. F. Bigg-Wither*:—

WITHER.

No.	Date.	
1	1653	*William Wither* i, of Manydown.
2	1671	*William Wither* ii, ,,
3	1679	*William Wither* iii, ,,
4	1692	*Joan Wither* (*née* Geale, widow of William Wither ii).
5	1700	*Mary Wither* (widow of William Wither iii).
6	1700	*Mary Wither* (spinster, daughter of above).
7	1701	*Thomas Wither*, of Andwell (father of William Wither iv).
8	1733	*William Wither* iv, of Manydown (will below).
9	1735	*Elizabeth Wither* (*née* Nicol, widow of above; will below).
10	1789	*William Wither* v, of Manydown.

BIGG.

11	1670	*Richard Bigg*, of Hainshill, Berks.
12	1677	*Richard Bigg*, of New College, Oxford (in full below).
13	1711	*Mary Bigg* (*née* Wade, widow of Richard of Hainshill).
14	1717	*Dorothy Bigg* (*née* Wither).
15	1724	*Lovelace Bigg* (father of Warden Bigg and Walter Bigg).
16	1740	*Henry Bigg*, Warden of Winchester College (abstract below).
17	1770	*Walter Bigg*, Rector of Worting (father of Lovelace Bigg-Wither) (memorandum instead of will).

BIGG-WITHER.

18	1813	*Lovelace Bigg-Wither*, of Manydown (abstract below).
19	1833	*Harris Bigg-Wither*, of Manydown.
20	1874	*Lovelace Bigg-Wither*, of Manydown and Tangier.
21	1586	The will of *George Wither of Dummer*, third son of John Wither of Manydown, and grandfather of George, the first Wither of Hall, is among the Oakley Hall archives. It was proved 16th January, 1587, and is printed in full below.

LIST OF WILLS AND ADMINISTRATIONS CALENDERED IN THE INDEX LIBRARY, BRITISH MUSEUM.

Lichfield.

1587 *Wither, George.*
1588 *Wither, Margery.*
1591 *Wither, Thomas.*
1601 *Wither, Gabriel.*
1605 *Wither, John.*
1616 *Wither, Jerome.*
1622 *Wither, George.*
1626 *Withers, Thomas.*
1642 *Withers, Thomas Drayton.*

Bristol.

1578 *Wyther, Richard*, of Bushley.
1609 *Withers, Richard.*
1684 *Withers, Edward.*
1684 *Withers, Philip.*
1712 *Withers, Thomas.*
1752 *Withers, Henry.*

Gloucestershire.

1545 *Wyther, Thomas*, of Strode or Stroud.
1549 *Wyther, Joan*, of Oldbury on Severn.
1550 *Wether, William*, of Stonehouse.
1557 *Wyther, Thomas*, of Thornbury.
Wether, Robert, of Thornbury.
1570 *Weathers, Robert*, of Tidenham.
1571 *Wither, John*, of Oldbury on Severn.
1571 *Wyther, John*, of Rockhampton.
1572 *Wyther, Richard*, of Rockhampton.
1573 *Whither, Joan*, of Oldbury on Severn.
1583 *Wether, Richard*, of Rockhampton.
1584 *Wether, John*, of Rockhampton.
1584 *Wether, Ellen*, of Rockhampton.
1585 *Wether, John*, of Westbury.
1585 *Wyther, Nicholas*, of Horton.
1587 *Wither, John*, of Thornbury.
1590 *Wither, John*, of Thornbury.
1596 *Wether, Walter*, of Newnham.
1597 *Weether, William*, of Thornbury.
1607 *Whether, John*, of Oldbury on Severn.
1608 *Wyther, Annie*, of Thornbury on Severn.
1608 *Whyther, Thomas*, of Morton.
1612 *Wither, Henry*, of Shepardine.
1618 *Wyther, Thomas*, of Little Dean.

Norwich.

1743 *Withers, Elizabeth*, of Holt.

BERKSHIRE WILLS AND ADMINISTRATIONS.

FROM OXFORD HISTORICAL SERIES (*Phillimore*).

1557 *Withers, John* (Chipping Farringdon), D. 157.
1558 *Withers, Thomas* (Chipping Farringdon), E. 25.
1609 *Withers, Edmund* (Inkpen), K. 608.
1609 *Withers, Catherine* (Halford).
1615 *Withers, John* (Standford-in-the-Vale), 119. ii.
1626 *Withers, Richard* (Longworth).
1628 *Withers, John* (Abingdon).
1632 *Withers, David* (Hinton Waldridge).

LANCASHIRE WILLS IN ARCHDEACONRY OF RICHMOND.

FROM RECORD SOCIETY PUBLICATIONS.

1633 *John Wither*, of Overkellett.
1662 *John Wither*, of Cawood.
1666 *Brian Wither*, of Archolme.
1671 *Elisabeth Wither*, of Timerley, parish of Melinge.
1676 *Jane Wither*, of Archolme.
1676 *John Wither*, of Archolme.

WILL OF *RICHARD WETHER*, CITIZEN OF LONDON.

PROVED 5TH NOVEMBER, 1492. [*P.C.C.*, *114 Doggett.*]

I desire to be buried in the parish church of St. Peter "the Power" in the new Aisle before the Altar of St. Katherine there.

I bequeath to the High Altar there for my offerings forgotten 26*s*. 8*d*. I have granted £50 to the reparation of the new work of the said church, whereof I have already paid £30.

I will that a priest shall pray for my soul, the souls of my father and mother, and all Christian souls, in the said church, and there to be present and sing at Matins, High Mass, and Evensong, and daily to say his mass at the said Altar of St. Katherine; and every day after mass, he is to say at my tomb de profundis for my soul and the souls aforesaid, and on my burial to cast holy water, and he to have yearly for his salary ten marks.

I will that my obit shall yearly for ten years be kept in the said church,—13*s*. 4*d*. to be expended at every obit.

I will that the beadle of my craft shall have 12*d*. a year to give warning to the wardens and my Fellowship of haberdashers to be at my obit, and each of the said Wardens coming to my obit to have 12*d*.

I will that yearly there shall be expended at my mansion in the said parish 13*s.* 4*d.* for my said Fellowship and other honest people coming to my said obit during the said ten years.

I bequeath to the use of my said craft and Fellowship of Haberdashers my best standing cup silver and gilt, covered.

I will that four of the said Fellowship shall bear my body to my burying, and shall have 3*s.* 4*d.* each.

I will that during the said ten years, every Sunday 13 poor men and women, not being common beggars, shall be present during mass at the Altar of St. Katherine, and shall pray at my tomb for my soul and the souls aforesaid, and afterwards shall be rewarded in good beef or mutton value 2*d.*, a penny loaf and a penny in money.

I will that every summer, during the said ten years, two cart loads of coals of charcoal shall be bought, to be given to the poor of the said parish in winter.

I will that every year, during the said ten years, an obit shall be kept for my soul and the souls aforesaid, by the Prior and Convent of the Friars Augustines, in their convent church, and they to have yearly for the same 13*s.* 4*d.*

I bequeath 13*s.* 4*d.* to the Crutched Friars of the city of London to pray for my soul.

I bequeath 5*s.* to every house of the poor Lazars next the city of London.

I bequeath 20*s.* to the "Frirers observaunces" at Greenwich to say one Trentall of masses and Placebo and Dirige for my soul.

I will that within the said ten years there shall be dealt in shirts and smocks of canvas and strong linen cloth for my soul, to the value of £10.

I bequeath 6*s.* 8*d.* to the Brotherhood of Pappey to sing Placebo and Dirige for my soul within the time of my month's mind in my said parish church.

I will that four orders of Friars shall bring my body to the burying, and sing Placebo and Dirige one after the other within my parish church, and every order to say a trentall of masses within their convent church for my soul and the souls aforesaid; and I bequeath each order for their labour 40*s.*

I bequeath 10*s.* for a trentall of masses of St. Gregory to be said for my soul within my parish church.

I will that twenty poor men shall hold my torches and tapers at my burying and month's mind, and each of them is to have a black gown and hood, 12*d.* in money, and meat and drink. Of which said torches I bequeath four to my parish church, four to the Friars Augustines, two to the Charter House of London, two to the Nuns of Halywell, one to the parish church of All Hallows in the wall of London, one to the church of St. Mary Stanyng, one to the parish church of Newington in Surrey, and one to the Charnel House.

I bequeath to my godchildren 6*s.* 8*d.* each.

I will that in every prison in London, Southwark, and the Fleet, 6*s.* 8*d.* shall be bestowed in bread among the poor prisoners.

I bequeath to every poor householder in my parish 20*d.*

I will that there shall be given in alms ten marks at my burying and month's mind, every person to have a penny.

I bequeath £20 to acquit prisoners out of the prisons in London for the debt of 20*s.* or under, and a like £20 for prisoners at Her*t*ford (*sic*); and if there is any overplus it shall be given to the poor in the town of Her*e*ford aforesaid.

I bequeath 12 dozen silver spoons, each dozen worth 36*s.* 8*d.*, to the marriage of poor maidens of good name, whereof six dozen to be given in London, and six dozen in Hereford. The eldest daughter of Johan a Woode shall have a dozen, and Eliz. Takley and her daughter shall have a dozen between them.

I bequeath to Cecily my wife, the residue of my goods.

Executors.—Cecily my wife, William Wordeboys, and Henry Somer. I bequeath to the two latter £5 each. I ordain Wm. Curteys, one of the Customers of the King in the city of London, and I bequeath to him £40.

Witnesses.—Wm. Sutton, Doctor in Divinity, Wm. Barton, priest, and Wm. Camp, notary.

Proved 5 November, 1492, by the three said witnesses, and commission was issued to Cecily relict and executrix, etc.

THE WILL OF *RICHARD WYTHER* (SALTER) OF LONDON.

PROVED 31ST AUGUST, 1521. [*P.C.C., 14 Manywaring.*]

"In the Name of God Amen. The XXVIIth day of Marche the yere of our Lord God M V XXI and the XIIth yere of the Reigne of King Henry the VIIIth I *Richard Wyther* Citezen and *Salter* of London holy of mynde and in my good memory beying Laude be to Almyghty God Make and Ordeyn this my present testament conteyning my last will in this wise following That ys to say First I bequeth and recommend my Soule unto Almyghty Jhu my Redeemer and Saviour to his most Glorious Moder our Blessed Lady Saynt Mary the Vgyn and to all the hooley company of Hevyn and my body to be buried wtin the Conuentuall Churche of the Black Fryers of London after the discrecions of myn executors under wrytyn and I will that all such debtis and dueties wiche I shall owe of right or conscience unto any psone or psones at the time of my disceas be wele and tryly content and paide wtout any delay Itm I will that according to the Laudable custome of this Noble Citie all and singuler my goodis plate juellis redy money catallis and debtis shalbe equally devyded in twoo partis or porcions of the wiche I give and bequeth unto *Alice my wyf* the oon parte or moytie of the same in the name of hir parte and porcion of right to hir belonging accordyng to the Ancient use of the saide Citie and thother parte or moytie I reserve to myself for the pforming and fulfilling of this my saide testament of the which I bequeth unto the High Altar of the Pisshe of Allhalowes in Bred Street for my tithes and affryngges necligently wholdyn in discharge of my soule XIIIs IIIId Itm I bequeth unto the same High Alter to Bren afore the Blessed Sacrament at the tyme of the Elevation two new torchis Itm I bequeth unto the Fraternitie of our Ladie holdyn in the saide Churche VIs and VIIId and oon new torche Itm I bequeth towards thadmendyng of the defaultis in the Southyle of the same Churche XXs Itm I will that myn executors by the ousight of parte of the preshens of Saynt Nichas of Newport in the County of Salop shall provide a cope a vestment Deacon and Sub Deacon of Blewe velvet and all thingys requisite and necessary to the same to thuse of the saide Churche of Saynt Nicholas in the whiche pisshe I was born Itm I bequeth unto the saide Churche a Chalice silver and gilt of the weyght of XX[li] uncis in the foote wherof I will there shalbe gravid pray for the soule of Richard Wyther of London Salter and I woll the saide suyt shall be of the value of XX[li] sterlingis in redy money Itm I bequeth unto the saide churche Nichs a Corporace and case for the same for the saide Chalice to be occupied at Principall Festis and a writyn Masse Boke wt all the newe service to thentent that the parishens ther shall have my soule the soules of my fadir and moder and all my friendes soules spially recomended in their devout prayers Itm I will that myn executors under wretyn shall provide an honest Seculer Prest of good name and fame to sing for my soule the soules above saide and all xpen soules in the saide pisshe Churche of Saint Nichas in Newport aforesaid by the space of three yers next ensuyng after my diseas and that the saide Preste at the first lavatory shall say for my soule and the soules above saide the psalms of Deprofundis with suffragis and collectis accustumed and that he shalbe aidyng and helpyng to his pour to alle man of Dyvyne servyce to be song and saide there and that he oon time evy woke shall say for my soule and the soules above saide Placebo Dirige and Comendacions and I bequeth yerely for his stipend and salary quarterly to hym to be paide by evyn porcions VI[li] sterling I woll that my saide executors shall cause a solemn obit or anniversary by note to be kepte in the same pisshe churche for my soule and all the soules above saide by the space of three yers next ensuing after my saide diseas that is to say Placebo and Dirige at afternone and Masse of Requiem the day next following and I bequeth for the saide yerly obit or anniversary to be kept there XXs sm VIII[li] to be disposed in this wise First to the Warden or his depute present at the saide obit XIId Itm to every Prest of the saide Churche being present at the saide Obit VId to the Clerke for the same Obit and ringing of bells according as it is ys ther used for II convenyent taps to bren about my hers XIId to either of the Churchewardeyns there for the tyme beyng for his labor about the same VIIId and the rest of the saide XXs yerly by the ousight of the Warden to be distributed amongis pour householders there dwelling in the saide pisshe to pray for my soule and all the soules above saide Itm I will that immediately after my saide deceas I have a trigental of Masses to be saide for me in the saide pisshe churche of Allhalowen and I bequeth for the same XIs Itm I will that in likewise that I have another Trigentall to be saide for my soule at the Croched Fryers besides the Tower of London by the Bredrein of the saide place and I bequeth for the same XIs Itm I woll that by the space of oon yere I have said by oon of the bredern of the saide place daily mass at Scala Celi in the saide churche and I bequeth for the same unto the use of the new building of there churche VII[li] Itm I bequeth unto the Black Fryers aforesaid for a trigentall of Masses and for fetching of my bodie to their churche and for my burying ther to be had III[li] VIs VIIId Itm I bequeth to the Grey Fryers besidis Newgate for a trigintall of masses there and for bringing my bodie to the said churche of Black Fryers XXXs Itm I bequeth unto the White Freers in Flet Streete for a trigintall of masses for my soule and for the bringing of my bodie to the saide Black Fryers XXs Itm I bequeth unto evy pour householder of my Feliship of Salters to pray for my soule IIs Itm I bequeth unto evy pour householder in the saide pisshe of Allhalowen willing and disposed to take it XXd Itm I bequeth unto Thomas Jonys my neyghbor Xs Itm I bequeth unto Elizabeth Best to pray for my soule my Hope of Gold Itm I bequeth unto the coialtie of Salters of London of whom I am a pour membre for a remembrance a standing cup with a cover gilt hanging in the knopp thereof III saltes weying XXIX unc Di Itm I bequeth unto Frannces Burwell Mcer XXs praying hym that he will forgeve me for all varianncis wiche lately were bitween me and hym Itm I will that by the space of VII yeres next ensuying after my disceas I have a solemn obit or anniversary by note to be kept in the said pisshe churche of Alle Halloen in Bred Street that is to say Placebo and Dirige at after none and masse of Requiem the morrowe than next ensuyng and I bequeth for the saide yerly obit XXXs at the wiche yerly obit I heartily require the Wardens and coialtie of the saide crafte of Salters for the time being in their lyvy or clothing as is accustomed at other obits to come and the wiche XXXs I woll yerly shalbe distributed in this wise following to pson or his depute their present at the saide Dirige and Masse XIId to every Prest of the saide churche being there helpying at the saide obit VId to the pisshe Clerke ther VId to the sexten of the saide churche IIIId for II taps to bren at the saide obit XIId for the bellis XVId to the Bedill of the Crafte for the warning of the Company and bringing of the Pall Clothe VId and the rest of the saide some to be convertyd to thuse of the saide crafte at the discrecions of the Wardyns of the saide crafte of the time being Itm I bequeth toward the gildyng of the Alter of Corpus Xpn in the Salters Chappell ther soo it be bigonne to be doon wtin II yeres next after my disceas III[li] VIs VIIId and if it shall happeyn that it be not begonne to be gilded wtin the saide II yeres then I will the saide III[li] VIs VIIId shalbe distributed in Colys in the Coldest tyme in Wynter amongis pour householders dwelling there in the saide pisshe of Alle Halowen and nygh about the same by the discrecions of myn executors Itm I bequeth unto my cousyn *Elyn Wither* to be delyved unto her at her marriage or lawfull age of XXI yeres XX[li] marc sterlying Itm I bequeth unto her a good fedirbed my payer of Shetis and alle other thinges necessary and complete for a bed a table clothe a towell a dosin napkyns alle of good Diap a brasse potte and a brasse panne Itm I bequeth unto *Laurence Wither* myn apprentice XX^{li} in redy money Itm I bequeth unto *Richard Wither* his brother X^{li} I bequeth unto my broder *Thomas Wither of Stafford* X^{li} oon of my gownes a dobblet and a jaket Itm I bequeth unto his wyf XLs and to Eviche of their children IIIs IIIId and evy of them to be heir unto other Itm I bequeth unto my brother *Robert Wither* XXs and a black gown Itm to his wyf Xs and a black gown and to eviche of their children VIs VIIId and evy of them to be held unto thothis Itm I bequeth unto *Agnes my sister* a black gown and IIII^{li} in redy money to be delived unto her at the discrecion of my executors Itm I bequeth unto her husbond a black gown Itm I bequeth unto Geffrey Lee son of the saide Agnes XX^{li} and to his sister Agnes XX^{li} sterlyng a good fedirbed a mattresse IIII payer of shetis and alle other things necessary and complete for a bed a table clothe a towell a dosyn napkins alle of diap and a pot and a panne of brasse and either of the saide Geffrey and Agnes to be heire unto othis and if the saide Geffrey and Agnes his sister disceas befor their lawful ages of XXI yeres or marriage of the same Agnes and my saide sister their mother than levying than I bequeth the moytie of the saide bequests of hir children unto my saide sister to be delivered to her at the discretion of my saide executors and the other moytie to be disposed by them in charitable deadis for the most proufit of my soule and the soules above said Itm I bequeth unto *my sister Elnor* XL^{s} and a black gown Itm I bequeth unto Adam Pickard a gown a doblet and a payer of hosyn of myn and III^{li} VIs VIIId to be delyved unto hym from tyme to tyme at the discrecion of my executors Itm I bequeth unto his wfy a black gown Itm I bequeth unto Johane the wyf of Miles Cheyny Goldsmyth to pray for my soule XXs and a black gown Itm I bequeth unto Elizabeth Killick my servant VI^{li} XIIIs IIIId a fetherbed a mattresse a cilor and tester my pair of shetis and all other things necessary and appteynyng for a bed complete a tabull clothe a towell a dosyn napkyns all of diap a brasse pot and a brasse panne Itm I bequeth unto Elizabeth Crosse XLs Itm I bequeth to Sir John Haryson Prest to pray for my soule a black gown and XXs Itm I bequeth unto eviche of myne apprenticis that is to say Thomas Dichefeld John Cockis Thomas Duckyngton and John More XLs sm VIII^{li} Itm I bequeth unto Thomas Bull towards his exhibicion to scole at Cambrige to be spent at the discrecion of myn executors XX^{ti} mrc Itm I bequeth unto William Cockis Salter a black gown and to Richard his sonne IIIs IIIId Itm I bequeth unto John Bateman Salter oon of my gownes and XL^{s} in mony to be delyvered unto hym at the discrecion of myn executors Itm I bequeth unto Jamys Walwyn Mcer XXs a black gown oon of my doublettes and oon of my cappis the residue of all and singular my goodes plate puellis catills and debtis whatsoever they be not bequethed my debtis paide my burying and funallis doon and this my present testament and last will truly in all things parformed and fullfilled I will shalbe distributed and disposed in deadis of mcy and chartie most acceptable to God by myn executors for the proufit of my soule and of this my present testament and last will I ordeyn and make the forsaide Alice my wyf and the saide John Cootis myn executors and I bequeth unto the said John Cootis for his labor and business in that behalf to be had V[li] and a black gown and overseer of the same my testament and last will I ordeyn and make my welbeloved frend Nicholas Waryng Citezen and Salter of London to whom I bequeth for his labor and for his good connsell in that behalf to be had III[li] VIs VIIId and a black gown IN WITNESSE whereof to this my present testament and last will I have set my seal yevyn the day and yeres above specified these being present Syr Thomas Sowth Parisshe Prest of the saide Parisshe Churche of Allehalowen my gostly fader Syr William Este Syr John Haryson Prestis William Rede Citizen and Fremason of London and John Devereux Notary Itm I freely forgeve and pardon Thomas Soffyngale Salter all such sommes of money wiche he oweth me to pray for my soule Itm I bequeth unto my cowsyn *Syr Richard Wyther* Parson of Holcot XXVIs VIIId and a black gown Itm I bequeth unto Maister Andrew Harwod Bachiler of Holy Dyvynytye III[li] VIs VIIId Itm I bequeth unto his brother Robert Harwod a black gown."

ABSTRACT OF WILL OF *ELIZABETH WETHERS*,

OF THE PARISH OF BOROWCLERE (BURGHCLERE), 12TH AUGUST, 1539.

Winchester Registry.—Archdeacon's Court, Book C, fo. 294,

"My body to be buryed in the church porche of the said borowclere."

Bequeaths to Winchester, *2d.*; to Burghclere church 6/8; "to my gostelye father iijs iiijd." "Itm to eu'y one of my meny childrey iiij shepe & a cowe. Itm to Margaret Hardynge a cowe & iiij shepe. Itm to Katryn Howlldwe (?) a cowe & iiij shepe, a pott and a panne. Itm to Thomas Holdway a cowe & iiij shepe, a pott and a panne. Itm to Thomas Holdwaie the leste ij bolockes, v shepe, & a calfe. Itm to Elizabeth Holdwaye a cowe iiij shepe a pott & a panne. Itm to Rychard Holdwaye one bolocke & v shepe. Itm to eu'y one of my godchyldrey iiij[d]. Itm to Johan Smythe one kyrtell. Itm to the pyshe clarke xij[d]. The Resydewe of my goodes not bequethed I amitt (?) to Wyllyam & Xpofer my sonnes whom I make my executors to bestowe it to the pleasure of gods & soule helthe. Itm I wylle that Nicholas Atwell and Edward Clyffe shuld be my ou'seers to se that my wyll be fulfylled . . . . . ."

Witnesses—S[r]. PETER, Curat',
S[r]. WILLYAM OF LUDSHELFE (LITCHFIELD),
WYLLYAM FOOLOER,
WYLLYAM WETHER, and others.

Proved 28 Augt. 1539.

ABSTRACT OF WILL OF *JOHN WYTHER*, OF ECCHINSWELL.

PROVED 16TH JUNE, 1570. [*P.C.C. 20 Lyon.*]

6 Oct. 1558. John Wyther, of Echinswell in the parish of Kingesclere. Bequeaths his soul to Almighty God, our blessed Lady, St. Mary, and all the holy company of heaven. "My body to be buried in the churches new yle of Kinges-

clere." To the cathedral church of Winchester, 4[d]. "Item unto the churche of Kingesclere, to be praied for as a benefactor, one good shepe. Item unto the chappell of Echinswell ij shepe. Item to the chappell of Sydmanton one shepe. Item my tapers to be lighted and to burne the Sundaies aboute my hearse, and the man that shall so lyght them, xij*d.* for the space of the moneth." Mentions Mr. John Fawkener "my godson"; also John Beckensall, who also was probably a godson. To Margaret his wife he leaves "my best fetherbed with almanner of parrel thereto belonging, a dozen of platters, half a dozen of pottengers, two sawcers, the best salte seller, the best candlesticke. Item a caudron at Babbes, a pott and a skyllet and a mydle pott here, and a freng panne and a girde yron, a kettell and suche housholde stuffe of treue vessells as there is at Babbes, and xxx cheses. Item thre pownds of money, a silver spone, and a maser. Item a carte and a plowe, iiij oxen and a couple of geldings to drawe them withall." Also bulls, sheep, geese, etc., wheat, barley, etc.

His son John is to occupy one of the leases "in Strattons" until he provides other by marriage or otherwise. Testator leaves to John kine, sheep, poultry, etc. "Item a flocke bed with allmanner of apparell, half a dozen of platters, two pottingers, the next best salte seller, and a candlesticke." Also wheat, barley, etc.

To his son Peter he leaves kine, sheep, poultry, etc. Also "a flockebed with all the apparell, half a dozen of platters, two pottingers, a salte seller and a candlesticke." Also wheat, barley, etc., and the occupancy of a parcel of ground "in Strattons, on the north parte."

To "Borowclere churche" he leaves a sheep.

The residue to Henry Wyther. his son, who is also appointed executor.

Witnesses—John Carter, clarke, Mr. Peter Fawkner [who in 1575 married testator's sister Joan], and Richard Legatt.

Short codicil, dated 4th June, 1570:—

"All suche Rowe tymber as is at Babbes to Henry my sonne, saving I woulde Margaret my wife to have one borde stocke thereof to repaire her house."

Witnesses—James Warde, clarke, Francis, Wall, Dorothie Winckworthe, and Elizabeth South.

Prob. 16th June, 1570.

WITHER AND BECONSHAW.

In his will dated 28 Mar., 1542, and proved 6 June, 1543, *John Bekynsawe* of Borowclere [Earlstone] appoints his uncle *Richard Wither* one of the overseers of his last will and testament. He also bequeaths to *William Wither* "XXs and a heyfer." Wm. Wither is also one of the witnesses of the will. [*P.C.C. 21 Spert.*]

Richard Wyther is appointed one of the overseers of the will of Edward Bekynsawe [of Earlstone], dated 22 Oct. 28 Hen. viii, and proved 16 Aug., 1538. [*P. C. C. 20 Dyngeley.*]

Vide Pedigree of Beconshaw of Earlstone and Moyles Court. *Proceedings of Hampshire Arch. Soc.*, Vol. IV, Part II, p. 163.

WILL OF *GEORGE WITHER*, OF DUMMER.

PROVED 16TH JANUARY, 1587 (*Oakley Hall Archives*).

"In the name of God Amen. 25 Feb. 1586. Acc[d] to the accomptor of the Church of England I *George Wyther* of Dummer of the Co. of South, being of sick of body but of perfect remembrance thanks be unto God do make this my last will and testament in manner and form following. First I bequeath my soul unto the hands of the Al. God my Saviour and Redeemer Jesus Christ by Whose blessed passion and bloodshedding my hope is to be saved and my body to be buried in the Church of Dummer near unto my wife's burial. Item I give to my son *Thomas Wethers* £40. Item I give to my son *John Wethers* £40. Item I give and bequeath to Edward Lyllywhite £20 and £20 sheep in the custody of *Gilbard Wethers* my son. All which sums of money before bequeathed I will that my exor hereafter named shall discharge and pay unto the said parties within 2 years after my decease. Item I give to the Cathedral Church of Winchester VI[d]. Item I give to *Avelyn Wethers* and *Joan Wethers* daughters of my son Gilbert Wethers each of them a sheep. Item I give and bequeath to Richard Weston and Joan Coppe each of them a sheep. Item I give to my well beloved landlord Mr. William Dummer one old angel of 10/-. Item I give to every servant now dwelling in the house XII[d] apiece. Item I give to my son John Wethers one feather bedd with the bowlster and Coverled one pair of sheets and one blanket. Item I give to such two coffers and all things therein contained now being in the upper loft.

"Item I give to every one of my godchildren 4[d] apiece. Item I give to John Bayley, Mother Hopegood, Gilbert Ingines, Henry Smythe, Edwin Wayte, and to Mother Bolegate VI apiece. Item I give and bequeath all my lands lying in Laurence Wootton and East Ockley and my lands called Staples alias Gawlds and Roast lying in Kemshott in the parish of Winslade in the Co. of Southampton unto Gilbert Wethers my son and to the heirs of his body lawfully begotten. Item I give to the Church of Dummer one sheep. Item I give to *Reginold Wethers* my son one malt myll guerne and one parchment mill with the cast thereonto appertaining to big grain. The residew of my goodes not given nor bequeathed I give and bequeath to my son Gilbert Wethers whom I do ordain and make my sole exor of this my last will and testament. And I desire Mr. William White parson of Dummer, and my cousin Richard Ayliff and my cousin John Wethers of Manydowne to take the pains to be my overseers of this my last will and testament and I give to each of them for their pains VI[s] and VIII[d] apiece. In witness this my last will and testament I have put to my hand and seal in the presence of Mr. Wm. White parson of Dummer Richard Ayliff of Ewhurst and *John Wethers of Manydowne*."

ABSTRACT OF WILL OF *GILBERT WITHER*, OF DUMMER (SON OF GEORGE).

PROVED 1599 (*Bishop's Court, Winchester*).

Body to be buried in the body of the Parish Church of Church Oakley before the seat belonging unto the farm house of Rastowelles.

Bequests.—Church of Oakley, 6/8; Cathedral, Winchester, *6d.*; Parish Church, Dummer, 5/-.

To Poor of Dummer, 6/8; of Oakley, 3/4; of Laurence Wootton, 3/4.

To Daughters Avelyn, Joan, Agnes and Elizabeth, £100 each.

To Sons Reignold [Reginald] and William, £100 each.

To Son George all my lands and hereditaments in Deane, Oakley and Wootton, then in default of heirs to son Reignold, then to Henry, then to William.

To wife for life £10 rent of Rastowelles.

Provision that heirs should not enter for twelve years upon the lands and tenements now in the testator's tenure or occupation, *viz.*, Bullbushes park and barn, Northdowne, Evinger Copse and Barton Allins.

"I will that my exors. do provide a stone of marble a foot square to lay over my burial place, and that the grave be dug deep."

Residue to my well beloved wife. She and my son Henry exors. until my son Henry attains twenty-one.

Overseers: my cousin John Wither of Manidown and Walter Madgewick.

Inventory attached to will value £936. 4*s.* 8*d.*

ABSTRACT OF WILL OF *GEORGE WITHER*, OF WINCHESTER, SECOND SON OF HENRY WITHER, OF SOUTHWARK,

Who married—(1) Ann Searle, sister of James Searle, 1641.
(2) Catherine Chester, sister-in-law of Nicholas Love, 1657.

PROVED 9TH APRIL, 1662. [*P. C. C. 56 Laud.*]

No mourning to be given at funeral except to wife and daughter.

Bequests.—To wife Catherine £50 and annuity of £20, desiring her to be loving and careful of my daughter Mary.

To my uncle George Wither, of Hall, guardianship of daughter Mary [afterwards married to William Wither iii, of Manydown].

To mother-in-law Mrs. Anne Searle, brother Gilbert, sister Mrs. Anne Pinke, rings value 20/- each.

To nephew and niece William and Mary Pinke £5 each.

To daughter Mary, diamond ring, silver tankards with arms engraved, guilt wyn bowl given by Aunt Wither to her mother.

To trustee of dead wife's jointure, lands in Bramley, Strathfieldsaye, Baghurst, Pamber, with the manors of Wonston * and lands in Cranborne.

Trustees of will: Brother Gilbert, Brother-in-law Henry Pinke of Kempshott, Kinsman William Wither of Manydown.

Exor: Uncle George Wither, of Hall.

ABSTRACT WILL OF *ANNE PINCKE* (*née* *ANNE WITHER*, OF HALL).

PROVED 22ND SEPTEMBER, 1703.

[1703]. Anne Pincke of Kempshott in the parish of Winslade co. Southton widdow, being weak etc.

To be buried in Winslade Chancell as near to my husband etc. Stone to be laid on ye grave etc.

To my son Thomas Pincke, all the household goods which I have at Kempshott etc. for his use during life and after to his heir. My wedding ring to my son Thomas Pincke.

To my Grand son Henry Pinck, 1 large silver tankard with ye Pincke's and Wither's arms engraven on it upon condition etc. that he surrender etc. one other sylver tankard of smaller size with ye Pincke's arms on it and marked H. P. to his brother Gilbert Pincke another of my grand son's for ye use of ye said Gilbert his heir's To son Thomas £100 for the use of his *five* children, *i.e.*, Elizabeth, Henry, Gilbert, Mary, and Thomas, equally to be divided etc. to be paid at 21. If any die portion shared equally by survivors. Son William's children £18 which with the £82 he formerly had of me make up £100 for use of his five children, Jane, Elizabeth, Anne, Edward and Alured equally to be divided etc. (as above) To two grand-daughters Elizabeth and Mary daughters of Thomas 1 Table Cloth, 1 Dozen napkins, 1 pair sheets, 1 pair of pillow cases, Best of linnen, and my pewter to be divided between s[d] grand-daughters Elizabeth and Mary. To Elizabeth my said grand-daughter my little silver cup; and my six silver spoon's to be disposed of thus two to 2 grandsons and God-sons Gilbert Pincke and John Butler, and the four remaining to my four grand daughters Elizabeth and Mary daughters of Thomas Pincke and Jane and Elizabeth daughters of son William. To grand-daughter Mary a feather bed and bolster. To son Thomas Pincke and my daughter in Law Jane Pincke widdow and to my son in law John Butler and my daughter Catherine his wife £5 a piece to buy mourning. To Grand-son John Butler 40/-

* The manor of Wonston, in George Wither's first marriage settlement (1641), is described as "leased from the Dean and Chapter of Winchester"; in the second marriage settlement (1657) it is referred to as "my manor of Wonston." Probably George Wither, of Hall, uncle to the above testator, bought the manor of Wonston from the contractors of the Long Parliament after the Act of 1649 in the same way as William Wither bought the manor of Manydown (see page 33).

MRS. CHARLES WITHER,

(*Née* Elizabeth Wavell).

Died 1752.

to poor of Dummer 10/- poor of Winslade 20/-. To son Thomas residue of household goods which are not here by etc. Son Thomas Ex^{or} and do give him all my estate which is not hereby or otherwise disposed of.

Signed by mark.
Witnesses—THOMAS TERRY.
WALTER KNIGHT.
JAMES ARNILL (or ANNELL).

22nd Sept., 1703. Proved by THOMAS PINCKE, GENT.

WILL OF *GEORGE WITHER*, OF BENTWORTH (FATHER OF THE POET). DATED 14TH OCTOBER, 1629.

The Archdeaconry Court of Winchester.

The last will and testament of *George Wither*, gent., late of Bentworth, deceased.

"Perticulars concerning ye last will and testament of George Wither of Bentworth if it shold please god to p^{r}vent a more and full declaratio or expressio of his minde. After my Soule and bodye recommended to God in Christ Jesus in whome I trust for my eternall salvation and ye recomendatio of my dear wife and chilldren for whome I am much bound to praise him and in my troble praies to his gratious providence and protectio.

Concerning my worldly goods this is my minde and will First I geve and bequeath to my daughter Mary ye sume of fourescoure pounds of good and lawfull monie of England Item to my daughter An ye same sume of fourescoure pondes Iten to my daughter Pollyxena ye same sum of fourescore pouds Item to my son Jeames ye same sume of fourscore pouds Item to my son Antonye ye sume of twenty poundes Item to my daughter Jane ye sume of Five poundes. Item I geve to *my wife Mary Wither* ye sume of twentie poundes to be disposed of as she shall see good. These Legacies dulye paid wth in 4 or 5 yeares as I maie heraft more expresslye mention if God shall permitt and my funerall fitlye performed I geve all y^{t} shall remaine of my landes & goodes to my deserving & beloved *wife Marye* & to my beloved & *eldest sone George* [the poet] whome I doe by these make and appoint ye executors of this my will and testament. Item I do give unto Thomas Martin [son-in-law] and his three children an ewe sheepe.

dely^{d} wth mine owne hand the fourtenth day of October, 1629,

GEO. WYTHER.

Subscribed in ye p^{r}sence of
THOMAS SPARKE
the marke of ANTONYE BULBECKE.

for overseers of this my last will and testament I desire to have Mr. John King of Weston Patrick and Lawrence May of Alton.

and that the sd George Wither about fortnight before his death in declaracon of his will and concerning the disposcon of xx^{li} aforesd given to his wife, he did will that the sd xx^{li} should bee paied to his son Anthony at such time as his former legacies were willed to bee paied unto him. & whereas he hath given to his daughter Jane five pownds he willed that that 5^{li} should be in satisfaccon of a Legacy of xx^{li} wch he had pmised to the sd Jane to be paied at the birth of her first child. the sd Jane now being unlikely to have any child."

N.B.—The testator was buried at Bentworth 17 November, 1629.

ABSTRACT OF WILL OF *ELIZA WITHER* (WIDOW OF THE POET), OF GATWEEKE, PARISH OF BENTWORTH, HANTS.

PROVED 2ND JANUARY, 1682. [*P. C. C. 11 Drax.*]

Whereas by indenture dated 1666 between John Hunt of Theddon parish of Alton and Robert Wither my son the said John Hunt has sold to Robert Wither for £240 a barn 5 closes etc. containing about 40 acres called Gatwick and whereas Robert Wither by deed poll declares his name is used for sole and separate use of me Eliza Wither his mother: and whereas in 1674 Robert Wither sold to Eliza Wither 2 closes called Heathcroft containing 20 acres, I give Gatwick to my only daughter Elizabeth Barry wife of Adrian Barry citizen & merchant of London. Whereas my late husband George Wither Esquire bought certain lands with manors called Bishops lands, I give and bequeath to Eliz. Barry all the manor of Bentley and farm called Berry Court also all the Borough and privileges of Gosport and the advowson of Alverstoke. I give and bequeath to my grandson Hunt Wither the son of my said son Robert 12^{d} to Elizabeth eldest daughter of Robert 12^{d} to Sarah 12^{d} to Robert son of Robert 12^{d} to Mary daughter of Robert 12^{d} to Joan youngest daughter of Robert 12^{d}. I make Elizabeth Barry my executrix.

ABSTRACT OF WILL OF *THOMAS WITHER*, OF ANDWELL.

PROVED 17TH FEBRUARY, 1700–1. [*P.C.C., 31 Dyer.*]

To be buried in Church of St. Laurence Wootton in or near grave of dear wife [*née* Mary, dgt. of Dr. Fulkes, Bodley's Librarian, Oxford].

Bequests.—To eldest son William and his heirs all copyhold lands in the parish of Yateley, manor of Crondall, Hants, in trust to brothers in law, Mr. Thos. Bethell and Mr. Lovelace Bigg, William to pay to the testator's daughter Mary and sons George and John the legacies given by their grandmother Mrs. Eleanor Fulkes [*P.C.C., 132 Pett*] and £100 to said son George and £200 to John when each aged 21.

To Daughter Mary £100 and her mother's wedding ring.

"The reason testator gives George and Mary so little is that they have grievously offended God, but if they repent their brother William to be kind to them."

To Son John five 20/– pieces of broad gold.

Mourning rings of 10/– each to nephew William Wither [iv of Manydown], niece Mary Wither, sister Barbara Wither, brother [in law] and sister Bethell, brother [in law] and sister Bigg, uncle and aunt Ernle, aunt Bigg, cousins William, Mary, Dorothy, Henry, Alethea, Elizabeth, Sarah and Thomas Bigg; cousins Alethea Cotton, Chambers Slaughter and Susanna his wife, John and William Pottinger, Elizabeth Ernle, Thomas Pleydell and Rachel his wife, Mary and Edward Ernle, each a mourning ring of 10/–.

Residuary legatee: son William Wither.

Executors: son William, brothers-in-law Thomas Bethell and Lovelace Bigg.

NOTE.—The grandson of the above testator inherited in 1732 the Manydown estates, and was the last Wither of Manydown, dying in 1789. See Pedigrees III and IV for persons mentioned in above will.

MINUTES OF THE WILL OF *WILLIAM WITHER* (IV), OF MANYDOWN, ESQUIRE,

(DATED JANUARY 4TH, 1732), WHO DIED 25TH SEPTEMBER, 1733.

Testator devises: *1st* All his freehold estates to his wife for life After that to Sir Henry Maynard and Edward Ernle (trustees) for 500 years from and after decease of his wife [Elizabeth *née* Nicol] upon the *Trusts* hereinafter mentioned and after the determination of the said term to *William Wither of Andwell* during his life, and then to his 1st 2nd and 3rd son and the heirs male of their bodys; and next to *Thomas Wither* in like manner and to his heirs male in like manner: and for default of these to *Thomas Bigg* and his heirs for ever:—provided it shall be lawful to his wife and others seised of the premises to make leases for 21 years upon the most improved Rents, without Fines etc.

Trustees to pay out of the premises one annuity or yearly sum of £40 to and amongst M. Blackstone, D. Bethell and A. Banister in equal portions during their lives and the life of the longest liver of them etc. and also the sum of £1500 to and amongst the brothers and sister of William Wither aforesaid or of Thomas or Charles, whichsoever shall come to the estate (after the decease of testators wife) in even and equal portions—and also the further sum of £5000 to the daughters and younger son or sons of the said William Wither (or others possessed of the estate) or of £3000 to one daughter or younger son as aforesaid.

2ndly All his leasehold estate of Manydown etc. held of the Church of Winchester to the same trustees Sir H. M. and E. E. in Trust to surrender and renew the said leases from time to time—to suffer his wife to enjoy them for her life and next the possessors of the Freehold estates for their several terms in the said estates respectively; with power to her and them to make such leases as aforesaid. And also it shall be lawful to the persons entitled to the said Freehold and Leasehold premises to make settlements or jointures of the same, or any part thereof, to any wife or wives of theirs during her life only.

3rdly All his leasehold estates of Andwell (held of Winchester College) and Up Nateley Tithes etc. (held of Magd. Coll. Oxon) to the same trustees on trust to renew the said leases from time to time, to permit his wife to enjoy them for her life and after her decease gives the said premises to Thos. Bigg aforesaid his exors and administrators: charged with the pay[t] of £1000 to and amongst the children of M. Blackstone, and A. Bannister share and share alike at the age of 21 or day of marriage £50 apiece to Mary, Henry, Dorothy, Elizabeth, Walter, and Anne his (Thos. Bigg) brothers and sisters within six months after the decease of his said wife.

4thly Gives unto William Wither aforesaid one annuity or yearly sum of £100 and to Mary Blackstone, Dorothy Bethel, and Anne Banister one annuity of £40 to be paid unto them respectively during the life of his wife by 4 quarterly pay[ts] clear of all taxes. To all and every one of his Godchildren £10 apiece. To Wm. Wither, Mary Wither £10 each for mourning. To Sir H. Maynard and E. Ernle £100 a piece for mourning. To his 2 men servants who shall wait on him at the time of his decease £5 apiece and mourning and to each other servant (except Mary Bignall) who shall have lived with him one year next before his death £2 apiece and mourning and to Mary Bignell £50 to be disposed of by his exors for her separate use without her husbands intermeddling. To the poor of the parish of Wootton £20; to the poor of other parishes (where he has estate of upwards of £10 per annum) £5. All his debts of simple contract to be paid with lawful interest.

His wife to pay Mary, Henry, Dorothy, Elizabeth, Walter, and Anne brothers and sisters of Thos. Bigg £2 10 yearly apiece as interest for their respective legacies of £50 apiece before given and also £5 yearly to Thos. Bigg during her life. Trustees to reimburse themselves all charges relating to the Trust out of the estates devised.

5thly All the rest and residue of his personal estate given to his wife charged with the pay[t] of all Debts, Legacies and pay[ts], and if not sufficient then on the other estates before given to his wife during his life. Wife made executrix, and desired to dispose of Rings (not exceeding 50 among his relations as she shall think fit. Sir H. Maynard and Ed. Ernle desired to assist the said Executrix in the management and execution of this will.

ABSTRACT OF WILL OF *ELIZABETH WITHER* (*née* NICOL).

DATED 21ST MAY, 1735.

Body to be buried in the Church of St Laurence Wootton in the grave with my late Husband.

SIR CHARLES GOUNTER NICOLL, K.B., 1732.

Nephew of MRS. WILLIAM WITHER (*née* Nicol), of Manydown.

Bequests.—To my cousin William Wither of Andwell all my household furniture at Manydown and farm instruments and £10 for mourning.

To Sir Henry Maynard £500.

To my niece K. Maynard £1500 for pocket money and my best diamond ring.

To Master Wm Maynard, son to my niece, £500 and my gold watch.

To my sister Gounter, Lady Maynard's picture set with diamonds.

To daughters of my late nephew Sir Charles Gounter Nicol £500 apiece.

To my God-daughter Mrs Eliz: Gounter Nicol my pearl necklace and diamond stay buckles.

To my cousin Elizabeth Bigg £200 and my diamond girdle buckles.

To Dr Henry Bigg [Warden], to cousins Tom. Bigg and Walter Bigg [Rector of Worting] £20 apiece.

To cousins Blackstone and Bethell £20 apiece.

To godsons Charles Blackstone and George Prince and Mr. Richardson £10 apiece.

To cousin Rainer £29 annuity.

To cousin Anne Banister £300. To god-daughter Elizabeth Banister £200.

To cousin Elizabeth Wither of Andwell £300.

To Lady Nicol £20 for mourning.

To Church of St Laurence Wootton a Silver Plate for the Communion.

To Mrs Fenton [wife of the Vicar of Wootton] a legacy of £10.

To apprentice poor children £100. [See Appendix IV.]

To poor of St Laurence Wootton £20, to poor of Worting £10, of Sherborne St John £10.

To servants James and Mary Bignell £25, others 40/- apiece, and 40/- apiece to those day labourers that have constant work at Manydown.

Sister Judith Gounter and sister Francis Nicol to dispose of my wearing clothes.

The rest of my estate real and personal I equally give to my sister Gounter and sister Nicol, making them executrixes in this my will, being all written with my own hand this 21st May, 1735, and sealed with my own seal.

[Signed] ELIZABETH WITHER.

ABSTRACT OF THE WILL OF *RICHARD BIGG*, OF HAINES HILL, HURST.

PROVED 3RD OCTOBER, 1670.

N.B.—Richard Bigg married first the *Lady Phœbe Ley*, and had issue by her, who died 1653, four sons: James, John, Richard and Daniel. By his second wife *Mary Wade* (widow), *née* Cooke, three sons: Nathaniel, Samuel and Lovelace, and a daughter Mary. (See Pedigree VI.)

Bequests.—Poor of Hurst, £5; poor of St Giles-in-the-Fields "where I was born," £10.

Wife Mary, £500, linen, plate, jewels, furniture in the wainscott room, Hurst, coach and 2 horses, rent for life of 3 houses in St Giles-in-the-Fields.

Son John, all furniture at Hurst except above.

Stepson Robert Cooke £500.

Son Richard £1000 and £100 to furnish his rooms at Oxford.

Son Nathaniel £1000 and the three houses in St Giles-in-the-Fields.

NOTE.—Nathaniel died in 1676 and left the three houses to his half-brother Richard, who left them to the poor of Hurst. (See Richard Bigg's will below.)

Son Lovelace [who married Dorothy Wither of Manydown], £1000.

ABSTRACT OF THE WILL OF *LOVELACE BIGG*, OF CHILTON FOLLIAT.

PROVED 26TH APRIL, 1725.

N.B.—Lovelace Bigg married first *Dorothy Wither* and had issue by her, who died 1711, twelve children, of whom eight survived him, *viz.*, *Mary*, wife of Charles Blackstone, *Dorothy*, wife of Thomas Bethell, *Henry*, Warden of Winchester, *Elizabeth*, *Thomas*, *Walter*, Rector of Worting, *Richard*, and *Anne*, wife of Richard Bannister. By his second wife, *Rachel Fettiplace*, who died 1759, he had no issue. (See Pedigree VI.)

Bequests.—Poor of Chilton and Kingsclere, £5 each parish.

Wife Rachel, £250 and £100 annuity charged on estates in Market Stanton, Lincolnshire, two houses in Bond St. for life, "unless my son Henry permits her to live at Chilton Folliat," moiety of furniture at Chilton, jewels, rings, pair of silver candlestics, one silver hand candlestic and snuffers, silver coffee pot, and four silver spoons marked W B, etc., etc.

Daughters Elizabeth and Anne, £600 each and £25 annuity each, or £500 additional on marriage in lieu of annuity; to Elizabeth, two silver porringers; to Anne, the silver salver which was her sister Sarah's.

Daughter Mary [Blackstone], £300.

Son Thomas, £100 and lease of the Warren called Shibbington in Kingsclere.

Son Walter, £600 and lease of Chappell lands in Kingsclere.

Son Richard, £800 and my two silver tankards.

William Wither of Manydown, £10, as likewise to all my children, sons and daughters in law, £10 each.

Grandsons, Charles Blackstone my silver bason, Thomas Bethell my diamond ring.

Grand-daughter Alethea Richmond, £10.

Mary Bigg (*née* Wade).

Widow of Richard Bigg, of Haines Hill.

Mother of Lovelace Bigg, who married Dorothy Wither.

Aged 43 years, 1674.

Rest and residue of all my estates real and personal to my son Henry, exor.

I revoke former wills and the settlement relating to the estate late of my cousin Bigg late of Haynes Hill in co. of Wilts bearing date Nov. 17, 1723.

[Signed] Lo. Bigg.

WILL OF *RICHARD BIGG*,

Fourth Son of Richard Bigg, of Haines Hill, Hurst, and of the Lady Phœbe Ley. Dated 20th July, 1677.

"In the name of God Amen. I Richard Bigg lately Fellow of New College in Oxon being at this time in perfect health and memory doe make constitute and ordayne my Last Will and Testament to be as followes, viz.: Imprimis I commend my soule to God that gave itt me in sure and certain hopes of a joyful Resurrection, merited by the death of Jesus Christ my Redeemer. Item I give my body to the ground and I desire that I may be buryed in the parish Church of Hurst, it being the place where my father lived many years and was also buryed. And I desire that I may lye in that part of the Church where a monument may be raised upon my grave like to that monument which is in the Churchyard of the said place upon the grave of Mr. Maynard. Item I make constitute and ordayne Hugh Hunt, Citizen and Scrivener of London the sole executor of this my last Will and Testament to whom I give during his natural life the full entire revenue, rents and profits of the George Inn in St. George in the Fields: And after his decease to the use of the parish of Hurst, and all my study books, watches and rings whatsoever not otherwise disposed of. Item I give William Barker Esq. one gold ring of 20/- value. Item I give to Mr. Francis Simpson of London, upholsterer, all my goods as Lumber sheets wearing apparrell together with all debts that is due from him to me. Item I will and desire that my buryal may be with all privacy that is possible without any mourning scutcheons or any of the like formality. And I desire that there may not be drunk at my funeral one drop of wine as the usual custom of England is; But that a sermon may be preached at my funeral upon this text viz 'He that giveth to the poor lendeth to the Lord'; and I desire that 10/- maybe given to the Minister for his pains. Item that 40/- maybe laid out for bread to be given to the poor of the said parish according to discretion of the Overseers of the poor of the said parish. I desire that the grave wherein my body is buried may be dug nine or ten feet deep if it may be permitted. Item I desire that every year on th 4th day of Nov. may be preached a sermon in the said parish Church on the above named words viz 'He that giveth to the poor lendeth to the Lord,' the said day being my birthday. Item I give and bequeath 20/- to the preacher of the said sermon every year to be paid unto him for his pains. Item I desire that the overseers of this my Will and Testament may yearly appoint and nominate the Minister or Priest to preach the aforesaid Sermon. Item I constitute ordain and will that the Annual Rents of my three Messuages or Tenements in the parish of

St. Giles in the Fields, the said annuities of twenty pounds and except which I have already disposed of, be, according to the discretion of the overseers of the poor and Minister of the said parish of Hurst for the time being, laid out in Bread and every week viz on Sunday mornings be put into a basket appointed for that purpose and set upon my grave stone in the Church during divine service and after divine service is ended to be distributed to the most indigent and houseless poor creatures of the said parish either men women or children. Item I will that if any person be either blind or sick and really in great want and poverty and so by that means is disabled from coming to hear divine service that care maybe taken to allow them or him or her some sustenance to support them or him or her in such a condition. Item that a book be kept of all disbursements of moneys and to be examined by the justices of peace of the said parish yearly. Item I will and require the Minister and Overseers for the time being as they will answer it at the great and terrible day of judgment that these said Alms may be given to those that really stand in need and whom they in their own consciences do believe to be most in poverty and want and that they do not at any time give any greater alms for favour or affection or any other means whatsoever. Item that my Will may publicly be read in the Church immediately after divine service is ended on the 4th day of Novbr every year. Item that a double proportion of bread maybe bought and distributed that day of my Commemoration although it happen not upon a Sunday. Item that the 44th chapter of Ecclesiasticus be read instead of the 1st lesson of my Commemoration Day: and I constitute and ordain the Minister of the said parish of Hurst and the witnesses of the poor to be the overseers of this my last Will and Testament to see it be duly and truly observed. Item that the said Overseers shall have power from time to time to let leases of those my said three messuages or tenements of St. Giles in the Fields London. Given this twentieth day of July in the year of our Lord God one thousand six hundred and seventy seven. I do hereby revoke all former wills by me made and that this stand in force and virtue."

[Signed] Ri: Bigg.

Note.—For the way in which the above bequest is now administered, see p. 131.

ABSTRACT OF WILL OF *HENRY BIGG*, D.D.,

Warden of New Coll., Oxford, 1724; Warden of Winchester Coll., 1730–40.
Proved 11th August, 1740

Body to be buried at discretion of exor. "either with my relatives at Chilton, or in one of the two Colleges to which I have been related as shall be nearest to the place where I happen to die." [It is not known where he was buried. His name is not recorded in the Chilton registers, and the Win. Coll. registers are missing between 1711—1759.]

Bequests.—£10 to poor of Chilton.

£5 each to poor of Market Stanton, Farrington, Hurst.

HENRY BIGG, D.D.

Born 1690; died 1740.

Warden of New College, Oxford, and of Winchester College.

From a picture in Winchester College Hall.

£20 to apprentice 2 children of the Charity School in the City of Winchester.

£20 to Winchester County Hospital.

To wife: all plate, jewels and furniture at both my lodgings in Winchester, and in my house at Chilton and elsewhere; coach, chariot, horses and harness; also £1200 and £50 for mourning, 3 closes of meadow ground in Speen (Berks) for life, and after her death to my nephew Henry Blackstone for ever.

£200 to my niece Dorothy Bethell on death of my mother Mrs. Rachel Bigg.

£10 to Brothers and Sisters each and to Brothers and Sisters in law.

£5 to nephews and nieces each.

£20 annuity and all plate in her use at Chilton to my honoured mother.

£20 annuity to my cousin Mrs. Katherine Woscomb, sister of John Bigg, late of Hainshill, Esq.

£100 to sister Elizabeth on her marriage. [She did not marry.]

To brother Walter, house in Bond St., saddle horses and books, except certain specified books to the Library Winchester College.

£100 to my friends the Warden and Scholars of New College, Oxford.

£200 to my friends the Warden and Scholars of Winchester College.

The latter sum to be invested for the benefit of the most poor and deserving scholars of Win: Coll: either in aid of the superannuates fund, or after the manner of Dr. Cheyney's Exhibitions acc[d] to the will and discretion of the Warden and Fellows with the advice of the Schoolmaster and Usher.

Also to the said College of Winchester for the use of my successors in the said College all my Furniture in or belonging to the Chamber over 4th Chamber.

Also rings to the value of 20/- apiece to the Warden of New College, and to every Fellow, Schoolmaster, Usher and Chaplain.

Also gloves to every Child, Commoner and Chorister of the School and to the survivors of the servants of Win: Coll: at my decease.

To all men and maid servants a legacy of so many pounds respectively as each of them shall have completed years in my service.

To brother Thomas Bigg, of Chilton, my gold watch, seals, diamond rings and picture of relatives, to my wife the pictures of me, leaving to the Warden's lodgings of Win: Coll: my picture of the late Warden Dobson.

All residue of real and personal estate to brother Thomas Bigg, particularly my lands and tenements in the parish of Hurst, and I appoint my s[d] brother Thomas sole heir and exor., and in case he die before me then brother Walter on this further condition that Walter shall then immediately resign and make over to my nephew Charles Blackstone and his heirs the house in Bond Street aforesaid.

Signed, 21 April, 1740, HEN: BIGG.

CODICIL dated July 20, 1740. I bequeath £315 to my three friends, Dr. John Coxhead, Warden of New Coll., Mr. John Coker, Fellow of the s[d] College, and

Wm. Pescod, Esq., of Winchester, and my hope and confidence is that they will be guided in the disposal thereof by a letter which I have written to the said three gentlemen and enclosed with this my codicil or last will.

HEN : BIGG.

ABSTRACT OF WILL OF *LOVELACE BIGG WITHER*, OF MANYDOWN.

SON OF REV. WALTER BIGG, RECTOR OF WORTING.

PROVED 1ST DECEMBER, 1813. SWORN UNDER £35,000.

To Trustees James Blackstone, of Woodstock, D.L., and son Harris; freehold estates in Bramley and Pamber (Lechmere Green, 99 acres), to be sold, and money held upon under-mentioned trusts of residuary personal estate.

Bequests.—To daughter Margaret Blackstone for her use for life; leasehold farm and estate in Sherfield and Bramley (232 acres) held on life under Lady Bolton in lieu of and in full satisfaction of £100; then to uses of my residuary personal estate.

To son in law Sir John Awdry; Kennett and Avon and Wilts and Berks Canal shares.

To grandson Fred: Charles Blackstone £1000 when 25 if he do not accept benefice of Worting.

To daughter Alethea Bigg £150 annuity while unmarried, or £2000 and £300 on my death; also £3000 in lieu of any sum settled on her by my marriage settlement or as next of kin to her uncle and aunt Thomas and Jane Blachford.

To Trustees; freehold estate at Woolston to secure bequests to daughter Alethea and grandson F. C. Blackstone, rest for sole use of son Harris. [Security altered by codicil and Woolston freed for Harris.]

To Trustees; leasehold estates at Manydown and elsewhere; also money, stocks and shares not before disposed of in trust to raise and pay £500 to daughter Margaret Blackstone, £100 to daughter Jane Awdry, £1000 to daughter Elizabeth Heathcote, £100 to daughter in law Ann How Wither, £500 to daughter Catherine Hill, £100 to Herbert Hill [these two last were paid before death by testator], £100 to James Blackstone, £100 annuity to grandson William Heathcote during lifetime of his uncle Sir Thomas Heathcote.

Exors: James Blackstone and son Harris.

Residuary Legatee: son Harris.

Signed, LOVELACE BIGG WITHER.

Date 3 Feb., 1809.

APPENDIX IV.

A.—NOTES ON PARISH REGISTERS.

B.—EXTRACTS FROM HAMPSHIRE PARISH REGISTERS.

C.—RECORDS FROM HOLT AND NORTH WALSHAM, Co. NORFOLK.

D.—MARRIAGE LICENCES FROM HARLEIAN MSS., LONDON, WESTMINSTER AND ESSEX.

CONTENTS OF APPENDIX IV.

APPENDIX IV.

A.—*Notes on Parish Registers.*

Parish Registers in England were established in consequence of a Royal injunction issued by Thomas Cromwell A.D. 1538, at the command of Henry VIII, who ordered "That every Parson, Vicar or Curate . . . . shall for every Church keep one Book or Register, wherein he shall write the day and year of every Wedding, Christening and Burying made within the parish, ... and also there insert every Person's name that shall be so wedded, christened and buried."

In 1558 an injunction of Elizabeth provided that the incumbent of each parish should annually send to his bishop a *transcript* of his year's register. Both injunctions were, it seems, generally disregarded, or the early registers have been lost, for a return of the early part of the last century showed that out of about 11,000 parishes in England, only 812 registers began in 1538.

In 1597 the Convocation of Canterbury, with the approval of the Crown under the great Seal, issued an ordinance that *parchment register* books should be purchased at the charge of each parish, which order has greatly tended to their preservation.

In 1653 a registrar was appointed by Act of Parliament for each parish, but the Registers were, during the Commonwealth, very badly kept, the reason being, no doubt, partly the unsettled nature of that period, and partly, as a note in the Wonston registers says, beause "the Registrar deputed had not what was due to him for it." Moreover a Justice of the Peace was substituted for the Rector or Vicar of the parish to perform the marriage ceremony, which was seldom entered in the parish register.

In 1678 an Act was passed called the "Woollen Act," which ordered that "for the encouragement of the woollen manufacturers . . . . no corpse should be buried but in woollen" under a penalty of £5. Attached to many burial registers is a list of "affidavits" to the effect that the Act had been carried out. The Act was always unpopular, and was repealed in 1812, but long before that date it had become a dead letter.

In 1753 Lord Hardwick's Marriage Act prescribed a special form of the entry of banns and of marriages, from which date the registers of births, marriages and deaths are usually in separate books, in addition to a Register book for the Publication of Banns of Marriage.

N.B.—For convenience of reference the dates in the following extracts are given at the beginning of each entry in uniform manner, instead of in the varying place of the original registers. The spelling of the names has not been altered.

B.—*Extracts from Hampshire Parish Registers.*

1.—WOOTTON ST. LAWRENCE.

The Registers at Wootton begin A.D. 1560. [*Mixed Births, Marriages and Deaths.*]

1560, Jan. 19. Margaret Whither, the Daughter of Richard Wyther, buried.
1561, July 14. Barbara Wyther, the daughter of Rychard Wyther, baptised.
1562, July 14. George Wyther, the sone of Rychard Wyther, baptised.
1563, Apr. 27. Olyfe Wyther, the wife of John Wyther, buried.
1564, Oct. 14. Edithe Wyther, the Daughter of John Wyther, baptised.
1565, Jan. 24. Elenor Wyther, the Daughter of Rychard Wither, baptised.
1567, June 3. Elyzabeth, the Daughter of John Wyther, baptised.
1568, May 5. Otho Wither, the son of Rychard Wither, baptis'd.
1568, July 26. Nicholas Whetland and An. Wither were married.
1569, June 6. Joane, the daughter of Rychard Wither, baptised.
1570, May 23. Persall Wither, the son of John Wither, baptised.
1573, Aug. 14. Savage Wither, the son of John Wither, baptised.
1573, Sept. 8. William, the son of Rychard Wyther, baptised.
1573, Sept. 11. William, the son of Rychard Wither, buried.
1574, Oct. 28. Fernando Wither, the son of Rychard Wither, baptised.
1576, Oct. 7. John, the son of John Wyther, baptised.
1577, July 23. Rychard Wyther, the *fermor* of Manydowne, buried.
1580, June 5. Jane, the daughter of John Wither, of Ramsdale, baptised.
1580, Oct. 22. Margaret, the wife of Rychard Wyther, buried.
1582, Nov. 8. John Wither, of Ramsdale, buried.
1584, June 21. William, the son of John Wither, of Manidowne, baptised.
1585, July 19. Antonie, the sonn of John Wither, baptised.
1587, Aug. 17. John, the son of John Wither, baptised.
1588, Sept. 29. John, the son of John Wither, buried.
1589, Jan. 13. Elizabeth, the daughter of John Wither, baptised.
1590, July 15. George, the son of Rychard Wyther, baptised. [Not placed in pedigree.]
1591, Feb. 16. An, the daughter of John Wither, baptised.
1592, May 23. Rychard, the son of John Wyther, baptised.
1597, Aug. 17. John, the son of John Wither, baptised.
1599, Nov. 27. James, the son of John Wyther, baptised.
1600, Mar. 15. Richarde, the sonne of John Wither, baptised.
1602, Mar. 31. Henricus, filius Johannis Wither, baptizat.
1602, Apr. 2. Henricus, filius Johannis Wither, sepult.
1604, Feb. 11. Georgius Wither and Anna Serle, nupt. [Erroneously supposed to be the parents of the poet George Wither. See p. 85.]
1605, June 16. Edmundus Hungerford and Eliz. Wither, nupt.
1620, June 2. Mgr. Johannes Wither, sepult.
1620, Oct. 22. Ricardus Wither, sepult.

7. Anna, fla Mri Guilielmi Wither, baptizat.
7. Jana, fla Mri Guil: Wither, baptizat.
22. Guilielmus, flus Mri Gulielmi Wither, baptizat.
22. Stephanus Evered and Jana Wither, nupt.
6. Robertus, flus Mri. Guil: Wither, baptizat.
5. Alethia, fla Mri. Gulielmi Wither, baptizat.
4. Annabella fla Mri. Gulielmi Wither, baptizat.
10. Brigeta fla Wilhelmi Wither, baptizat.
21. Briget Wither, sepult.
14. [not legible] flus Georgii Wither, baptizat.
18. Maria fla Guilielmi Wither, baptizat.
8. Robertus flus Georgii Wither, baptizat.
22. Susanna Wither, sepult.
26. Elizabetha Wither, sepult.
4. vid. Wither, sepult.
4. Joannes Wither, sepult.
19. Guilielmus flus Mri Ricardi Wither, baptizat.
20. Guilielmus Wither, sepult.
7. M[rs] Joanna Wither, sepult.
9. Alethia, filia Dni Gulielmi Wither, sepult.
23. Mag[r] Samuel Smith and M[rs] Gratia Wither, nupt.
9. Thomas filius M[ri] Gulielmi Wither, Junioris, bapt.
14. Mag[r] Crescenti[s] Risley, sepult.
26. Mag[r] Gulielm[s] Wither, Senior, sepult.
N.B.—*Vide* additional entries for years 1655, 1656, 1657.]
14. Anna, filia Roberti Wither de Okley, baptizat.
15. Anna, filia Roberti Wither de Okley, sepult.
4. Georgius, filius Roberti Wither de Okley, baptizat.
2. Elenor, filia Roberti Wither, baptizat.
15. Dorothea, filia Gulielmi Wither Armig., baptizat.
5. Anna, uxor Roberti Wither, sepult.
19. Ricardus flus Ricardi Wither Gen., sepult.
29. Gulielmus Wither sen[r] Armig., sepult.
12. Gulielmus Wither de Manidowne Armig: et Maria Wither de civitate Winton: in Ecclia paroali Steventon in hoc Comtu, virtute licentiæ iis datæ Novem[s] 12° die nupti.
16. Mag[ra] Joanna Wither, sepult.
24. Maria filia Guielmi Wither, Gener., baptizat.
27. Guielmus flus Gulielmi Wither, Armig., baptizat.
30. Gulielmus Wither, Armig., sepult.
9. Robertus Wither, Armiger, sepult.
3. Thomas Bethel de Paroch: Sancti Gregorii Londons et Magistra Alletheia Wither nupt.
2. Maria uxor Thomæ Wither, Gen., sepult.

1683, Dec. 25. Fulks Wither, filius Thomæ Wither, sepult.
1684, May 10. Robertus Wither, sepult.
1685, June 26. Thomasina Wither de Basingstoke, sepult.
1685, Aug. 27. Robertus filius Lovelacii Bigg, Gener., baptizatus.
1687, May 8. Maria filia Lovelacii Bigg, Gener., baptizat.
1689, Sept. 20. Dorothea filia Lovelacii Bigg, Generos, bapt.
1692, Mar. 25. Magistra Joanna Wither de Andwell, sepult.
1696, Sept. 12. Thomas filius Thomæ Wither de Andwell, Gener., sepult.
1699, July 22. Magistra Fulks de Andwell, sepult.
1700, Jan. 3. Thomas Wither de Andwell Generos, sepult.
1700, Jan. 25. Magistra Maria Wither, vidua, sepult. [N.B.—For fuller description see add. register.]
1701, Apr. 30. Magistra Maria Wither, sepult.
1703, Aug. 31. Catharina Bigg, vidua, sepult.
1708, Jan. 18. Magistra Alletheia Bethel, sepult.
1727, Nov. 23. Carolus Gounter Nicol, Armig., de Racton in Com. Sussexiæ, et Eliz. felia Gulielm., Basingstoke, Armig., nupti.
1732, Sept. 28. Gulielmus Wither de Manydown, Armiger, sepultus.
1735, July 31. Elizabetha, Gulielmi Wither, de Manydown, Arm., vidua, sep.
1735, Dec. 22. Elizabetha Wither, soror unica Gulielmi Wither de Manydown, Arm., sep.
1749, Feb. 2. Carolus Wither, A. M., sepult.
1753, Nov. 29. Maria Wither, sepult
1789, Nov. 5. William Wither, Esq[r] of Manydown, buried. [N.B.—The last of the Withers.]

Additions to the Wootton Register taken from the Supplementary Register (1653—1657) Martin Miller, Registrar, appointed by Act of Parliament, 1653.

1655. Allathea Wither daughter of William Wither, Esq., borne the 7th day of Aprill.
1656. Michael Ernle of Ashlington, gent, and Mrs. Mary Wither. Feb. second.
John Walker of Highclere and Amey Wither of Burclere. March 24.
1657. Joane Wither, daughter of William Wither, Esq., borne the 30th day of Oct.

A register of ye b. d. m. in pursuance of an act of Parliament made An. D. 1695, contd. to 1706.

1696. Thomas the son of Thomas Wither, of Andewell, gent, was buried Sep. 12.
1700. Mrs. Wither of Manydown, ye wife of Wm. Wither of Manydown, Counsellor at Law, was buried Jan. 25th.
1701. Mrs. Mary Wither, dyed April 25 and was buryed Aprill ye 30th.
(On Sep[t] ye 25th, 1703, a note of ye births and buryalls wh. were within ye last half year was delivered to George Wither.)

N.B.—These add. entries are continued to 1706. At end of them is following memorandum:—

MEMORANDUM.

"That ye Births, marriages and buryalls entered here were done to signify the taxes quarterly paid to King William for everyone born, married, and buryed, this distinguisheth ye births, marriages and berths (burials) where there is not account of ye quarterly entry of births, etc."

Entries since 1789 (Wootton Registers.)

BAPTISMS.

Children of Harris Bigg-Wither.

1814, Aug. 27. Anné (sic) Frances Bigg-Wither.
1817, Nov. 4. Elizabeth Mary Bramston Bigg-Wither.
1819, Aug. 13. Marianne Bigg-Wither.
1822, Apr. 27. Charles Bigg-Wither.

Children of Lovelace Bigg-Wither.

1835, June 18. Arthur Fitz Walter Bigg-Wither.
1836, June 22. Guy Carleton Bigg-Wither (rec[d] July 21).
1837, Nov. 5. Edward Julian Bigg-Wither.
1839, Nov. 26. Lancelot Frith Bigg-Wither.
1841, Jan. 4. Emma Sophia Bigg-Wither.
1842, Jan. 9. Reginald Fitz Hugh Bigg-Wither (rec[d] Feb. 24).
1843, May 18. Ferdinand Courtenay Bigg.Wither.
1844, Nov. 6. Archibald Cuthbert Bigg-Wither.
1845, Nov. 28. Thomas Plantagnet Bigg-Wither.
1851, Nov. 6. Henry St. John Bigg-Wither.

MARRIAGES.

1792, Dec. 3. Charles Blackstone and Margaret Bigg.
1795, Jan. 15. John Awdry, Junr. and Jane Bigg.
1798, Jan. 11. William Heathcote and Elizabeth Bigg.
1808, Oct. 25. Herbert Hill and Catherine Bigg.
1847, Oct. 5. Walter J. P. Bigg-Wither and Sophia Dixon Stubbs.

BURIALS.

1793, Sept. 16. Dorothy Bigg (3rd d. of Lovelace Bigg-Wither).
1794, Mar. 8. Lovelace Wither Bigg-Wither (eldest son of Lovelace Bigg-Wither, aged 14).
1813, Mar. 3. Lovelace Bigg-Wither.
1833, Mar. 30. Harris Bigg-Wither.
1866, Nov. 20. Anne Howe Bigg-Wither.
1874, Dec. 18. Ann (sic) Frances Bigg-Wither.
1876, Mar. 20. Walter John Percival Bigg-Wither.

1879	Elizabeth Mary Bramston Bigg-Wither.
1883	Margaret Eliz[th] Anne Bigg-Wither.
1900, June 26.	Marianne Bigg-Wither.

Extracts from Register Books of Wootton St. Lawrence.

Bigg, Mary.—"Anno Dom[ni] 1674. Mem.—That in the year above written Mrs. Mary Bigg, the relict of Richard Bigg, lately of Haynes Hill, in Hurst, in the co. of Berks, Esq., she being a sojourner at Manydowne did this year give unto our parish church of St. Lawrence, Wotton, a fair carpet for the communion table with a large cushion of velvet, both of a purple colour, and upon both of which the two first letters of her name are embroydered in gold. Ita testor Gulielmus Manning, Vic."

[This lady was the mother of Lovelace Bigg, of Chilton Folliat, Wilts, who married in 1684 Dorothy Wither, of Manydown, grandparents of Lovelace Bigg-Wither, who succeeded to the Manydown estates in 1789.]

Wither, Mary.—"Anno Dom. 1689. At Easter, in the year above written, Mrs. Mary Wither, now of Manydowne, the relict of William Wither, late of Manydown, Esq., and mother to William Wither, the young gentleman and heir of Manydowne, now living [he was then aged 11], gave a fair silver flagon to the parish church of St. Lawrence, Wotton. Ita testor Guielmus Manning, Vicar."

[This lady was Mary, daughter of George Wither, of Winchester, who married in 1673 William Wither (iii), of Manydown. By her will dated 30th August, 1699, she gave "a handsome velvet cushion for the pulpit in Wootton Church in the roome of that which my dear Husband gave suitable to the pulpit Cloath, and the same letters put on this as was on that, only dated according to the year it shall be brought in." She died the next year.]

Wither, Elizabeth.—"The Exors. of Elizabeth [*née* Nicol], the relict of William Wither, Esquire, in pursuance of her last will and testament dated May 31st, 1735, gave a handsome silver Patten and Chalice for the Communion Table of the Parish Church of St. Lawrence, Wotton, Nov. 3rd, 1735. Tho: Fenton, Vicar."

"The said Mrs. Wither gave likewise in her will the sum of a hundred pounds for putting poor children to apprenticeships, and appointed her two sisters, Mrs. Judith Gounter and Mrs. Frances Nicol, together with the Vicar of this Parish, to be Trustees for the disposal of the said hundred pounds, with which the following persons were accordingly apprenticed:—

	£	s	d
(1) *George Dicker* to Francis Wyeth, of Odiham, Blacksmith ...	12	0	0
(2) *Stephen Goddard* to Thomas House, of Odiham, Wheelwright ...	12	10	0
(3) *Thomas Jones* to Wm. Drewitt, of Monk Sherborne, Wheelwright	14	10	0
(4) *Richard Hankin* to Wm. Cooper, of Deane, Taylor	13	0	0
(5) *John Sparvill* to Jos. Hill, of Basing, Blacksmith	10	10	0
(6) *John Hall* to Wm. Harbord, of Overton, Wheelwright	12	0	0
(7) *Wm. Savage* to Th. Goodyer, of Cliddesden, Wheelwright ...	13	10	0
(8) *Stephen Hunt* to John Carter, of Cliddesden, Carpenter	12	0	0
	£100	0	0

Thos. Fenton, Vicar."

2.—WICKHAM.

From the Wickham (Hants) Registers.

1601, Oct. 10.	Catheryne Withers was baptized.
1604, Mar. 29.	Elyoner Wythers " "
1605, Mar. 9.	ffrances Withers " "
1608, Aug. 21.	Elizabeth Wythers " "
1609, Mar. 5.	William Withers " "
1612, Jan. 21.	Anne Wythers, ye daughter of John Wythers, was baptized.
1616, Apr. 28.	Mary, the daughter of John Wythers, was baptized.
1617, Dec. 1.	John, the son " " " " "
1620, Feb. 11.	Edward Withers, the son of John Withers, was baptised.
1622, Aug. 15.	John Withers was buryed.
1632, July 2.	Jacobus Hawkesworth et Anna Wither, married.
1635, Nov. 13.	Gulielmus Wither et Joanna Dunce, married.
1638, Nov. 18.	Anne, the daughter of William Wither and Joane, his wife, baptized.
1638, Jan. 5.	Anne, the daughter of William Wither, sepult.
1640, Nov. 13.	Thomas Lunne and Elizabeth Wither de Wickham, married.
1644, Nov. 16.	Frances Wither vidua sepulta fuit.
1652, May 21.	John Wither juvenis sepultus fuit.

The above entries are interesting as (*a*) illustrating the way in which "Wither," "Withers" and "Wythers" are used interchangeably, and as (*b*) explaining the following extract from the *Survey of Manydown*, taken in 1649:—

All those five Crofts of ground called Newlands lyeing and beinge in the Parish of Wotton, within the Mannor of Manydowne, consisting of one Messuage, and three rod of ground thereto adjoining, which wee value worth 35*s*. p. a. 0 . 3 xxv*s*.

Five inclosures of Arable cont. 18a. by est. wee value att 6*s*. 8*d*. the a. p. a.
Am. to 18 0 vj *li*.

William Withers, Katherine Withers, and Edward Withers, the sonnes and daughters of John Withers, of Wickham in the county of Southampton, yeoman by Indenture by Lease, dat. 23 Junij, 6° Caroli (1630), granted by the Deane and Chapter of Winton, hold all the last mentioned premisses with the appurtenances for and dureing the natureall life of the said William Withers, and after his decease, surrender, or forfeiture, unto the aforesaid [Katherine Withers] for her life, and after her decease, surrender, or forfeiture, unto the aforesaid Edward Withers, for and dureing his natureall life, under the reserved yeerely rent of twelve shillings, But is worth upon improvement over and above the said Rent seaven pounds three shillings p. a. } vij *li*. iij *s*.

The Lessee, etc., by covenaunte to Comm. . . . . waste on the said ground in any way . . . . . . there, under the paine of forfeiture, ... thereof, dureing the said tearmes . . . . . nor alien or sell the premisses without Lycense.

[A page lost here between fol. 24 and 26 of the MS.]

3.—DUMMER.

The Registers at Dummer begin A.D. 1540.

1543, Nov. 21.	Gilbert Wythers, child of George Wythers, bapt.
1545, Mar. 2.	Thomas Wythers, " " "
1549, Mar. 30.	John Wyther, " " "
1551, May 12.	Raynald Wythers, " " "
1578, Sept. 15.	Gilbert Wythers and Annie (Agnes) Page, married.
1579, Sept. 6.	Avelin Wythers, daught. of Gilbert Wythers and Agnes his wife, baptized.
1581, Aug. 15.	Joane Wyther, daught. of Gilbert Wythers and Agnes his wife,
1583, Mar. 4.	George Wether, son of Gilbert Wither, bapt.
1584, Apr. 3.	Avelin Wethers, wife of George Wethers, buried.
1586, Oct. 7.	Raynold Wythers, son of Gilbert Wythers and Agnes his wife, bapt.
1586, Oct. 22.	George Wythers, buried [3rd son of John Wyther of Manydown].
1589, Aug. 2.	Henrie Wither, son of Gilbert Wythers and Agnes his wife, bapt.
1590, Dec. 10.	Philip Kiftell, parson of Dummer, and Elizabeth Wither, were married.
1593, Oct. 27.	William Wyther, son of Gilbert Wyther and Agnes his wife, bapt. [Rector of Dummer, 1624].
1596, Sept. 12.	Agnes Wyther, daugh. of Gilbert Wyther and Agnes his wife, bapt.
1599, May 5.	Elizabeth Wyther, d. of Gilbert Wyther and Agnes his wife, bapt.
1599, July 7.	Gilbert Wyther was buried the 7 day of July, 1599, in the Parish Church of Church Oakley.
1600, Jan. 18.	John Millingate of the Grange, senior, was married unto Agnes Wyther, widow, the late wife of Gilbert Wyther.
1603, Jan. 16.	Walter Knight, of Kingsclere, and Jane Wyther, d. of Gilbert Wyther and Agnes his wife, married
1609, Mar. 5.	Raynold Wythers was buried.
1614, Sept. 11.	Raynold Wyther was buried.
1616, Jan. 20.	Christopher Cox of Northbrook and Agnes Wyther were married.
1624, July 30.	William Wither, clerk, M.A., and parson of Dummer, being presented thereto by the presentation of John Millingate of Dummer (the younger), was inducted into the church and Parsonage of Dummer.
1694	In hoc signo vinco.
	† Thomas Terry, clerk, ffellow of New College in Oxford, Master of Arts and Parson of Dummer, being presented thereunto by the gift and presentation of his ffather, Mr. John Terry, of Sutton (near Odiam), upon the death of Mr. Hugh Davis (who was presented to the same parsonage by Mrs. Jane Terry, daughter of John Millingate the youngest, of Dummer, and Avelyn, his wife, about the year 1656, upon Mr. Will. Wither's Resignation and Egeation), was instituted the 24 Dec., 1694, and inducted into real Possession the 5th Jan[y] following.

MRS. GILBERT WITHER (*née* Elizabeth Hall).

Born 1633; died 1694.

1696, Nov. 22. Bennet Wither, widow, was buried in Wollen (aged 83).
1783 William Withers and Jane Loader (Licence), from Banns Book.
1839, May 8. Harris Jervoise Bigg-Wither (clerk in H. Ord.), widower, married Elizabeth Maria Blunt.

4.—OVERTON.

1655, May 27. Banns of marriage and marriage by William Wither, Esquire, of Manydown, and Justice of the Peace. [Two marriages by the same.]
1655, July 29. Thomas Small, yeoman, of the parish of Dean, and Ann Wither, of the parish of Overton, were married with the consent of both their parents.

5.—WHITCHURCH.

1656, Apr. 8. "Wee, the Inhabitance of Whitchurch whose names are subscribed, have made choyce of Mr Robert Billings to the parish Register the day and yeare above written." [*Signed.*] "Upon ye Removall of ye former Register Mr Robert Billing above menc'oned was sworne and approved Register. Before us, Ric: Kingesmyll, W^m. Wither."

Marriages.

1750, Nov. 4. Robert A'Lee and Anne Withers.
1801, Dec. 17. William Withers and Rebecca Buffin.
1810, Mar. 14. Jason Withers and Elizabeth Hendy, minor. (Licence.)

6.—DEAN.

The Registers at Dean begin A.D. 1655.

1659, Oct. 29. Mrs. Agnis Wither, of Hall, buried in Chancel of Dean.
1677, Oct. 3. Mary Wither, ye daughter of Guilbert Wither and Elizabeth, his wife, buried.
1677, Oct. 6. Guilbert Wither, ye son of Guilbert Wither and Elizabeth, his wife, buried.
1677, Nov. 29. George Wither and Elizabeth, his sister, ye son and daughter of Guilbert Wither and Elizabeth, his wife, were buried in one grave.
1678, Feb. 9. William Wither, ye son of Guilbert Wither and Elizabeth, his wife, buried.
1679, Oct. 9. Guielmus Beach, filius natu maximus Gulielmi Beach de Fiddelton in agro Wilts Generos et Anna Wither filia Elizabethæ Wither de Hall in com. Southton matrimonium contraxere in ecclesiâ parochiali de Dean in Com ult. praedict. nono die Octr. An Dm 1679.

1680, July 15. Elizabeth, ye daughter of William Beach and Ann, his wife, was baptized.

1681, Feb. 27. Ann, ye daughter of William Beach and Ann, his wife, was buryed.

1683, June 17. Dorothy, ye daughter of Charles Wither, Esq., and Dorothy, his wife, was baptized.

1684, Aug. 8. Charles, ye son of Charles Wither, Esq., and of Dorothy, his wife, was baptized. [Commissioner of Woods and Forests.]

1685, Dec. 7. William, ye son of Charles Wither, Esq., and of Dorothy, his wife, was baptized. [Died 1687.]

1697, July 18. Charles Wither, of Hall, Esq., was buried under Hall seat next ye wall in ye Church of Dean.

1710, Oct. 26. Dorothy, the daughter of Charles Wither, Esq., and of Frances [*née* Wavell], his wife, was baptized.

1711, Dec. 11. Frances, daughter of Charles Wither, Esq., of Hall, and of Frances his wife, was baptized.

1711–12, Feb. 13. Maria, the daughter of Gilbert and Elizabeth Wither, formerly of Hall, whose body lay interred in ye chancel, dyed in London, 7th February, 1711, was buried according to her desire in ye Churchyard close under ye wall of ye chancel on ye left hand of ye chancel door on 13th Feb. aforesaid in the year afterward, 1711.

1712, July 11. Frances, ye daughter of Charles Wither, Esq., and of Frances his wife, was buried in ye chancel under the stone yt lays upon her uncle William's grave.

1713, June 10. Henrietta Maria, ye daughter of Charles Wither and Frances his wife, was baptized [afterwards Mrs. E. Bramston].

1718, July 30. Anne, the daughter of Charles Wither, Esq., and Frances his wife, was baptized [afterwards Mrs. Beach].

1719, Dec. 27. Charles, ye son of Charles Wither, Esq., and Frances his wife, was baptized.

N.B.—No Register kept from 4 Oct., 1720, to the latter end of the year 1729.

1731, Nov. 25. Charles Wither, of Hall, Esq., was buried in a new vault made for him and Mrs. Wither his wife, on the left hand within the Communion rails, between eleven and twelve at night.

"Quando ullum invenieret parem" (Æn. 4).

1732, June 3. Dorothy Wither [*née* Smith], mother of the aforementioned Charles Wither of Hall, Esq., was buried under the great seat belonging to that family, in a brick grave, just as you enter the door of the seat. She lies on the arch wherein her daughter Dorothy was buried in the year 1696.—Aet. 73.

Mrs. William Beach,

(*Née* Anne Wither).

Born 1662; died 1742.

DOROTHY.

Daughter of Charles Wither, the younger.

Born 1710; died 1783.

1746, June 29. William Beach, Esq., of Fiddleton, Wilts, and Miss Anne Wither of Hall, were married in Dean Church, they bringing the Bishop's Licence for the same.

1747, June 3. William Wither, the son of William Beach, Esq., of Fiddleton, Wilts, and Anne his wife, was baptized.

1748, Oct. 25. James Harding Beach, the 2nd son of William Beach, Esq., of Fiddleton, and of Anne his wife, was buried.

1752, Oct. 3. Frances Wither of Hall, and Dorothy her daughter, were buried in the Vaults of the Chancel.

1763, June 27. Edmund Bramston, Esq., of Hall, was buried in a new vault within the Communion rails on south side [married Henrietta Maria Worsley, *née* Wither].

1771, Aug. 16. Henrietta Maria Bramston, daughter of Edmund and H. M. Bramston of Hall Place, in the parish of Dean, was buried in a vault within the Communion rails.

1788, Jan. 11. Ann, wife of William Beach, Esq., of Netherhaven in the County of Wilts, and daughter of Charles Wither of Hall Place, and of Frances his wife, was buried in the Chancel within the Communion Rails, aged 69.

1790, May 26. Henrietta Maria, widow of Edmund Bramston, Esq., and daughter of Charles Wither, of Hall, and Frances his wife, was buried in the Chancel within the Communion Rails in the same vault with her late husband, aged 76.

7.—CHURCH OAKLEY.

The Registers of Church Oakley begin A.D. 1559.

1599, July 1. Gilberte Wither, of Dummer, buried. [Dummer Register says July 7, 1599.]

1632, Oct. Robert Wither, son of George Wither, of East Okeley, in the parish of Lawrence Wootton, was baptized here, licence being first had of Mr. Butler, Vicar of Lawrence Wootton aforesaid.

1634 Richard, son of George Wither, of East Oakley, baptized.

1636 George, " " " " "

1640 Anne, daughter " " " "

1678, Nov. 25. Elizabeth Cumia, wid., was buried. The said wid. Cumia was buried in Wollen according to ye act as appears by an affidavit brought Dec. 2, 1678, and attested by Mr. William Wither, Justice of ye Peace.

1685 Jane Goodall was buried in Wollen as appears by a certificate under the hand of Mr. Charles Wither, one of H.M. Justices of the Peace for this County.

1762 William Wither and Mary Blackburn, of Wonson.

8.—NORTH WALTHAM.

The Registers of North Waltham begin A.D. 1650.

1656, Aug. 16. Gilbert Wither, the son of Gilbert and Elizabeth Wither, buried.
1682–3, Feb. 7. Elizabeth Wither, widdow, buried.

9.—BENTWORTH.

The Registers of Bentworth begin A.D. 1554; *irregular till* A.D. 1603.

1558–9, Feb. 18. John Wither, buried.
1604, Apr. 1. Pollixina, the daughter of John Wither, christened.
1605, Mar. 15. Thomas Wyther, buried.
1606, Jan. 4. Alice, daughter of George Wither, baptized.
1607, Nov. 16. Alice Wyther, buried.
1610, Dec. 10. Thomas Martin and Elizabeth Wither, married.
1616, Dec. 16. William Gregorye and Anne Wither, married.
1621, Feb. 18. William Cooper and Mary Wither, married.
1622, June 19. John, the son of George Wither, buried.
1622, Oct. 29. Anthoney Wither and Margery Mageweeke, married.
1624, Apr. 4. Marye, daughter of Anthonye Wither, baptized.
1625, Nov. 21. George, son of Anthonye Wither, baptized.
1628, Mar. 18. Anthonye, the sonne of Anthonie Wither, baptized.
1629, Nov. 17. George Wither, buried. [Father of the poet.]
1630, Sept. 5. James, the sonne of Anthonye Wither, baptized.
1630, Sept. 13. Margaret, wife of Anthonye Wither, buried.
1636, Nov. 28. William Swan and Pollyxena Wither, married.
1643, Apr. 29. Mary Wither, widow, buried.
1656, Jan. 31. William Hunt and Polexina Whither, married.
1667, Nov. 13. Margret, daughter of Mr. Robert Whithers, of ffidine [Theddon], buried.
1677, Apr. 25. Robertus Wither de Theddone, in parochia Alton sepultus fuit.

10.—ALTON.

The Registers at Alton begin A.D. 1615.

1662, Sept. 15. Hunt, the sonne of Mr. Weethers [of Theddon Grange], christened.
1664, June 9. Elizabeth Wither, the daughter of Mr. Wither, baptized.
1666, May 30. Sarah, the daughter of Mr. Wethers, baptized.
1671, May 15. Mary, the daughter of Mr. Robert Wither, baptized.
1675, Oct. 10. Joanah, the daughter of Robert Withers, baptized.
1681, Sept. 9. Elizabeth Withers, buried.
1695, Apr. 3. Elizabeth [*née* Hunt], ye wife of Robert Withers, buryed.
1729, Dec. 20. Philip Wither, buried.

BASINGSTOKE.

The Registers at Basingstoke begin A.D. 1638.

1654, Sept. 4. The Rev. Gilbert Wither, Rector of North Waltham and of Dean, married Elizabeth, da. of Walter Pincke, of Kempshott, Esquire.

1658, Sept. 10. Mr. James Wyther, buried. [Mayor, 1650; brother of the poet.]

1659, May 5. Mr. William Barnweek the elder, of Andover, and Mrs. Margaret Wither, married at Eastrope by Mr. Web, minister.

1665, Nov. 26. William Whither, son of William and Mary, born.

1672, Feb. 13. Mr. Richard Wither, buried.

1686, Sept. 29. Richard Grantum and Elner Wither, of N. Oakly.

BASING.

The Registers at Basing begin A.D. 1655. *B. D. M. separate.*

1662, Sept. 7. Jane Wither, the wife of Will. Wither, buried.

1663, Jan. 7. John Wither, buried.

1678, Dec. 21. William Whother, deceased.

1671, Oct. 20. Tody Whother, baptized.

UP NATELEY.

The Registers at Up Nately begin A.D. 1692 *(on fly leaf)* "*Ex dono Thomæ Wither de Andwell, gent, vicesimo quinto Decembris Anno Dmi., 1692.*"

1703, Jan. 24. William Wither, son of William Wither of Andwell, gent, and of Elizabeth his wife, baptized.

1708, Oct. 22. Dorothy, ye daughter of William Wither, gent, and Elizabeth his wife, baptized.

1709–10, Mar. 13, Mary, daughter of William Wither, Esq., and Elizabeth his wife, baptized.

1713–14, Apr. 1. Charles, son of Mr. William Wither and Elizabeth his wife, baptized.

1734 Note.—"The body of Mr. Wither of Andwell and of his wife and children were removed from the Chancel of Nately Chapel and interred in ye parish Church of Wootton St. Lawrence in ye Burying Place of ye Ancestors of William Wither of Manydown, Esq."

KINGSCLERE.

The Registers at Kingsclere begin A.D. 1538, *the date of the order of Henry VIII.*

N.B.—The day of the month is seldom inserted in the earlier entries.

Baptisms.

1545, Jan. 10. Editha Whyther.

1547, Oct. 30. Winifreda Wyther.

1579, Aug. Ellen Wither, daughter of Nicholas Wither.
1581, Feb. Roger Wither, sonne of " "
1584, Sept. Jane Wither, daughter of " "
1586, Jan. Thomas Wither, sonne of Nicholas of Okeley. [N.B.—Okeley is a part of the Parish of Kingsclere near Hannington.]
1589, June. Wineffride Wither, daughter of Nich.
1600, Mar. Brigett, Wither.
1603, May. Elenor Wither, daughter of Richard.
1605, Dec. Ann Wither, daughter of Richard of Okeley.
1619, Nov. Roger Wither, sonn of Mr. Roger Wither. of Okly.
1621, July. George, sonne of Roger Wither.
1622, May. Nickholas Wither, sonn of Roger.
1625, Aug. James Wither, sonn of Roger.
1626, Aug. { Ffrancis Wither, sonn of Roger of Okly / Elinor Wither, daught. of Roger " } twins.
1628, Mar. Henry Wither, sonn of Roger, baptized at Hanytown.
1701, Sept. 29. Nicholas fil. Guilhelmi Wyther et Susannae ux.
1703, Feb. 20. Margeria fil. Thomæ Wyther et Janæ ux ejus.
1729–30, Jan. 18. Gulielmus fil. Nicholai Wither et Mariæ ejus Uxoris.
1730–31, Jan. Gulielmus fil. Johannis Wyther et Eliz. ejus Uxoris.

MARRIAGES.

1557, June. Willm Hunt and Joone Whythier.
1567, Feb. William Byllette and Wenefryde Wether.
1568, Jan. John Upton and Edith Wether.
1598, Nov. Richard Wither and Elizabeth Elliat.
1621, Jan. William Withers and Ann Aubery.
1677, May. Richard Willmot and Margery Wither.
1743, July. Thomas Wither of Burgclere and Sarah House of Kingsclere.

BURIALS.

1601, July 15.. Anne Wyther.
1614, Oct. 1. Nicholas Wither, senior, of Okeley.
1619, Jan. 2. Mary Wither of Strattens. [Strattens is a small property on the road to Newbury.]
1625, Sept. 10. James Wither, sonn of Roger, a child.
1632, Mar. 5. Henry Wither, son of Roger, a child.
1635, June. Anne Wither, the wife of Roger.
1644, Dec. Roger Wither.
1648, Oct. 30. Richard Wither of Beename Court. [Beenham Court is just beyond Strattens, a large property.]
1650, Aug. Mrs. Wether of Bennam Cort, widow.

ITCHINGSWELL AND SYDMONTON.

1626, Dec. 4. Peeter Wether, buried.
1632, Aug. 30. Joonne Wethers, widow, buried.
1634, Apr. 12. Anne Wether, the daughter of Edward Whethers, baptized.

ST. MARY BOURNE.

1662, July 3. Dorothea Wither, married Thomas Locke.
1663, April 6. Richard Wither, son of Richard, buried.
1666, Sept. 15. Dorothea Wither, daughter of Richard, baptized.
1700, April 12. Edith Wither, " " buried.
1720, Mar. 1. Elizabeth Wither, married Paul Holdway.
1788, May 1. Philip Withers of Faccomb and Elizabeth Webb, married.

HURSTBOURNE PRIORS.

1745-6, Feb. 17. Mr. Charles Wither, clerk, of Lichfield, and Mrs. Mary Ley, of Dolton, Downshire, married.

BURGHCLERE.

The Register of Baptisms and Burials begins in 1561; of Marriages in 1559. There are gaps in the Burials from December, 1618, to December, 1631: and in the Marriages from 1623 to 1656.

Baptisms.

1561, Nov. 14. Thomas Wither.
1572, May 28. John, s. of Edward Withers.
1574, Apr. 4. Margaret, d. of Edward Wither.
1575, June 21. Margaret, d. of John Wither.
1577, Dec. 28. Margery, d. of Edward Withers.
1578-9, Feb. 19. Francis, s. of John Withers.
1580, Apr. 4. Agne, d. of John Withers.
1580, Aug. 15. Francis, s. of Edward Withers.
1581, May 7. Richard, son of John Withers.
1583, Sept. 20. Mary, d. of John Withers.
1586, Apr. 24. John, s. of John Withers.
1586-7, Feb. 24. Constance, d. of Edward Withers.
1588, Dec. 22. Agnis, d. of Edward Withers.
1589, Oct. 19. Willm, s. of John Withers.
1592, Nov. 19. Francis, s. of John Withers.
1594, June 14. William, s. of Edward Withers.
1595, July 20. Thomas, s. of John Withers.
1595, Aug. 3. Jone, d. of Thomas Withers.
1595-6, Feb. 1. John, s. of Edward Withers.

1596, Sept. 4. Thomas, s. of Thomas Withers.
1598, June 29. Phebe, d. of Edward Withers.
1600, Aug. 17. Jone, d. of Thomas Withers.
1603, Aug. 28. John, s. of Thom^{s}: Withers.
1604, Nov. 21. Edmund [or Edward ?], s. of Francis Withers.
1613. "The 28th of March was baptized Richarde Withers, the sonne of Richard Withers, of *Babs*." [Babbs has not been located.]
1614–5, Jan. 6. Mary, d. of Richard Withars, "of *Babbs*."
1615–6, Mar. 10. Thomas, s. of Thomas Withers.
1616, Aug. 25. Margrie, d. of Richerd Withers.
1618, May 3. John, s. of Thomas Withers.
1618, July 19. Jone, d. of Thomas Withers.
1618, Nov. 1. Winifrith, d. of Richard Withers.
1619, July 25. Margaret, d. of Thomas Withers, junior.
1619, Oct. 16. Henry, s. of Thomas Withers.
1620, Dec. 24. Elizabeth, d. of Richard Withers, "of *Babs*."
1620–1, Jan. 28. Joanne, d. of Thomas Withers.
1621, Sept. 3. [blank] d. of Thomas Withers, "of Attbury" [Adbury].
1622–3, Mar. 17. Anne, d. of Richard Withers, "of *Babbs*."
1623, Oct. 1. Ursula, d. of Thomas Withers.
1624, May 8. Ursula, d. of "Thomas Withers the younger."
1625, Dec. 5. Sara, d. of Richard Withers.
1626, Mar. 26. Edmund, s. of Thomas Withers.
1628, Apr. 13. Abraham, s. of Thomas Withers.
1628, June 6. Thomas, s. of Thomas Whithers.
1629, Nov. 6. Edward and Joseph Withers, sons of Edward Whithers.
1630–1, Feb. 13. Amy, d. of Thomas Withers.
1631, Oct. 2. Elizabeth, d. of Edward Wither.
1632, Nov. 25. Mary, d. of Edward Withers.
1637–8, Feb. 18. Robert, s. of Edward Withers.
1640, May 31. Francis, s. of Edward Withers.
1643, Aug. 27. Rebeckah Withers.
1647, Nov. 10. Elizabeth, d. of Thomas Withers.
1649–50, Mar. 5. Mary, d. of Thomas Withers.
1651, Oct. 18. Thomas, s. of Thomas Withers.
1653, Apr. 25. Margaret, d. of Thomas Withers.
1654, May 6. Edward, the s. of Thomas Withers.
1657, Apr. 8. William, the s. of Thomas Withers, *born*.
1658–9, Jan. 8. Joane, the d. of Tho: Wither.
1660–1, Mar. 13. John, the s. of Tho: Withers.
1662, Nov. 7. Ann, d. of Thomas and Elizabeth Withers.
1665, July 1. Martha, d. of Thomas Wither.
1666, May 9. Susanna, d. of Thomas and Elizabeth Withers.

1666, Sept. 5. Joane, d. of Francis Wither.
1667, June 28. Francis, s. of Thomas Withers.
1670, Sept. 2. Elizabeth, d. of Thomas and Elizab. Withers.
1685, Sept. 28. Joseph, s. of Thomas and Ann Wither.
1686, July 25. Dorothea, d. of John and Dorothea Wither.
1687, May 11. Benjamin, s. of Thomas and Ann Withers.
1689-90, Mar. 16. Will., s. of Will. and Martha Withers.
1689-90, Mar. 18. Moses, s. of Tho. and Ann Withers.
1691, Dec. 11. Martha, d. of William and Martha Withers.
1693, Nov. 15. John, s. of William and Martha Withers.
1739, May 8. Hannah, d. of Willm Withers.
1742, Sept. 28. Willm, s. of Willm and Mary Withers.
1743, Nov. 9. Benjamin, s. of Thos. Withers.
1744, Dec. 26. Ann, d. of Willm Withers.
1745-6, Feb. 16. Thos., s. of Willm Withers.
1749, May 19. Elizabeth, d. of Willm and Mary Withers.
1750-1, Jan. 26. Dinah, d. of Wm and Mary Withers.
1766, June 22. John, the s. of a daughter of William Withers.
1771, Dec. 30. Joseph, the s. of Wm Withers, junr.
1776, Dec. 15. Sarah, the d. of Thomas Withers.
1780, Feb. 6. Hannah, the d. of Thos and Sarah Withers.
1784, Aug. 22. Thomas, the s. of Thomas and Sarah Withers.

MARRIAGES.

1577, Nov. 25. Richard Waldron and Jone Withers.
1585-6, Feb. 8. Edward Withers and Dorothie Rives.
1591, Nov. 1. Francis Tomson and Sibill Withers.
1591, Nov. 22. John Brooker and Mary Withers.
1593, June 16. Edward Withers and Jone White.
1594, Aug. 5. Thomas Withers and Jone Alie.
1600-1, Feb. 5. Edmund Mason and Margaret Withers.

[A gap from 1623 to 1656.]

A note at beginning of Vol. II:—"I doe hereby approve of Andrew Pearse being a Register (sworne by Sr. Richard Kingsmyll) for ye Parish of Burgclear within this County, to ye Intent yt Hee duely keepe a Register accordingly in this Booke being to yt end Confirmed this 4th of February, 1655. By mee Willm. Wither."

1655-6, Mar. 24. John Walker and Amee Withers.
1673, Apr. 2. John Cross, *alias* Baker, and Mary Wither.
1674, Oct. 31. Richard Digweed and Winifrith Wither.
1679, Sept. 22. John Alee and Margaret Withers.
1684, Oct. 6 Thomas Wither and Ann Reade.
1685, Sept. 28. John Withers and Dorothea Wheler.

1689, Apr. 5. William Withers and Martha Browne.
1692, Oct. 10. William Holdway and Elizabeth Withers.
1701, Oct 9. Clement Hawkings and Elizabeth Withers.
1729, Aug. 17. James Crate, of Itchenswell, and Frances Withers, of Burghclere.
1731, Aug. 2. Francis Withers and Marjery Dearlove.
1771, Oct. 21. Ambrose Young and Elizabeth Withers.
1772, May 28. Thomas Withers and Sarah Smith.

BURIALS.

1563, May 31. John, s. of Edward Withers.
1569, Apr. 20. Andree Withers.
1575, July 1. Margaret, w. of John Wither.
1575, Aug. 21. William Withers.
1576–7, Jan. 2. Margaret, d. of John Withers.
1578–9, Feb. 21. Francis, s. of John Withers.
1580, Apr. 11. Agne, d. of John Withers.
1582–3, Jan. 5. John, s. of Edward Withers.
1585, July 24. Marjery, w. of Edward Withers.
1588, Dec. 29. Doritye, w. of Edward Withers.
1593, June 2. John, s. of John Withers.
1598, July 16. Phœbe, d. of Edward Withers.
1602–3, Feb. 2. Jone, w. of Edward Withers.
1603, Nov. 15. John, s. of Thomas Withers.
1603, Dec. 14. Marjery, d. of Edward Wethers.
1604, July 4. Jone Wethers, widow.
1605, Apr. 25. Mary, d. of John Wither.
1605, Aug. 12. Agnes, w. of Francis Wythers.
1605–6, Jan. 5. Agnes, d. of Edward Withers.
1606, Apr. 21. John Withers.
1607–8, Mar. 2. Francis Withers.
1613–4, Feb. 21. Edward Wythers, of Erlestone.

[On 16th Jan., 1618–9, Thomas Wither signs as one of the witnesses of the induction of William Lucy to the Church of Burghclere.]

[There is a gap here till 1631.]

1632, June 12. Annes Wither vidua of Babs.
1633, Nov. 22. Francis Withers.
1634, Apr. 30. Joane, w. of Thomas Withers.
1634, Sept 8. Ursula, d. of Thomas Withers.
1643, May 7. Thomas Withers.
1643–4, Jan. 30. The wife of Richard Wethers, of Babes.
1646–7, Jan. 28. Richard Wither.
1651, Nov. 23. Elizabeth Withers.

1653, Apr. 27. Margaret Withers.
1655-6, Mar. 12. Mary Withers.
1657, Aug. 19. Thomas Withers.
1659, June 2. Edward Withers.
1663, Apr. 19. Robert Withers.
1667-8, Feb. Marthay Wither.
1667-8, Mar. 20. Susan Wither.
1668, Aug. 28. Elizabeth Withers.
1669, Nov. 1. Edward Withers?
1670, Dec. 18. Winnifrith Withers.
1678, Aug. 6. Francis Wither.
1680-1, Mar. 5. Joane Wither.
1681, Sept. 9. Elizabeth Wither.
1694, July 5. Martha, w. of William Withers.
1695-6, Jan. 31. Thomas Withers, junior.
1696-7, Jan. 6. John Withers.
1700, Oct. 14. Thomas Withers.
1728, Oct. 24. Mary, w. of Francis Withers.
1729, Apr. 1. William Withers.
1739-40, Jan. 12. Ann, w. of Benjamin Withers.
1742, Nov. 17. Francis Withers's wife.
1747-8, Feb. 8. Anne, d. of the Rev. Mr. *E.* Withers. [See inscription later.]
1748, Nov. 8. Francis Withers.
1749, Mar. 26. William Wither's child.
1751-2, Mar. 20. Mary, d. of Benjamin Withers.
1752, Apr. 24. Thomas, s. of Ann Withers.
1774, Feb. 19. Benjamin Withers.
1777, Jan. 17. Mary, w. of William Withers, Aet. 65.
1778, Mar. 24. William Withers, Aet. 67.
1793, Apr. 28. Moses Withers.
1793, Sept. 1. Sarah, d. of Thomas Withers.
1794, Dec. 10. Ann Withers, wid.
1795, Apr. 28. Sarah Withers.

NEWTOWN.

BAPTISMS. [Earliest entry 1666.]

1667, May 11. Edmund, the son of Thomas Withers, baptized.
1722, June 22. John, s. Wm Withers.
1749, May 6. Sarah, d. W^m and Catherine Withers.
1750-1, Feb. 4. W^m s. " " "
1753, Aug. 15. John, s. " " "
1757, Nov. 13. Anne, d. " " "
1760, June 1. George, s. " " "

1762, Aug. 29. Mary, d. W^m and Catherine Withers.
1773, Mar. 6. Ann, d. Thomas and Sarah Withers.
1782, July 21. Mary, d. „ „ „

BURIALS. [Earliest entry 1750.]

1757, Nov. 25. Anne, d. W^m and Catherine Withers, buried.
1759, Apr. 22. Rebekah Withers, aet. 86.
1765, July 28. Catherine, w. of Wm Withers.
1773, Sept. 15. Ann, d. Thos. and Sarah Withers.
1777, May 19. Wm Withers.
1779, Oct. 21. Esther Withers, widow.

HIGHCLERE.

1696, May 18. Mary, daughter of Widow Withers, was buried in Wollen.

In the old churchyard of Burghclere, on the N. side of the chancel, is a small marble headstone, inscribed :—

Ann daug^r of the Revd Mr Chas Wither and Mary his wife,
died ye 6th of Feby 1747, aged 9 months.
of such is the kingdom of God.

Benjamin Withers was Churchwarden of Burghclere in 1735.
„ „ „ Overseer „ „ 1729.

EAST WOODHAY.

BAPTISMS.

1611, June 30. John, s. of John Wythers.
1613-4, Jan. 9. Peter, s. „ „
1617, Apr. 22. Edward, s. „ „
1619, Nov. 27. Stephen, s. „ „
1619-20, Jan. 30. Alice, d. of Thomas Wytheres.
1622-3, Feb. 16. Mary, d. of John Wither.
1625-6, Mar. 19. Thomas, s. of Thomas Withers.
1639, Nov. 9. Richard, s. of Richard and Elizabeth Withers
1642-3, Feb. 4. Elizabeth, d. of Richard Withers.
1645, July 27. Mary, d. „ „ „
1671, Oct. 10. Elizabeth, d. of Richard Withers.
1674, Nov. 29. Richard, s. „ „ „
1677, Oct. 6. Thomas, s. „ „ „
1679-80, Jan. 20. An, d. „ „ „
1681, Aug. 19. Jane, d. of Thomas Withers.
1683, Apr. 11. William Withers, baptized.

1686. "John, ye son of Tho: Withers, was, being weak, baptised privately, Nov. ye 18th."

1686, Nov. 20. Richard, s. of Thomas Withers.

1688, Nov. 9. Elizabeth, d. of Thomas Withers.

1702, Nov. 16. Mary, d. of Thomas and Mary Wither, *alias* Shipway.

[Also three more children in 1704, 1705-6 and 1706-7. The name is also spelt "Widdoes."]

1716, Apr. 23. Mary, d. of Richard and Sophia Withers.

[Also other children in 1718, 1722 and 1729.]

1719, May. Ann, d. of Benjamin Withers.

[Also another child in 1721.]

1731, May 2. [blank] d. of Joseph and Sarah Withers.

[Also other children in 1733, 1737, 1740-1 and 1744.]

1740-1, Mar. 15. Frances, d. of Richard and Sophia Withers.

1749, Apr. 30. William, son of John and Mary Withers.

BURIALS.

1629, Sept. 27. Elizabeth Wither, widdow.
1637, July 20. Alice, wife of Thomas Wither.
1638, Sept. 29. Alice, d. of Thomas Wither.
1648-9, Mar. 23. Nicholas Withers.
1654, Aug. 10 Jone, d. of Richard Withers.
1670, Aug. 31. Richard Withers, senior.
1675, May 5. Elizabeth Withers, widow.

At *Linkenholt* there is a *marriage*: 1728, Oct. 7. John Horne and Mary Withers.
At *Whitchurch*, a *burial*: 1612, Oct. 27. "Father Withers."

ROMSEY.

The Romsey Registers begin A.D. 1569.

BAPTISMS.

1650, June 3. Ann Withers, dgt. of Edward Withers.
1651, Dec. 29. John Withers, son of Edward.
1653, Jan. 24. Edward Withers, sonne of Edward.
1655, Nov. 6. Peter Withers, sonne of Edward.
1660, Aug. 20. Frances Whither, dgt. of Edward.
1661, Nov. 10. William Withers, son of Edward.
1663, April 15. Mary Withers, dgt. of Edward.
1667-8, Mar. 8. Edmond Withers, son of Edward.
1684, May 28. Edward, son of Richard Withers.
1687, Sept. 27. Anne, dgt. of Edward Withers.
1689, June 18. Thomas, son of Thos. Withers.
1701, Nov. 19. Richard Withars, son of George.

1703, Sept. 2. Richard, son of George Withers.
1727, Sept. 13. Rachel, dgt. of Richard and Mary Withers.
1728, Sept. 25. Peter of John and Sarah Withers.
1728, Oct. 21. Elizabeth of Richard and Mary Withers.
1728, Nov. 17. Benjamin of Benjamin and Elizabeth Withers.
1730, Sept. 15. Ann of Richard and Mary Withers.
1731, Feb. 26. Joseph, son of Richard and Mary Withers.
1732, Feb. 4. Richard of Richard and Mary Withers.
1733, Jan. 19. Sarah of John and Sarah Withers.
1733, July 12. John of Edward and Ann Withers.
1734, Dec. 30. Edward of Edward and Ann Withers.
1735-6, Mar. 9. Peter of John and Sarah Withers.
1735-6, July 3. Joshua of Joshua and Lydia Withers.
1736, June 3. William of John and Sarah Withers,
1737, Apr. 6. William of Richard and Mary Withers.
1737, Sept. 6. John son Joshua and Lydia Withers.
1739, Mar. 11. Joshua of Joshua and Lydia Withers.
1740, Apr. 30. Peter of Richard and Mary Withers.
1740, May 6. Thomas of John and Sarah Withers.
1741, June 9. George of Joshua and Lydia Withers.
1742, Sept. 1. Elizabeth of John and Ann Withers.
1742, Sept. 17. Joseph of John and Sarah Withers.
1742-43, Feb. 2. George of Richard and Mary Withers.
1743, Dec. 27. Edward of Joshua Withers.
1744, June 21. Catharine, daur. of Benj. Withers.
1744, Oct. 31. Sarah, daur. of John Withers.
1745, Dec. 17. Edward, son of Richard Withers.
1745-46, Feb. 5. Edward, son of Richard Withers.
1746, June 22. John, son of Benjamin Withers.
1746, Dec. 26. James, son of Joshua Withers.
1747, July 5. Rachel, daur. of Edward Withers.
1748, July 26. Joshua, son of Richard Withers.
1749, Oct. 16. Aaron, son of Joshua Withers.
1751, Dec. 27. Moses, son of Joshua Withers.
1755, Apr. 17. Ann, daur. of George Withers.
1756, Feb. 3. George, son of Joshua Withers.

Registers not searched after this date.

MARRIAGES.

1631, May 1. Thomas Adam and Dorothy Whethar.
1638, Feb. 4. William Withors and Jane Whale.
1731, Nov. 29. Richard Withers and Mary Savage.
1733, Jan. 22. John Withers and Ann Elcomb.
1734, Mar. 11. Joshua Withers and Lydia Purchas of Minstead.

1736, Feb. 24. John Carden and Elizabeth Withers.
1745, Oct. 31. Edward Withers of Hursley and Rachel Jenvey.
1753, Dec. 25. John Randall of Portsmouth and Ann Withers.

Registers not searched after 1755.

BURIALS.

1638, Jan. 13. Edward Withers.
1649, June 22. Jane Withers, widow.
1669, Nov. 22. Edmund, son of Edward Withers.
1670, Dec. 21. John, son of Edward Withers.
1683, Aug. 23. Christine, dgt. of Henry Withers.
1728, Oct. 16. Edward, of Edward and Elizabeth Withers.
1728, Nov. 6. Elizabeth, wife of Edward Withers junr.
1728, Nov. 17. Elizabeth, wife of Benjamin Withers.
1730, Apr. 5. Peter, son of John and Sarah Withers.
1731, Aug. 24. Elizabeth, dtr. of Edward Withers.
1732, May 28. Jane, of Edward and Ann Withers.
1733, June 12. Elizabeth, of Mr. Richard and Mrs. Mary Withers.
1736, Oct. 19. Joshua, of Joshua and Lucy Withers.
1736, Dec. 11. Mary, of Mr. Richard and Mrs. Mary Withers.
1741, Feb. 23. John, of Joshua and Lydia Withers.
1742, June 28. Thomas, of John and Sarah Withers.
1745, June 21. Catharine, daur. of Benj. Withers.
1745–6, Mar. 15. Edward, son of Richard Withers.
1747, Dec. 8. Ann Withers, w[d].
1748, Aug. 22. Mary Withers, w[d].
1749, Oct. 16. James, son of Joshua Withers.
1749–50, Mar. 6. John, son of Benjamin Withers.
1749–50, „ 23. Richard Withers.
1750, Apr. 22. Joseph, son of John Withers.
1750, Oct. 31. Ann, wife of Benjamin Withers.
1750–1. Feb. 12. George, son of Joshua Withers.
1752, Feb. 6. Edward, son of Edward Withers.
1752, June 5. Margarett, wife of Richard Withers.
1752, July 20. Moses, son of Joshua Withers.
1752, Dec. 3. Rose, wife of Edward Withers.
1755, Mar. 1. John Withers.
1755, June 8. Sarah, daur. of Edward Withers.
1755, July 17. Ann, daur. of George Withers.

Registers not searched after 1755.

N.B.—On N.E. wall behind the altar of Romsey Abbey Church is a tablet in memory of Godwin Withers, died Nov. 21, 1829, aged 43 years, and of his widow, Mary Elizabeth, died 1886, aged 90, and of their children, Seward, Margaret, Gustave, Josiah and Godwin drowned at sea.

C.—*Holt and North Walsham, Co. Norfolk.*

The registers and Churchyard monuments of Holt are full of the name Wither or Withers.

There are none of the name living in Holt now (1907), but the demolished "Church House" was the home of a Withers family within the memory of present parishioners. New Street in Holt was originally called "Withers Street."

The present Rector (Rev. L. B. Radford), to whom I am indebted for the following information, is writing a history of the parish.

There are also many monumental inscriptions to members of the family of Wither(s) in North Walsham Church (see below), where the arms are the same as Wither of Manydown with slight differences.

I have appended some further references to Norfolk Withers taken from Blomfield's *History of Norfolk* and Dew's *Monumental Inscriptions.*

The Holt Registers begin in 1557.

BAPTISMS.

1793, June 23.	Mary Ann, daughter of William Withers and Ann Trotter, both of Holt.
1795, Feb. 1.	Martha, daughter of William Withers and Ann Trotter, both of Holt.
1804, Dec. 16.	William Woodcock, son of William Withers, and his wife Elizabeth (*née* Woodcock).
1806, Mar. 2.	John Showell, son of William Withers and his wife Elizabeth.
1807, July 13.	Henry Press ,, ,, ,, ,,
1809, Mar. 5.	Louisa, daughter of ,, ,, ,,
1810, July 5.	Elizabeth, ,, ,, ,, ,,
1811, Dec. 8.	Charles, son of ,, ,, ,,
1813, June 5.	Martha, daughter of William and Elizabeth Withers.
1815, May 12.	Frederick, son of ,, ,, ,,
1817, May 4.	Henry ,, ,, ,, ,,
1830, Feb. 7.	Henry Percy, son of Wm Woodcock Ann } Withers.
1835, Mar. 27.	Anna Margaret Ainslie, da. of W. W. W. A. W. }
1835, Nov. 6.	Amy Martha, da. of John Showell Amy Caroline } Withers.
1836, Dec. 28.	Louisa ,, ,, ,,
1837, Nov. 14.	John Tucker, s. of ,, ,,
1841, Dec. 5.	Charlotte Jane, da. of ,, ,,
1844, Nov. 9.	Wm Geo., s. of ,, ,,
1846, July 26.	Robt Barnes, ,, ,, ,,
1848, Mar. 29.	Henry Cooke, ,, ,, ,,

1849, May 13. Rob[t] Barnes, s. of John Showell / Amy Caroline } Withers.
1851, July 27. Thomas Woodcock, " " "
1851, July 27. Martha Elizabeth, da. of Fredk. and Eliza Withers.

Marriages.

1791, June 30. William Withers and Ann Trotter, both of Holt.
1839, Oct. 10. W[m] Barker, silk manuf[r], of Macclesfield, and Martha Withers, da. of W[m] Withers, attorney-at-law. Witnesses—W. Withers, Chas. Withers, Fred. E. Withers, W[m] Woodcock Withers, E. A. Withers, Amy Withers, Anne Withers.
1844, July 18. Charles Withers, surveyor of taxes, Bury S. Edmunds, son of W[m] Withers, solicitor, and Anna Maria Ellis, widow (formerly Back), of Holt, da. of W[m] Back, gent.

Burials.

1644, Nov. 18. Robert, son of William Whithers.
1807, July 19. Henry Press, son of W[m] Withers and Elizabeth, his wife (late E. Woodcock), 8 days.
1817, Jan. 13. Henry Withers, 8 months.
1827, Apr. 29. W[m] Withers, 72 years.
1830, Nov. 21. Martha Withers, 74 years.
1831, Jan. 23. John Withers, 73 years.
1841, Sept. 6. Anna Margaret Ainslie Withers, 6 years.
1848, Jan. 15. W[m] Withers, 66 years.
1848, June 1. Robert Barnes Wither, 2 years.
1851, July 18. Elizabeth Withers, 63 years.
1853, May 6. Fredk. Wither, 38 years.
1859, June 29. John Showell Withers, 52 years.
1863, July 13. Albert Edward Withers, 4 weeks.
1873, July 18. Elizabeth Ann Withers, 63 years.
1888, Sept. 23. Fredk. W[m] Withers, 45 years.
1894, Jan. 15. Martha Elizabeth Withers, 42 years.
1897, Mar. 5. Louisa Withers, of Bale, 87 years.

Will.

1743, May 15. Archdeaconry of Norwich. Elizabeth Withers, of Holt, Spinster. "To be buried in the parish Church of North Walsham as near as may be to the remains of my family."

Bequests.—£5. 5*s*. to John Withers, of North Walsham; £5. 5*s*. each to children of Daniel Press, of Holt; £10 to Ann Press, his wife.

From Dew's Monumental Inscriptions in the Hundred of Holt, Co. Norf.

HOLT.

1827, Apr. 24.	William Withers, d., in 72nd yr.	altar tomb.
1835, Jan. 24.	Ann. W., d., aged 84 yrs.	
1848, Jan. 9.	William Withers, d., aged 66.	
1851, July 13.	Elizabeth Withers, d., aged 63.	
1853, Apr. 30.	Frederick Withers, d., aged 37.	
1873, July 14.	Elizabeth Ann Withers, d., aged 63.	

LANGHAM.

1860, Dec. 8.	James W., d., aged 62.	altar tomb.
1866, Oct. 14.	Sarah W., d., aged 64.	

THORNAGE.

1826, Oct. 13.	Ann W., d., aged 74.	altar tomb.
1833, Mar. 31.	Wm W., d., in 82nd yr.	

References to Wither (s) family in Blomfield's History of Norfolk.

1. Subsidy Roll. 21 James I, 1623. Nicholas Withers of Trunch. Estate, xls. Asset, viijs.
2. Fines. 25 Geo. II, 1752. John Withers v. Rd Fray and Susan his wife in Cromer ats., Shipden.
3. *Robert Withers*, chaplain, or perp. cur., of St. John Timberhill, Norwich in 1590 (Bl. iv, 128). Rector of All Saints' (next ch. to St. Jo. Timb.) 1584, burd in All SS. Ch. 1597 (Bl. iv, 131), was R. of St. Edmund's, Norwich, 1595—1597 (Bl. iv, 406).
4. *William Withers*, presd to Ry of Gt Ryburgh, Norf., by Robt Bacon, 1624, succeeded by Nathaniel Bacon (presd Robt B.) in 1628. (Bl. vii, 167.) Possibly same person as
5. *William Withers*, M.A., rector of Diss, Norf., 1613—1647; also rector of Wetheringsett. (Bl. i, 18.)
6. *Samuel Withers*, died, vicar of Honingham, Norf., not long before 1672. (Bl. ii, 452).
7. *John Withers*. (Bl. xi, 79.) Monument at N. Walsham in memory of John Withers, gent, died Aug. 29, 1712. Arms: Argent—a chevron, gules, between three crescents, sable, impaling ermine, on a chief, a billet between 2 annulets.
8. *Thomas Withers* (Bl. iv, 463), died Feb. 16, 1723, aged 49. "Black marble slab in West Alley" of old independents' meeting house, Norwich.
9. *Robert Withers* (Bl. ix, 506) says that Ralph Anesley became vicar of *Gateley*, Norf., in 1718, on the death of Robert Withers.

There is no Wither or Withers in index of *Visⁿ Norfᵏ* (*Harleian* MS.); but in the third list of names printed in *Three Norfolk Armories*, ed. by W. Rye, Norwich (Codex C) there is "Withers . . . . a chevron, gules between crescents." This list is an index to a collection of heraldic notes. *cp.* No. 7 of these extracts fr. Bl., Norf.

Monumental Inscriptions of the Hundred of Tunstead.

(Edited by W. RYE, Norwich.)

North Walsham—in the Church.

Hannah, wife of Joseph Withers, d. 1722, aged 63.
Joseph Withers, senior, d. 1730, aged 70.
Elizabeth, of Holt, daughter of Joseph and Hannah Withers, d. May 15th, 1743, aged 58.
Joseph, son of Joseph and Hannah Withers, d. 1744, aged 54.
Bridget, wife of John Withers, d. 1765, aged 66.
John Withers, d. 1766, aged 73.
Inscription speaks of their forty-four years of married life, and their being almost united in death.
Joseph Withers, son of John and Bridget, d. 1761, aged 33.
Sarah Withers, daughter of John and Bridget, d. 1760, aged 26.
John Withers, d. 1785, aged 62. [? Son of John and Bridget.]
Ann, wife of John Withers, junior, d. 1766, aged —6.
Inscription speaks of premature death. Near her lie two of her children :—
Mary, d. 1759, aged 5.
George John, d. 1762, aged 4.
Priscilla, widow of Thomas Withers, d. 1825, aged 81.
Thomas Withers, Captain R.N., d. 1813, aged 71.
Melissa, his wife [apparently second wife], d. 1851, aged 68.

D.—*Marriage Licences (London).*

(See *Harleian MSS.*, Vols. 23, 24, 25, 26, 30 and 31.)

1557. Robert Wythers and Margaret Parke, of St. Martin's, Outwich.
1574. John Wythers, of St. Michael's, Cornhill, and Dorothy Newman, of St. Mary's, Colechurch.
1578. John Withers and Johanna Drood (widow), of St. Michael's, Cornhill.
1584. William Wither, of St. Mary ab Church, and Jane Lysby, of Stepney.
1592. Robert Taylor, Esq., and Elizabeth Wythers, of St. Lawrence's, Jewry (widow).
1608. Robert Snell, clerk, A.M., Vicar of Matching, co. Essex, and Elizabeth Wither, of Theydon Garnon in said county, daughter of Henry Wither, S.T.P., Rector of Theydon Garnon.
1610. James Ellis, Esq., and Elizabeth Withers, of St. Stephen's, Coleman.

1614. Abel Gower, Gent., and Anne Withers, daughter of Antony Withers, of the City of London, Gent.

1615. Candishe Sanderson and Elizabeth Withers, daughter of Antony Withers, of the City of London, Gent.

1620. John Willis and Anne Withers, daughter of Mr. George Withers, late of [ ], co. Somerset, Gent.

1635. Henry Withers, Gent., of Chigswell, co. Essex, and Phoebe Norris.

1639. Henry Withers, Gent., of Little Thorrock, co. Essex (widower), and Mary Parshlowe.

1670. Antony Wither, of St. Margaret's, Westminster, Gent., and Mrs. Elizabeth Russell (widow).

1673. John Withers, of Middle Temple, Esq. (widower), and Katherine Gill.

1679. William Withers, of St. Giles', Cripplegate, and Mrs. Francis Shaler (widow).

1681. William Withers, senior, of St. Mary-le-Bow, alleges the marriage of William Withers, October 28th [afterwards Lord Mayor], and Margaret Hayes, of Bray, co. Berks.

Memorial in Wootton Church.

Winchester College Cloisters.

Grandson of above. Only surviving son of the Author of this book.

INDEX.

N.B.—No attempt has been made to form a complete index of ALL *the names occurring in the various pedigrees and parish registers.*

Lightning Source UK Ltd.
Milton Keynes UK
UKOW06f2227070814

236574UK00010B/300/P